I0819936

Quertext

Quertext

An Anthology of Queer Voices from German-Speaking Europe

Edited by
Gary Schmidt *and* Merrill Cole

THE UNIVERSITY OF WISCONSIN PRESS

The University of Wisconsin Press
728 State Street, Suite 443
Madison, Wisconsin 53706
uwpress.wisc.edu

Gray's Inn House, 127 Clerkenwell Road
London ECIR 5DB, United Kingdom
eurospanbookstore.com

Printed in the United States of America
This book may be available in a digital edition.

Library of Congress Cataloging-in-Publication Data
Names: Schmidt, Gary, 1967– editor. | Cole, Merrill, 1966– editor.
Title: Quertext : an anthology of queer voices from German-speaking Europe / edited by Gary Schmidt and Merrill Cole.
Description: Madison, Wisconsin : The University of Wisconsin Press, [2021] | Includes bibliographical references.
Identifiers: LCCN 2020055855 | ISBN 9780299333805 (hardcover)
Subjects: LCSH: Gays' writings, German—Europe, German-speaking—Translations into English. | German fiction—Europe, German-speaking—21st century—Translations into English. | Gay men—Fiction. | Lesbians—Fiction. | Sexual minorities—Fiction. | LCGFT: Fiction.
Classification: LCC PT1335 .Q44 2021 | DDC 833/.920892067—dc23
LC record available at https://lccn.loc.gov/2020055855

To queers everywhere

Contents

III. INTERTEXTS

IV. INTERCULTURAL ENCOUNTERS

V. YOUTH

VI. RELATIONSHIPS

From the Editors

Translating literary texts penned by authors with such varying styles and themes as those represented in this volume presents a number of challenges. In our efforts to make these texts accessible to English-speaking readers, we have sought to find a balance between promoting readability and conveying culturally specific terms and concepts. In the words of Lawrence Venuti, rather than "domesticating" such concepts and rendering the translation "invisible," we have attempted to maintain readers' awareness of the "foreignness" of the originals while at the same time providing additional information in notes that will enhance understanding and appreciation of the rich cultural and historical contexts in which these texts are embedded.

Acknowledgments

The idea for this volume was inspired during a stay in Berlin in May 2017 on a Professional Enhancement Grant from Coastal Carolina University (CCU), when I participated in the workshop and discussion "What Makes a Man? Sexuality and Representation in Europe–Middle East Encounters," organized by Peter Rehberg at Berlin's Institute for Cultural Inquiry. In discussion with Merrill Cole, we agreed that an anthology of English translations of contemporary queer German fiction was needed to bring the diversity of experience and expression of authors writing in German to Anglophone students and scholars, and Merrill graciously agreed to assist as coeditor and translator. Through the generous funding of a second grant from CCU, I was able to travel again to Germany, Austria, and Switzerland in June and July 2019 to interview many of the authors represented in this anthology. I wish to express a special thanks to all of the writers who were able to meet with me, including Jürgen Bauer, Claudia Breitsprecher, Gunther Geltinger, Joachim Helfer, Odile Kennel, Friedrich Kröhnke, Marko Martin, Michael Roes, Angela Steidele, Jana Walter, Antje Wagner, Tania Witte, and Yusuf Yeşilöz, as well as all authors in this volume for their e-mail correspondence. Thank you also to Jim Baker of Querverlag, in Berlin, for speaking with me and providing important insights regarding the conditions of queer publishing in Germany today. A special thanks to Antje Rávik Strubel and Joachim Helfer for the suggestions they made during their visit to South Carolina to read from their works at CCU in March 2018. I also wish to express my appreciation to my colleague Simone Boissoneault for agreeing to assist with the translation of some of the texts. A special thanks to Robert Tobin for his careful review of the manuscript and extremely helpful suggestions. Finally, the support of the staff at University of Wisconsin Press has been invaluable: thank you to Dennis Lloyd, Jacqulyn Teoh, Adam Mehring, and Mary Sutherland for her very helpful suggestions in the editing process.

Gary Schmidt, September 2020

Quertext

Introduction

Contemporary Queer German-Language Fiction in Historical Context

Gary Schmidt

Given the global diversity of queer cultural production today across all forms of media, one might rightly ask why an anthology of English translations of fiction by contemporary German-speaking authors is needed. What do queer authors who write in a language whose speakers inhabit a relatively small area in central Europe have to contribute to the global dialogue on sexuality and gender that has accompanied a revolution in how lesbian, gay, bisexual, transgender, nonbinary, and queer individuals are represented? In order to do justice to this question, one must first challenge the assumption that the depictions of queer bodies and identities that circulate most widely today in the Anglophone world truly represent a global diversity rather than an Anglo-American hegemony in literary and cinematic production. This assumption continues to limit the access of monolingual readers and viewers in the United States, Britain, Canada, and other English-speaking countries to a relatively small amount of fictional works in translation and a small group of films identifiable as "foreign," which have been subtitled or dubbed for niche markets.

This anthology is intended to be part of a broader project of decentering queer culture in all its manifestations, including representations of contemporary life and explorations of a queer past. German-speaking authors have much to say regarding the current possibilities for fashioning nonheteronormative identities; they also help us reimagine queer histories. Indeed, one can argue that the history of homosexuality as an identity is largely traceable to German-speaking central Europe. Michel Foucault's overstated and overcited claim that in the late nineteenth century the sodomite became the homosexual, a unique "species" defined by medicine, psychiatry, and secular law," can now be seen as the mere starting point for more recent scholars.[1] Through the careful curation and analysis of textual archives from a wide range of public and private sources, these scholars have woven a complex tapestry that depicts how doctors, lawyers, journalists, novelists, activists, and even agents of law enforcement in late nineteenth and early twentieth-century German-speaking Europe engaged in the practice of naming, explaining, and justifying practices, identities, and forms of expression that appeared to many others as deviant, criminal, degenerate, or pathological. In *Gay Berlin: Birthplace of a Modern Identity* (2015), Robert Beachy claims that modern homosexuality is a specifically German invention, a thesis also supported by the Germanist Robert Tobin in *Peripheral Desires: The German Discovery of Sex* (2015). These studies attest to a productive tension between historical and literary scholarship: Beachy examines mostly nonliterary sources; Tobin looks at fictional texts, some of which reinvent a Greek model of love between men to which middle- and upper-middle-class German, Austrian, and Swiss males had access through the classical training emphasized in the *Gymnasium*; other literary writings engage with the new typology of sexuality that evolved in the interplay between self-identified homosexuals and the new science of *Sexualwissenschaft* (sexology).

Recent scholarship by and about women has brought a necessary corrective to the emphasis on male homosexuality in late nineteenth- and early twentieth-century German-speaking Europe, examining the intersections of gender identity, performance, and sexual orientation in the Weimar Period, the interplay between psychoanalysis and sexology, the complicity of sexological scholarship in discourses of race and colonization, and the establishment of a limited public sphere for the circulation of queer writing between the end of World War I and the Nazi takeover of Germany in 1933.[2] The work of these scholars demonstrates that in spite of male homosexuality's criminalization under Paragraph 175 of the German penal code, queer communities and subcultures flourished in early twentieth-century Berlin and other German-speaking cities. These entities were often merely tolerated at best, but sometimes they also enjoyed support from institutions such as the Social Democratic Party. The achievements in LGBTQ+ rights in Europe and North America are inconceivable without the contributions of German-speaking intellectuals, writers, and activists of the world's first homosexual emancipation movement, which might be said to have officially begun with the founding of the "Scientific-Humanitarian Committee" in Berlin in 1897 under the leadership of Dr. Magnus Hirschfeld. The origins of this movement can be traced back even farther, for example, to Karl Heinrich Ulrichs's impassioned plea for the rights of "urnings," at the Congress of German Jurists in 1867.[3] Hirschfeld's politically progressive activism on behalf of the rights of those whom we now refer to as members of the LGBTQ+ community notwithstanding (most notably consistent advocacy for the repeal of Paragraph 175), sexology and its practitioners were not universally affirmative of queer lives. Many individuals drew upon Ulrich's characterization of *Urninge* (biological males with feminine psyches) and *Dioninge* (biological females with masculine psyches) and embraced new labels coined by sexologists, self-identifying as "inverts" or members of the "Third Sex"; however, they did not simply swallow whole the new theories and taxonomies. As Tobin notes, Aimée Duc (pseudonym for Minna Wettstein-Adelt), the author of the novel *Sind es Frauen?* (*Are They Women?* 1901), takes issue with the pathologizing of female "inverts" by Richard von Krafft-Ebing, whose *Psychopathia sexualis* (1886) was the standard work on sexual "deviance" for the generation of sexologists that followed, including Hirschfeld. Duc's novel appeared twenty-seven years before Radcliffe Hall's *The Well of Loneliness* (1928), which invoked an obscenity trial in Great Britain.[4] While Hall's novel was translated into German and became highly influential on the lesbian community there, as early as 1919, Anna Elisabet Weirauch's novel *The Scorpion* had been published in Germany.[5] Weirauch's protagonist is Metta Rudlof, a young upper-class woman who develops an intense friendship with Olga, an older woman. When the intensity of her attachment to Olga becomes increasingly obvious to her family, Metta's father first has Olga followed by a detective, then turns to a doctor for help, who assists the family by sending Metta to her uncle's house. Later, after the death of her father, Metta discovers materials in her father's library that appall and disgust her; if anything, these writings make it more difficult to come to terms with her desire for Olga and appear irreconcilable with her bourgeois identity:

> On his desk she now found from time to time books, pamphlets, brochures, apparently of a quite varied character, novels, medical works, daily papers with passages underlined—but all treating one theme. / There were strange and weird stories of countesses who dressed in men's attire and frequented various dives until they were lured into a trap and brutally murdered. / Or accounts of sickening orgies in well-known clubs where hundreds of women dressed and disported themselves like men. [. . .] / Or descriptions of the soul life

> of sexual inverts which led one to suppose that these thousands of human beings constituted a vast community, a community bound together by no ties of common interest, no similarity of education, origin, taste or attitude toward life, and never by love, but by a common lust for a common form of excess.[6]

Although neither authors nor texts are identified in this passage, one can reasonably assume that the writings Metta finds in her father's library are of a sexological nature: some appear to pathologize gender-transgression and same-sex desire, while others do not. Even though the descriptions of drag balls and other gatherings gesture toward a queer community, one that transcends boundaries of class and nation, Metta rejects such a vision as perverse and unnatural.

Weirauch's *The Scorpion* is instructive regarding continuities and ruptures in German history that have conditioned the possibilities for queer voices to express themselves. This is true for several reasons: first, as Laurie Marhoefer states, *The Scorpion* initiated a genre of lesbian "penny novels" (*Groschenromane*) that were available to a niche market and highly popular among lesbians.[7] Relatively liberal censorship laws in Imperial Germany had allowed the publication of materials on homosexuality and gender nonconformity as long as they fell within the domain of scientific research and thus could be considered to have redeeming value. This principle continued to be operative in the Weimar Republic, although, as Marhoefer writes, many queer activists themselves saw the birth of representative democracy as the opportunity to end censorship and abolish Paragraph 175. In reality, again according to Marhoefer, the Weimar Republic compromise on such matters did allow some greater degree of expression for queer voices but was far from abolishing censorship altogether, as indicated in her analysis of the magazines *Die Freundin* (*The Girlfriend*) and *Die Freundschaft* (*Friendship*). Marhoefer writes that advocates for homosexual emancipation "won a restricted public sphere for magazines like *Friendship*. Homosexual emancipation publications were nevertheless bound by restraints, such as the Filth and Trash Law, which often kept *Friendship* and similar publications from being publicly displayed or sold to minors."[8]

The concept of a restricted public sphere for queer publications is highly useful for a number of reasons. First, it complicates the skewed image of Weimar Germany as a liberated (or decadent, as viewed from a less progressive perspective) society. Second, it explains at least in part why openly queer voices remained largely restricted to a niche readership. Finally, Marhoefer's concept helps us to consider the writing strategies, including self-censorship, masking, and camouflage, that authors with aspirations to enter the literary mainstream felt compelled to utilize. Those authors who found critical and commercial success beyond niche markets in Imperial Germany, the Weimar Republic, and after the demise of National Socialism were not those who wrote about or for a clearly recognizable homosexual subculture but rather writers whose depictions of same-sex relationships or gender transgressive behaviors could be interpreted as metaphors for broader philosophical and aesthetic questions. For such writers as Thomas Mann, Hermann Broch, Robert Musil, or Arthur Schnitzler, there was little to no overt engagement with the terminology or progressive politics of sexologists such as Hirschfeld.[9] Instead, Freudian psychoanalysis was clearly favored for a number of reasons, not least of which was the apparent suitability of psychoanalysis for veiling and masking, which in turn contributed to the perceived quality of literariness associated with complexity and ambiguity. Such writing strategies also made it possible for various readerships to interpret texts through completely different lenses. Thomas Mann (1875–1955), for example, in *Death in Venice* (1913) effects a half-open closet, one that allows those in the know to read his texts as queer (including his own children), while making it possible for others to overlook queer subtexts or interpret even more explicit examples of homoerotic expression in terms of allegory and philosophical musings on aesthetics. Although Mann wrote at a time when others were openly calling for the abolition of Paragraph 175 and shaping the new German discourse on sexuality, Manns's choice for the respectability of bourgeois heterosexual family life kept him at the margins of the burgeoning homosexual rights movement. His literary treatment of sexuality was intimately linked with the nurturing of a humanistic practice, one that was dissatisfied with the alleged reductionism of medical-scientific discourse and saw aesthetics as inimical to purely physical expressions of sexuality. One need only contrast Mann's philosophical musings on aesthetics in *Death in Venice* to a novel like John Henry Mackay's *Der Puppenjunge* (*The Hustler*, 1926), which describes specific locations in Berlin where men met to find other men to have sex with, often for pay.[10] Or even Karl Friedrich von Linden's *Die Süßen* (*The Sweet Ones*), first published in 1909, four years before Mann's Venetian novella, in which the threat of blackmail for upper-class homosexuals in Imperial Germany is a major theme.[11] Linden's and Mackay's descriptions of Berlin's queer nightlife and cruising locations are a kind of literary counterpart to Magnus

Hirschfeld's *Berlins drittes Geschlecht* (*Berlin's Third Sex*, 1904), which Manfred Herzer describes as "the first independent publication that undertook the exclusive depiction of this city's world of gays and lesbians."[12]

The divide between literary respectability and full emergence from the closet ran straight (or perhaps queerly) through the Mann family, a topic that Hans Pleschinski engages with in his novel *Königsallee* (2013), an excerpt from which appears in this anthology. Klaus and Erika Mann, unlike their father, were intimately familiar with the Berlin queer scene of the 1920s; Rick Chamberlin describes Klaus Mann's novel *Der fromme Tanz* (*The Devout Dance*, 1925) as the "mapping out of a gay identity where no such thing had ever existed before in German literature."[13] Rolf Goebel identifies *Der fromme Tanz* as an important contribution to the genre of the queer Berlin novel, with which such contemporary authors as Friedrich Kröhnke, Peter Rehberg, and Joachim Helfer, all represented in this volume, continue to engage.[14] Klaus Mann did attain a degree of commercial success, but he never received the critical recognition enjoyed by his father. Although the younger Mann continued to explore homosexuality more or less directly in later writings—for example, in historical novels and stories about Alexander the Great, Pyotr Ilyich Tchaikovsky, and King Ludwig of Bavaria—his writing was also subject to the restraints imposed by the limited public sphere, with mainstream critics sometimes reacting negatively to the thematization of homosexuality, sometimes ignoring it, and sometimes subsuming it in a broader discussion of "eros."[15]

It is telling that in Hans Pleschinski's satirical novel *Königsallee* (2013), excerpted in this volume, Thomas Mann's daughter Erika becomes the vehicle for an attempt to thwart a reunion in postwar Düsseldorf between her father and Klaus Heuser, a young man with whom he had fallen in love while vacationing on the island of Sylt in the 1920s. Erika was herself a lesbian who was briefly married to the homosexual dramatist Gustav Gründgens and later, during the Nazi period, married the homosexual English poet W. H. Auden, reportedly to obtain British citizenship. For Pleschinski's fictional Erika, her father's continued literary production far outweighs the fleeting value of any sentimental encounter between the two men. This novel, which became a Spiegel Bestseller, demonstrates the continued relevance of the Mann family legacy on queer German writing: it offers both an analysis of what one might call the "Mann complex" and an aesthetic project to overcome it—not through the oedipal pathos underlying Klaus Mann's writing but via the lighthearted critique of parody.

Queer women's writing suffered just as much, if not more so, from the restricted public sphere: Annamarie Schwarzenbach (1908–42), who was a friend of Klaus and Erika Mann and romantically pursued by Carson McCullers when she visited New York City in 1940, is a prime example. Schwarzenbach's first novel, *Freunde um Bernhard* (*Friends around Bernhard*, 1931), maintains a precarious balance between private revelation and camouflage, which went too far even for some of the author's friends.[16] Homosexuality is thematized in the context of aesthetics, youth, and generational conflict; the sexual ambiguity of the main characters is linked to an androgyny reflecting Schwarzenbach's own gender expression. As Michael Töteberg points out, the photograph on the sleeve of the first edition, interpreted by one critic as an illustration of the eponymous Bernhard, is actually the author. Schwarzenbach gave a new twist to her strategy of projecting herself into a male protagonist and utilizing a disembodied third-person narrator in her second novel, *Lyrische Novelle*, which is narrated in the third person by an androgynous young man consumed by desire for a woman outside of his social circles. Significantly, Schwarzenbach's openly queer novel *Eine Frau zu sehen* (*To See a Woman*), in which narrative voice and authorial queer identity are allowed to meld, was first published in 2008, more than six decades after her death in 1942.

In the twenty-first century, following the definitive abolition of Paragraph 175 in reunified Germany in 1994, the establishment of domestic partnerships in 2001, and, finally, full same-sex marriage rights in 2017, the concept of the limited public sphere as described by Marhoefer in the context of the Weimar Republic may no longer seem relevant. Nonetheless, the fictional Erika Mann's admonishment to Klaus Heuser in *Königsallee* that literature must take priority over love is an apt metaphor for the position of queer writers in Germany, even following reunification in 1990. For a time, achievement of literary quality and recognition seemed to be inimical to the description of actual bodies and their physical encounters with one another, seen, for example, in the critical response to Joachim Helfer's semi-autobiographical novels, which appeared with the prestigious literary publisher Suhrkamp in the late 1990s. Helfer also engages with *Death in Venice* in his *Cohn & König* (1998), rewriting Aschenbach's encounter with Tadzio in the protagonist's more directly physical encounter with a younger male. Helfer's writing represents a kind of breakthrough of queer themes into the mainstream; his first two novels' critical success, however, appeared to be partly a result of their perceived avoidance of the particularity of gay experience in favor of so-called universal themes, a heteronormative code for desexualized, de-queered writing. One critic, for example, praised *Cohn & König* for avoiding digressions into the homosexual milieu of train stations and hustlers, embracing instead an "education of the heart."[17]

Just as queer authors struggled to obtain a voice in the world of German literature, another challenge arose in the notion that the abolition of Paragraph 175 and establishment of same-sex partnerships heralded a post-homophobic era in which the LGBTQ+ rights movement was no longer relevant. In 1997 the journalist Werner Hinzpeter, in his *Schöne schwule Welt* (*Beautiful Gay World*),[18] had already proclaimed the end of the gay rights movement, since gays and lesbians had allegedly already reached all their goals (significantly full gay marriage was not deemed to be important, and trans issues were ignored); a few years later, Berlin's mayor Klaus Wowereit, in his successful bid for reelection, could state "*Ich bin schwul, und das ist auch gut so*" (I am gay and that's also ok).[19] The belief seems to be so widespread now that Germany is indeed in a post-homophobic era that Johannes Kram identifies this very notion as central to a new homophobia. Akin to claims of a post-racist society that disavow the continued effects of past and present racism, homophobia today manifests itself precisely in contemporary German political and cultural discourse's unwillingness to acknowledge and interrogate the persistence of homophobia and its causes.[20]

An aspect that distinguishes contemporary queer German-language fiction writing and that of early twentieth-century authors such as Aimée Duc and Anna Weirauch is the notable absence of the need to explain or justify, let alone take recourse to a "scientific" discourse of sex and gender. In our days, at least in the examples presented in this volume, queer authors seem neither highly concerned with sexological impulses to label and categorize nor terribly bothered with further exploration of the implications of Freudian theories, which contrasts rather sharply with successful straight-identified authors such as Christian Kracht, whose novels *Faserland* and *1979* link queer sexuality with a new, post-reunification German sexual decadence.[21] This does not mean, however, that contemporary authors no longer engage with the discourses of sexuality that burgeoned in the late nineteenth and early twentieth centuries and continue to exert influences on contemporary culture. In the historical fiction of Angela Steidele, when the medicalization of homosexuality appears as a theme, it is precisely to turn the tables on those who engaged in that practice; when transgender expression is discussed in Tania Witte's contemporary Berlin novel, *beziehungsweise liebe* (*and/or love*), it is in a pointed response to the intrusive and obviously ill-informed inquiries of a straight-identified male.

Engagement with contemporary queer writing in German is also important to break the tiresome repetition of images and stereotypes that focus primarily on National Socialism and the ostensible decadence of the Weimar Republic, which is often portrayed as leading directly to Hitler's ascension to power. The success of the German-language television series *Babylon Berlin* with American audiences attests to this ongoing obsession. In the series, based on novels by Volker Kutscher, Detective Gereon Roth negotiates the intrigues and tawdry secrets of a late 1920s Berlin, which is once again both deliciously decadent and on the brink of succumbing to fascism. In a never-ending loop initiated by Bob Fosse's 1971 film version of the musical *Cabaret*, itself an adaptation of Christopher Isherwood's *Berlin Stories*, viewers' fascination for sex German-style begins and ends with the rise and fall of National Socialism, for which the Weimar Republic serves merely as decadent prelude.[22] Such a narrow window onto sexuality and German history serves to render queer experiences prior to the early twentieth-century invisible and ignores the diversity of queer communities of German-speakers in Europe today. In addition, the close thematic linkage of sexual diversity and decadence in historical productions that center on the Nazis not only obscures the emancipatory achievements of queer communities but also limits our understanding of the scope and impact of queer practices and the multiple intersections of identities and communities.

This volume seeks to expand the window through which English speakers view German, Austrian, and Swiss culture by making contemporary queer fiction available in translation, which exemplifies the diversity of styles, themes, settings, and subjects addressed by twenty-first-century queer authors who write in German. At a time in which queer studies and LGBTQ+ studies have gained academic recognition and the field is growing, students and scholars now need to have access to literary sources that challenge cultural stereotypes and push the discipline beyond US-centered insularity. The texts collected and translated in this anthology open up new worlds of experience for students, scholars, and general readers interested in queer life beyond their borders.

The author Michael Roes, when asked in an interview about gay (*schwul*) literary forebears, immediately mentioned Heinrich von Kleist's tragedy *Penthiselea* as an "outsider drama" in which the playwright's identification with the mythical Amazon is paramount.[23] An overemphasis on the development of the modern discourse of sexual orientation might cause one to suggest that in making such a statement, Roes utilizes the term *schwul* anachronistically or even that he can recognize the gay element in Kleist only from his own contemporary positionality. From a different angle one might object to Roes's identification of a male author with a mythical Amazon as "gay," claiming that it should more rightly be dubbed "queer." Yet, I would argue that Roes uses *schwul* in a much broader fashion than the English term "gay," and even more broadly than many Germans would use the word, which unlike its English counterpart rarely refers to women, *lesbisch* (lesbian) being preferred. Roes does not associate *schwul* with a particular fixed identity and its subculture but rather with a whole range of feelings, thoughts, and actions that exceed and transgress the limitations of heteronormativity; indeed, he uses it in a manner more akin to the way "queer" is used today by Anglophones and some German-speakers who identify as part of the community. In doing so, the author employs language in a manner open to the reimagining of identities and transformative potentials. Such a principle is also in force in his fiction. In a similar fashion to Roes's use of *schwul* and in recognition of literature's potential to interrogate not only heteronormative but also homonormative identity categories, we decided to title this book *Quertext: An Anthology of Queer Voices from German-Speaking Europe* rather than using the acronym LGBTQ+ or some variation thereof. We also made the decision to include two straight-identified authors in recognition of the queer voices they construct in their writing: Christoph Poschenrieder's novel *Das Sandkorn*, set in Berlin during the First World War, presents a complex, closeted, gay male protagonist with whom readers can empathize instead of offering a voyeuristic eye to straight readers and the opportunity for titillation in perversion or instrumentalizing homosexuality to critique an ostensible lack of authenticity or a new form of decadence as does Christian Kracht, in *Faserland* and *1979*. Yusuf Yeşilöz, a Kurdish-Turkish immigrant to Switzerland, courageously addresses a topic—one that is often taboo in Muslim immigrant communities in Europe—by writing the coming-out story of a second-generation Turkish immigrant.

Germanists have dedicated considerable scholarship to unpacking the queer potential of the Classical and Romantic periods.[24] Unfortunately, relatively little attention has been paid to contemporary authors who see themselves as the inheritors of this queer literary tradition.[25] Perhaps the success of approaches that endeavor to unearth queer desire prior to the alleged invention of the modern homosexual is, in part, responsible for the relative lack of interest among Germanists in contemporary queer fiction. Is the idea that since categories of identity have now become available—nomenclature for all possible orientations, gender expressions, performances, etc.—literary fiction is no longer interesting, bereft of its potential for subversion, subtlety, and nuance? The authors represented in this volume refute such a claim. Rolf Goebel suggests that literary scholars themselves are responsible for overlooking contemporary queer German fiction because the methodological tools suited for uncovering the queer in canonical literature are no longer suitable for identifying the ways in which queer experience is contextualized in the broader themes of contemporary life: "Queer literary theory has to move from the decoding of hidden same-sex subtexts to the analysis of the multiple ways in which contemporary fiction openly foregrounds queer lifestyles as conformist or subversive performances in the present world of multiculturalism, global affairs, and postindustrial consumer capitalism. Since the complexity of this situation requires the analytical tools provided by interdisciplinary cultural studies, queer theory must expand and cultivate its affiliations with other disciplines, such as urban studies, film criticism, media theory, ethnic discourses, and global studies."[26] If one follows Goebel's lead, it is necessary for Germanists to take greater interest in the considerable cultural labor being undertaken by queer writers today in Germany, Austria, and Switzerland, thus making their texts accessible to the large number of English-speaking students, teachers, and scholars engaged in queer studies who do not read German. Contemporary queer writing in German is valuable for its insider perspective on central European history and culture and also for its outsider perspective on Anglophone cultural developments, including the US-dominated LGBTQ+ rights movement and the rise of queer theory and queer studies as an academic discipline.

Even as the notion of a gay or lesbian identity and community arose in the late nineteenth and early twentieth centuries, literary texts continued to offer alternative, more complex understandings of sexuality that did not reduce sexual expression to a nomenclature of types. This is no less true today than it was then; the authors represented in this volume cross multiple boundaries, refusing to conform to either heteronormative or homonormative standards. They reflect critically on their own communities and practices and, at the same time, bring new angles of vision to familiar aspects of German culture and history: some write semi-autobiographically, others play with the genres of science fiction, historical fiction, youth literature, and travel writing. Almost all see themselves within a tradition of queer writing that is not synonymous with a political definition of a queer community. Moreover, their writing engages with multiple literary traditions, not just German, Austrian, and Swiss but French, British, Irish, American, Greek, Czech, and Russian.

Sadly, contemporary queer German-language authors are virtually unknown in the Anglophone world, suffering from the general imbalance in literary translation between German and English. Unsurprisingly, English-language anthologies of queer literature usually contain texts from the late nineteenth and early twentieth century, and German literary giants of that time period continue to inspire contemporary English-language cultural production, as in Michael Cunningham's *By Nightfall* (2010). There, the story of a heterosexual New York art dealer who falls in love with his wife's younger brother prompts critics to see ghosts of Thomas Mann's Gustav Aschenbach. Or one could point to the success of the Broadway musical *Spring Awakening* (2006), adapted from Frank Wedekind's revolutionary dramatization of youth sexuality by the same name (1891), which also appeared in a new English translation by Jonathan Franzen in 2007. Such adaptations and inspirations indicate that American authors remain interested in German sexuality in the late nineteenth and early twentieth century, but interest in queer German literary production appears to fall off abruptly in the post-Nazi era.

The Nazi seizure of power in 1933 brought an end to the homosexual rights movement in Germany;[27] the stricter version of Paragraph 175 enacted by the Nazis and the more intense censorship of queer writing remained in force in the post-Nazi West Germany until 1969, when sex between men over the age of twenty-one was legalized (the age of consent for heterosexual activity was sixteen), and the paragraph was not completely abolished until 1994, four years after reunification. Compounding the chilling effect of Paragraph 175 and continued enforcement of the Filth and Trash Laws (Schund- und Schmutzgesetze) were postwar representations of the Nazi past that attempted to explain its unique evil as a form of sexual perversion and which led to numerous cultural productions that circulated the stereotype of the gay Nazi.[28] Thus, in the immediate postwar period (1945–69), Austria and Germany, whether East or West, offered very few opportunities for openly queer writing.[29]

The apparent caesura in the German-language queer literary tradition brought about by the rise and fall of Nazi Germany perhaps made it more difficult for English-speakers to recognize the reemergence of queer German writing as, for example, in the wake of the Generation of 1968 (68ers), a term used to describe a range of protests associated with student groups against the continued influence of fascism and the alignment of the West German establishment with the United States in pursuit of capitalist imperialist objectives in Vietnam. Hubert Fichte (1935–86), for one, is absent from most English-language accounts of queer literary history. An admirer of the modernist author Hans Henny Jahnn (1894–1959), whose unfinished novel *Perrudja* (1929) might best be dubbed pansexual and can only with difficulty be co-opted for any particular sexual identity, Fichte's writing has inspired many of the authors of this volume for his open portrayal of homosexuality and for his project of bringing subjective reflection on the self to the understanding of the foreign and vice versa.[30] The post-1968 era did see some noteworthy breakthroughs of gay men's writing into the literary mainstream, as in the appearance of the anthology of gay men's writing *Entstellte Engel* (*Disfigured Angels*, 1983) with the mainstream publisher Fischer, and Ronald Schernikau's *Kleinstadtnovelle* (*Small Town Story*, 1980). Written by the author when he was just twenty years old, *Small Town Story* received critical recognition by the national German press for its portrayal of West German youth.[31]

As in the United States, women's activism and writing in German-speaking Europe had a complex and not unproblematic relationship to the student movement. While the critique of bourgeois sexual mores and the proclamation of an era of sexual liberation by the 68ers opened up new opportunities for exploration of non-heteronormative sexuality and gender identities/expressions, women's voices were often marginalized. Significantly, the Swiss lesbian author Verena Stefan's (1947–2017) *Häutungen* (*Sheddings*, 1975), a foundational text in the German women's movement, grapples with the position of women confined by both patriarchy and heteronormativity. Stefan revisited these themes more than thirty years later in *Fremdschläfer* (*Alien Sleeper*, 2007).[32] The legacy of 1968 and its radicalization in the terrorism of the Red Army Faction is highlighted in this present volume by Odile Kennel, whose narrator of the novel *Mit Blick auf See* (*Lakeside View*) is a lesbian who attempts to restore a continuity with a repressed personal and political past. Other important lesbian authors began writing at this time as well: Christa Reinig, whose novel *Mädchen ohne Uniform*

(*Girls without Uniform*, 1981) revisits the theme of Leontine Sagan's late Weimar-era film *Mädchen in Uniform* (*Girls in Uniform*, 1931), based on a play by Christa Winsloe about the all-girls boarding school she attended in the early twentieth century. As Simone Pfleger and Faye Stewart write, Reinig "suggests that some institutional spaces—like the Prussian school and its later iterations in the Weimar Republic and the postwar Federal Republic—affirm hegemonic discourses of gender and sexuality, the text, and particularly the preposition *ohne* [without] in its title, also points to the potential for resistance and change."[33]

Reinig's work illustrates the intersections between queer literary and cinematic traditions, and indeed the Generation of 1968 saw considerable important queer cultural production. Rainer Werner Fassbinder's groundbreaking but not uncontroversial films *Faustrecht der Freiheit* (*Fox and His Friends*, 1975) and *In einem Jahr mit dreizehn Monden* (*In a Year of Thirteen Moons*, 1978) present queer identities in the context of bourgeois capitalism's repression of difference but with what can also be seen as a critique of homonormativity avant la lettre.[34] Rosa von Praunheim's *It Is Not the Homosexual Who Is Perverse, but the Society in Which He Lives* (1971) also casts a highly critical eye on German gay men's efforts to conform to the demands of West German capitalism's bourgeois values; this piece raised considerable ire in the gay male community since it was perceived as revealing faults and weaknesses of the community to a straight audience.[35] It is not surprising that films such as these were not embraced by the emerging gay rights movement in the United States. Furthermore, as the American gay liberation movement transformed from its original anti-identitarian and liberationist approach to one focused on identity and assimilation, filmmakers such as Monika Treut used a feminist lens to interrogate what Gayle Rubin described as the limits of acceptable sexuality in her groundbreaking article "Thinking Sex."[36]

The emergence of the world's second gay-rights movement was a largely American phenomenon: Anglophone voices predictably exercised immense influence on the new politics that soon became a worldwide movement. Anglophone hegemony is also reflected in literary production: post-Stonewall queer literary voices such as Andrew Holleran, Edmund White, Felice Picano, Armistead Maupin, and Rita Mae Brown are all available in German translation. Holleran's *Dancer from the Dance* appeared as *Tänzer der Nacht* in 1997 with Bruno Gmünder, a publisher that specialized largely in fiction, nonfiction, and photography for gay men; White's

The Beautiful Room Is Empty in 1991 with Kindler Verlag, and Maupin's *Tales of the City* with the mainstream publisher Rowohlt. Felice Picano, when traveling to Berlin in the summer of 1994 to promote a new translation of his book *The Lure* (1979), concluded that "if there was a gay German literary scene it was hard to find," but noted "that might be changing," and lauded Michael Roes, who in 1992 had published *Jizchak. Versuch über das Sohnesopfer* (*Yitzhak: Essay on the Sacrifice of the Son*), which revisits the Abraham and Isaac story.[37] Twenty-six years after Picano made his observation, one can state unequivocally that there *is* a queer German literary scene, although it remains virtually unknown to Anglophone readers due to the continued imbalance of literary translation between German and English.

The richness and diversity of queer German literature today can be traced in part to developments in the 1990s, which saw the founding of important queer-niche publishers that continue to play a role in the literary life of German-speaking Europe. Such presses offered a venue for scholarship that pursued a project of rediscovering queer German history: Claudia Schoppmann's *Zeit der Maskierung* (*Days of Masquerade: Life Stories of Lesbian Women in the "Third Reich"*), originally published with Orlanda Frauenverlag in Berlin in 1992 and then with Fisher Verlag in 1998, or with any of the publications of the Verlag Rosa Winkel, whose name refers to the pink triangle assigned by the Nazis to homosexuals. Two significant contributions to the historical exploration of queer lives under National Socialism and East German communism captured attention on the other side of the Atlantic: Charlotte von Mahlsdorf's *Ich bin meine eigene Frau* (1992) appeared in English in as *I Am My Own Wife* and was adapted by Doug Wright into a Pulitzer Prize–winning play by the same name. Mahlsdorf dressed in women's clothes under four different regimes in the twentieth century and was obsessed with collecting antique furniture. Any attempt to classify her, whether as trans, gay, or something else, would fall flat. The Austrian feminist author Erica Fischer's documentary narrative *Aimée und Jaguar* (1995) on the life of the Jewish lesbian Felice Schragenheim was translated into English and adapted into a German-language feature film by Max Färberböck, released in both Germany and the United States in 1999. Schragenheim lived underground in wartime Berlin and entered into a romantic relationship with the "Aryan" housewife Lilly Wust until she was deported to Theresienstadt and then to Auschwitz. The relative level of recognition obtained by Mahlsdorf's and Fischer's writing demonstrates that the explorations of twentieth-century queer German histories, which had begun in West Germany (the Federal Republic of Germany) after 1968 and somewhat later in East Germany (the German Democratic Republic), entered mainstream discussions after reunification.[38] The public acknowledgment of the suffering of queer men and women under the Nazis led to the construction of the Memorial to the Homosexuals Persecuted under National Socialism, which opened in central Berlin in 2008 in close proximity to the Memorial to the Murdered Jews of Europe.

Today, queer voices are flourishing throughout German-speaking Europe, not merely in niches but in mainstream publishing. Queer presses such as Querverlag, founded by Ilona Bubeck and the American expatriate Jim Baker in 1995, Krug & Schadenberg, which calls itself "the publishing house for lesbian literature," and Männerschwarm in Hamburg, which has published primarily gay male literature since 1992, continue to play important roles in disseminating fiction and nonfiction relevant to queer communities in Germany, Austria, and Switzerland. Authors represented in this volume whose work is published with queer presses include Claudia Breitsprecher, Marko Martin, Peter Rehberg, Lovis Cassaris, and Tania Witte. At the same time, broader audiences are being reached with mainstream publishers such as dtv (Odile Kennel), btb (Angela Steidele), Suhrkamp (Gunter Geltinger and Sasha Marianna Salzmann), Kiepenheuer und Witsch (Alain Claude Sulzer), and Fischer (Antje Rávik Strubel). Antje Wagner first published with Querverlag, achieved her literary breakthrough with a series of short stories and a novel with Kiepenheuer und Witsch, and now chooses to write youth fiction, where she feels there is a greater scope of impact in fostering openness to diversity. Under the pseudonym Ella Blix, she collaborates with Tania Witte in this endeavor. Their success in this market inherits the legacy of Andreas Steinhöfel, whose novel *Die Mitte der Welt* (*The Middle of the World*, Munich: Carlsen Verlag, 1998) achieved remarkable success given its open and explicit depiction of the adolescent protagonist's budding homosexuality; a film version directed by Jakob Erwa was released in 2016.

Anja Kümmel's writing explores the literary implications of queer theory through the vehicle of dystopia. The *Frankfurter Allgemeine Zeitung* critic Dietmar Dath, who in Kümmel's novel *Träume digitaler Schläfer* (*Dreams of Digital Sleepers*, 2012) sees George Orwell and Aldous Huxley "waving from a distance,"[39] finds that Kümmel writes narratives that no longer distinguish between present, past, and future but instead constructs these categories only in reference to one another.

This anthology attempts to incorporate the multiple perspectives represented by the diverse identities, publication venues, thematic interests, and geographical settings of contemporary queer writing in German without claiming to offer an exhaustive representation of the contemporary German-language queer literary scene.

A central theme of many of the authors represented here is the narrativization of a queer German history that situates non-heteronormative sexuality and gender expression at the heart of watershed events, for example, the ascension of Frederick the Great to the throne. Under Frederick, Prussia became the premier military power in German-speaking Europe, challenging the preeminence of the Hapsburgs and setting the stage for the eventual unification of Germany under Prussian domination with the exclusion of Austria. The tension between the ideals of militaristic masculinity and homoerotic bonds, accompanied by the omnipresent fear of disgrace, imprisonment, scandal, and emasculation is a theme central to Thomas Mann's portrayal of Gustav Aschenbach, who, hailing from Silesia—the Austrian province wrested from the Austrian Empress Maria Theresa by Frederick the Great—exhibits many of the same tendencies toward "effeminacy" that caused the young Frederick to be despised and persecuted by his father. Michael Roes, in grappling with the story of the Crown Prince's relationship with Hans Hermann von Katte, works with the conscious awareness of this story's weight in German history and culture. His decision to write from Katte's perspective brings both a queer perspective to this story and a fruitful violation of the boundaries between historical documentation and fantasy. One also sees such an aesthetic at work in the fiction of Angela Steidele, Christoph Poschenrieder, and Odile Kennel, all of whom examine the relationship between politics and sexuality.

Significantly, writers such as Roes, Steidele, Poschenrieder, and Kennel leave judgments on the sexuality of their characters to the readers, thus opening up perspectives on alternative ways of being that the characters are still trying to come to terms with in the context of societies whose values allow little room for them to unfold publicly. Steidele's *Rosenstengel* brings the added complexity of viewing—from the perspective of a nineteenth-century doctor charged with the evaluation and care of King Ludwig of Bavaria—the gender transgressive behavior of a female who lived as a man and fought as a Prussian soldier in the early eighteenth century. King Ludwig, widely understood to have been homosexual, was the subject of Klaus Mann's novella *Vergittertes Fenster* (*Barred Window*, 1937). Steidele employs the epistolary form and masterfully imitates the language of the time to allow readers to imagine the possibilities of how one might have spoken of forbidden desires and transgressive gender practices in an age before the birth of modern sexual identity . . . and long before the circulation of trans and queer identities.

Other authors, while not explicitly writing queer histories, clearly situate personal narratives within a political context shaped by the history of German-speaking Europe. Joachim Helfer's semi-autobiographical narrative contrasts the current openness of Berlin, which offers perhaps unprecedented opportunity for queer expression, with that city's dark history as capital of National Socialist Germany; the achievements attained coexist with attitudes that led to the very horrors of Nazism. Sasha Marianna Salzmann's contemporary Berlin seems more a city at the brink of disaster than a cosmopolitan, sexually liberated utopia. The changes associated with the arrival of hundreds of thousands of refugees from the Middle East and the mixed responses of Berliners have inevitably become a theme in queer niche fiction beyond what is represented in this anthology, for one example, the crime novel *Schöneberger Steinigung* (*Stoning in Schöneberg*, Berlin: Querverlag, 2019) by Peter Fuchs, an Austrian who lives and writes in Berlin. Fuchs's novel pits a gay German police detective against queer alt-righters who wish to exploit the killing of a gay priest in order to fan xenophobic sentiment against Syrian refugees in Berlin. Perhaps more significantly, writing in German by queer authors born outside Germany is rapidly emerging into the mainstream to a degree that could not be represented in this volume. For example, journalist Ronya Othmann's semi-autobiographical debut novel *Die Sommer* (*The Summers*, Munich: Carl Hanser Verlag, 2020) narrates the coming of age of a Kurdish-Yazidi-German girl who spends her summers in her grandparents' village in Syria until the advance of ISIS troops forces her relatives to seek asylum in Germany. The sexual awakening of the protagonist presents far less of a conflict to her than the apparent indifference and insensitivity of her German friends to the fate of the Yazidi people.

Tania Witte's Berlin trilogy, compared in the German media to Armistead Maupin's legendary *Tales of the City*, which Witte had not yet read when she wrote her novels, portrays a metropolis in flux whose queer inhabitants are constantly reinventing themselves in response to outside and inside influences.[40] It would have been possible to compile an anthology of queer authors whose texts are set entirely in Berlin, but this would have failed to give voice not only to writers from other major German-speaking urban centers such as Cologne, Munich, and Vienna but also to depictions of queer life outside the metropolis. Unfortunately, the Swiss and Austrian contributions are far outweighed by those from Germany, something that can hopefully be corrected in a future anthology. This reflects, however, the pull of Berlin as a center for artists and writers, especially queer ones. Jochen Bauer is notably the sole Austrian voice in this volume; the excerpt from his novel *Das Fenster zur Welt* (*The Window to the World*, 2013) presents a triply queer perspective. Here, the protagonist lives not in Vienna, a city already marginalized in comparison to Berlin, but somewhere on the commuter train line; he is not integrated into the Viennese gay community and has "failed" to find happiness in partnered domesticity.

The group of Swiss authors represented is also small, yet the three contributors bring great diversity to this volume. Alain Claude Sulzer is a well-established figure in contemporary German-language literature; his success attests to an emerging acceptability of queer themes in literary fiction. Sulzer's novel, *Ein Perfekter Kellner* (*A Perfect Waiter*, 2004), brings a new form of engagement with Thomas Mann's legacy, one that is both lighthearted and serious: in the choice of a waiter as protagonist, Sulzer flaunts literary conventions according to which, as one critic writes, waiters would "not even come into consideration as secondary figures";[41] the author also plays upon the aging Mann's infatuation with a young Bavarian waiter named Franz Westermeier who inspired him to write an essay on Michelangelo.[42] Lovis Cassaris, in contrast, is a Querverlag author whose debut novel, *Ein letztes Mal wir* (*Us for the Last Time*, 2016), tells the story of a young professional who leaves Berlin to settle down with her partner in Zurich, who then becomes terminally ill with cancer. Yusuf Yeşilöz, along with Christoph Poschenrieder, is one of the two straight-identified writers represented in the anthology. Yusuf was born in Turkey but emigrated to Switzerland at the age of twenty-three to escape oppression as a Kurd. Learning German only upon his arrival in his adopted homeland, he chose to write in this language so to embrace a new identity that was not solely Turkish, Kurdish, or Swiss in order to communicate to his new compatriots. His decision to write two novels on the theme of the difficult topic of homosexuality in the Turkish diaspora in central Europe reflects his own journey in overcoming the beliefs he was brought up with, according to which, in his own words, being gay is akin to being a thief or a murderer.[43]

J. Walther, as a woman writing about a gay male couple, offers a double queer perspective in *Im Zimmer wird es still* (*A Hush Falls over the Room*,

2011). The rural setting and theme of non-HIV-related illness defies genre expectations for gay male writing, which is significant given that the novel was originally published with the gay-male press Bruno Gmünder. Walther's sparse German prose is reminiscent of the American author Jim Grimsley's succinct but evocative writing and, indeed, Walther's novel begins with an epigraph from Grimsley's *Comfort and Joy*. Other authors in the volume explicitly thematize the contrast between Berlin and rural German village life. For example, Antje Wagner in her youth novel *Unland*, or Claudia Breitsprecher in *Hinter dem Schein die Wahrheit* (*Behind the Appearance, the Truth*, 2017), in which a Berlin lesbian returns after a long hiatus to her hometown when her nephew goes missing after having been outed to the whole community.

Any anthology of contemporary German-language fiction would be remiss not to include literature depicting what is described by the German phrase "*das Selbst in der Fremde*," which means something like "the self in a place that is not one's home" or somewhat more reductively "the self in a strange place." The writers in this volume depict traveling and living away from home for various purposes: to overcome relationship crises, to pursue professional opportunities, in search of sexual encounters, or even to continue to lead an outsider existence that seems no longer possible in the consumerist culture of contemporary Germany. Gunther Geltinger's novel *Benzin* (*Gasoline*, 2019) reflects on the privileged position of a white gay male couple traveling through South Africa and Zimbabwe who not only due to their sexuality but also to their race and first-world status are marked as "other." Marko Martin's literary texts are overwhelmingly set outside of Germany; they combine an unapologetic depiction of gay male sexuality with a boundless curiosity and a lens on the world that is highly self-conscious of being mediated through the experiences of writers, filmmakers, and artists who have gone before him. Friedrich Kröhnke has written extensively based on his experiences traveling and living outside of Germany. The protagonist of his novel *Ciao Vaschek* (2003) chooses to leave Berlin for Prague in order to "search for or find on every corner the possibility of indecent behavior."[44] Both Antje Rávik Strubel and Peter Rehberg write about the United States, based on their own personal experiences there with the academic and literary communities. Their texts offer not merely a German or a queer view of America but a queer *German* view, while also subjecting their narrators and protagonists to a queer American gaze.

In defining contemporary queer voices as those of living authors, we admit to having drawn an arbitrary line for the purpose of limiting the selections to the space available for this volume. In doing so, some significant voices have been excluded, for example, Jan Stressenreuter, who died in December 2018. Stressenreuter's novels and stories, all published with Querverlag, span two decades and include AIDS narratives, erotica, and his wildly popular crime novels set in Cologne. All authors represented here were born after the end of the Nazi regime; for those from Germany, most were old enough to have grown up in either the West or the East, such that they were shaped by these different experiences. Only a few are old enough to have been affected by the most stringent version of Paragraph 175 that remained in effect in West Germany until 1969, but all have certainly lived through tremendous changes in Europe and the world in the status of people who identify as queer. Finally, given the significant changes in the past two decades regarding the availability and circulation of queer themes in literature, all texts selected for inclusion in the anthology were written in the twenty-first century, although several authors represented here began their literary careers in the prior century.

Selections in the anthology have been grouped into six categories in order to assist readers who are interested in particular themes and may not wish to read in a linear fashion. While all such categorizations are necessarily reductive, given that many of the selections address multiple themes, we believe that the headings provide guides to central aspects of the texts included under each of the following rubrics: History, Berlin, Intertexts, Intercultural Encounters, Youth, and Relationships. For example, while Michael Roes's *Zeithain* deals with the relationship between Hans Hermann von Katte and Crown Prince Frederick of Prussia, it is primarily an effort to provide a new, queer perspective on a topic of great significance to Germany history and thus listed under "History." Texts grouped under the categories of "Relationships" treat challenges experienced by same-sex couples in the context of contemporary German, Austrian, and Swiss society's relative acceptance and openness to queer bodies and identities. Selections found under the rubric of "Berlin" are set in the German capital and interrogate the possibilities for queer expression in this city, which has undergone and continues to undergo such radical transformations. The section titled "Intercultural Encounters" contains writing that in some manner involve interactions between German-speakers and inhabitants of other regions of the world, whether these encounters occur between characters or are implicitly those of the author with another culture, for example, Antje Rávik Strubel's selection of the American West as a setting for many of the episodes in her novel *In den Wäldern des menschlichen Herzens* (*In the Forests of the Human Heart*). In the "Intertexts" section, the selections by Anje Kümmel, Hans Pleschinski, and Friedrich Kröhnke all frame how self-perception and presentation of the self to others is mediated through prior representations. In the section titled "Youth," two of the texts are explicitly from the genre of *Jugendroman* (youth novel), another portrays the coming out of an adolescent in rural Germany, and the fourth depicts an epiphanic moment in the sexual awakening of the narrator.

Contemporary queer literature in German offers a more complex assessment of queer experience than what can be accounted for by the historical development of a modern gay identity or by political assessments, which, building on the homogenization of gay experience, equate attainment of full personhood with a legal status that benefits largely middle- and upper-class white Europeans without an immigrant background. The voices represented in this volume attest to identifications with queer literary traditions reaching much farther back than the late nineteenth century; these writings also undermine the facile equation of white hegemonic metropolitan queer cultures with the reality of *all* queer experience, bringing into account rural and migrant spaces and gesturing toward an inclusiveness that goes beyond the designation *schwullesbisch* (gay-lesbian) to imagine bisexual, trans, and still-undefined modes of being. Regrettably, queer voices of color are absent from this volume. Although Afro-German filmmakers, journalists, and writers have become more prominent over the last several decades and have increasingly been studied and written about by Germanists, their representation in queer fiction is still minimal. Authors of fiction who identify as trans are also absent, although some of the contributors to the anthology identify as nonbinary. Clearly, much work needs to be done in German-language cultural production and scholarship to create a more inclusive picture of queer life. We hope that this volume also inspires others to continue the project of identifying and making accessible a greater diversity of queer voices.

Notes

1. Michel Foucault, *The History of Sexuality*, vol. 1, *An Introduction* (New York: Vintage, 1990), 43.

2. Katie Sutton, *The Masculine Woman in Weimar Germany* (Oxford: Berghahn, 2011); Sutton, *Sex Between Mind and Body: Sexology and Psychoanalysis in the German-Speaking World, 1890s–1930s* (Ann Arbor: University of Michigan Press, 2019); Heike Bauer, *The Hirschfeld Archives: Violence, Death, and Queer Culture* (Philadelphia: Temple University Press, 2017); Laurie Marhoefer, *Sex and the Weimar Republic: German Homosexual Emancipation and the Rise of the Nazis* (Toronto: University of Toronto Press, 2015).

3. Robert Beachy, *Gay Berlin: Birthplace of a Modern Identity* (New York: Vintage Books, 2015), 85ff. The term "urnings" is from Ulrich's series of booklets, published 1864–65.

4. See Catherine Bailey Gluckman, "Constructing Queer Female Identities in Late Realist German Fiction," *German Life and Letters* 62, no. 2 (July 2012): 318–32.

5. See, for example, Katie Sutton, "Female Masculinities and Conflicting Lesbian Identities in Anna Elisabet Weirauch's *Der Skorpion*," in *Quer Durch Die Geisteswissenschaften: Perspektiven Der Queer Theory*, ed. Elahe Haschemi Yekani and Beatrice Michaelis (Berlin: Querverlag, 2005), 267–81.

6. Anna Elisabet Weirauch, *The Scorpion* (Paris: Olympia Press, 2009), Kindle: Location 1759 of 4087.

7. Marhoefer, *Sex and the Weimar Republic*, 56.

8. Marhoefer, *Sex and the Weimar Republic*, 51.

9. Katie Sutton problematizes the dichotomy often constructed between sexology and psychoanalysis in her study of the dynamic interplay between these two groupings in *Sex Between Mind and Body*.

10. John Henry Mackay, *The Hustler*, trans. Hubert Kennedy (Boston: Alyson Publications, 1985).

11. Karl Friedrich von Linden, *Die Süßen: Ein Berliner Roman* (Hamburg, Männerschwarm, 2007).

12. Manfred Herzer, "Nachwort," in Magnus Hirschfeld, *Berlins drittes Geschlecht* (Berlin: Verlag Rosa Winkel, 1991), 145–61.

13. Rick Chamberlin, "Coming Out of His Father's Closet: Klaus Mann's *Der fromme Tanz* as an Anti-*Tod in Venedig*," *Monatshefte* 97, no. 4 (2005): 615–27.

14. Rolf Goebel, "Queer Berlin: Lifestyles, Performances, and Capitalist Consumer Society," *German Quarterly* 79, no. 4 (Fall 2006): 484–504, here 485.

15. Samuel Clowes Huneke, "The Reception of Homosexuality in Klaus Mann's Weimar Era Works," *Monatshefte* 105, no. 1 (2013): 86–100.

16. Michael Töteberg, "Nachwort: Annemarie und ihre Freunde," in Annamarie Schwarzenbach, *Freunde um Bernhard* (Basel: Lenos, 1993), 196.

17. Gary Schmidt, "The Homosexual Text in Joachim Helfer's *Cohn und König*," *Gegenwartsliteratur* 4 (2005): 185–210.

18. Werner Hinzpeter, *Schöne schwule Welt* (Berlin: Querverlag, 1997).

19. Goebel, "Queer Berlin," 484.

20. Johannes Kram, *Ich habe nichts gegen Schwule, aber . . .* (Berlin: Querverlag, 2018).

21. David Clarke, "Dandyism and Homosexuality in the Novels of Christian Kracht," *Seminar: A Journal of Germanic Studies* 41, no. 1 (February 2005): 36–54;

Gary Schmidt, "Fear of the Queer? On Homosexuality, Masculinity and the Auratic in Christian Kracht's Anti-Pop Pop Novels," in *German Pop Literature: A Companion*, ed. Margaret McCarthy, 209–36 (Berlin: Walter de Gruyter).

22. See Marhoefer, *Sex and the Weimar Republic*, 194–98.

23. Michael Roes interview with Gary Schmidt in Berlin on June 26, 2019.

24. See, for example, Paul Derks, *Die Schande der heiligen Päderastie: Homosexualität und Öffentlichkeit in der deutschen Literature, 1750–1850* (Berlin: Verlag Rosa Winkel, 1990); Alice Kuzniar, ed., *Outing Goethe and His Age* (Stanford, CA: Stanford University Press, 1996); Robert Tobin, *Warm Brothers: Queer Theory and the Age of Goethe* (Philadelphia: University of Pennsylvania Press, 2000).

25. Some notable exceptions include Goebel, "Queer Berlin"; Faye Stewart, "Queer Elements: The Poetics and Politics of Antje Rávic Strubel's Literary Style," *Women in German Yearbook* 30 (2014): 44–73; Claudia Breger, "Postmoderne Inszenierungen von Gender in der Literatur: Meinecke, Schmidt, Roes," in *Räume der literarischen Postmoderne: Gender, Performativität, Globalisierung*, ed. Paul Michael Lützeler, Ingeborg Hoesterey, Alexander Honold, and Doris Kolesch (Tübingen: Stauffenburg, 2000), 97–125.

26. Goebel, "Queer Berlin," 502.

27. For an account of the possibilities of queer literary expression under the Nazi regime, see Christian Klein, *Schreiben im Schatten: Homoerotische Literatur im Nationalsozialismus* (Hamburg: Männerschwarm, 2000).

28. See, for example, Andrew Hewitt, *Political Inversions: Homosexuality, Fascism, and the Modernist Imagination* (Stanford, CA: Stanford University Press, 1996); Dagmar Herzog, *Sex after Fascism: Memory and Morality in Twentieth-Century Germany* (Princeton: Princeton University Press, 2005); Gary Schmidt, *The Nazi Abduction of Ganymede* (Bern: Peter Lang, 2003).

29. Switzerland appears to be somewhat of an exception, as described in Hubert Kennedy's study of the gay journal *Der Kreis*. Hubert Kennedy, *The Ideal Gay Man: The Story of "Der Kreis"* (San Francisco: Harrington Park Press, 1999).

30. Christoph Schmitt-Maaß, "Erbrechen oder Einverleiben? Zwischen eigenmotivierter Fremdforschung und Gefährdung des Subjekts: Ethnographie im Spannungsfeld von Wissenschaft, Poesie und Autobiographie," *Monatshefte* 100, no. 2 (2008): 191–212.

31. See Karl-Ludwig Stenger, "Introduction to Small-Town Story," *New German Critique* 23 (Spring–Summer 1981): 97–99.

32. Sonja Klocke, "'Committed from Head to Toe?' Cancer, Immigration, and Kinship in Verena Stefan's *Fremdschläfer*," *Women in German Yearbook* 26 (2010): 117–35.

33. Simone Pfleger and Faye Stewart, "In and Out of Uniform: Imagining and Illustrating Queer Subjects, Institutional Spaces, and Counterpublics in Christa Reinig's *Mädchen ohne Uniform* and 'Die ewige Schule,'" *Seminar: A Journal of Germanic Studies* 55, no. 2 (2019): 166–85.

34. See, for example, Stephen Tropiano, "Fassbinder's Not-So-Pretty Picture," *Gay & Lesbian Review Worldwide* 8, no. 2 (March 2001): 18–20.

35. Randall Halle, "From Perverse to Queer: Rosa von Praunheim's Films in the Liberation Movements of the Federal Republic," in *German Cinema since Unification*, ed. David Clarke (London: Continuum International Publishing Group, 2005).

36. Gayle Rubin, "Thinking Sex: Notes for a Radical Theory of the Politics of Sexuality," in *The Lesbian and Gay Studies Reader*, ed. Henry Abelove, Michele Aina Barale, and David M. Halperin, 3–44 (New York: Routledge, 1993). The scholarship on Treut's cinematic oeuvre is too large to cite in full, but for an interesting consideration of the relationship between feminism and pornography, see Muriel Cormican, "Pro-Porn Rhetoric and the Cinema of Monika Treut," *Women in German Yearbook: Feminist Studies in German Literature and Culture* 19 (2003): 179–99.

37. Felice Picano himself noted the imbalance in translations in queer literature between English and German in his article "Letter from Berlin: The Gay Male 70s Live On—In Germany" in *Lambda Book Report: A Review of Contemporary Gay and Lesbian Literature* 4, no. 10 (May–June 1995): 8–9.

38. See, for example, the concentration camp memoir of Josef Kohout, *Die Männer mit dem Rosa Winkel*, written by his friend Hans Neumann under the pen name Heinz Heger, available in English translation as Heinz Heger, *The Men with the Pink Triangle: The True, Life-and-Death Story of Homosexuals in the Nazi Death Camps* (Boston: Alyson Publication, 1980). The memoir inspired Martin Sherman's play *Bent* (1979), which was made into an English-language film with the same name (dir. Sean Mathias, 1997). In East Germany, Heiner Carow's film *Coming Out* (1989), in which Charlotte von Mahlsdorf makes a cameo appearance, includes a scene where an older man in a gay bar tells younger listeners about how gay men were treated in the camps during the Nazi period. The film was one of the last productions of the East German state film studio DEFA and premiered on November 9, 1989, the night the Berlin Wall fell. See Dennis Sweet, "Bodies for Germany, Bodies for Socialism: The German Democratic Republic Devises a Gay (Male) Body," in *Gender and Germanness*, ed. Patricia Herminghouse and Magda Mueller, 248–62 (Providence, RI: Berghahn, 1997).

39. Quoted in *Perlentaucher*: https://www.perlentaucher.de/buch/anja-kuemmel/traeume-digitaler-schlaefer.html.

40. Tania Witte interview with Gary Schmidt in Mannheim, Germany, on June 12, 2019.

41. Gieri Cavelty, quoted in *Perlentaucher*; https://www.perlentaucher.de/buch/alain-claude-sulzer/ein-perfekter-kellner.html.

42. Anthony Heilbut, *Thomas Mann: Eros and Literature* (New York: Alfred A Knopf, 1996), 433.

43. Yusuf Yeşilöz interview with Gary Schmidt in Winterthur, Switzerland, on June 13, 2019.

44. Friedrich Kröhnke, *Ciao Vaschek* (Zurich: Amman, 2003), 12.

I

HISTORY

Michael Roes

Michael Roes lives and works in Berlin. He studied psychology, philosophy, and German literature at the Freie Universität in Berlin and worked in the theater before writing a dissertation on the sacrifice of Isaac. Roes has received numerous stipends and residencies to pursue literary, cinematic, and ethnographic projects in countries such as Yemen, the United States, Algeria, Hungary, Mali, and China. His writing is in part inspired by Hubert Fichte's aesthetic project of blending the representation of the foreign and of the self in interaction with it. This approach foregrounds ethnography as narrative construction while also seeking to ground literature in "empirical" and "logical" processes.[1] Roes describes his own work as part of an "ethnological turn" rather than a postmodern one and sees the task of literature as preparing readers to "take the jump from the self to the other."[2]

Roes engaged early in his literary career with gender and sexuality across cultures and time periods, for example in the novels *Rub' al-khali—Leeres Viertel* (*Rub' al Khali—Empty Quarter*, 1996) and *Der Coup der Berdache* (*The Coup of the Berdache*, 1999).[3] *Zeithain* (2017), from which the excerpt below is taken, is written largely from the perspective of Hans Hermann von Katte, intimate friend of Crown Prince Frederick of Prussia, later Frederick the Great. Frederick's father, King Frederick William I, had Katte executed before the eyes of his son after he was condemned for aiding the Crown Prince in an attempt to flee to England. Roes was interested already at a young age in the Katte story, seeing in the young Prussian lieutenant a symbolic victim who took the place of the king's son, who was detested by his father for his putative effeminacy and love of the arts. Roes waited thirty years until he felt prepared to write a novel on a topic that is both well-known and hotly debated in German culture. The broader themes of religion, duty, masculinity, sexuality, and sacrifice lie at the core of Germany's historical development; in particular, the centrality of militaristic masculinity to the nation's identity proved fateful. Thus, queering narratives of masculine duty gives a voice to previously suppressed perspectives on relations between men in all-male institutions; it also has larger implications for the understanding of the relationship between sexual oppression and political manipulability. Roes notes that he did not wish to write a historical novel but one that blends fantasy and realism.[4] So that readers are constantly reminded that they are engaging with a work of fiction, Roes includes a frame narrative in the form of a fictional stand-in for the author-ethnographer, who searches for the historical Katte by visiting the locations that serve as setting for the inner narrative. In this manner, Roes's approach to the historical material remains consistent with his greater ethnopoetic project. The following excerpt is taken from that inner narrative, in which Katte is the first-person narrator.

from *Zeithain* (2017)

If I asked myself what happened between me and the Prince in Leipzig I would tell myself: nothing more than fleeting nocturnal encounters like those in the *Hasenstall* in Glaucha.[5] Yet, no one demands that I account for the nights we spent together. Therefore, I entrust our adventure to silence, for so long as no one utters a word about it, there is nothing to remember.

If one feeling remains from this night, it is a shadowy one that warns me to be on my guard.

The more the Crown Prince looks for opportunities in the following weeks to meet and be together, the more I keep my distance from him, often even dismissing him gruffly in order to avoid encouraging him with imprudent signs of affection. Through the scrutinizing eyes of a naturalist I observe the virtues and weaknesses of the Prince, so that in the future I might sustain him in his weaknesses and be wary of his strengths.

Yet, the unhealthy arousal of these imprudent nights is not quickly forgotten. The ways of the flesh are inscrutable. The changes creep in slowly and almost unnoticed, tiny changes that, taken as a whole, signify a complete transformation. For the time being, I don't know if it is my perception that has changed or if the things themselves have become brighter, clearer, more radiant.

Suddenly, all aspects of daily life appear upended and yet only now in their rightful place in this new order. It is as if my ears and eyes have been rinsed out, and yet I am aware that this extraordinary clear-sightedness cannot last. For like all sharpness, it dulls, it grows weary. It is difficult for me to differentiate between flesh and spirit, between elation and melancholy. What is soft and nondescript refreshes me; what is loud and piercing evokes my physical disgust. And then I think I have gone mad from so much clear-sightedness and clairaudience.

Zeithain, the tenth of June. Infantry maneuvers. Twenty-four battalions of infantry squares demonstrating how they beat their drums and fire their rifles one after the other in a square, consecutively in a line, and in reverse.[6]

"Woe betide us, if my father sees us together like this!"

"Don't think of it!"

"He *always* thinks of it: when he sees his Potsdam Giants,[7] when he sees you or Keith with me. For him, it is as if he has already sinned by thinking of it."

"That's why Pastor Francke[8] has such any easy time with him."

"Indeed, he considers himself dirty, so he must wash himself constantly and yet never gets clean, because he has not once touched what day and night he longs to touch. He believes that God sees everything and that his sinful desires already suffice to condemn him to eternal damnation."

"And you? Do you also think what we are doing is a sin?"

"I rejoice in it because my father forbids it to himself and the whole world!"

"That does not sound very flattering for me."

"I would not have thought that you were susceptible to flattery, Katte! I have always considered you to be the least vain person whom I have ever encountered and have learned to love you above all for that."

Scores of riffraff are bustling around in neighboring hamlets. Yet, great effort is being made to ensure order and cleanliness on the grounds of the encampment. Just today, eight vagabonds who had snuck into the camp were delivered by the village socager to the authorities at Grossenhain. One of them carries a valuable watch, which he must have stolen, although no one has reported the theft of a watch.

A few days after my visit to his apartment I received the first letter from Friedrich, sent from Wusterhausen. He writes that he finds himself in the most inane company imaginable. He could surely say another thing or two about the people his father surrounds himself with, but he had to get up at five o'clock in the morning and only now, at midnight, can he finally write to me.

"You know Wusterhausen," he writes. "If there is a hell, then it will look like this, at least for me: my very own hell, created just for me. At the entrance to the palace courtyard two bears are standing watch: wild, maleficent beasts that can only lumber around on their hind legs because the paws of their forelegs have been hacked off. Regardless of the weather we eat our noonday meal outside under a tent pitched under the large linden tree. When it rains heavily we sit in water up to our calves, since our dining quarters are in a small hollow. There are always more than twenty of us at the table, three-quarters of whom fast, for there are never more than six bowls served, and their contents have been cut so small that even a person who is only semi-hungry could empty them all by himself. And you know that my father, the king, is a heavy eater with an insatiable hunger. If the king is in a bad mood, the already paltry fare is reduced even further, and if he considers me worthy of punishment, I not infrequently sit before an empty plate. On all the autumn days that have led us annually to this bleak place, which is only good for my father's hunting pleasure, I have lived on nothing but bread and water. As a child I was always hungry. Although we are part of the royal family, my siblings and I often almost died of hunger.

"While the king takes his afternoon nap after dinner, the whole family must sit gathered around him completely still. Only on beatings does the king not skimp; he always has his cane at hand.

"The rooms in Wusterhausen resemble cells more than chambers," he writes, "and the whole crude facility is more of a barrack than a palace, so it is my father's favorite place. His sleeping quarters are right behind the guardroom of the artillery, his guardsmen closer to him than his lawfully wedded wife, who is lodged on a different floor in her own cloistral cell. And my sister and I are housed like doves in narrow attic garrets of this royal penitentiary.

"I am so weary of these things, dear Hans! Every day here I experience the most abominable scenes; I am so tired of it that I would rather beg for my bread than to keep living in this condition."

Zeithain, the 11th of June. Camp service.—In contrast to St. Augustine or the Eleatics, I am convinced that only the external world is the essential path that allows us to advance to the internal world. Maybe they will prove to be one and the same at the end of the journey.

Last night the Saxon Uhlans[9] tried to play a trick on us, most certainly not without the permission of their king. They sneak into the Prussian camp in order to steal the Prussian flag raised before Friedrich Wilhelm's tent but are discovered by the vigilant guards and repelled with appropriate force. His Majesty takes it in stride and calls the bloody incident a nice military jest.

On the way back to my lodging in Riesa, close to the banks of the Elbe and the nearby barrel bridge over the river, I run into an enormous swarm of mosquitoes, so bizarre that it almost resembles an infernal nightmare. It is as if they filled in every bit of air, flying up from the dank meadows into my mouth, eyes, ears, and nose, not maliciously, since they did not bite, but in such a dense swarm that they threatened to suffocate me.

I swat at them and manage to grab one of these beasts, small as a kernel of corn, in my fist, but I can hardly recognize what kind of a winged bug it might be, let alone am I able to describe it. Even the good Orfraie[10] feels plagued and threatened by the suffocating swarms and steers her hooves without further guidance from me toward the river, diving in along with her rider in order to fend off the invading army by immersing herself completely.

When I tell my roommates about this diabolical attack, they shake their heads in disbelief and say it must have been a swarm of June bugs gone wild. Whatever the case may be, my mare and I should be happy that they didn't bite.

"Hans? Are you asleep already?" Fritz awakens me in the middle of the night.

"Well, not anymore."

"Sorry." We have arrived safely back in Wust. Our leave is over, tomorrow my valet, Lieutenant Keith, and I must escort the Crown Prince in all haste back to Potsdam, so that his stern father does not make him pay for exceeding the leave he was granted.

"What is it?"

"One day I will no longer be afraid of anyone!"

"Maybe, one day. But I don't know if that is really so desirable."

"Fear destroys us, eats us up, makes life into a living hell!"

"And sometimes, albeit seldom, it saves us."

"The only thing that I still want to fear is that someday you will grow tired of me."

"You are talking nonsense."

"One day I will build us a house with many windows that face south, so that it is always bright in the beautiful, large rooms. And no servant will be allowed to wait on us, for I myself will be the one who removes your coat and rapier and pours your wine."

"Of which you have drunk too much today, undoubtedly! Try to sleep or I will bring you back to Potsdam tonight."

"Do you think we will still know each other in heaven? Or in hell?"

"In heaven there are probably so many distractions and so little misery that one has no need of friends."

"If hell were the price for our being together, I would prefer it to heaven."

"Yet at the moment you can't escape it quickly enough!"

"Heaven or hell, it's all the same to me. The main thing is that the judge does not send me where my dear departed father is."

"He is still alive. Go to sleep now!"

Zeithain, the 12th of July. Uninterrupted rain since early morning. Regardless of this, the artillery maneuver is taking place with forty-eight cannons and two regiments of infantry cover. The rain has long since saturated everything, yet the cannoneers succeed in firing quickly.

Friedrich Wilhelm commands us officers to observe the maneuver from start to finish. He himself perseveres in the rain in spite of his gout and his cold. He says he has not brought us along to feast and gawk but, above all, to carefully study the military techniques of the Saxons and learn from them.

The next letter from Fritz reaches me via messenger from Potsdam: "You will not believe it, Hans, but the king strikes me daily and treats me like a slave. And never does he let me rest or grant me the least possible recreation. He has forbidden reading, music, and instruction. I am hardly allowed to speak with anyone anymore and am constantly surrounded by spies and overseers. God knows when and in what circumstances we will see each other again!

"I lack even the most basic clothes necessary. And then the last scene I had with my father in the palace: he has me summoned in the morning and as soon as I enter he grabs me by the hair, throws me to the floor, and mauls me with his fists and boots. Then he drags me to the window, loops the curtain chord around my neck, and pulls it taut.

"Luckily, I am able to grab both his hands and call for help with my last bit of strength. Old Gummersbach rushes up and frees me from the king's grip, only himself to feel my father's cane.

"I still do not know the reason for his murderous rage. I have no other way to explain it but to say that madness has taken hold of him!"

Zeithain, the 13th of June. Lance throwing at straw pyramids and wrestling. Infantry, cavalry, and artillery maneuvers.

The field hospital is located two hours away on foot from the encampment, in Kreinitz. The devil only knows why it was set up so far off the beaten path, for the doctors do not lack for work. After the presentation of the artillery today, the powder residue left in the tube exploded in the face of the artillery master while he was cleaning the barrel, and three other cannoneers were also injured. In addition, a few sparks hit a munitions cartridge and caused it to blow up, injuring nine more soldiers.

Perhaps they placed the field hospital so far away so that less seriously indisposed soldiers are reluctant to report sick, preferring to stay on duty rather than hobbling for two hours all the way to Kreinitz because of a sprained ankle or an upset stomach. Yet, for those who are gravely injured like the artillery master, the long transport to succor can end fatally.

Late in the evening, shortly before ten o'clock when the gates to the Potsdam Court are shut, I slip into the garden and wait until the guard strides past. My gaze falls on the dark windowpane. The king has long since gone to bed. It is his custom to rise by five o'clock, and he compels all family members who are present to conform to his rhythm. It is no wonder that the queen always yearns for her summer relocation to Monbijou Palace.[11]

Friedrich inhabits two modest rooms in an isolated wing of the palace. Never before had I been in the palace at such a late hour. Moreover, I have come without the knowledge of the Crown Prince, even though he had urged me in his letter to visit him soon.

The Crown Prince's rooms lie at the end of the unlit corridor. When I knock quietly the heavy door is opened by Lieutenant Keith, who looks at me in astonishment. "Oh, Lieutenant von Katte!"

"Good evening, Keith. Is the Crown Prince not present?"

"No, Lieutenant. He accompanied the king this morning to Berlin."

"And why are you here then?"

"Actually, he wanted to return this evening to Potsdam. Is there a special reason for your visit?"

"No, nothing special. Just a surprise. I will let you go back to sleep now."

"Where will you sleep? You have your apartment in Berlin, don't you?"

"Yes, indeed."

"It is much too late for you to return to Berlin now."

"I'll hunker down at Wietersheim's or Ingersleben's."

"I can let you stay overnight here if you don't betray me to anyone."

"To whom?"

Keith is silent for a moment and turns red. Then he quickly says: "The Prince will scold me if I just send you out into the night."

I look around in Friedrich's small chamber and wonder what all has been discussed here and—even more—what all has been concealed or kept secret here. A table, a chair, a smoking candle, a narrow bed.

"Friedrich is a most lovable boy," says Keith. I say nothing in response to this unseemly judgment, for Keith is barely older than the Crown Prince. "But when you have to spend longer periods of time with him then sometimes you have enough for a while."

"Have you no fear that the Crown Prince could learn of your loose statements?"

"No, Fritz knows and loves my loose lips."

I rise from the narrow cot, grab my hat and rapier, and take my leave. "I must go now. Thank you for your openness, Herr Lieutenant. But do not overdo it!"

Tired and somewhat indignant I walk down the dark corridor, then I hear bootsteps coming toward me. I stop at a window, through which a little bit of moonlight falls into the corridor, so that whoever is coming toward me notices my presence and is not startled.

"Katte?" It is the voice of the Crown Prince.

"Yes, it is I, your Highness."

"At this hour?"

"A spur of the moment idea."

"You weren't leaving already?"

"I was told you were in Berlin."

"I informed Keith that I wished to return this evening at all costs."

We retrace the few steps back to Friedrich's apartment. Keith casts a dirty look at us when we cross through the anteroom, continuing immediately into Friedrich's parlor. I feel my stomach churn as if I had consumed rotten food.

Friedrich makes a light, then fans the almost extinguished flame in the fireplace.

"Should Keith prepare a coffee for us?"

"It's a bit late for coffee."

"Then he should bring us beer!"

The Prince looks tired. I cannot possibly stay.

In the morning, my body awakens at the usual time, but my head does not want to follow suit. It harkens inward, my heart beats blithely, unburdened.

Next to me lies Friedrich, now no longer a child but a seventeen-year-old man. I let him rest, dress silently, and leave the Prince's spartan apartment.

Notes

Translated by Gary Schmidt.

1. Christoph Schmitt-Maaß, "Erbrechen oder Einverleiben? Zwischen eigenmotivierter Fremdforschung und Gefährdung des Subjekts: Ethnographie im Spannungsfeld von Wissenschaft, Poesie und Autobiographie," *Monatshefte* 100, no. 2 (2008) 191–212.
2. Michael Roes interview with Gary Schmidt in June 2019.
3. Claudia Breger, "Postmoderne Inszenierungen von Gender in der Literatur: Meinecke, Schmidt, Roes," in *Räume der literarischen Postmoderne: Gender, Performativität, Globalisierung*, ed. Paul Michael Lützeler, Ingeborg Hoesterey, Alexander Honold, and Doris Kolesch (Tübingen: Stauffenburg, 2000), 97–125; Robert Tobin, "Postmoderne Männlichkeit: Michael Roes Und Matthias Politycki," *Zeitschrift Für Germanistik* 12, no. 2 (2002): 324–33.
4. Michael Roes interview with Gary Schmidt in June 2019.
5. Literally, "rabbit pen," as the boys referred to their quarters in the boarding school of August Hermann Francke, a leading pietist whose ideas influenced Frederick William I. Pietism was a reformed branch of Lutheranism that stressed biblical doctrine and individual responsibility.
6. Military terms: *Carre-feuer*, *Lauffeuer* (running fire), and *Heckfeuer*.
7. "Lange Kerls" in German, a regiment commanded by Frederick William I of Prussia, for which he recruited tall soldiers.
8. Reference to the pietist August Hermann Francke (1663–1727), whose ideas influenced Frederick William I; see also the excerpt from Angela Steidele's *Rosenstengel* in this volume.
9. Light cavalry common in central and eastern European armies.
10. Katte's horse.
11. A rococo palace that was located in what is now central Berlin on the north bank of the Spree River, now the site of a park with the same name.

Angela Steidele

ANGELA STEIDELE, who lives and works in Cologne, completed a doctoral dissertation on the topic of love and desire between women in German-language literature. Her biographical writing includes *Geschichte einer Liebe: Adele Schopenhauer und Sibylle Mertens* (*Story of a Love: Adele Schopenhauer and Sibylle Mertens*, 2010) and *Anne Lister: Eine erotische Biografie* (*Anne Lister: An Erotic Biography*, 2017), which recounts the life of the English aristocrat with passions for women, travel, and keeping a diary. In *Zeitreisen* (*Travels through Time*, 2018), Steidele revisits the trip she took to Russia and the Caucasus in preparation to write her biography of Lister.

The excerpt below is taken from *Rosenstengel: Ein Manuskript aus dem Umfeld Ludwigs II* (*Rosenstengel: A Manuscript from the Milieu of Ludwig II*), an epistolary novel, which was awarded the Bavarian Book Prize in 2015. The novel builds upon Steidele's study of Catharina Linck, *In Männerkleidern* (*In Men's Clothes*, 2004); Linck was a Prussian soldier executed for dressing in men's clothes and engaging in lesbian relationships in early eighteenth-century Prussia. Steidele's letters mimic not only the spelling and style of Linck's era but also of the late nineteenth century itself, when a certain Doctor Müller, charged to evaluate and tend to King Ludwig of Bavaria by conspirators who wish to declare him unfit to rule, comes across letters referring to Linck and shows them to the king. Ludwig, whose homosexual proclivities are widely known—they were thematized, for example, in Klaus Mann's novella *Vergittertes Fenster* (*Barred Window*, 1937)—encourages Dr. Müller to pursue the research on Linck; both king and doctor see in her story an affirmation of their own same-sex affections and a counternarrative to the ongoing pathologizing of same-sex desire in the medical community in the mid- to late nineteenth century. Letters 60 and 108, translated in the following section, represent an exchange between an officer who arrested Linck, Friedrich Wilhelm von Grumbkow, and Christian Thomasisus, a renowned jurist and philosopher associated with the German Enlightenment who was entangled in a feud with the pietist August Hermann Francke, in whose orphanage Linck had spent time. Once Grumbkow discovers that the cross-dressing Linck was a product of Francke's orphanage, he writes to Thomasius, believing Linck can be used as a weapon by the Enlightenment reformer in his struggle against Francke's brand of pietism. Letters 175 to 177 represent an exchange between Ludwig, Dr. Müller, and Empress Elisabeth of Austria, more commonly known as "Sissi," in which Linck is discussed, as is Sappho, as a historical model for lesbian love.

from *Rosenstengel* (2015)

[60] Grumbkow to Thomasius

Leuven, May 28, 1713

Most Noble and Learned
Professor of Widespread Fame

I bow wholly to your judgment of the pietistic sacrilege. If the weeds of pietism be not ripped out decisively, their damaging seeds will soon spread everywhere. Yet, let my Most Esteemed Sir moderate his just wrath: The King knows the ends of such pietists be not active Christendom but the thousand-year realm in which they might stomp across the Kings and Potentates of this world. From the City of God which they erect before the gates of Halle they hope in the course of time to transform our Prussia into a Theocracy. Yet I beseech you, Illustrious Sir: esteem neither the King nor his Privy Councilors so pious or stupid they should consent to be Francke's stooges.

I bid you, most worthy Benefactor, deign to hear what followed in Linckin's[1] story. Such curious circumstances as were in the matter should not easily occur a second time. Whilst we awaited Francke's answer the examination of the body was decreed. Thus was a local Midwife summoned, who with the Regiment Surgeon examined Linckin in my presence. They unclothe Linckin first above, to discover, as the Pastor said, first the tin plate and then two beautiful, young, and full, albeit not overly large proofs of her Womanliness. Says Linckin, the tin plate veiled not only her female breasts but served also to protect her in battle, wherefore none of her tentmates has ever wondered. As men sometimes too have fat breasts, the Surgeon demands to proceed to further inspection. Linckin resists and struggles and becomes tame only when I impress on her that only full proof of her Womanliness can save her, lest the Judgment on her, already made, be executed forthwith. What astonishment befalls us all, Midwife and Surgeon too, as Linckin's breeches at last drop and both a horn and certain leather instrument appear, which both she had bound before her birthing part by means of a leather strap. When asked, answers Linckin, the horn was for pissing so she could do as her comrades. From a young ox it comes, is none too big and just slightly bent, has a right broad opening on the shaft and in its tip, Linckin had bored a little hole. Enjoined by me, Linckin shows us how she hath employed it. Many a man should wish as mighty a gush as that which Linckin, standing, whizzed into the bucket.

Asked of the leather instrument, Linckin was mute. As I signify to her yet again that full Truth only might save her, she answers reluctantly, she had to do what her comrades did. Once the midwife and surgeon were released, she finally relates how in winter camp she fashioned the manly member from leather and stuffed it, first attaching a sack fashioned of pig bladders and, when that would not stay, the two stuffed testiculi likewise made from leather. She sewed the strap from saddlery, which wisdom she taught herself; in Halle she also apprenticed with a button maker, of whom she learned many an art. With this instrument bound to her pudenda, Linckin visited many a wench and for two pence stuck the leather thing in her body. Various widows did she also caress and employed the leather thing likewise; the widows felt the dildo and played with it but did not recognize it. At times she walked whole miles to chase a pretty hussy. I confess, my esteemed Sir, to have felt the same, without always having the right instrument at hand as Linckin did, tactically erected and not from weak nature's vain chance.

I need not further elucidate, most famous learned gentleman of laws, that the Truth spares Linckin a Deserter's fate yet drives her into new Calamities, for an unmerciful Judge could, well founded, bring forth the charge of Sodomy. I pursue henceforth, however, with Linckin my own intentions, who, witty and smart, is more valuable to us in living flesh. Thus, have I said in the field not a word to a living soul of said interview and sternly admonished Linckin to silence, gathering to myself the corpora delicti. To surgeon and midwife gave I each a guilder that they should affirm the Inquisition her uncontested Womanliness and mention only briefly the horn, whilst keeping all else to themselves. Thereat was determined Linckin is indeed a Woman and as such belongs not in War, wherefore neither shall she be punished as Deserter.

After Francke hath now acknowledged Linckin and pleaded she be spared, tomorrow she shall be dispatched with a pass to Halle and must reach anon the Saale. I send to you, my most esteemed Sir, the finest of gunpowder in the form of a sly maiden, who, as wished by us and God, shall explode the pietistic parsons.

In hopes of serving my most esteemed Sir, I remain
your most devoted, loyal Servant
Friedrich Wilhelm von Grumbkow

[108] Thomasius to Grumbkow

Halle, July 5, 1713

Most Honorable and Esteemed Sir

I live in the hope that my most esteemed Sir yet lives in this enduring war and finds himself still in a desirable state. The sly maiden, thus returned so grandly adorned to Halle by my most Esteemed Sir, hath exceeded our greatest expectations. After Catharina Linckin arrived here safe and sound I summoned her at once to me and offered her refreshment that I might bind her to me. That Francke should not have the occasion to likewise offer her good deeds, I led her to the Cloth-Maker of the University, that the Master be shown her arts and, upon completed examination, retain her in his charge. There she now makes flannel, dyes calico with many colors and keeps eight, nine, and more spinning girls under her command.

After I held forth on tolerance and forbearance to the Cloth-Maker, giving him also a few kreutzer, he now lets Linckin walk according to her will, dressed betimes as Man, betimes as Woman. And should the wicked street urchins shout after her, she has a riposte at hand for each to bring to silence the most malicious scoffer. As Linckin hath more wit than many a Latin journeyman whose snores disrupt my lectures, I have bestowed upon her a place in my heart. That haughtiness not seize her, believing she might wrap me around her finger, I revealed to her what I learnt of her prior life from the epistles of My Most Honorable Sir.

That a former Orphan Maid from the Glaucha Asylum[2] who served as musketeer in war with Prussian troops now strides in breeches through the streets of Halle, hath set all city tongues to wag. I rub my hands with glee seeing Francke pass by my house to make his way to St. Ulrich, where soon he shall be installed as Pastor Primarius, and the same lads who now almost reverently allow Linckin to pass, set upon him, who in Christ can poorly defend himself. He is received by the venerable men who elected him with faces of stone and deafening silence.

Could hitherto Linckin not have reigned more blessings upon us, yesterday hath brought yet more: Soldiers have seized Linckin and will not release her. Beknownst to my Most Esteemed Sir, the most despicable Crimpers walk about in Halle, who lead Craftsmen, Apprentices, and Students to the tavern, plying them with brandy, more forcing than persuading them to sign the contract of recruitment. Indeed, at time the Crimpers surround a church and tear all able-bodied men from worship, waylay at night the townsmen's homes and farmyards, not releasing those whom they have captured. So did it come to pass with Catharina Linckin, who in manly garments strolled in the gardens before the gates. Since she had her fill of Soldier's craft she refuses to sign the Contract. When the Crimpers still will not release her, she reveals herself as Woman. In spite of this, the Crimpers still wish not to let her go. Whoever can wear breeches is not too weak to bear a musket. Linckin has no choice but to send Johanna Sophia, Francke's daughter, who accompanied her, for help. But my words, be they good or bad, count for naught with those soldiers: Linckin is brought to City Hall and placed under arrest.

Hardly is this made known in the city than hastens Anna Magdalena Franckin, my Colleague's Dearly Betrothed, her daughter Johanna Sophia and the Brothers Pott, two studiosi, to City Hall and demand entrance. Refused access to Linckin they do not turn back but rather start to pray and sing on open market, read chapters from the Holy Scripture, and cause in summa such ghoulish racket as has not been heard since the Turk besieged the Imperial Residence. Francke comes at last and mildly bids Wife and Daughter to return with him to home, yet they remain steadfast and will only yield when Linckin is again free. Blessed and praised be Women!

Thus arises from the gunpowder sent by my Most Highly Esteemed Sir, now a Conflagration that, God willing, will reduce the Glaucha Asylum to ash and rubble.

To My Highly Esteemed Sir eternally obliged,
Christian Thomasius

[175] Müller to Ludwig

Halle, February 20, 1886

My Gracious King!

I report to have arrived safely in Halle on the Saale, an ancient and proud city most worthy of a visit. Francke's asylum lies directly outside the city gates in the former village of Glaucha and is as large and expansive as a city district in its own right. The famous orphanage is executed in stately stone, adjoined in the rear by two rows of half-timbered houses, which form an elongated courtyard. As in Francke's time, boys and girls still live and learn here in diverse schools. In the so-called Canstein Bible Facility, Bibles are printed in octavo and folio in German, Polish, Czech, Sorbian, and other languages. There is a pharmacy, a publishing house along with a bookstore—I have not yet the full overview of this buzzing swarm of protestant bees. Two sights entice visitors from afar: one of these is the Chamber of Wonders, with its collection of most unlikely objects that were sent back from all over the world by missionaries from Halle. There you can see a stuffed crocodile, Chinese women's shoes, a Greenland kayak, an Indian folding altar to the god Vishnu, human miscarriages "in spiritu conservante" (almost as in Nissl's laboratory), "a Malabar barber's knife, which only Malabars let themselves be shaved with," as the catalog for the 1741 collection enumerates, as well as a "Japanese silver-plated belly ripper, which they must use to rip open their own bodies when they have erred." The second place of interest is the library, which brings every bibliophile to rapture, so beautiful is it arranged and so rich its treasures.

In this library I sit now day after day and read printed and handwritten texts from the early phase of the asylum, which began in 1695 in Francke's rectory as an improvised school for the poor and for common citizens. Can you imagine, I have discovered the entry of Rosenstengel's[3] matriculation in the very first orphan album! Catharina Linck was only the seventh girl to be taken in by the orphanage. She was born in "Gehoffen four miles from Halle," wherever that may be. Her "Qualitates accedentium" were: "knows her letters"; that means she taught herself to read even before she entered the orphanage. Her certificate of completion ("Qualitates abeuntium") reads: "followed her own path"—She was headstrong even early on!

And if this is not enough, I have also discovered Rosenstengel's picture! It is the frontispiece of an anonymous pamphlet titled *Intricate and Truthful Description of a Deceiver of People and Country*. It shows Catharina Link on the left side "as a female-person and inspiring prophet" and on the right "as a disguised male-person and soldier under the name of Anastasius Rosenstengel." So that my friend can imagine the portrait I have traced it, touching it up somewhat, and enclosed it with this letter. Say, my friend: would the superb title of this brochure not also be something for my book? Oh, I thank you, I have no words for my thanks, for the incitement and command to make this journey.

Yours in Glee,
Franz

[176] Müller to Elisabeth

Halle on the Saale, February 25, 1886

Your Imperial Majesty!
Dear Elisabeth!

My deepest thanks for the dried everlastings and your poetic portrayal of Sappho's grave. There perhaps lies a higher truth in the legend, and yet: I have never believed that Sappho jumped from the Leucadian cliff. The story of her unrequited love for the young Phaon, who scorned the aging woman, was invented by the Roman poets. Since in poetry they could not hold a candle to her, they brought the immortal one down from Mount Parnassus and drowned her in the sea. I might perhaps upon this occasion allow myself the following observation: All women who strive for emancipation, who are rightly famous for their intellect, exhibit manly traits. The very first according to chronology is Sappho, and from her is derived the designation of a sexual relationship between women among themselves, named Sapphic or Lesbian love.

The philologists have zealously sought to purify Sappho of the suspicion that she entertained true love affairs with women, relationships that exceeded mere friendship, as if such an accusation, if warranted, would of necessity mean a woman's moral debasement. Far from being so, a homosexual love pays homage to women perhaps even more than a heterosexual bond. Catherine the Great of Russia, Queen Christina of Sweden, as well as certainly George Sand, belong to such circles, and also my Catharina Margaretha Linck—you recall, our Rosenstengel—whom, whether as man or woman, I endeavor here to discover. I have already been able to locate several letters here which illuminate her life. An error that occurred while copying them has given me a fruitful idea for the definitive form of my manuscript: after my midday repast I mistakenly copied on a half-filled sheet not the letter I had already begun but a different one. When I noticed my error, the resulting "blended" letter read more favorably and succinctly than the genuine one. As an experiment, I am now extracting quotations from the original letters and compiling them in new ones which characteristically tell the story. I know not yet, however, whither that will lead me—.

Your communication of the rumors surrounding the lineage of our common friend have opened my eyes for many of his hobbies. Lohengrin, already adored by Ludwig at a young age, must conceal his origins to the people of Brabant: "Never shall you question me!" he commands Elsa, with the well-known tragic ending. More recently the king is inclined more toward Parsifal, who knows not whence he comes nor who his father is![4] I fear not only Ludwig himself but also others believe the veracity of such rumors or rather wish them true that they might derive their own claims from them.

I bid that you might hold your shielding hand over our friend.

Yours in Constancy,

Franz

[177] Ludwig to Müller

Hohenschwangau, March 1, 1886

Dearest Friend!

How can I thank you for the vivid description of Halle and Francke's asylum there located, yet even more for the glimpse into your most personal workshop, your research, combining, and weighing. I think almost your work must take not only Rosenstengel herself as object but also the story of how you came across her. Thus, that the title of that pamphlet on the "Deceiver of Country and People" be suited, seems doubtful to me. Less than ever, I can freely confess to my friend, am I convinced by your talk of the distance that is said to gape between us and the past and that you like to call unbridgeable. Perhaps my friend has simply not yet sought thoroughly enough to fill the gaps? What is still painfully absent from the epistolary novel your collection of sources amounts to are the letters which Rosenstengel and Mühlhahnin[5] must have written to one another. If we were afforded to find such unmediated attestations to the love of the two, oh how irresistible were the whole story!

Again and again I take out the precious double portrait which you crafted and sent to me.—Thank you, thank you from the bottom of my soul!—and study the differences and commonalities of the two Rosenstengels. While pondering occurred to me a thought that I must discuss with you.

From the inheritance of my grandfather I possess superb engravings of Dürer,[6] of which there were always several in circulation, since with printed graphics there are never per se originals. Could we not come to the aid of the world and delight it with more Dürers! For the world wants to be deceived, after all! You have such a skilled hand! How splendidly you copied Rosenstengel that a rhinoceros must be a trifle for you! Write to me at once what you think of my plan and how you imagine to implement it. "Whatever I longed for, I saw it in you; in you I found what I have always lacked!"

You remain until our concurrent death my King and God, the Lord of my life, the foundation of my being. My crown I wear for your sake.

Yours,
Ludwig

Notes

Translated by Gary Schmidt.

1. In the original German, Catharina Linck is repeatedly referred to as "die Linckin," given the feminine definite article "die" and the feminine noun ending "in," which was common practice.

2. Francke's facility that housed the orphanage where Catharina Linck was housed as a girl, as well as the boarding school attended by Katte in Roes's novel.

3. Literally "rose stem," the name assumed by Catharina Linck when dressing as a man and which provides the title of Steidele's novel.

4. *Lohengrin* and *Parsifal* are operas composed by Richard Wagner, of whose music Ludwig was an ardent admirer. The Bavarian king re-created scenes from Wagner's operas in the palaces he built, for example, the Venus Grotto from *Tannhäuser* at Linderhof and multiple rooms at Neuschwanstein.

5. Mühlhahnin is the woman wed by Catharina Linck as Rosenstengel.

6. The German Renaissance artist Albrecht Dürer of Nuremberg.

Christoph Poschenrieder

Christoph Poschenrieder is the author of five novels, including *Das Sandkorn* (*The Grain of Sand*), from which the following excerpt is taken. A self-identified heterosexual ally of the queer community, the author creates three complex queer characters in a narrative set in a time period when in Europe, and particularly in Germany, the notion of fixed sexual identity was emerging that has shaped our contemporary discussions of queer issues. The protagonist of *Das Sandkorn*, Jacob Tolmeyn, is a young art historian forced to leave Berlin shortly before the outbreak of the First World War, when he suddenly falls victim to blackmail at the hands of a former soldier. As a garrison city, the German capital had a long history of association with male homosexuality, and specifically male prostitution[1]—indeed, the Prussian Guard Corps was garrisoned there since before the time of Frederick the Great, whose affinities for men have long been a subject for German authors. The presence of so many soldiers in Berlin attracted men seeking sex with other men even before the invention of the word "homosexual."[2] At the same time, Prussian law, codified in the notorious Paragraph 175 for the new German Empire after 1871, criminalized sex between men until decades after World War II.

Das Sandkorn begins when Tolmeyn is picked up by the Berlin police and interrogated by Head Commissioner Treptow in the Blackmail Department. As the author himself notes, Treptow is based on the historical figure Hans von Treschkow, who collaborated with Magnus Hirschfeld and developed special techniques to pursue blackmailers.[3] Treptow's interrogation of the suspicious art historian provides the frame narrative for the imaginative heart of Poschenrieder's novel. On Tolmeyn's trip to southern Italy, while under order from the Ministry of Culture in Berlin, he unearths traces of the Holy Roman Emperor and Crusader Frederick II and enters into a complex relationship with his Swiss male colleague and an Italian feminist that cannot be disentangled from what Eve Sedgwick aptly described as the epistemology of the closet.[4] In the following excerpt, Tolmeyn returns to Berlin from Italy for a short time in order to learn the art of photography. Shortly before his scheduled return to Italy, Tolmeyn is unable to resist a foray into Berlin's gay night life, and so he runs into the very pursuer who forced him to flee the city so precipitously several months earlier.

"Schulze Takes a Swim," from *The Grain of Sand* (2014)

Berlin, June 19, 1914, Evening

To start out, he walks for a while up Friedrichstraße, all the way to Jägerstraße to the Weihenstephan beer hall. Past the Bavarian lion with the coat of arms and under the fat boy riding the beer keg, into the pub. He looks for a seat behind one of the numerous columns where he has an unobstructed view without attracting attention—hopefully. He orders a mug of dark beer and a beer warmer, a nickel-plated metal cylinder filled with hot water that he hangs in the mug. That does him good; slowly they warm up, he and the beer.

He recognizes a few old acquaintances at distant tables: the Countess and the Princess Elector hold court in union with Georgette and the unavoidable Dorchen; yet neither the Countess nor the Princess Elector can claim noble birth: the nicknames come from the streets they live on: Kurfürstenstraße and Landgrafenstraße.[5] He himself had lived at the end of Friedrichstraße, north of the Spree River, so some had thought they could call him Fritzi. He had refused to tolerate any and all nicknames: Jacob it was, and Jacob it remained. With a *c*. If anything at all was possible then Jacopo, like the great painters Tintoretto, Bellini, and Bassano. Or Jaco for short. But no one calls him that anymore.

And no one, he thinks, would recognize him. He wears his hair longer than before, falling well below the collar from a part almost in the middle in a dark rich wave on each side. He could have effortlessly closed the curtain over his eyes by slightly lowering his head. He resembles Oscar Wilde a little when he was the same age. In any case not like the close-cropped curator who put on finely woven cotton gloves in the Kaiser Friedrich Museum (how long ago was it, really just four months?) in order to dust off medieval carvings with a soft brush and the greatest conceivable tenderness—

if the basswood object (a Madonna or saint) were sentient it would have felt caressed. Sometimes he even took off the gloves. That was against the rules, but how else was he to sense the peculiar warmth of the wooden figures? A tree comes into being from light and the warmth of the sun. Or the fine and finest surfaces turned into naked skin, fur, or scales by a master like Riemenschneider: He had run his fingers along every square millimeter of the sculpture of St. George slaying the dragon and found George's armor somewhat cooler, the nostrils of the horse somewhat hotter. He missed that. Most of the papers and parchments he dealt with in Rome were only the bearers of signs, insignificant in and of themselves. You could copy them and then destroy them—someone like Stammschröer would bellow at that, but what would you have done other than pour the wine from one bottle into another?

Be that as it may, don't screw this up, Tolmeyn thinks, or you will be sorting through documents again in the basement.

In the meantime, a few more guests have arrived at the other table: Miss Wine Grape is there too, who had been given this nickname due to her excessively pronounced sentimentality. She is once again in tears because of something or other, if only to dry them on the all-consuming consolation of the Stable Mistress and the Queen of Poland, who arrived with her. Things seemed to be stepping up, the contours of the crowd are getting fuzzy and starting to move.

Tolmeyn leaves the pub through the back door and decides to take a stroll. But careful: he would keep to the edges and peer far ahead, always prepared to step into a doorway or examine a shop window. And avoid those very bars that he had liked to frequent. He takes a long detour, crossing Spittelmarkt and Moritzplatz.

This early in the evening, there are mainly older gentlemen sitting in Hannemann's pub in Simeonstraße, waiting for the opportunity to buy someone a beer. They take note of Tolmeyn's arrival with a brief flicker of interest: probably they think he has lost his way or is a tourist. He drinks a tea with rum at the bar, his back turned to the customers. He just cannot get in the mood to enjoy this outing. Go back, something says inside him, but it would not have been the first time that the voice of Tolmeyn's conscience lacked the power to convince. Why have a conscience at all if it was so weak and made such a poor case?

It is only a few steps from Hannemann's to the Schöne Müllerin[6] in Brandenburgstraße—but there he finds only women in men's clothing smoking cigars—how quickly a place's clientele can change. Tolmeyn has already turned around when the proprietress comes at him in Berlin dialect.

"So, mademoiselle, what'll it be? The usual?"

Dammit, she recognizes me, thinks Tolmeyn. He hears something like "Wait a minute, you can have one on the house," but now he really doesn't feel like it anymore.

One more thing, just one. Next thing—*last thing*—straight to Lichterfelde.[7] But he walks along the canal down the Waterloo Bank, skirts so close to the Katzenmutter bar[8] that he can feel its warm walls, and finally contents himself with a glance through the window that yields nothing, for the Katzenmutter is a dingy dive and blind eyes are its windows.

With this last loop he has almost returned to the starting point of his exploration: the beltway trains rumble along the overpass in reliable intervals and endless circles.

If you don't take this one, you'll take another one, Tolmeyn thinks, and stands back from the Number 96 that should have whisked him out of the city. He crosses the canal again and turns down Königgrätzerstraße. Just one more try: the Mikado. To see what's going on there. And then back to Master Lampe in Lichterfelde like a good boy to say good night and blow out the candles.

Already buzzing, Königgrätzerstraße—more of a concert hall than a street, with stage, main floor, mezzanine, and balcony—receives him as one more man in the orchestra pit. He jumps over the staves of the streetcar tracks, oscillating from one side of the street to another as if striking an eighth note over and over. He is by no means the only one adding to the music: everyone walking here succumbs to the allure—of adorned shop windows (saccharine violin sounds), neon signs (clarinets and harps to Tolmeyn's ear), a barker (tenor). Men, women, and children careen back and forth, shooed away by the streetcar bell (carillon), startled by a car that races up (trumpets). He almost starts directing—he's already flailing his hands a bit. You'd have to stand on one of the highest balconies and photograph the human notes on the staves of the streetcar tracks. Then you'd have part of the score to which Berlin dances every day and every night. A player piano gone mad that punches its own holes in the roles of music that make it play.

Halfway to the Anhalter Train Station he takes a quiet side street: but what does quiet mean? The snorting of a cart horse haltered for the night, voices and shouting in all pitches, from *piano* to *fortissimo*, a man beating a rug prayerfully, the poker in a cast-iron oven, a squeaking pump filling a tin pail, the *fffft-fffft* of a brushwood broom on pavement, *tssss-chhh* of a match lit by someone right behind him.

Now he's standing at a crossing, catty-corner from Das Mikado. Some say Der Mikado.[9] Either way, an asinine name, for in that place whoever doesn't move loses out. From the outside, the Mikado always looks like it is about to burst at any moment from the pressure, heat, and noise. The music—he listens for the sound of piano keys being struck—is being performed today by Sadler-Grün, the baron, or baroness, depending on which clothes he is wearing. Or she: nobody cares. As long as he plays well. Or she.

So: two possibilities, Tolmeyn lectures himself. Either you throw all care to the wind, go inside, have a good time, put up with old Niethe's final photography lecture and return to Rome—with one last nice memory of Berlin. Or exactly the same plan minus the good time in the Mikado with old friends, and minus at least *one* nice memory of this outing to Berlin.

Once again someone strikes a match right behind him. When he turns around it takes a moment before he recognizes the face behind the dying flame.

Niki puffs twice on the cigarette and says: "Now the cat's got your tongue, huh? The Miller Woman put me on the right track."

Tolmeyn freezes for two or three seconds. He pushes the man a few steps farther into a gateway. Just don't be seen—with him.

"You've made yourself scare lately," says Niki. "Where'd you go?"

"Of all people, you think I'll tell you that?" says Tolmeyn, perhaps a little too aggressively.

"Ah, new hair style, *très chic*," says Niki and tries to grab Tolmeyn's hair. He slaps at his outstretched hand but misses.

Niki takes a cigarette case out of his jacket. He snaps it open and shut skillfully.

Tolmeyn watches and waits. He wants something from him, well then out with it. Half a minute goes by.

Niki is like his cigarette case: from the outside quite handsome, polished, chiseled, even engraved: N. S. The dapper Niki Schulze. With the minimum required manners, even a little bit more. Able to use a knife and fork, knows the difference between white wine, red wine, and port glasses. Who taught him that? Tolmeyn, of course. Drinks it all too. Doesn't just read the tabloids but has a certain education, but more than that he is skilled at concealing the gaps in his learning. Above all, very agreeable to look at when he still wore the uniform of the Guard Grenadiers. Like his cigarette case: inside self-rolled cigarettes that resembled unearthed roots, bent and rough, brownish yellow. He can't afford real ones. The Manoli Monte Bello or a Garbaty—of course he would gladly have accepted the most expensive ones—Queen of Sheba!—as a gift from Tolmeyn. On holidays he indulges at his own expense in an Okassa Zarotto, a soldier's tobacco. Other than that, the self-rolled ones. Doesn't he realize it? He sticks those vile things in his far from ugly face. Why did Tolmeyn never notice this before? Like the snapping shut of the case: clear and sharp and tinny. Precisely not silver.

"Come on, let's go inside the Mikado, drink some champagne," says Niki. "My treat, of course."

While speaking, he makes an exaggerated gesture, as if here were pulling a fat wallet out of his pocket. Tolmeyn almost has to laugh. That would be the first time. Well, maybe it will be enough for the first glass.

"I am not going anywhere with you, Niki. Leave me in peace."

The Mikado spits out a pile of people that quickly disintegrates. When the last of them have disappeared around the corner, he leaves the gateway and goes toward Wilhelmstraße. Quickly enough to seem determined but not so quick as to look like he is taking flight. He simply walks away, the free man that he is.

Niki follows.

"You still owe me something."

"I owe you nothing, nothing at all."

"We had an agreement."

"You call that an agreement? Preposterous."

"Then, all of a sudden, you were gone."

"I am not accountable to you."

"And I sit here broke. Flat broke. I had already counted on the cash, you know? Friends don't do a thing like that."

Tolmeyn heads up Wilhelmstraße, then turns left toward Askanischer Platz. His plan, which he should have hatched while he was walking, still consists of just four words: *get rid of Niki*. But how? Hail a carriage and then take off in a wild gallop? When you need one, none comes. Then two taxi autos cross paths. Tolmeyn would have waved to the first, but then Niki would have jumped in the second and followed him all the way to Lichterfelde. It occurs to him too late that his pursuer, notoriously broke, could not have afforded the long ride. But who knows that for sure.

Take cover over there in the Anhalter Station? Now—toward eleven o'clock at night—there is clearly too little bustle on the platforms. Streetcar? Niki would catch the same one Tolmeyn did. Run away? Niki is faster. He played sports in the barracks, is a member of the Neptune Swimming Club of Berlin, boasts of his immense lung capacity and can stay under water for who knows how long. Which from the outset rules out the possibility of settling the matter by fighting. Maybe it would be better to fill him up with masses of champagne or wine and beer in one of the bars. Only, Niki won't let himself get drunk in this situation; he is capable of that much calculation.

Niki follows him at a consistent distance along the north side of the train station and farther toward the Landwehr Canal. He stops once and lights a cigarette but after a few quick strides catches up again. He never loses sight of Tolmeyn when he tries to lose himself in the crowd pouring out of the Philharmonie; among all the black tailcoats, he is the only pure idiot in a bright summer linen suit and straw hat adorned with a bright blue ribbon. Tolmeyn hears Niki laugh.

At the older harbor basin protruding from the Landwehr Canal he stops, less from being exhausted than from being tired of this whole matter, which offers him so much opportunity to berate himself. All the result of wrong decisions: the apartment at the end of Friedrichstraße (that had resulted in the silly nickname "Fritzi"); the job on Museum Island (he had rejected an offer from a private collector in Charlottenburg); the barracks in between. He had to pass by them twice a day (no, he didn't have to, there were other routes, but also other barracks on all corners of this uniform-infested city). Either way, the Kaiser Alexander Guard Grenadiers wore long white trousers and dark blue uniform jackets with shiny gold buttons. They looked good on Niki in their simple elegance, these uniforms (oh, all right, they looked good on everyone, that was the point of the uniform). No, especially good on him.

The same Niki now in a slightly rumpled leisure suit, nonchalantly rummaging around in his pocket for his cigarette case and looking down placidly at Tolmeyn, sure of his victory. That's what you get from all this!

There are a few dozen retired freight ships in the harbor basin, some of them almost drowned, held close together in the turbid broth by creaking ropes. Tolmeyn gazes at this forced brotherhood and then at his pursuer, who again shoves one of his crippled cigarettes between his lips.

"I don't have what you want with me anyhow. So, what's the point?"

Niki hadn't said anything, but he always wanted money, why should it be different now? He had certainly wanted money back then, four months ago, a lot of money, or . . . and Tolmeyn had left Berlin in a hurry.

"You put me in a difficult situation," says Nikki, "and you aren't going to do it again. You understand that I'll have to charge an extra fee this time, and a mighty big one."

"You are the only one to blame for your situation. Besides, I'm not in Berlin anymore."

"Oh, no? And that's the Thames right there?"

"Just here for a visit. Tomorrow I am going back."

That's wrong. The day after tomorrow. Is it good to put the other guy under pressure? The less time he thinks he has, the more he'll feel driven to act.

"Listen here, Fritzi," says Niki, "it doesn't make a damned bit of difference where we are, I just need to write a little letter to the museum. You know, a reputation like that doesn't precede you; it creeps after you. Clop, clop, clop, and there it is cozying up to everyone. Sticks like tar."

"You are a miserable little vulture."

"You bet I am," says Niki. "And you're a huge idiot for not noticing it earlier."

Niki pretends to have pen and paper in hand and scribbles in the air something he must have read somewhere, for it's not how Niki normally expresses himself.

"Most esteemed Sir! I have learned by chance but with the greatest of credibility that your valued employee, the Curator Jacob Tolmeyn, is also one of those unhappy men whose proclivities fall under threat of punishment in our barbaric age. If you would please consider the precious materials that your man handles every day . . . and so forth and so on."

He folds the imaginary letter and sticks it in an invisible envelope, licks the adhesive strip around the tab with an unsavory grimace, and sends the letter on its way like a paper airplane. Tolmeyn feels like vomiting.

There had once been a different Niki, one with big plans for the time after the army: he wanted to start up an "Athletes Club." Wrestling, gymnastics, weightlifting, and a boxing ring. There was a demand for that among young men who, in spite of hard workdays, wanted to put their bodies to the test in fights and games. And there were many who just came to watch and tossed plenty into the club till. Niki had long since chosen the place, the back rooms of a tavern. What he lacked was capital to purchase the equipment, the weights, the wrestling mats, the boxing ring. It's an investment, he had always said, when receiving money from Tolmeyn; the iron-eaters and the money will work for us. And the old cash cows that only want to stare, if we tickle them hard enough.

It's just that he did not invest. He bought no weights and no mats, he paid off gambling debts in order to incur new ones. Had dress uniforms tailored and bought drinks for his army buddies.

"We could have long since been the best of friends again, even at a distance," says Niki and takes a step toward Tolmeyn, who, standing two feet away from the edge of the basin, cannot back away. Perhaps Niki got an idea from his Guard Grenadier's perspective (his regiment, after all, was the one of the famous "Potsdam Giants")[10] and with an undisguised glance at Tolmeyn's brand-new straw hat: in any case, his hand shot out for the hat, his greedy fingers grown long. And Tolmeyn, as he pulls his head back to avoid Niki's rapid grasp, thinks: yes, of course, there is a label inside: *Mario Modica, Cappellaio, Roma.*

Tolmeyn's movement is hindered to his left by a bollard and to his right by a rolled-up rope of the kind that is thick as an arm; Niki does not notice the loose end lying over the pavement as he storms ahead.

"Like to see, where . . ." Niki says then suddenly needs both his arms for a fruitless spinning and fluttering that neither steadies him nor saves him from his dangerous lurch. He tries to land his splayed-out hands on Tolmeyn's shoulders or at least grab the lapels of his jacket, or in case this did not succeed, to clutch at his belt-reinforced waistband. All to no avail: Tolmeyn jumps aside. As his right knee gives way, he hits his hip against the rolled-up rope, his elbow catches him. If it hurts, he doesn't feel it. One light touch and Niki flies over the edge in an irreproachable high diver's pose.

He smashes his torso against the stern of a boat with a loud bang, slides back, hangs on the smashed railing for one or two seconds, moans, and falls in the water. Quickly he goes under. Two seconds later, Tolmeyn sees his white face and closed eyes in the light of a distant gas lantern. A light current pulls Niki between the stern and the bow of the boat moored next to it. Tolmeyn loses sight of him. He frees himself from the tangle of the coiled rope and walks a few steps to where the harbor basin is open to the canal. At this spot, the current of the canal pulls water out of the basin and creates the undertow that the moored boats resist, creaking lightly, but to which the motionless body completely succumbs. Tolmeyn looks around: no life preserver, no pole. Now face down, Niki drifts out and away. It takes just a few seconds until Niki Schulze is no longer to be seen.

Tolmeyn sits on a bollard. He has always been able to think better sitting down. Seated, slouching slightly, he feels his belly resting securely in the slight bend of his torso. His head, with its presumptuous reason and clarity, gains a bit more humility when it recognizes where it (and all the other organs) are fed. It was certainly not wrong to get out of Niki's way; if he had crashed into him, Tolmeyn could also have ended up in the basin. An attempt to catch Niki as he ran toward him would not have been advisable given his momentum and the difference in their weights. Throwing himself on the coiled rope—and here his stomach and head were in agreement—was self-preservation: unobjectionable even in the pettiest of interpretations.

But leaving his left leg out?

Notes

Translated by Gary Schmidt.

1. Robert Beachy, *Gay Berlin: Birthplace of a Modern Identity* (Vintage: New York, 2015), 9.

2. Karl Heinrich Ulrichs, "described by some as the world's first open homosexual," is one prominent example (Beachy, *Gay Berlin*, 9).

3. Beachy, *Gay Berlin*, 58–59, 81. Rosa von Praunheim includes a scene in his film *The Einstein of Sex* (1999) in which Hirschfeld takes the Berlin chief of police on a tour of Berlin's gay/lesbian bars and drag balls.

4. Eve Kosofsky Sedgwick, *The Epistemology of the Closet* (Berkeley: University of California Press, 1990). Sedgwick complicates a dichotomous understanding of the closet as a state of either being "out" or "in," analyzing the apparently limitless ways in which knowledge of sexuality can be both concealed and revealed at the same time.

5. "Prince Elector Street" and "Landgrave Street."

6. "The beautiful miller woman," the name of the bar but also the title of a song cycle composed by Franz Schubert to poetry by Wilhelm Müller.

7. Prussian village just outside Berlin that housed the Prussian Main Military Academy since 1882 and was later incorporated into Greater Berlin.

8. The Mother Cat bar.

9. The bar "The Mikado" is given the masculine article "der" by some and the neuter article "das" by others.

10. In German "Lange Kerls," the regiment commanded by Frederick William I of Prussia, father of Frederick the Great, for which he recruited tall soldiers, also mentioned in Roes's *Zeithain*.

Odile Kennel

ODILE KENNEL, who lives and works in Berlin, grew up bilingual in French and German. She has published two novels, *Was Ida sagt* (*What Ida Says*, 2011) and *Mit Blick auf See* (*Lakeside View*, 2017), from which the following excerpt is taken, as well as two collections of poetry: "oder wie heißt diese interplanetare Luft" (*Or what is that interplanetary air called*, 2013) and "Hors Texte" (2019). She has also translated poetry from French, Portuguese, English, and Spanish into German. As a reader and writer, she desires protagonists who are not defined as women or men but as autonomous subjects.[1]

Having grown up in a small village in southwestern Germany, Kennel was confronted with a mixture of personal and collective memories while writing *Mit Blick auf See* during a residency in the small town of Hausach. These memories were in part awakened by the upcoming fortieth anniversary of the so-called German Autumn of 1977, in which Hanns Martin Schleyer was kidnapped and murdered by the Red Army Faction (RAF). The narrator of *Mit Blick auf See* is a journalist named Béatrice, or Béa, who has been commissioned to write a book on how Germans today remember the terrorist activities of the RAF, a topic to which she claims to have no close connection. Béa has just bought a house in the country, a "mill," and moved there from Berlin, much to the consternation of her daughter and friends. Shortly after moving in, a young man named Alexander shows up at her door. He is eager to have information about Béa's relationship with Helga, his mother, who once lived in the mill and disappeared for three years in 1977, a few months before the German Autumn. At first Béa resists, claiming never to have known Helga or to have ever visited the mill. Before Béa has even unpacked her belongings and arranged her new living space, the frame narrative is invaded by recollections from the past that suggest that Béa had indeed known a brother and sister who were active in the left-wing student movement and had become involved in a complicated relationship with both of them. In the following excerpt, the italicized passage represents the book that Béa is working on, while the third-person passages are flashbacks to the 1970s, which might be interpreted as dreams, memories, or both.

from *Lakeside View* (2017)

I am awakened by the wild geese. Their calls scrape across the sky, bearing witness to the real life that exists up there, to a world of its own that keeps turning no matter what happens down here. I am surprised, indignant: it's the wrong soundtrack for the country, the scratchy screams of the geese should be in the night sky of Berlin, transforming houses, streets, and human quarrels into things that exist only by chance, having thrust themselves in the path of the migratory birds, soon to disappear again. I imagine how the geese at flight look down upon the city, agreeing with a knowing glance: oh, look at that, still there, the city, their glance says, still there, those humans with their frivolous activities. I never noticed the wild geese until Katharina, with her soft spot for ornithology (which Nelly must get from her) drew my attention to them, and since then I wait for the geese. In autumn and at the end of winter I look forward to their arrival, lying awake like a spellbound child who listens to their calls from above.

I am surprised and indignant, for here in the country the wild geese seem to fly lower, as if the sky were none of their concern when they don't have to avoid high-rises, radio towers, and airplanes. I am disappointed that they have lost some of their power of enchantment because their presence is more taken for granted or because their nearby calls sound less mysterious.

I have a headache and the feeling that I really have been here in the mill before. Have I spent four nights here, or is it five? After how many nights does a feeling of déjà vu begin? I have to stop thinking about Alexander's story. I have to concentrate on my work. What time is it? Should I take a headache tablet? But where did I put the medicine chest?

I listen to the waning cries of the geese until they fade into the distance and then I try to fall back to sleep. I hear the wood of the floor and the beams snap, hear the silence that spreads between, the nocturnal intimacy of a house that can only be deciphered in the course of time. Until then, with my adult mind I'll try to ward off the attacks of childish fear that turn every creak into the steps of an attacker. Someone is surely sneaking up the stairs right now and will push open the door any second to stand next to my bed.

It would truly be sensible to get a dog, but I've already bought a house and am having difficulty adjusting to this role; becoming a dog owner would exceed my current powers of conformity. If anything, then a cat. I force myself to breath calmly; the best thing to do would be just to fall asleep again,

But I am awake, and my headache gets stronger every minute, the punishment for last night; I truly should have drunk a glass of water. Shouldn't there still be a headache tablet in the toiletry bag? I switch on the bedside table lamp, get up, and grope from the dark room for the light switch in the hall like I used to do in my parents' house when I climbed into my attic room. In order to get to my bedroom, I had to go out of the kitchen and step onto a small platform in the barn, from where the steps led upwards. It was a simple wooden set of stairs with dark spaces in between that swallowed up fallen slippers and would swallow me up too if I took a false step. With bated breath and a frozen gaze aimed at the door to my room I climbed up, always careful to step in such a manner that the tip of my foot did not extend over the step, always careful not to look beyond the pale glow of the lightbulb over the entrance into the darkness where shadowy creatures were waiting for the opportunity to snatch at me. I could have pressed the light switch to my mother's studio corner, but her uncanny pictures would have made me even more afraid. If I wanted to go back downstairs, I had to stretch my hand outside my room in order to switch on the stairway light, every time with the expectation of touching something undefinable . . . and dying of fear. It never occurred to me to ask my father to install a light switch inside my room. At some point he would renovate the barn and convert our cramped house into the spacious, luxurious home that he dreamed of and for which he had precise plans that he never implemented, but someday he would realize his dream and then the issue of the light switch would be resolved.

When my father told me the story of my mother I understood why our house was never finished. I always thought it was a question of money, which my parents did not have, because it wasn't important for them to have money, but the much more decisive factor must have been that my father used up all his energy on my mother and that, after she died and my brothers and I moved out, he saw no more sense in finishing the renovation. He lived up to his death on a construction site and never really got a foothold in the village, but the house was more important to him than anything else, being all that remained of his life with my mother.

I step into the lighted hallway, lumber down to the living room and by a hair avoid kicking down the wine glass I had left on the landing. I take it with me, rinse it out in the bathroom, and fill it with tap water. A light plop, followed by a fizz, and the tablet dissolves. The water is so cold that it hurts my teeth. My bare feet are cold too; now I really won't be able to sleep before my feet get warm again.

I get a sofa cushion from the living room, my laptop with headphones, put my socks back on, and get comfortable in bed. I rarely work at night anymore. When Nelly was still little and climbed into my bed because she had had a nightmare, it sometimes happened that I couldn't fall back to sleep so I got up and went to my desk.

[. . .]

Shortly after the Berlin Wall opened I had my coming out and through my first relationship became familiar with the West Berlin Autonomous Lesbian scene. And the mood at the beginning of the nineties was that there was a lot of discussion about what would become of Germany: Greater Germany, racism, and all that. The reason I'm telling you that in this context is that forms of action were discussed: how far could and should you go and stuff like that. And Red Zora[2] *was a point of orientation, I would say. Violence against people no, but violence against things is okay. I still believe that. I am certain that some of them were involved or at least very close to it. I was in love and excited because everything was new, and for a while I noticed this temptation, how should I say it . . . you're against the system but it's a fact that you constantly benefit from it: you study, receive financial aid, shop, travel, go to parties. And the temptation is to be on the right side. Once and for all not to have to grapple with these contradictions. That's the one thing, and the other thing is that I wondered how you know when the right time has come, when do you take the step and give up your prior life, do illegal things, always have one foot in the underground? When does it become clear that there is no other way forward? When did the few people who fought against the Third Reich decide? How long do you still accept what is happening? That was always the point of reference and although it was clear to me that the comparison isn't so easy to make, I still asked myself again and again if there is not a creeping development toward fascism now that this Germany is unified and if I, just as creepingly, am getting used to it. And then at some point it's too late. I really tried to imagine that, in more and more detail, just how it would be to go underground until I became dizzy, since the next step would have been to do it. But the curve of my imagination kept approaching the X-axis without ever touching it. Because, when is the moment there? But I imagine it must have been like that for the people in the RAF*[3] *and all the others. At some point they decided. This temptation to be absolutely on the right side, that's central, I believe that. In my case, however, it was, on the one hand, a different time and, on the other hand, there was indeed this certain something that prevented me from completely identifying with these radical women; I had grown up in the German Democratic Republic and sometimes I found them completely messed up with their West German socialization and pretty darn despicable toward the East Germans.*

[Jenny, *1970]

When does a curve bend to become a straight line that crosses the X-axis? There is a need for explanation, for linearity, for reassurance. If I can explain when and why someone steps over the line and is willing to accept that other people will die so they can reach their political goals, then I can shield myself from it: for me, it would never come to that, because . . . for such reassurance one goes so far to conserve brains in formaldehyde[4] in order to find evidence of madness as an explanation. But there does not exist a chain of cause and effect that necessarily leads to this and not to that, no logic, line, or protection from oneself. Everyone who has at one time decided to take this step could have decided differently. And everyone who has decided against it could have decided in favor of it. That has nothing to do with morality but rather with facts and factors. Factors that in all probability play a role: time period, personality, love, chance. Factors that in turn can be broken down into incalculable causal chains that can never be traced back to the last atom. There is always just approximation. A different fact, a different factor, and it would have turned out quite different. Which factors may have played a role for Hah, if she had gone underground at the beginning of 1977, that is to say: before what we now call the German Autumn?

I need some fresh air. I turn off the light again, open the window and lean out. The lake is not visible from here, but I can smell it, mossy, musty, metallic, with a note of earth, clay, and wet straw. I stare into the dark where gradually the outline of the garden becomes visible, the paths between the flower beds and the hedges. The garden where possibly I petted a cat with Nelson. Or with Clogs.[5]

She liked the smell in the house, of woodfire and a little bit of stable; it smelled like that at her house too after they had been gone for a few days; stable smells clung to houses even a hundred years later, not intrusively, but noticeably. She entered the house almost reverently with Nelson, as if it was already a legend, because Nelson lived here with Hah and his mother, and with Hah's child. Involuntarily, she looked for traces of Hah, wondered which jacket in the entryway belonged to her, which shoes, and wondered why she wondered that. It was dark when they arrived; they had stopped at the house of friends of Nelson and loaded wood, and while with steaming breath in the cold she handed him log after log, she felt lighthearted and cheerful in a way she hadn't for a long time. Nelson wanted to go right to the lake. He took her hand and pulled her to the patio door. Down there, a surface stood out from the darkness, a lake house, she thought in astonishment; why had Nelson never mentioned that to her? The thought had never crossed her mind that someone she knew could live directly on a lake.

We can unload the wood tomorrow, Nelson said and ran down to the shore. He crouched down and, as far as she could tell in the darkness, felt the surface of the lake.

Frozen, he called up to her. Another cold night and we can go ice skating!

Ice skating? I thought we were getting ready for the party? Besides, I don't have any skates with me.

You can use my mother's. They might fit you. Wait a second!

Nelson ran back to the house and shortly after that she heard a window open.

I found them, Nelson called down.

Nelson held a pair of ice skates out of the skylight that shined in the dull light of the attic: white skates with fur borders like the ones her mother had given her.

I'm not putting those on, she yelled back up to him. I'm not a ballerina. And besides . . .

Besides what?

Nothing, it doesn't matter, forget it.

Shortly after that he was standing in front of her again, waving the skates like a trophy.

I can't offer you Hah's. She'll definitely want to go skating herself; she loves ice skating. Hers are really fancy, with black and red leather and black laces. Anarchist skates, he said. Only anarchists can skate with them. Well?

He looked at her teasingly and raised an eyebrow in the way she liked.

But they'd be too big for you anyhow.

Is Hah an anarchist?

It felt strange to say "Hah" instead of "your sister," as if she was only allowed to use her name after having met her.

Anarchist? Naw! In any case, not a proper one, ideologically speaking or such. More of a feminist. On the other hand . . . ask her yourself, when she comes.

Nelson handed Béa the skates and she slid them on. They fit. She stood up carefully and took a few teetering steps on the blades.

Have you ever been ice skating before, asked Nelson.

She shook her head.

We only had an indoor ice rink. But I didn't want to go there: I think that either the weather is cold enough and you have a lake or you just don't skate. But I always went roller skating. It's similar.

She took the skates back off and handed them to Nelson.

Well, we'll see, she said. Let's first wait and see if we have time for that tomorrow.

There's always time for some ice skating. And now let's get a blanket and something to eat and have a picnic down at the lake.

In February? In the dark? It's much too cold! And when, actually, is Hah coming?

What does Hah have to do with it? I don't know when she's coming. She wanted to find someone to give her a ride, and that's always worked out before. Especially since she's been traveling with the kid. She'll be there on time. After all, it's her party.

Where did she go, actually?

No idea, Nelson answered impatiently, I'm not her guard dog. To Paris, I assume. Or Brittany. Or both. Or in the South; sometimes she goes there, to Larzac. Or do you say "to the Larzac"?

"To the Larzac" I think.

Faites labour pas la guerre,[6] printed on the bright red poster in her parents' house. She knew it was a military base that was supposed to be expanded, against which local farmers and many others were protesting. To hear about that here astounded her. The thought had never crossed her mind that anyone in Germany besides her family could be interested in the Larzac and know what was going on, let alone go there. Not because she thought that wasn't possible but because those were two unconnected worlds for her, worlds that couldn't be connected, so unconnectable that she never even attempted to make a link between the inside and the outside. And at that moment she didn't even want to. She didn't want to think about home or about the fact that the poster no longer hung in her parents' house but in her father's. She didn't want her throat to close up, hadn't come here to be sad but to spend time with Nelson, to have a celebration, and get to know Hah.

Is your sister often in France?

Yes, rather often.

And why?

Why not? answered Nelson. She speaks French; she has friends there. . . . Why are you so interested in Hah all the time anyhow?

Later, wrapped in a blanket, they smoked in front of the fire.

The warmth emanating from Nelson and the fire, the slight dizziness from the joint, the bright surface of the frozen lake in the darkness, the night sky, where only a few stars were visible—she drifted through space without starting point or destination, and she wanted to keep drifting forever, without past, without death, without nonexisting death-days, without inside and outside. Only what was now counted, and that tomorrow she would meet Hah.

Something tore inside of her. She couldn't stand it; she didn't have the right to be happy in this moment; she didn't have the right to look forward to tomorrow while her mother was dead and her father and brother at home without her. She wanted to quash this moment, say something mean, hurt Nelson, hurt Hah. She jumped up. Nelson looked at her surprised.

Hey, what's up?

I'm cold, she said, let's go in.

Cold? You were just totally warm!

But I'm cold now.

She trudged up the slope to the patio, fought back tears, hated herself for it, for always ruining everything.

Was there a lake by Clogs's house? Did I perhaps go ice skating there the only time in my life? Am I remembering the wrong white skates?

There was no lake by Clogs's house, but the house stood like this one somewhat outside the village. He told me that: it was something like a *lieu-dit*, one of those places that as a child I imagined existed only after they had been named. Did Clogs ever mention a *mill*? But I wouldn't have forgotten a *Frenchman's mill*, so it can't have been my current mill. Especially since my mill does not smell of stable. It smells of wood coal, but not of stable.

Didn't I want to look at the map yesterday already, or even the day before yesterday? A book, maps; I really have to start unpacking. Certainly, I'll recall the name of the village that Clogs was from when I read the place names on the map.

In the middle of the night she woke up, needing to go to the bathroom. She slid out of bed and quietly left her room. There was a light shining through one of the doors. Muffled voices could be heard: women, a man. Apparently, Hah had returned. Although she was cold, she stopped in front of the door and listened. Which of the voices was Hah's? With whom had Hah come from France? She didn't understand what was being said, but it was German, not French. Then someone put a record on and after a few notes she recognized the song. *J'suis ni l' œillet ni la verveine, je ne suis que la mauvaise graine qu'on a semé comme un caillou sur un chemin à rien du tout.*[7] Her mother had listened to this song over and over a few weeks before her death. Once, Béa had even heard her mother singing it when she apparently thought she wasn't being observed and didn't know that Béa was upstairs in her room spying through the cracked door. Béa had never heard her singing before and was surprised by the sound of her voice, "clear as a bell," were the words that occurred to her; she pushed the door ajar and watched her mother sing while painting. When the song was over, her mother placed the arm of the record player carefully back to the beginning of the song and kept singing. Béa remembered this scene because it didn't fit with her other memories; it seemed to her as if her mother was happy at that moment, as if she even had a mischievous air, as if she would show the world, and Béa had thought that everything would be okay with her after all.

The door was wrenched open, and Béa jumped back startled.

Can I help you with something?

Hah's voice was the dark, somewhat throaty voice that she had picked out from among the others. Her hair was shorter than in the photo, and it wasn't red but light brown, as far as she could tell with the light coming from behind. Hah had her hand on her hip and, with the other hand, held the door so that Béa could not see into the room. Her bearing had something defiant about it, as if she had to defend something. She looked Béa up and down, and Béa felt like she was being X-rayed. She realized she would rather not have encountered Hah at this moment, with her clothes hastily thrown on and her hair tousled from sleep. She wanted to please her.

No, she stammered, I . . . it's just the song . . . I was on my way to the bathroom . . .

You're Béa, aren't you?

She stressed the "a." Béa nodded.

Aha.

It sounded as if Hah had already speculated about her and was comparing her vision with what she now saw. Béa felt her face turning red.

Under no circumstances did she want Hah to notice how confused she was to be standing in front of her in the middle of the night; under no circumstances did she want to show that she had speculated about Hah, that she desperately wanted to meet her, for how could she have explained that? She couldn't even explain it to herself.

I really was just standing here because of the music, she managed to say, happy that she had come up with something that was at least true.

Hah's face relaxed.

Oh, I see. Ferré. I just brought it home with me. We can put it on again tomorrow, if you like. Are you staying for the party?

Béa couldn't imagine listening to the song again, but she nodded.

Nelson thought we could help you with the preparations.

She immediately regretted her words; she had sounded awkward and childish.

Aha, help us with the preparations.

Hah had the same wry tone that Nelson sometimes had, and Béa wished she were far away, not knowing how to answer.

Ok, then, see you tomorrow, said Hah, and closed the door in her face. She opened it again and added, Don't worry, I'm sometimes a bit gruff. Don't take it personally. Sleep well anyhow.

Béa remained standing in front of the door for a moment and tried to comprehend what had just happened, trying to understand her confusion when she suddenly found herself standing in front of Hah, her feeling of humiliation when Hah had slammed the door in her face and her joy when the door opened again and she apologized, although there was nothing to apologize for. She was glad, so glad that she was wide awake when she slipped back into bed with Nelson.

What happened, he asked sleepily. Is Hah back? What were you talking about? Is she with someone?

She has company, but I didn't see who it was. And we didn't really talk. She just wanted to know if I'm Béa and if I'm staying for the party.

Nelson grunted and turned over, and Béa lay awake next to him, replaying the short scene in front of Hah's door over and over in her mind, varying her own answer, varying what Hah said and what happened. She suddenly felt aroused and considered whether she should wake Nelson. With a guilty conscience she touched herself, imagining Hah. She stroked herself, rubbed, stuffed the blanket in her mouth, and stifled her exhalation when she came.

"And who are you going to do it with there?" Katarina asked me full of malice when she found out that I was moving to the country. A few years earlier I had refused to even consider such an idea with her.

"Do you think the housewives in the new housing developments are sitting there waiting for a fifty-year-old from the city to seduce them?"

I didn't respond; she was hurt and confused, and any answer on my part would have led to an escalation. But she was right: that is a question that arises in the country, even if a university town is not far away and, besides, I don't feel any need for intimacy with anybody. Or maybe I do? Right now, it would be nice if someone were lying in bed waiting for me, someone who would tell me to close the window, saying it's too cold, come back to bed, I want you now.

I listen for sounds in the night and hear nothing, no matter how hard I strain and hold my breath without stirring. Shouldn't there be water birds on the lake, mice in the garden, or do they hibernate? There must be something to hear, a rustling, sniffing, or whimpering; the silence is a dark wall surrounding the house, pressing up against it and pushing the darkness together into an even blacker mass, compressing the air and stealing my breath. I stand rigid at the window, holding the handle, not daring to close it, clear my throat, breathe out loud.

I don't know how long I have been standing there. Headlights sweep across the night sky beyond the fields; after a short time lag the sound of the motor catches up, connecting me again to the outside world. People are out and about, in the country, at three o'clock in the morning during the week. Today is Friday, if I'm not mistaken, or Saturday already; on the weekends the country youth drive themselves to their deaths. My mother drove herself to her death on a Sunday morning, on a February 29th, and I still don't know where she wanted to go or even if she wanted to go anywhere.

My headache has subsided. Tomorrow, namely in a few hours, I'll start unpacking; it is easier to work in an orderly house than a disorderly one. I will proceed systematically: first the office, where I will finally connect the computer, since in the long run it is much too uncomfortable for my neck to constantly use a laptop. Then the kitchen, pots, dishes, silverware, so that I am not always offering Alexander the same cup, another habit that could creep in and should be avoided. And I'll go grocery shopping; I'll drive to the nearest available supermarket and buy the essentials. And sometime next week I'll drive to town, and perhaps that will jog my memory. Unless tomorrow is Sunday already, in which case Alexander is coming over and I would have to wait until Monday to go shopping.

I could just ask the neighbors for a package of noodles and a few eggs; they would surely be glad to help me out a bit; that would be a start. I try again to calculate when I moved in. When did Alexander show up? But I don't have any firm point of reference; I need a calendar. Somewhere in my boxes is the kitschy wall calendar with the flower-covered houses, *maison fleuries*, that my friend and colleague Lise brought back from her vacation in France. "It is so kitschy I couldn't help but give it to you for your country house." It would be even easier to cast a glance at my pocket calendar, which must be in my backpack. Then I could figure out how many days I have been here and what day of the week it is. Without clear, visible segmentations on paper, time decays into approximations, and I am surprised how quickly I have fallen out of the socially agreed-upon system of measuring it. And did I really set a date with Alexander for Sunday? Can a cook take Sunday off? I said "the day after tomorrow," I am sure of that, and he must have meant Monday, but on what day did I say "the day after tomorrow"? I have to look at the calendar; we absolutely must not miss each other.

The next morning the sky was blue, frost had covered the trees and fields. She had not slept well, feeling like she had dreamed strenuously, and yet she was excited, as if something special were in store . . . but she first had to remember what it was. She recalled the previous evening, and she once again felt aroused; she observed Nelson, who was breathing calmly beside her, felt a tinge of shame, and left the bed. She walked to the window, looked down, and, next to the car in which Nelson had picked her up she saw the tracks of another car that must have been parked there overnight on the other side of the lane. The dark rectangle that was not covered with frost stood out clearly from its surroundings; Hah's visitors must have left just a short time ago. She crept down the steps and saw a baby carriage in the entryway: exactly, the child! She had forgotten that Hah had a child, and she couldn't succeed in imagining the woman who had been standing in front of her last evening with a child. She put on the parka, slipped into her shoes, and stepped onto the patio. The cold hit her in the face but she found it pleasant; her body was not cold. As she went to pull the patio door shut behind her, a red striped cat slipped outside. It must have come into the house yesterday with Hah; in any case, it had not been there yesterday evening. The animal pressed up against her leg, purring. Béa stood frozen: animals were okay as long as they kept their distance; such trustfulness frightened her when it did not originate with her. Then the cat sprang off as if following a sudden intuition.

The lake lay frozen in the still pale morning sunlight, stiff and cheerful at the same time. [. . .] She crouched down on the shore, sitting there for a while looking at the lake and observing the sprinkling of frost crystals on the icy surface. It was pleasant not to think of anything concrete, to let the world slowly trickle into her consciousness. What had happened yesterday? Why was she here? There were answers to these questions, but they circled around the margins of her thoughts, following their own orbits, not bothering her. She scraped a pile of frost together on the ice, observing with fascination the icy blue in the spaces in between, then let a little frost melt on her tongue. Like snow, she thought, only bluer, and she noticed that she was cold after all.

I brought you a blanket. It's much too cold to just sit here like that.

Béa dropped her fingers and jumped up; she had not heard Hah coming. She thought about the previous evening and a wave of heat surged into her face; she heard her blood rushing in her ears and felt her groin start to throb. Hah had stopped six feet away from her as if she suddenly hesitated to come closer, as if she were suddenly embarrassed. In the pale winter sunlight her hair had a reddish sheen, and she seemed approachable now, standing there with the blanket over her arm. Then Hah closed the final distance and stood directly in front of Béa.

Last night, she said, and Béa could feel the warmth emanating from Hah's body, those were friends I met in Paris. They gave me a ride. They wanted to go to Munich and just decided spontaneously to make the detour here, since I still had nobody to drive me back, really nice of them. Otherwise I would have had to hitchhike, but try hitchhiking with a child and baby carriage! And since they didn't want to get stuck in traffic they left early at the crack of dawn.

It sounded like a justification that Béa had not asked for. She felt flattered that Hah thought she had to justify anything to her, even if she did not understand why one had to leave at the crack of dawn to get to Munich without traffic. It didn't matter to her anyhow. The essential thing was that Hah was standing in front of her, and, in fact, very close.

It's okay.

She tried to sound indifferent.

You know what, Hah said, as she squatted down, almost happy now, as if she were relieved to be rid of her explanation, we'll share the blanket. It's nice to look onto the water in the morning. It is so calming.

It would have been simple to settle down next to Hah, but her body was suddenly an assemblage of components that were difficult to coordinate; she pattered in place indecisively next to Hah until she, Hah, grabbed her arm and pulled her down. Somewhat awkwardly, Hah put the blanket over their shoulders, brushing against Béa's neck and touching her arm. When they were finally squatting next to each other under the blanket, Hah's knee was leaning on Béa's, a glowing point that demanded all of Béa's attention to make it seem like she was indifferent to the contact. She had necked a few times with a female classmate but that had been different; she hadn't taken that seriously, and then she had been head over heels in love with a teacher, but she had not sat with her in the early morning under a blanket on the lake. She could not under any circumstances show that her body was reacting to the contact; Hah would have laughed, made an ironic comment; Béa was just her brother's girlfriend; she had better come to her senses right away.

You are French?

As if she had moved away from Hah, there was suddenly distance again. That was not ground she wanted to cover again, her mother had just been far away and she didn't want anyone at all on this ground, not even Hah. Especially not Hah.

Me? No, nonsense.

Then Nelson must have misunderstood.

I never misunderstand anything.

Nelson stood behind them, looking down on them teasingly with crossed arms.

Béa rose hastily, almost losing her balance.

No, he didn't misunderstand, she said turned toward Hah. Or only half misunderstood. I am just half French. But I don't have much to do with France. I can't even speak French properly.

Hah laughed.

Who wants to be proper?

She stood up and folded the blanket.

Come on, she said, let's go inside and make breakfast. Alexander will surely be hungry soon. And there is no way to overhear that. My son, she added in explanation.

There was the child again, and Béa noticed that it bothered her, bothered her like Nelson, who had suddenly turned up, bothered her like the question about her being French; she would like to be alone now with Hah, on this lake and in her head. She had to come to her senses: Hah was not interested in her, and even if she put the blanket over them both, it was only because it didn't matter to her if she sat knee against knee, and her hesitation before, her embarrassment—she had just imagined that. On the contrary, it was good there was a child and a Nelson, so she wouldn't work herself into a frenzy; perhaps she shouldn't even stay for the party but drive home instead, to her father and brother, who needed her,

Nelson put his arm over her shoulder and left it there while they both trudged up to the house. Béa still felt Hah's knee against hers, the warmth next to her under the blanket, and suddenly Nelson's arm felt heavy on her shoulder.

It is eleven in the morning, when I look at the alarm clock. I can't remember lying back down in bed. My head feels good. Did I really take a headache tablet last night and then work at my desk? Stand at the window? Long for the warmth of a body? My computer is next to the bed on the floor, the sofa cushion next to it; the wine glass I dissolved the tablet in must still be downstairs in the bathroom. I still don't know what day it is and whether Alexander is coming today or tomorrow. Did I dream of a cat? Of Hah sitting next to me on the lake? I still feel the spot on my knee where we touched, feel the arousal from the dream in my body. Something must have pressed against my knee while I slept; I reach under the blanket, but nothing is there.

Notes

Translated by Gary Schmidt.

1. Odile Kennel interview with Gary Schmidt in June 2019.

2. In German, "Rote Zora," a far-left feminist terrorist organization active in West Germany from 1974 to 1995 that explicitly rejected violence toward people but found violence against objects legitimate, unlike the Red Army Faction (RAF), which embraced armed struggle.

3. Red Army Faction (RAF), also known as the Baader-Meinhof Group, in reference to its first-generation leaders Andreas Baader and Ulrike Meinhof. The RAF was a leftist militant group formed by individuals who had been close to the student movement (also called the Generation of 68 or the 68ers) and had become radicalized by what they saw as the West German government's collusion with capitalist imperialism, US aggression in Vietnam, and the failure to denazify German society. After Baader and Meinhof were arrested in 1972, the group continued terrorist activity, culminating in the so-called German Autumn (Deutscher Herbst) in 1977 with the kidnapping and murder of Hanns Martin Schleyer, a former SS officer, who at that time was president of the German Employers' Association.

4. A reference to the fact that after RAF leader Ulrike Meinhof's alleged suicide in prison her brain was removed, preserved, and examined by psychiatrists.

5. Béa, the narrator, recalls having had a boyfriend named Clogs who lived with his sister Hedda, called "Hah," in the country, but she at first claims not to remember that his name was actually Nelson or that his sister's name was in reality Helga.

6. French for "Make work, not war!" A play on the slogan "make love, not war."

7. French for "I am neither carnation nor verbena, I am nothing but the bad seed that has been sown like a pebble on a road to nothing at all." Lyrics to the song *La Mauvais Graine* (The Bad Seed) by Léo Férre.

II

BERLIN

Tania Witte

TANIA WITTE is an award-winning author, journalist, and spoken-word performer who lives and works in Berlin and in The Hague (Netherlands). Between 2014 and 2018 she was one of three writers of the weekly queer-themed column "Anders rum ist auch nicht besser" (The Other Way Around Isn't Any Better) for the *Zeitmagazin*, contributing essays with titles such as "Und jetzt wollen die auch noch Kinder!" (And Now They Want Children Too!), "Schwul ist das neue Cool" (Gay Is the New Cool), "Und wer ist bei euch der Mann?" (And Which One of You Is the Man?), and "Ich bin etwas, was du nicht siehst" (I Am Something That You Don't See). In addition to her three Berlin novels with Querverlag, she publishes young adult novels with Arena Verlag, one of Germany's biggest publishing houses for youth literature, and, since 2018, also collaborates with Antje Wagner to write young adult novels under the name Ella Blix. Authors past and present who are important to her include Carson McCullers, Margaret Atwood, Sylvia Plath, Ian McEwan, Marlen Haushofer, Virginia Woolf, Audre Lorde, Jeffrey Eugenides, Siri Hustvedt, Chimamanda Ngozi Adichie, Andrea Gibson, and Annemarie Schwarzenbach.[1]

The following excerpt is from *beziehungsweise liebe* (*and/or love*), the first book in her Berlin city trilogy. The trilogy centers on the lives of a group of friends (and occasional enemies) in Berlin. In contrast to Armistead Maupin's *Tales of the City*, to which the German press compared Witte's trilogy, the central characters are all lesbian, transgender, or bisexual rather than gay men. Witte's stories, like Maupin's, contain many intricate plot twists, but the surprises tend toward plausibility and run contrary to stereotypical genre expectations. In *beziehungsweise liebe*, Nikoletta, a die-hard opponent of long-term relationships, becomes romantically involved with Liza, a transgender American of German heritage living in Berlin. Their affair becomes more complicated when Nikoletta's roommate, a straight man named Clemens, falls madly in love with Liza. Ultimately there is a surprise for all, and Nikoletta turns for succor to her friend Manu, who lives in coupled domesticity with her partner Sandy in a Berlin suburb, provoking their friends to teasingly call the pair collectively Sandyunmanu.

from *and/or love* (2011)

September

Manu

Everything in Berlin is somewhere in limbo. You can look for clarity, but you won't find it. Instead, you constantly run the risk of losing yourself in all the murky in-between spaces.

Everything here is always in transition. It's possible that's the reason Berliners move so often. You never arrive in this city because you are obsessed with looking for something better, a calm harbor—and when you see one, you veer off right away. Your next apartment will have a balcony, the one after that most definitely a bathtub, and the one after that at least one more room and a window looking onto green.

In Berlin you can search so much without ever even coming close to arriving that you never need to leave the city again. You can become addicted to searching, and to floating in limbo, somewhere between unemployment and hoping for a job, between lovesickness and the next great sensation, between comic exchange, *Wigstöckel*,[2] exhibit openings, and the next open-air film season. There are days when Manu forgives the city for nothing, and others for everything and even lovingly. Today she has pangs of longing for her very own private harbor at the Erkner train station.[3] In spite of the September sun, she wraps her sweater more tightly around her body.

[. . .]

Loud screams of "Happy Birthday" and the jingling of bicycle bells herald the arrival of Nikoletta and Clemens. Nikoletta is a fan of dramatic entrances—obediently, Manu and Marte turn around and wave.

"Who is that next to her?" Manu wants to know and appraises the person on the third bicycle.

"Some new flame," says Marte.

"Of Clemens or of Nikoletta?"

The answer never comes, since the trio arrives within earshot.

Nikoletta's bike lands in the grass and she herself, still singing, in Marte's arms, then in Manu's.

Manu gives her a squeeze and then points toward the unknown person. "Who is that you brought with you?"

Nikoletta skips over to the woman who has observed the spirited greeting from a safe distance, grabs her hand, and pulls her toward Marte and Manu.

"This is Liza," she says and reddens slightly. "Liza is from the US but her mother is German. And Liza, this is Marte, the birthday girl, and Manu."

"Hi," says Liza and, turning toward Marte: "Happy Birthday!"

"Thanks," Marte replies. "Nice that you all are here!" Then her attention shifts to Clemens, who is still trying to wrap his bicycle lock around the thick elm tree that the blankets are lying under. "Clemens, leave it, nobody is going to steal that while we are sitting here!"

"You don't think so?" he doubts. "Recently a friend of mine was sitting along the canal, his bike right behind him and even protected by one of those mini-fences. After an hour, when he wanted to leave, it had disappeared. Swiped behind his back." He wrinkles his nose. "That, by the way, is also Berlin," he adds, turning toward Liza, and proceeds to explain to Marte and Manu: "We were just talking about this. Liza is head over heels in love with the city because everyone here is so open and everything is always somehow possible. I just tried to get her to see that not everything is as great as it looks."

"I know that!" Liza has a dark, clear voice. "I'm not stupid! Do you think it is any different in the States? Still—Berlin is something special. Maybe it's because people here don't have any money and therefore are more creative . . ."

"Or are creative and therefore have no money," interjects Marte, thinking of all her artist friends.

"Or that," nods Liza. "In any case, you can't help but feel the energy, and I like that."

"Liza is a performance artist," boasts Nikoletta, and if it wasn't clear before, it is at least clear now whose new flame is standing in front of Manu. She can't help but admire Nikoletta's taste. Liza is beautiful in an awkward way. Somewhat taller than Nikoletta and definitely much too thin, which is why her nose appears more pronounced. High cheekbones, straight brows, and a large, narrow mouth. Much too angular for Manu's taste, but you have to give credit where credit is due: Nikoletta has a hand for extraordinary women who are the complete opposite of herself. The mysterious beauty at my side, the usual cliché. "That's not a cliché, that's a predator-prey system," moaned Nikoletta on a wine-soaked evening when Sandy accused her of looking like the homo-version of the couples on the glossy mags, regardless of which one of her temporary conquests she had at her side. The blond, blue-eyed, butch Nikoletta and the smashing, dark, feminine and exchangeable lover—the blond prince and the brunette princess. Hollywood. Disney. "Watch out that you don't end up like Rod Stewart. Or like Donald Trump," jabbed Manu lightly as she pulled Nikoletta aside for a moment. "Their wives always look the same."

"Oh, leave me alone," Nikoletta whispered back. "You and Sandy look like sisters." And then adds, clearly in a good mood: "In your place I would feel like I was having sex with myself."

Well, at least we have sex, thinks Manu and grins at Nikoletta indulgently.

Clemens

The kitchen floor is full of multicolored works of art. Like in the final round of a "creative baking" workshop, Clemens thinks. You can't set foot on the floor between all the baked goods decorated with pink, turquoise, and/or silver pearls.

"We were hard at work, weren't we?" Liza queries in his direction as he sits exhausted at the table and hypnotizes a cup of coffee.

"You can say that," Nikoletta answers for him, "four and a half hours of solidarity baking is truly not for beginners."

"I can't even look at all this sweet stuff anymore," he moans. "Why don't we order a pizza?"

"We could bake a pizza," suggests Liza, who is met from both sides with an aghast "Forget it!"

"You both are funny." Her laughter is deep and rolling. "In San Francisco we had real baking marathons before any and all charity events, and you all wimp out after eleven batches."

"Phh," Nikoletta waves her off, "The *Amis*[4] always have to overdo it with everything!"

She shoves the second to last batch of pastries over to Clemens to be decorated. He pastes one tartlet after the other with green decorator icing—with the same conscientiousness with which he otherwise ties his shoes, reads the newspaper, or does the dishes. Nikoletta sprinkles some red sugar confetti on top and puts the result in the last free corner under the radiator.

With such clean freaks for roommates like we are you could shove the things under the sofa, Clemens thinks, and asks Liza: "What is actually the difference between muffins and cupcakes?"

Nikoletta giggles in an oddly exhilarated manner, which is probably the result of exhaustion and lack of oxygen: "You are asking me that after all the hours we spent baking together?"

"Well, up until now it was just a question of with or without chocolate, with walnuts or pecans, vegan or not," Clemens defended himself with raised sticky green hands. "With all the decision making I had no time to think about something so basic."

"Yes, the basics," Nikoletta teases and tries to look profound. "If it were so simple to explain all that. How should I start?"

"Man, are you going to rib me for half an hour just because of this one simple question?"

"It's indeed very simple," Liza tries to defuse the situation. "Cupcakes are something like the femmes in the gender landscape," says Nikoletta, interrupting her and getting a tap on the nose in return. And a broad grin.

"Exactly. Actually, they have almost the same thing inside, but they are sweeter and more beautifully decorated," Liza philosophizes, then balances on her tiptoes to the table and sits down next to Clemens, whose cranky confusion has subsided. "Oh," he says, "I always thought that everything that came out of the oven in paper liners was a muffin."

"Big mistake!" Nikoletta makes fun of him.

Clemens does not often feel excluded, but the bubble of blind understanding surrounding Nikoletta and Liza is slipping out of his grasp. Until Liza puts her hand on his arm. His skin communes with its warmth. And suddenly he himself is sitting in the center of a bubble that surrounds just Liza and him. Liza's smile. "The main thing is that it tastes good."

"You sound like my mother," he quips. The bubble bursts. Amazed at his own abrupt reaction, he softens his comment by smiling back at her.

"Is that bad?" Liza wants to know, turning toward Nikoletta, who nods vigorously. "You can bet on that."

Clemens turns red. "That's one of her standard phrases. When everything goes wrong, she either says 'The main thing is that you're healthy!' or 'The main thing is that it tastes good,' depending on the situation."

The main thing is that it tastes good.

Besides this sentence there is really nothing that connects Liza with his mother. And she, in turn, Clemens thinks, would not at all like being compared to Liza, even without knowing all the unusual details. It was enough to irritate his mother simply that Liza truly had everything that you could want from a woman: she is feminine but not artificially cute, witty and warmhearted, smart and, above all: genuine. Moreover, probably because of her history, she exudes mysteriousness like others' exquisite perfume. Too much perfection for his mother, who actually only likes women twenty years older and forty pounds heavier than herself. And who are not as smart as she is, at least according to her own standards.

[. . .]

Liza, however, seems to have enough confidence even to put his mother in her place. A nice prospect, he admits, but absolutely impossible for various reasons. The most important of which is that although Liza is a gem, she is a lesbian one. And apparently completely infatuated with Nikoletta. At least, the two of them have seen each other almost every day during the last two weeks—and more than once shared Nikoletta's sacred bed. Regardless of how much Clemens broods, tries to comprehend, and fantasizes, the situation is more than clear. He sighs and gets up to pull the last batch out of the oven and pack the tartlets that have already cooled on the floor in cardboard boxes. Nikoletta and Liza emerge from the conversation they were immersed in during Clemens's daydream.

"Wait, I'll help you," says Liza.

Why is she so friendly? Why can't she just simply look nice like Nikoletta's other conquests and stare at him like a walking STD. Why isn't she tugging at the symbiotic leash instead of sitting here in the kitchen being charming and interesting? And why does he have to listen to the two of them have sex?

"Everything okay, Clemens?" asks Nikoletta and points to a bunch of cupcakes lying neatly upside down in the box. With her long fingers and short fingernails, Liza takes one tartlet after the other out of the box and carefully turns it over.

"All good," she proclaims, and looks at him searchingly with her blackish-brown eyes. "I believe he has overdosed on sugar. We really should order a pizza."

"Why is it that you have short fingernails?" The question shoots out of his mouth quicker than he can turn red.

Nikoletta and Liza look at him uncomprehendingly.

Okay, Clemens Scharnhofner, faux pas. So much for group harmony.

"Sorry, I didn't want . . ." he stammers, turning red. "I just . . ."

"Yes?" asks Nikoletta expectantly. There is no explanation here but the truth. Clemens takes a deep breath.

"So, the ones that I know all have long hair and long fingernails. And . . . I've never seen one in baggy pants."

Liza's eyes widen, but the car has already smashed into the wall and awaits its film-ready explosion.

"What I mean to say is: most women who were once men, that is: trans-women, or . . ." he brushes aside the missing words, "They always wear pink and little flowers and skirts and never sneakers but high heels. And makeup!" He digs himself in deeper and deeper. "You don't wear any makeup at all."

Embarrassed, he stares at Liza. She stares back. And Nikoletta looks like she wants the ground to swallow her up. Don't give me that, he thinks, I bet you already asked her the very same questions.

"Jesus, Clemens, could you be any more tactless?" Nikoletta blusters. "And honestly: women who were once men?" Liza looks back and forth from one to the other, bites into a cupcake, and chews.

"How do you know that?"

"Know what?"

"That you've never seen 'one of them' in loose jeans without makeup and with short hair?"

He knows how stupid he looks when he's slow on the uptake and takes his glasses off sheepishly, just to put them right back on.

"How would you have recognized her?" prompts Liza. "How would you have noticed that she is what she is?"

The gear clicks into place. Embarrassed, Clemens runs his hand along his face, leaving behind a trail of green icing.

"And fingernails . . . if you don't want to use your hands, then of course artificial nails work just fine." She sucks the chocolate off her fingers as if she were imitating a no-budget porn film, kisses Nikoletta, walks past her to the sink, and holds her hands under the stream of water. She lets Clemens squirm for a minute before she turns around and looks at him almost lovingly.

"I'm happy to answer all your questions, my dear, but to do that I really need a pizza and a glass of red wine." [. . .]

October

Nikoletta

Before meeting Liza, everything in Nikoletta's life stayed within excellently marked lines—at least since a few years ago. She likes her job, has awesome friends, a nice apartment, and has such a profound fascination for her own sex that she has been diagnosed in those silly internet tests as "completely pussy-fixated."[5] The test results hit the mark: she loves female bodies. Sometimes she is downright obsessed with them. Her sexual orientation is beyond question.

Was beyond question.

On the first evening at the sex party in Schöneberg[6] she did not even notice, because sex, after all, does not necessarily have anything to do with genitals. Liza is the epitome of what Nikoletta finds sexy. Her kisses, her breasts, and her butt all stoked the unease in Nikoletta's body, an unease that was later channeled by the hands of the one she desired. Nikoletta sighs blissfully at the thought of Liza's hands, smiling at her own blinders and how much time she needed before asking this one question.

"Why, actually, can't I touch you . . . uh. . . . *down there,*" she asked on their second date, visibly irritated and unaccustomedly shy.

"I thought that was obvious," answered a surprised Liza cryptically, continuing to insist on keeping her boxer shorts on, and it finally dawned on Nikoletta that she was not looking at a stone butch who was untouchable below the belt but a woman who was half in the body of a man. A realization that plunged her into a deep abyss.

That she was still stuck in.

Floundering.

And trying not to let Liza or anyone else notice her inner chaos.

She likes what she feels when she sees Liza. And that, in turn, she does not like, for two reasons: first, as she explained to Marte yesterday evening on the phone, because she feels somewhat more drawn to Liza than she normally allows herself to feel, due to Liza's openness, the resulting closeness, and the fantastic sex, and second, because she only likes dicks when they are made of pretty silicon, preferably bright-colored. She is confused. So, she called Marte yesterday, and since the thing with Liza cannot be explained by just hinting at it, Nikoletta had to be more precise. Marte listened, comprehended, and soothed: "You are just totally distraught, and that's completely understandable. It would be the same for anybody."

"Not for you," Nikoletta contradicted. "You like men too."

"Maybe. But I would also be confused. And you are demanding too much from yourself. It goes without saying that you are completely thrown off course when you suddenly feel attracted to a person who lived for twenty-five or thirty years in a body that from the get-go would be a sexual no-go for you but right now has become your embodiment of eroticism. Nobody expects you to act like you don't have any unresolved questions." And then, after a pause, she added pensively: "Having no questions can also be understood as lack of interest, you know?" Marte's propensity for honesty does not shy away from inflicting the brief stabbing pain of abrupt punches. As a reward, there is absolution, doled out light-handedly like gummi bears. Marte had competently played her role as mother confessor, and Nikoletta had gotten exactly what she had been looking for: the green light to have misgivings about the direction of her desire. About the fact that her lover was not a garden-variety lesbian but a trans-woman. Nikoletta had nevertheless also obtained from Marte the moral permission to yield to the obvious chemistry between her and Liza. After all, the fascination that Liza triggers in Nikoletta in no way means that Nikoletta is suddenly straight, right? Nor was it an absolution for the politically incorrect idea that this might be the case. For Liza is a woman. Period.

And apart from that: Even though Manu keeps making knowing comments. Even though Clemens gushes in such an obvious manner about Liza, as if he wanted to convince Nikoletta that he would be glad to see her bring Liza home with her any time. Even though she has butterflies in her stomach when she thinks about Liza and cannot get enough sex with her. And even though she gets a secret thrill from what confuses her about Liza's identity.

"I am not in love!" Nikoletta blustered into the phone, although Marte never even hinted at such a thing. [. . .]

November

Clemens

There is coffee instead of herbal tea. Good, strong coffee. Although Nikoletta herself has admitted having spent the last three days almost constantly hunched over the toilet bowl, and Clemens could really use some sleep. Nikoletta is sprawled on the kitchen chair with the hot water bottle on her stomach, and Clemens has tied a cherry pit pillow around his neck with his purple cashmere scarf. Both sip the pleasant poison and it almost feels like it used to, before Liza burst into their lives. Even sighing makes his neck hurt but he does it anyway. The third time, Nikoletta lifts her head and looks at him pensively.

"What, in fact, is going on with you?" she asks.

"Where, in fact, is Liza?" This evasion tactic costs him all the effort he can make. "I haven't seen her for a long time."

"That's because you are never here." That sounds like an accusation. Depending on the state of things, Clemens reacts to accusations with withdrawal or defiance.

In the state he is in today, option one is ruled out automatically.

"You should be happy, that you have the apartment to yourselves," he gripes.

Nikoletta blinks in astonishment but does not counterattack. Instead, she throws down the hot water bottle and runs out of the kitchen. From the bathroom comes a pitiful retching sound. Clemens hopes he doesn't catch this virus too; puking with a screwed-up neck must be a real bummer. Just like puking with screwed-up knees, he thinks, but before he can continue with this line of thought, Nikoletta has already sunk back into her chair. Her skin is the color of gruel, and a bluish web of veins has appeared under her eyes.

"Sorry," he mumbles, in a time lag.

"That's exactly what I mean." Apparently, both of them are too exhausted to argue.

"Whenever I set eyes on you, you are either more irritable than I am with PMS or you have the personality of a sleeping pill." [. . .]

Nikoletta crumbles a zwieback into bite-size pieces, but more crumbs seem to end up on her pajamas than in her mouth. Right on time for heating season, Nikoletta has dug up her collection of men's flannel pajamas, all of which are plaid and much too large. After the third morsel of zwieback she gives up, and the two of them fall silent again, briefly.

"By the way, don't think you can change the subject on me so easily," she says, tearing him away from his thoughts. "Of course, you can't possibly know about Liza, if you are almost never here."

Liza. He successfully casts an inquisitive glance at her without having to move his head.

"We ended it. Last week already."

The pressure builds up in the back of Clemens's throat, ensuring that supreme effort is required for his voice to pierce through the confusion in his head.

"What? Why?"

"Liza has fallen in love." Nikoletta's voice is completely monotone.

Voice from the tomb, Clemens thinks.

"And you?"

"What about me?"

"Well. . . ." Clemens falters. "Are you in love too?"

The answer is apparently in the coffee, for Nikoletta is staring deep into her cup. Her hands are almost white, so tightly is she pressing the turquoise-patterned porcelain between her hands. "I don't fall in love." She doesn't even lift her head.

"And it's not me she has fallen in love with."

Shit, thinks Clemens, and says it too.

Now Nikoletta looks up and stares right into him. Pensive, wounded, furious.

Furious? Clemens has the vague feeling that this fury has something to do with him. "Not with you?" he repeats obtusely. "Then with whom?" [. . .]

Manu

The kitchen table seems to bend under Nikoletta's weight. And that says something, for it is over five feet long and made of solid oak. And, moreover, it is only supporting Nikoletta's head! Sandyunmanu[7] stare exhausted at the blond strands of their friend's hair. Everyone knows that Nikoletta leaves the city center only to go to work and, on top of that, almost never makes a date with both of them at the same time. To find Nikoletta out here at all is already so unusual that the dog can barely contain himself, but the fact that she has come by bicycle, unannounced to Erkner, to stand trembling in front of the door and announce that she is pregnant puts the little family at a downright loss.

After uttering the four syllables she has headed straight into the kitchen and laid her head on the table. In light of the unfathomable, the befuddled hosts belatedly remember their duties.

"Would you like something to drink?" Sandy asks and, without waiting for an answer, pours a large stream of coffee into a cup from the 1997 Lesbian Spring Rally.

"Hey!" Manu stops her in the nick of time. "Didn't you listen? She is pregnant!"

The coffee gets dumped down the drain, and Manu puts a kettle on for tea. Nikoletta's head makes a sound as if someone had just twisted the arm of the woman wearing it. She is still shaking all over. Sandy fetches the reliable faux mink blanket from the living room and wraps it around the body on the chair. Then she puts on her jacket, the blue one with the large green patches on the back that they trade off wearing to walk the dog, whistles for

Rutherford, takes the car key, and says on her way out: "I think we need chocolate."

Manu manages to fall even more deeply in love with her thoughtful girlfriend. She sighs quietly and then turns back to Nikoletta, who in the giant blanket looks like a sad dancing bear.

"Can I do something?" she asks. A paw emerges from the mountain of fur, takes Manu's hand and lays it on her head. And Manu strokes without speaking, which is possibly the most bizarre occurrence of the whole evening—apart from the announcement.

How can this be? Manu asks herself. Her head is spinning. Nikoletta is indeed easygoing and adventurous, but she truly never was involved with men, and Liza, as Manu has come to understand, is not one. Who in the world is the father? Is Nikoletta also involved with Clemens? What is going on with these roommates? Manu thinks and thinks, and her thoughts falter. As does her hand.

Nikoletta's head moves demandingly from left to right beneath Manu's hand, and Manu resumes her soothing strokes. Could such a big decision have been made without Sandyunmanu knowing anything about it?

"None of that makes any sense, Nikoletta! You are fucking with us." The accused does not stir; instead, the door slams shut. "She's fucking with us, sweetie," Manu calls into the hallway. Sandy appears in the kitchen with a selection of all kinds of chocolate bars. The furrow between her eyes signals a coming storm.

"You aren't serious!" she says. "For that I drove to the gas station? Now please say that's not true." She throws Trauben-Nuss, Edelbitter, Weiße Vollnuss, and Kinder Riegel[8] onto the table. Manu's cold coffee sloshes back and forth in the Obelix cup. The hot water has not yet made it out of the teapot onto a teabag for their guest. Finally, Nikoletta lifts her head.

"It's not."

Her eyes are red. She reaches for a Trauben-Nuss, cracks it open, and sticks four pieces at once into her mouth.

"Not what? Is it *not* true?"

The last twist was too much for Manu's already overloaded system.

"It's not true that I'm fucking with you." Nikoletta struggles with the excess chocolate in her mouth. "But it is true. I am ten weeks pregnant."

"And you are surprised by that?" Manu asks, images racing through her head.

Nikoletta's vehement reaction does honor to a third-class soap opera actor.

She swallows the clumps of chocolate and squints her eyes indignantly.

"Excuse me?"

Even Sandy stares at her sweetheart with her head tilted slightly to the left. "What do you mean by that, sweetie?"

Manu hates her own tendency to get hot under the collar. The spots spread in nanoseconds across her head and neck. She leans back in annoyance.

"I mean . . . it could have been planned, couldn't it?"

In stereo: "Why would I plan a child?" and "What would Nikoletta want with a child?"

"Who knows?" Gradually, Manu is getting genuinely offended.

"It has to come from somewhere. I think we are all in agreement that the Virgin Mary story is a fairy tale. And the idea that Nikoletta would willingly sleep with a man, that is: with a real . . ." She searches briefly for an appropriate term and gives up. "I mean, one with all the paraphernalia—I really cannot imagine that."

Nikoletta unwraps a Kinder Riegel bar.

"Unless . . ." Sandy says. You can hear a pin drop. The lights go on all over at the same time, until Manu bursts out, almost inaudibly: "Don't tell me that Liza still . . . ?"

The Kinder Riegel hovers in space, completely unaware of its own metaphorical scope.

"Bingo," sighs Nikoletta and takes a bite. [. . .]

Nikoletta

"I can't sleep."

"Me neither."

"Just the thought . . ."

"Yes."

Nikoletta snuggles deeper into her warm blanket, Liza at her ear.

"Did you actually want children?" One of the many questions she had not managed to articulate during their short liaison.

"Absolutely. I love children!" Liza's enthusiasm sounds hollow through the receiver. "But it just never happened, and when it became clear that I really wanted to transition, well: I am just not calculating enough to have fathered a child beforehand just as a matter of principle."

They don't speak. Nikoletta's head spins and spins.

"I never wanted children," she says.

"I know."

They each start talking again at the same time, laugh nervously, and Liza says what she has said a hundred times in recent days. "I am so sorry. I should have known. I should have been careful."

"Nonsense! How should you have known *that*? And the sex . . . I wanted it too, even a lot. . . ." She stops. Thinks about the night more than two-and-a-half months ago, about the joy, and about how close she felt to Liza. Nikoletta starts to cry, and Liza's voice quivers at the other end of the line.

"It was beautiful, *sweetheart.*[9] Beautiful! And believe me, I do not regret a single second . . ." Nikoletta wants to feel arms around her instead of hearing platitudes on the telephone; she wants to undo what cannot be undone.

"I don't want a child!" she sobs. And behind her tears she hears Liza's soothing voice.

"Sweetie, we'll find a solution, I promise you. I am there for you. We'll manage this together!"

"Together?" Nikoletta surprises herself at how bitter this comes out of her. "In what way, together? You aren't even in love with me and now you have Clemens—what, please, can together mean?"

Self-pity spreads over Nikoletta like the blanket that she has just pulled over her head. She drops the receiver next to her on the mattress and wails and hiccups and whimpers. Only when the oxygen gets scarce under the improvised shelter does she use her finger to bore a hole out into the air and look for the receiver in the folds of the plaid cotton material. When she finally finds it, silence awaits her on the other end.

"Liza?"

A sad sigh. "You are not in love with me either, Nic."

But I would like to be, she thinks . . . and knows that Liza is right. After all, Nikoletta has emphasized it herself often enough.

Liza takes a deep breath before she continues speaking. "And you . . . you don't have to have it, if you don't want to."

I don't have to have it, thinks Nikoletta. And this from Liza. Although for her it is probably the last chance to have a biological child. Although Liza comes from an extremely religious family, in which abortion is murder and a deadly sin.

"You don't have to have it," she says, because Nikoletta's happiness is all she wants.

"You love me, don't you?" Nikoletta asks the telephone.

"Yes," Liza says. "I am not in love with you, but I love you."

"So, our baby was conceived in love?"

"Absolutely." The cheesy moment lingers until Liza adds with sacred seriousness: "In love and lust."

"Alright then," Nikoletta says.

And both of them start giggling hysterically.

Notes

Translated by Gary Schmidt.

1. Tania Witte interview with Gary Schmidt in June 2019.
2. A festival held in Berlin since 1996 to celebrate trans and nonbinary gender performance and identity (see http://www.wigstoeckel.de).
3. Erkner is a town near Berlin on the commuter train line.
4. Term used by Germans for Americans, more or less affectionately depending on the context.
5. "Completely pussy-fixated" is in English in the original text.
6. Neighborhood in Berlin with a significant LGBTQ+ community.
7. Short for Sandy and Manu; the lesbian pair is given this collective identity by their less blissfully coupled friends.
8. These are all types of chocolate bars commonly available in Germany and produced by different companies. Kinder Riegel is a specific brand of chocolate that literally means "children's bar."
9. "Sweetheart" is in English in the original.

Joachim Helfer

Joachim Helfer grew up in Schwalbach, a small town in Hesse in the foothills of the Taunus, a forested mountain range directly north of Frankfurt am Main. He studied English literature in Hamburg and traveled extensively through Europe, Africa, and the United States before becoming a writer and translator. Helfer's first novel, the semi-autobiographical *Du Idiot* (*You Idiot*), published with Suhrkamp in 1994, narrates the coming of age of the protagonist Florian König entirely in the second person. The novel received critical praise and was followed by *Cohn & König* (1998), which continues Florian's story after he meets the much older Pierre Cohn, who becomes his lifetime companion. In 2003, Helfer participated in a writers' exchange in the framework of the West-Eastern Divan program, which was sponsored by the German government and organized by the Goethe Institut, the cultural agency of the Federal Republic of Germany with worldwide locations. The program was intended to foster intercultural dialogue between German and Middle Eastern authors. The literary results of Hilfer's encounter with the Lebanese author Rashid al-Daif were published as *Die Verschwulung der Welt* (*The Gaying of the World*, 2006), triggering somewhat of a sensation due to the authors' differing views on their experience, particularly with regard to their discussions of homosexuality and gender. The volume appeared in English as *What Makes a Man: Sex Talk in Beirut and Berlin*, published in 2015 by the Center for Middle Eastern Studies at the University of Texas at Austin. In recent years, Helfer has devoted considerable attention to politics, coediting volumes on the 150th anniversary of the German Social Democratic Party, the 2017 German parliamentary elections, and the future of the European union.

The two excerpts are taken from the unpublished manuscript *Das Dritte* ("The Third"), the final novel of the Florian König trilogy. They narrate Florian's transition from being the younger partner in a relationship to the older one when, after finally being able to marry the now elderly Pierre Cohn, Florian falls in love with young Daniel. Helfer's views on male homosexuality run counter to the model embraced by activists who pushed same-sex marriage to the forefront of the political agenda, in which gay couples are usually assumed to be close to the same age. Helfer sees male homosexual relationships, regardless of age difference, more in line with the Greek model of sexuality, in which one partner fulfills the role of mentor and the other of student.[1]

"Wedding in Berlin after Two Decades of Marriage" (2021)

"Aren't you supposed to go to Venice on your honeymoon?"—the gentle sarcasm of the best man in front of the main gate of the Schöneberg[2] district city hall was justified after surviving the ceremony yesterday afternoon. In order to carry out an administrative act that came an entire generation too late, they had found, solemnly waiting for them that morning at 11 o'clock, a burning candelabra on a crocheted doily, a vase with pale pink stocks, and the Overture from Handel's *Music for the Royal Fireworks*. To top it all off, a young marriage registrar in pumps and a cocktail dress who first of all gave a warm welcome to Herr Pierre Cohn and Herr Florian König, or was it Mister Cohn? Monsieur Cohn? *Ja, ja,* Pierre still had command of his mother tongue in spite of his two foreign passports—but which was the right one here? Florian had foreseen the confusion and attempted to convince Pierre to choose one of them. "Better take the French one, as an American you aren't covered by EU law and we'll end up having trouble with the immigration office." All in vain. He could not talk this child of émigrés out of his obsession with proving his identity beyond a shadow of a doubt, preferably twice-over, since once was not enough: "I was born in Berlin and my parents were too! When Willy Brandt[3] was mayor here, before you were even born, he wrote to my mother in Los Angeles and invited her here." True, she had graciously declined and she was no longer living, but he himself had been in the city for ten years. "I would never have dared to do it alone, but with Florian . . . do you know, Madam, how long we have been together? Eighteen years! I mean . . . Florian was of course eighteen when we met each other. Here you have the proof of registration of address, and here you have the most recent tax return." Florian, shaking with embarrassment to see his boyfriend trembling before the authorities, interrupted him: "Just stop! The lady only wishes to know if you can speak German and which passport number she should enter!" After a very unbureaucratic and magnanimous completion of the paperwork—"According to your address registration you are French. If you were born here and your parents were German then you could also obtain German citizenship without any problem"—the lady gave a speech about their love and responsibility for one another: bombastic platitudes that Florian, unlike the older Pierre, could not just listen to with a pleasant smile. Then finally the partners could sign: with their prior names, of course! The question whether he wanted to take on a different name or add one to his own rubbed Monsieur Cohn the wrong way; as if the clueless young thing somehow thought his knee-length Indian silk shirt was a bridal gown: "Our partnership name is posted on our business!" Florian couldn't help thinking of how brusquely Pierre had refused to tolerate any public display of affection or togetherness, as if even walking arm in arm was an indecent display. In spite of the businesslike approach to the appointment beforehand—"This is just about making sure you are provided for and that you can take care of me when I turn senile"—he was apparently as tense as a string about to snap. Before this man, whose repressed and therefore all the more devastating feelings he knew better than his own, completely blew up, Florian took the analogy with the right to share names of married people to its absurd conclusion: "The children will just have to decide when they come of age." Only when he found himself to be the only one laughing at his lame joke did he realize that he was making fun of himself: that the young man who had just recently come of age, who had decided on Pierre, would also have gladly taken on his name, but above all would have been overjoyed to have children with him. Is that the reason why he had always avoided responding to Pierre's suggestion to follow the practice of the Roman emperors and adopt him as his chosen successor? No, all joking aside, there were no plans for an exchange of rings. "This here," said Pierre as he had reached for Florian's hand to hold up the jewel that he had put on his finger at breakfast just as ceremoniously as he had that first day of May watching the sunset in the most beautiful beach restaurant of the French Riviera, "is one of a kind, there is no equivalent to exchange." Florian mischievously seized on the wording—"Just like you!"—before Pierre proceeded with a lecture on Antinous[4] and how this was a symbol not for exchanging but for passing down. "No handcuffs, so to speak, but a baton." The lady made up like a Barbie doll found that "interesting," and Florian could not help noticing that she herself only wore a ring in the wing of her nose, that her shoes were hardly suited for running a relay, and that she even seemed to quiver involuntarily upon hearing the word "handcuffs."

Then he signed, as the second: as in a marriage the woman would, who was given the prerogative in both the "I do" and the signature of being able to change her mind after the man had already committed himself. Florian would have liked to ask what the actual basis was for deciding who to hand the document to first when there were two men or two women? Age? But isn't the ideal gay couple also same-aged? In every regard twin-like, as if hatched from one egg? But the marriage registrar was already on her feet extending them her hand: All the best! No, witnesses were not required by the law, and they had not invited any. Yes, they would be going to Florence for a few days, which, by the way, was where the ring came from! Before Pierre could start reforging every link of a story formed from a chain of improbabilities, Florian pushed him toward the door. The next couple was already waiting in the lobby, two extended families or maybe just one, with the women all in colorful Asian garb and the men in dark European colors, the head of the bride bent down to her breast under the weight of several kilos of gold. The dignified old man in Indian dress, perhaps a Kashmiri, who surely was ready to announce the birth of his grandchild, beamed like Jupiter, smiling beneficently at the group. Everyone smiled back amiably, a handsome young man with a black beard and a white pointed cap bowed with his hand on his heart—then they were outside.

"Visitors are requested to refrain from throwing rice in or outside of the city hall!" The district office's sign for newlyweds was not really all that funny, and he had certainly had wittier moments in his life than now, but after city hall, Florian couldn't help but make a wisecrack. Maybe he was just sad. He had expected that the legal act, which could add nothing to the intimacy between Pierre and him, would pass over him as a formality; but now it felt like he had lost something. Did the ring, which he preferred to stick in his pocket now that he was outside, seal not eternity but the loss of their beautiful illusion? Would Mr. and Mr. Zeus-Ganymede or Hadrian-Antinous not have fallen among the mortals by signing the civil union certificate? Did it not reek of transience when one repeated a promise they had already given each other half a life ago, joyful and generous as only young lovebirds could be, this time documented to provide for sickness, nursing homes, and the bereaved? Didn't it border on betrayal to make a contract legal and enforceable that they had always considered to be binding, even without witnesses and a piece of paper? For form's sake, even if form did not quite fit their alliance, since the one ring sealed nothing that resembled marriage but instead a kind of ersatz son's inheritance? Or was it just the bad style that bothered him in ending what had started at the bay in Cannes as a five-star dream among American captains, commanders, and admirals who had been invited by their grateful French allies to celebrate Independence Day in full dress uniform? Hearing Pierre say, "To believe that I lived to experience even this! Now I have really come home. Today Germany is truly the most decent country in the world!" Florian is mortified by his own narcissism and links arms with Pierre: while he had been staring melancholically—in his mid-thirties!—at his reflection in a puddle that was turning cloudy, good old Pierre didn't find it futile to be reconciled with the world yet again: "Come, children, we have to celebrate!" Luckily, Florian was not so dogmatic as to contradict Pierre in his high spirits; in a country that would have forbidden him from marrying young Peter Cohn even if he were a girl,[5] a little bit of joyful astonishment was all too appropriate. "I'm only saying it because you are forgetting that you are the one who refused to tolerate making a fuss about all this!" Not long ago Achim and Rolf had thrown the requisite festivities, at which Friedrich, ever the unrepentant bachelor, lamented the arrival of this fringe group in the societal mainstream as the foreseeable end of its cultural productivity: "Only wounded oysters give birth to pearls!"

"Finally, with Daniel" (2021)

"Hallo, Florian! Here then is the last step over the abyss: Wednesday, April 30th, but only if I don't have to play at revolution in the Berlin Wall Park. It would be a nice occasion for a belated Easter walk. Maybe in the Tiergarten?[6] Shall we meet at five o'clock at the Brandenburg Gate? Even I can find that . . . Looking forward to it! Daniel!"

Is Florian looking forward to it? Is his fluttering heart, stronger with every hour that separates him a little less from Daniel, truly a sign of anticipation and not fear? An evil premonition inextricably blending his fear of hurting Daniel with the fear that he himself will bleed to death from the contact? Isn't the same abyss that Daniel had already crossed now gaping in front of him, he asked himself as he was flying home over the North Sea to Berlin? Not the graves of royal children and not a generation gap, but the unbridgeable nothingness between dream and reality? He approaches the prospect so hesitantly that his prospect will come true, that he arrives too late instead of too early. If only Daniel had kept him waiting! But there he is already, a slender, slightly hunched line among the mighty half-columns of the gate, and waves at him from afar—with the little Pepita hat that he had never worn again since they had met two years ago. The gesture could not have been chosen more wisely and said two things, "I know that we are starting all over" and "We should find each other ridiculous from the start before we get too sentimental." Laughing, and more certain than ever that he had not just been smitten by Daniel, Florian crosses the remaining short distance between them and takes him in his arms: without words, since at that moment in which everything that can be said between them had already been said, and all barriers that divided them are removed. Arm in arm they make their way through the chaotic traffic of the Brandenburg Gate. At the beginning it is a bit awkward, because each of them wants to put his arm on the other's shoulder, and they also bump hips. But then Daniel executes a two-step, and Florian grabs the younger, more slender but no longer shorter friend around the waist, and they go sauntering side by side through the Tiergarten as if they had been doing it forever. . . . "Come to the park they say is dead and view!"[7] As easy as it is for him to resist the shallow jokes or suggestive remarks with which, for example, his brother or Friedrich gloss over moments of the unspeakable, he cannot remain forever as silent as the animals, who are perhaps happier but also dumber. As usual, Florian rescues himself from the embarrassment of uttering his own original text by reciting someone else's: What better fit for this Berlin spring walk over the large dog meadow by the pink granite boulder covered with graffiti, where already the first nudists lie under the spring sun, than the bombastic autumn poem of a big mouth like Stefan George? Daniel looks up grinning, recognizably grateful for the fine suggestion that he himself makes only at this moment: to bring the park to life. "Look . . ." he says, turning his gaze from one natural beauty to the next, "What a picture of a tree!" Knowing that Florian will call it beech, linden, maple, or oak. "Look, flowering bushes," Daniel shouts, and Florian calls them hawthorn or rhododendron, whitethorn or azalea. "And there, the birds, look!" Daniel rejoices with an enthusiasm that is not wholly mocking, and Florian lists them: Gimpel, Jay, Great Tit, Green Woodpecker, Chaffinch, "No, that was just a nuthatch. But there, the one trilling so sweetly without being seen, that is the blackbird."

And, as he continues undeterred to the daisies and orchids, he can't help but think of his mother, who has taught him the flowers; and of Pierre, who for the first time looked at the boy who he was smitten with through altogether different eyes when he had been able to identify the flowers on the grass in Botticelli's amorous spring painting in Florence. And can't help, with the boy on his arm, from shedding a few tears. Daniel would not be Daniel, if he did not sense Florian's change of spirits and have a remedy at hand: "Nothing against nature, but we could also just sit on a bench and read poems!"

The volume of the Goethe edition, which he pulls out of his jacket pocket, is the *West-Eastern Divan*,[8] but the bench he is heading for is already far to the west, beyond the Victory Column,[9] on the Duck Pond near the Lion's Bridge. Does he know that this is the edge of the hunting grounds where men in search of other men stalk through the bushes? Is it conceivable that Daniel might imagine that Florian himself has gone strolling here? Does he want to put him to the test? Or is he just curious? "Tell no one, just the wise man, because the crowd will jeer at once. . . ." The pupil reads from the page how the pubkeeper fills the poet's glass with tasty wine and a smile that seems completely pure and yet suggests ulterior motives—both intoxicating and charming. Florian knows the text: "I want to praise life that longs for a fiery death." "I thought you weren't interested in being burned at the stake anymore?" Daniel puts his finger to his lips—and then to the next line. So they indulge in blissful longing: the businessman in a midlife crisis and the politically committed high school student, hand in hand on a Berlin park bench, fallen out of their time and world like only ever a pair of lovers, spied on by God and turtle doves, passers-by, and a few troublemakers. A child's ball rolls over their feet again and again, which would have been more pleasant than annoying had the father, like the mother, pushed the buggy with the child's tiny sibling slowly and not suddenly rushed with a snapping voice at them to snatch their child away: "Jonathan! Get away from there!" So loud that the child wails in fear, lets the ball roll into the duckweed, and starts to pee like Rembrandt's too-young Ganymede.[10] Then follows a sneakered boy in his late forties, bleached locks and emaciated body pressed into jeans that are still too tight for him, whose smile Florian, seeing a specter of his own not-too-distant future before him, barely returns. He promptly creeps past them a second and third time until he stops right in front of them and listens, his mouth twisted not in a smile that would still be unreturned on the fourth attempt, but formed into an orifice excreting all the bitterness of the world: "Higher mating! That's what you dream of! You're just a child molester!" Whereupon the otherwise angelic Daniel lets go of a startlingly impatient sigh, slams the *Divan* shut with a loud bang, looks invitingly at Florian—and kisses him until the frustrated voyeur finally pisses off; and then two or three eternities later they hear "Off to Auschwitz!" invading their ears: more whispered than spoken, out of the dusk that has fallen around them as a protective cloak while their eyes were closed. Has Florian heard wrong? All he can make out are the shadows of the still quite bare trees on the other side of the lake—but aren't there also shadowy figures? Half-grown, a whole pack, certainly Arabs or Turks, in the holy war against Sodomites? Should he let himself be riled up by this outrage? Jump up, start shouting, and mobilize the leather queers from the bushes to rush the band of Nazis? Before he can move, shaking with rage, the haunting is over—and he realizes that it is Daniel who has held him back: that the hand, which is otherwise so soft in his, has him firmly under control. "Hey, Flori . . . Everything's okay! They were just a few idiots . . ."

Cradled on the bosom of his friend like a frightened child, Florian is reassured by the fact that Daniel's heart is beating faster than his. . . . But once again their embrace does not remain undisturbed: the darkness that befell them so suddenly when they had first kissed is not just nightfall but also dark purple clouds: gusts of wind are already shaking the trees and fat raindrops are falling. "Of course," thinks Florian, "nature will give us a push!"

Whereas Daniel, of course, ignores the signs: true, he sticks the volume of poetry under his jacket but otherwise acts as if the mere memory of the silly cloth hat that he has long since cast off is sufficient to shield these two men of intellect from the elements: he has no intention of getting up.

Florian cannot help laughing. "Why are you laughing?"—"Because this reminds me of a storm on another spring night. On our school trip to the South of France, I was exactly your age, and the woman with whom I sat hand in hand on the beach was my homeroom teacher." "Sounds romantic." "Yes, totally. Gudrun had invited me for a walk after dinner. As usual, we talked a lot. At some point we were seated in an amphitheater high above the French Riviera, and neither one of us felt like saying anything more. Of course, she expected me to kiss her—without the storm we would perhaps still be sitting there." "And then?" "And then there was a flash of lightning over the sea, and there was a rumble behind the mountains. In the Maritime Alps a storm like that comes out of nowhere. First there was such a strong wind that the pinecones and baobab fruit rained down. Then it started to pour. In no time we were drenched to the bone." "And then?" By then the driving rain forms a white veil around the park lights and the pale moon, falling like string from the naked black branches onto their necks. It is hard to tell if Daniel's question just sounds sly or if he is making a face to match it. "Then we ran laughing through the downpour to the youth camp where she, as a teacher, had a single cottage, tore off our wet clothes and crawled into bed." "Let's go!" Before Florian understands what is happening to him, Daniel has already raced ahead. But under the next lamp he stops, his dripping face so slick that Florian fears it will melt away on the spot: "You just have to show me the way to go!"

This time they know who should grab whom where, and they set off on the same foot: without haste, almost solemnly, past the zoo habitats where from behind barbed wire not a single ibis or flamingo shows itself in this godforsaken weather, past lines of shivering people at the bus stops and taxi stands in front of Bahnhof Zoo and down the Kurfürstendamm, whose sidewalks have been swept clean. Even back home on Fasanenstraße not a living soul was waiting for them: "Pierre and Isabelle always go to bed early. Would you like wine? Or rather hot tea?" Florian says this in the dark foyer with a hoarse, muffled voice: No, that's not really him speaking but just his damned cowardliness.

Maintain appearances at all costs, even if it means perfect unhappiness.

No, his mother had not raised him that way, he did it all himself. Luckily it was Daniel who was standing across from him with chattering teeth. "Café au lait, please—for breakfast! I just want to take a shower and then go to bed." Florian would not be Florian if he did not only nod solicitously and give his guest a fresh towel but also pick out bed linen and start babbling like he had to apologize for something—and yet he fervently hopes that Daniel will not hear him from the shower as he makes up the sofa in the office, since Isabella is occupying the guest room. "Good Night!" he calls through the bathroom door, before he goes into his bedroom, peels off his wet clothes, and in anticipatory modesty puts on pajamas that he normally would only wear if suffering fever and chills, before lying down. But he leaves his door open. . . . And Daniel? Daniel, who at the age of fourteen had already appeared before his school assembly wrapped only in a bedsheet to elucidate love according to Plato's *Symposium*? Daniel flits out of the bathroom into the office and calls softly into the dark, "Florian?" When nobody answers and no light goes on, Daniel floats over to him a heartbeat later, a nightmare in a toga.

Florian doesn't know. Not like that night with Gudrun, his first with a woman, when he truly did not know what he should do how and when. But rather he doesn't know if he should do what he nevertheless is about to do, to go as gently as possible, but without hesitation, where his overflowing desire leads him. No question of him just playing the role of Socrates who refrains from touching Alcibiades[11] when he lies down next to him. He neither wishes nor needs to prove his self-control to anyone, and he has never believed that wisdom lies in abstinence. But he would feel more comfortable in his skin if he knew that Daniel was not lying here next to him just because a chance storm had come up, not rigid but rather tenderly in an almost polite way, soft as tears, first waiting and then compliant? Has Daniel just surrendered to him as if to an unavoidable destiny? Is Daniel kissing Florian because Daniel wants to kiss Florian? Because Daniel wants to be kissed by Florian? Or only because Florian wants to kiss Daniel? How was it for Daniel with Andreas? Did he long for his first time? Was he carried along by curiosity? Or did he just tolerate it out of friendliness? Only one thing is certain: that Florian, who strangely cannot even remember his first time with a man, would never have dared to be the first one to touch Daniel. But then who is he to play the second to the other one? Is his scrupulous hesitation really better than unscrupulous action? Hasn't Daniel become much less unconditional under his influence? Didn't he protest an entire year against the impending attack on Iraq—the day after President Bush wanted to spin it as a job well done—but fell silent during the last six weeks when the invasion actually took place? Didn't this little apple that was still half green inside but bright red outside, whom *he* had found but Andreas had plucked, know much better what it wanted and did not want than the boy who was reading *Hamlet* today?

What if none other than Florian was seducing Daniel: not to indecent acts, of which he obviously was quite capable, but to a dubious attitude that weighed everything and risked nothing and was ultimately worried about its own advantage. Wasn't he about to turn Daniel around? To turn the revolutionary into a bourgeois? The idealist into a cynic? "Are you sure?" slips out of his mouth when it is already far too late for any uncertainty. For him, who has always experienced sexuality and language as irreconcilable, an embrace as the last refuge from pompous words that clomp around in the unsayable like conquerors in a defiled sanctuary? Daniel puts his fingers on his lips. As a sign that right now he is quite certain he does not want to speak, he turns away from him and buries his face in the pillow: all on his own and almost, but just almost, as if he would rather be left alone: "Don't think."

Notes

Translated by Gary Schmidt.

1. Joachim Helfer interview with Gary Schmidt in June 2019.

2. A Berlin district that historically and currently has a large LGBTQ+ population.

3. Willy Brandt was a Social Democratic politician who went into exile in Norway and Sweden during the Nazi period and was mayor of West Berlin when the East German government constructed the Berlin Wall. Brandt later became chancellor of West Germany.

4. Antinous was the adolescent lover of the Roman emperor Hadrian, who deified him after his early death.

5. Reference to the infamous Nuremberg Laws, which prohibited marriage between Jews and "Aryans" during the Nazi period.

6. Enormous park in central Berlin that extends from the Brandenburg Gate in the East to Bahnhof Zoo (Zoo Station) in the West.

7. Quotation from poet Stefan George. Original German: "Komm in den totgesagten Park und schau." George stylized himself as an almost cult-like leader and surrounded himself with younger male poets and artists and hence may signal queerness to some readers.

8. Refers to Johann Wolfgang von Goethe's most extensive collection of poems, which was inspired by the Persian poet Hafez. See Robert Tobin, *Warm Brothers: Queer Theory and the Age of Goethe* (Philadelphia: University of Pennsylvania Press, 2000), for queer readings of the *Divan*.

9. In German "Siegessäule," the monument in the center of the Tiergarten built in the nineteenth century to commemorate German victories in the wars of unification. The nearby woods are a popular cruising area for gay men, and the name of Berlin's premier gay magazine is *Siegessäule*.

10. "Ganymede" refers to the youth who in Greek mythology was abducted by Zeus, who had become enamored of his beauty, and was brought to Olympus to serve as cupbearer. In Rembrandt's painting *The Rape of Ganymede*, Ganymede appears almost to be an infant.

11. The Greek philosopher Socrates and the general Alcibiades were both historical personages but also characters in Plato's *Symposium*, in which Alcibiades gives a speech reporting on how he believed Socrates wanted to sleep with him but, after realizing he did not, began himself to actively pursue the philosopher.

Sasha Marianna Salzmann

Sasha Marianna Salzmann was born in Volgograd and grew up in Moscow. In 1995, their family emigrated to Germany after a decree of the German government granted asylum to people of Jewish ancestry who were living in the successor states of the Soviet Union. Salzmann studied literature and media at the University of Hildesheim and playwriting at the Berlin University of the Arts. While still a student, they already gained recognition for their plays: *Muttermale Fenster Blau* (*Birthmarks Window Blue*) was awarded the Kleist Förderpreis for young dramatists in 2012. Since 2013, Salzmann has worked as the in-house writer at the Maxim Gorki Theater in Berlin. They have written numerous plays, which have been performed in Germany and abroad to critical acclaim. In 2017, their debut novel, *Außer sich* (*Beside Oneself*), was published with Suhrkamp, on which they began working during a residency in Istanbul in 2012–13. The novel, which received high praise from critics, is about a pair of twins, Alissa and Anton, who grow up in post-Soviet Moscow, then in a home for refugees in Germany; Anton suddenly disappears, eventually leading Alissa to search for him in Istanbul, where she herself undergoes a radical transformation.

Salzmann wrote the following short story for the Cologne international literary festival. Set in current-day Berlin, which houses hundreds of thousands of refugees from the Middle East and other parts of the world, the narrator of this story walks through familiar neighborhoods that have become alien to them, a flaneur who, while seeking the familiar, finds only uncertainty.

"Berlin, September 18" (2018)

The field was scorched. At least it looked that way.

I couldn't tell her anything more than that.

I had been walking in circles, first around the block, then turning right several times, past the bakery open only until midday, whose assistants sat smoking in the doorway after closing time, but not today: it was already too late for that. I walked past the gas station that was long since out of business and now served as a meeting place for the homeless. I roamed through the streets, snapping my fingers as if I were trying to keep myself awake. Walked up the hill of the Hasenheide[1] and then across the busy street toward a marble-colored wall, behind which rose the turrets of the mosque. Although it smelled of rain, the sun was still burning; the woman at the bus stop in front of the neighboring cemetery shielded her face with one hand and peered through her fingers for the bus. I turned off onto the grounds of the abandoned airport and was dismayed by its rusty appearance, as if fires had raged there.

I used to walk for hours on this terrain, which had been transformed into a park, and was careful not to rouse the birds brooding in the high grass, where pink warning signs at the edge of the walking path called attention to their nests. Now the faded signs were standing around naked. The glimmering horizon was dotted by a few lone bushes and a small group of trees. I ventured onto the hay-colored ground; the dry, stubbly stalks of grass jabbed through the thin soles of my sandals and cut into my ankles. I stalked clumsily for a few meters and turned back to the runway. There were no families there today flying kites, no people drumming, the espresso cart had been taken away.

"It is such an odd feeling: I remember more and more what's missing," I said to her, "and at the same time I constantly forget everything."

When we bumped into each other by chance in the Weserstraße, I started to greet her and noticed that I no longer knew her name. I had wandered aimlessly from the Tempelhof field towards Neukölln.[2] On the lawn behind the little brick house at the next big intersection, there were scattered groups of people as always, unimpressed by the rain, leaning on each other, smoking, or gazing into nothing. I stopped several times in front of the display cases of the restaurants just opening up for dinner. The scent of garlic and oil penetrated my nostrils. Several times, a voice pierced the whoosh of the car tires rolling through the swelling puddles. The sun had finally disappeared behind the rapidly advancing clouds. The cries got closer: someone was shouting my name. I turned around and brushed up against an umbrella at the height of my shoulder. The child underneath looked at me indignantly, said something that I did not understand and kept going.

I looked up toward the houses to see if someone up there was calling to me. The façades looked darker in the rain; the balconies were empty. I sensed someone close behind me and spun around. She said my name over and over. And I couldn't ask her what hers was.

She said: "So nice to see you."

We had met right here last time, didn't I remember? Yes, right here, and it was a warm evening like today, was I alone or was there someone with me? And where was I going, did I want to have a drink with her, right here? She thought I had changed, but not so much that I looked worn out.

We had to wait for a table. They were just releasing the chains from the chairs. I didn't know what to say and harbored the absurd hope that the waiter on his way with the menus would know her and call her by her first name.

"This city has gone crazy, hasn't it?" she started, as we sat down. "It's pretending to be New York: when it's about reserving a table, people stand in line in front of the most ordinary restaurants. The bus never comes, because everything is always congested. All the tourists. I constantly am late to work because of it. I cannot afford a car and just barely the rent! There's a lot of building going on, but not for us: apartments with three bathrooms and heated floors. You feel like you're buried under concrete in them. And then all these people are coming from Damascus, Istanbul, Moscow, Tel Aviv, Paris, and also want to live somewhere. The city grows and grows and grows—and holds its breath."

She puffed out her cheeks, the sleeves of her jacket kept slipping over her reddened wrists when she gestured. I followed her movements with my gaze, as she drew horizontal eights before my face.

"And then—BUM,"[3] she pressed the air out of her mouth. "It must mean something that the whole world is coming here while everybody already here wants to leave. That must mean something. Everybody says they are going to leave, move to the country, apply for a visa in Canada. But why? Isn't this the best place there is?"

I asked her for whom.

She knows how things happen, she says, at least since she had been working as an intern in the intake facility for refugees in Hangar 2 of the abandoned airport. People were housed there in box-like cubicles with makeshift separators; the sleeping cabins were open at the top. Every morning, a voice from a loudspeaker woke them, and then the overseer turned on the lights. She was meeting a lot of people there. She doled out food, conversed—finally her Arabic studies were paying off. She had befriended two men; at first, they had often taken walks together on the runway. The two did not take her along to government offices. They didn't want that. She felt connected with them, the only one who knew they were a couple. Once, on one of their walks, she complained about her property manager, who had not reacted for weeks to one of her letters, and immediately she was ashamed because her problem suddenly seemed so petty. She carried this feeling around for days and then, one evening, she was sitting with the men outside in front of the hangar. They were trying to keep the coal glowing on the clay-head sieve of the water pipe, and she asked them both if they would like to move in with her. And one of them laughed, pointing to the lights of the airport field and said, only if she also had such a beautiful view in front of her window.

Living together was alright, they got along, they had a lot of visitors, the mountain of shoes in front of the door didn't bother her anymore; she just couldn't bring other people home anymore. Would they go to her place later then?

It came so abruptly that I doubted whether I had understood her correctly. I ignored the question. I still could not think of her name.

I told her that I also was planning to leave the city for a long time, maybe forever, whereupon she deduced that my apartment would be free, perhaps I could accommodate the couple that was living with her at the moment. She would love to look at the rooms; should we get going?

I said the Tempelhof field had been scorched. At least it looked that way. I had also been there.

Her restless, pointy face froze briefly.

I got up abruptly and took my leave, asking myself while walking if this lie about leaving the city perhaps indicated a need. I had lost my orientation in the city where I had grown up and also the feel for seasons. It was still raining, but at the same time the sun had come out, low on the horizon. I tensed my whole body so as not to slip on my thin soles.

Notes

Translated by Gary Schmidt.

1. A well-known park, a former hare-hunting area in the Kreuzberg district of Berlin, just north of the former Tempelhof Airport, site of the 1948–49 Berlin Airlift.

2. District of Berlin with a high percentage of immigrants and recently undergoing a certain degree of gentrification.

3. A beach volleyball tournament (Berlin Ultimate Mitte) held in the city center of Berlin.

III

INTERTEXTS

Friedrich Kröhnke

FRIEDRICH KRÖHNKE, whose essays, stories, and novels span four decades, is one of the most well-known voices in contemporary gay German literature. His prose is tersely poetic; pithy appraisals and enjoinders punctuate vivid, wistful images. Cultivating a tone that is at once contemplative and ironic, the author draws the reader into experiences that are intensely personal and yet viscerally political, offering a critique of global capitalism's pervasive influence on the daily life of human beings across the planet.

The three semi-autobiographical excerpts that follow address experiences of the author from the 1970s to the early twenty-first century. Kröhnke came of age in the wake of the Generation of 1968, the German student movement that took to the streets to protest West Germany's unfinished denazification, thus rejecting the previously unquestioned status of the United States as a model of democracy and identifying with the victims of American racial oppression at home and military aggression in Vietnam. The first excerpt, "How It All Started," is an unpublished manuscript provided by the author. The second, "Prague," is taken from his novel *Ciao Vaschek* (2003),[1] whose narrator, like Kröhnke, moved to Prague in the late 1990s in search of an enclave that had "not yet" been absorbed into global capitalist consumerism, where he could continue to lead the bohemian existence that had been possible in West Berlin before the fall of the Wall. The first-person narrator is obsessed with the idea of his own death, which has led him to research the most lurid and brutal details of capital punishment in the United States. A self-understanding as an outsider—both chosen and compelled—also characterizes the protagonist of the novel *Nach Asmara* (2011), from which the third excerpt, "Alexandria," is taken. Here the protagonist, given only the last name Frick, visits the residence of the Greek poet Constantine Peter Cavafy in Alexandria, Egypt. This short vignette interrupts longer reflections on Frick's encounter with a fellow patient, a certain Herr Burmeister, during a hospital stay eight years prior, during which a botched surgery necessitated the removal of Frick's left kidney (an incident also related at the end of *Ciao Vaschek*). Frick lied to Burmeister, claiming the recent death of a nonexistent girlfriend and concealing his nomadic existence and homosexuality in fear of losing Burmeister's esteem. Framed by the subjunctive expression "Erzählbar wäre . . ." (It would be possible to tell . . .), the narration of Frick's visit to the home of the Greek poet, whose homoerotic verses were never published while he was still living,[2] substitutes for a coming out.

"How It All Started" (2015)

A long time ago there was a late afternoon, probably in March and perhaps in 1970, perhaps 1971, when everything started. I felt new and different things, and I myself felt different. Did my twin brother feel the same way?

The season was not yet warm, but the weather was good. Cool evening air was alright. We roamed through the city, went downtown, which we did not take for granted: we had just turned fourteen or fifteen. Near the cafeteria of the technical university there was a bit of a commotion, a rowdy band of students calling out rallying cries and handing out leaflets.

We were curious, we were shy and bold at the same time. We learned that the students had carried a professor's desk onto the street—there it stood—because the professor conducted military research for US helicopters in Cambodia. We liked the fact that the students had carried the professor's desk onto the street.

And we also liked a pop song. There was a song we couldn't get out of our heads that day, just some song. It was called "Never Marry a Railroad Man." We didn't understand it. It was wistful and beautiful like the cold spring air toward evening. Such an odd sorrow that now it was becoming spring.

We were in love but didn't yet know with whom. We knew nothing of military research for the US Army in Cambodia. Nor did we understand "Never Marry a Railroad Man" . . . what did that mean exactly? It was peculiarly beautiful. Although it was already seven o'clock, by no means did we want to go home.

"Prague," from *Ciao Vaschek* (2003)

And in this city, I heard of Allen Ginsberg's death.[3] I frequented a hole-in-the-wall called Arcade Music Cafe, where in the vestibule, dimly lit even at midday, the schoolboys with their satchels descended the stairs after school.

Downstairs, bored by the wait, sit the pederasts from all countries, waiting daily for school to let out. Two dirty old men from Florida kill time with a game of chess, which they tend to bring along with them, just as they do the oilcloth on which they place the figures.

When a boy is in the mood for it, he walks toward the men or toward one of them in particular and says: "Beezeeness." It is a game and an affliction at the same time.

"Allen Ginsberg died," says one of the men from Florida. Across from me sits a fat man of indeterminate age, a Slovak. The Slovak says: "I knew Allen Ginsberg."

When he notices that I know who Allen Ginsberg was, the man leans over the table and colorfully narrates in detail how Allen Ginsberg had come to the Riviera Disco here in Prague a few years ago and entered into a conversation with the Slovak, standing next to him with a beer glass in his hand. The fat man tells with enthusiasm how Ginsberg wrote verses for him on the back of a Velkopopovický Kozel[4] beer coaster and how he knows Ginsberg's volumes of poetry very well, some even by heart, and he loudly recites, in English, the beginning of "The Howl."[5]

"Beezeeness?" they are interrupted by a peep. A towering, ungainly lad, a bit featherbrained-looking, has come to the table and picked me out with his eyes, proposing to me, "Beezeenez." I find him pleasing. "No," I say. "No" means "yes" in this country. "No" with a short open "o."

The next day at noon I am back there again and the men from Florida too. They are playing chess. At another table sits the boy, with a black eye and dried blood on his forehead. "He was beaten up," says one of the dirty old men. "The fat guy beat him up and robbed him, the Slovak." He was sitting with us at the table reciting "The Howl" and noticed that the boy was going to have some money afterwards. He waylaid him in the dark vestibule." The boy smiled at me from the next table, towering, feather-brained, dried blood on his forehead. Beezeeness, beezeeness.

"Alexandria," from *Nach Asmara* (2011)

It would be possible to tell how Frick commemorated a poet who shared his dreams and sorrows . . .

Even after searching doggedly, the house was hard to find: in a narrow street crammed between others behind an alleyway. And not a single sign in any language could be found pointing the way.

The alleys were not ugly, and they were full of life. Shops, carts, even donkey carts, in 2009. Children were running around everywhere in the streets and asked Frick, "Can we do anything for you?"[6] He laughed, answered in the negative, and did not want to ask about the house. Then suddenly he was standing in front of it.

To the left of the door were several plaques or signs, one above the other, that announced in English, Arabic, and Greek—in the Latin, Arabic, and Greek alphabets—that this was Cavafy's residence, "on the second floor," administered by the Greek Consulate. He climbed up and rang the bell.

You had to pay to get in—"lire," "pound"—not just a little, though the woman who came later, the other visitor, paid nothing.

An apartment in a pleasantly cool downtown house pressed up close to other downtown houses. Cavafy's furniture. Books and documents in glass cases. Besides Frick and the young man who had gruffly demanded his money, there wasn't anybody there. The young man squatted near the door to the apartment. Outside in the midday summer, a cat on a tin roof.[7]

Constantine Cavafy's bed! Why didn't he photograph it! Nobody would have prevented him. Nobody was there. It was as simple as it was beautiful. Metallic. Two could lie next to one another and yet it was monkish. It was a bed for two and yet also just for one, one who has to forego, one who remembers, one who hopes. And it must have been just like that.

And then an old witch came. At first, Frick thought she belonged to the house, to the Greek Consulate—later she asked him the question with which she addressed him: if he was Greek. She didn't pay the entrance fee and took a seat at Cavafy's desk. Her hair was completely unkempt and disheveled—an Agnes in the size of living people[8]—and she was toothless. On the bottom right there was still one tooth and one on the top right. Then Frick saw that she had flipped open a sketch book and was drawing Cavafy's furniture.

Frick talked for an hour with the toothless woman as they sat in Cavafy's armchairs. She claimed to be Armenian, that her name was Anna and she lived in Cairo. Frick took some of it to be a lie. "I've been coming here for twenty years to draw. At first there was a hotel in these rooms, but only for young men. Supposedly there was no room left for me. The boys had shoved the beds close together; I saw this when I went past the open doors to the rooms. There was more of Cavafy here then than there is now in all the display cases."

Noon. Summer. The city on the sea that you couldn't see from the windows. Here and there shouts, laughter, honking. A cat on a tin roof.

Notes

Translated by Gary Schmidt.

1. The title *Ciao Vaschek* alludes to the use of the Italian word "ciao" as both a greeting and farewell in Czech; "Vaschek" refers to the former president and playwright Václav Havel, who the narrator apostrophizes at the end of the novel when he decides to leave the Czech Republic to return to Germany after multiple encounters with an increasingly hostile police force.

2. Byrne R. S. Fone, ed., *The Columbia Anthology of Gay Literature* (New York: Columbia University Press, 1998), 469.

3. Beat Generation poet who wrote openly and unabashedly about homosexuality as early as the 1950s. He died in 1997 (Fone, *Columbia Anthology of Gay Literature*, 706).

4. The name of a Czech brewery founded in 1874.

5. The correct title of Ginsberg's poem is simply "Howl," but Kröhnke writes "The Howl" in English.

6. "Can we do anything for you?" is in English in the original.

7. Possibly a reference to Tennessee Williams's play *Cat on a Hot Tin Roof.*

8. Name of a stuffed doll that accompanies Frick on all his travels, often judging him for his lies and sexual forays.

Hans Pleschinski

Hans Pleschinski grew up in Lower Saxony when it was still part of West Germany, near the border between East and West. He studied German literature, Romance languages and literatures, and theater, and now lives and works in Munich as a freelance writer, journalist, and translator. Pleschinski has published numerous novels, memoirs, stories, and essays; he has also translated into German, among other things, Phillipe Besson's *Arrête avec tes mensonges* (2017), the title of which literally translates as "stop with your lies" but appeared in English as *Lie with Me* (2019). Pleschinski's novel *Bildnis eines Unsichtbaren* (*Portrait of an Invisible Man*, 2002) is based on the author's own experiences in the Munich gay community during the outbreak of the AIDS epidemic, which resulted in the death of his partner.

The following excerpt is taken from *Königsallee* (2013), Pleschinski's acclaimed novel about a fictional reunion in Dusseldorf in 1954 between Thomas Mann and Klaus Heuser, a younger man whom the famous author had met and fallen deeply in love with while vacationing on the North Sea in 1927. Heuser became the model for Mann's fictional Joseph in the tetralogy *Joseph and His Brothers* (1933–43). *Königsallee* became a Spiegel Bestseller and was praised by critics for its playful style and parody of Mann's late work, *Lotte in Weimar*, which narrates a reunion between the aging Goethe and his young love interest Charlotte Kestner, née Buff, whom Goethe had not seen for decades. In Pleschinski's fictional account, Klaus Heuser has returned to Germany with his Indonesian companion, Anwar, after an absence of twenty years, during which the Nazis committed the unspeakable crimes of the Holocaust and brought about the defeat and occupation of the country. Like Heuser, the Nobel Laureate Thomas Mann also spent two decades in exile, and for both men revisiting their homeland in a post-Nazi—although not fully denazified—era proves difficult. Mann's daughter Erika discovers that Klaus Heuser is staying in the same hotel as her father and pays a visit to Heuser in his hotel room to ensure that there be no reunion between the two.

from *Königsallee* (2013)

A Visit from the Daughter

Erika Mann took a seat in the cocktail chair. Strictly speaking, Anwar wanted to take a bath. He stayed. A disconcerting transformation occurred in the artist's face. The noticeably gray brow under her makeup was wrinkled, and one eyelid was twitching. She audibly took such a deep breath that she seemed about to make a significant confession. A bit of racket from the sparrows reminded them of the summer day outside.

"Klaus." The name sounded melancholic coming out of her mouth, its single syllable falling in pitch. Her addressee nodded obligingly. And, of course, a few things needed an explanation. It was not in the least bit clear why a phantom from the past, a woman with whom he had lived under the same roof for just a short time, had stormed into their strange double hotel room expounding on colossal twists of fate, and what was she doing in the Rhineland in the first place? As she herself admitted, she did not wish to pay a visit to her divorced husband.[1]

"When the opportunity arises, Klaus, you absolutely have to tell me more about yourself . . . about yourselves," she said, including the other man too with a glance. "I never made it to the depths of Asia. Klaus, I know what's going on. Of course, I don't know every detail. But one thing is certain, and you know it: you were like the blow of sword, the great red dawn, the menacing revelation."

Klaus Heuser smoked uneasily.

"You have stirred up things that had been put in order. It wasn't easy to go back to daily business after each of your departures, to smooth out the ruffles of his unease and misery—I ought to say his blissful misery. I managed it. But my mother had to deal with a breach of fidelity."

Anwar appeared to be straining to understand every word.

"She was used to dealing with a lot of intellectual escapades. She is permissive. She knows that he has to fall head over heels, love deeply, for his nature to warm up,[2] to be able to feel the power of love, that is to say: the greatest of all things. Young men bewitch him, that's why his female characters are, shall we say, more original than . . . doesn't matter. When two women love each other, a man has no power over that. When two men do it, women are without weapons. Mielein[3] could only count on his constancy, on his need for protection, his devotion. But for a while she was the one betrayed and deceived. I can see that his story lies in your hands."

"Pardon? What do you mean?" he asked uncertainly.

"The godhead arrived, let's call him Klaus Heuser, and he left behind a great pile of rubble. In *his* emotions."

"Oh . . ." He tried to brush it off.

"Be happy. His encounter with you was probably more intimate than with any other person. You will live on eternally, for the tender Joseph in Egypt, the blessed of the Lord, was cast from your mold.[4] And Krull is from the Rhineland."[5]

"That would be an honor for which I have no use, Eri. But it moves me so much, that . . ." And now he too turned his head away and sobbed briefly.

"Klaus. What happened? When I received confirmation that you were here, I suddenly remembered the lines he once wrote to me about you from Sylt: *At this roiling sea I have lived deeply.* When you were still in Munich and I had already departed, he seemed to need to confess to me: *I call him Du and with his express approval pressed him close to my heart as we said our good-byes.*[6] He never calls anyone else *Du*. I smuggled his diaries into Switzerland,[7] and I will have to publish them at some point. Under a thinly veiled pretext he visited your parents in Dusseldorf just to be able to breathe the same air as you, so deeply did you affect him. And what do we read? *His temples pressed against mine.*"

"Erika, that is private."

"Of course. Nevertheless. *Lived and loved. Eyes that shed tears for me, lips, that I kissed—it was there, I too had it—.* And you visited him one more time before you emigrated, in 1936 you said, during our first Zurich exile.[8] Hardly anyone knows about that. You stayed in contact with each other for almost a decade."

"And we wrote to each other when I was in Asia." He went on the offensive. "And why not? The postcards are in my luggage on their way to Hong Kong. It was Thomas Mann. It was an endless love that met me halfway. I was good for him, and I sensed that. He touched me more tenderly than anyone else at the time. He elevated forbidden feelings to something sacred. Yes, indeed: he sanctified our closeness. He told stories and explained lots of things, beautiful things, exciting things about the gods of Egypt, the monk Savonarola, whose picture was on his desk, about human freedom that must not bow down to tyrants. Even if afterwards I gladly ran back into the summery garden. Yes, perhaps it was from him, from all those things that were so extraordinary for me, even ethereal, that I gained the strength to say goodbye to this place and veer off my narrow path to board the freighter to Belawan.[9] He helped my petty nature lift itself up. And he was a friendly Jupiter.[10] I understood his sighs about his duties. Why shouldn't he have pressed his cheek against mine? He did it. We sat there, for a long time. It seemed to me that he was losing his senses. It was love, yes, absolutely!" said Klaus Heuser with certainty. "Briefly, very briefly, when I told him about my desires, my longing to go abroad, he looked at me, and his look said, Yes, away, risk everything, inconceivable to upend my existence, who am I, that I cannot be free? Always a yoke! Indeed, during the time of that look, which quickly became sadder and calmer, the family and all that existed might have been in danger. But to go to Sumatra? To a plantation? And me serving him tea? It is a story between men, Erika. It does not concern you. He continued to love you and support you. I found Anwar." He called for the hand of his companion, who gave it to him.

"You became his 'Du.'"

"It just happened that way."

"You must not see each other again. Not now."

"Excuse me?" Klaus Heuser said, puzzled. "I too am older and more withered."

"Not now," she clarified. "He forgets nothing. Especially feelings. He is in a creative crisis. He is well advanced in years and does not have much more time. After *Krull* he doesn't know if he can dedicate himself to new material or even which material. Perhaps he wants to continue with *Krull* or even venture writing a play about Martin Luther, which I rather think is an act of desperation. He needs the utmost protection and orderliness. What would you talk about? It is impossible for a conversation between the two of you to be unselfconscious. Any new emotions would confuse him, upset him, make him sad. Lola Montez couldn't suddenly come back from America either and appear before her Bavarian King.[11]

"Lola Montez?"

"Let him calmly follow his path to the end. Perhaps you were the only one whom he kissed and who returned the kiss, *tears shed for me* . . . Do you want him to suddenly notice you at the reading? Lose his train of thought, lose his composure at the lectern? Do you want the evening, perhaps one of his last public appearances, to end with a catastrophe? You cannot justify that for one brief moment that is perhaps more significant for him than for you. You mustn't, Klaus. Spare him and us, shun past love, leave everything in proportion without introducing disruptive sentimentalities. If you absolutely must hear him, I will try to arrange two chairs by a door. Klaus Heuser will not meet Thomas Mann again."

"Chairs at the reading?"

"In the Schumann Hall."

"Is here?" asked Anwar.

"Where else?" responded Erika with almost angry amazement. "Of course. You are both here right on time too. He is resting in the Heuss suite. The full program. Reception in the Malkasten.[12] Address by the minister. Visit to a theater museum with a certain Herr Lindemann. Expiation for Düsseldorf through his mere presence. You cannot get in the way of that."

"Where?" asked Klaus Heuser, and ash fell on his golden jacket.

"He is sleeping downstairs. And you up here. That's all there is to it. Of course, you are both welcome to stop by and see us in Zurich after allowing me time for thorough preparation. That could be considered. An outing to the Grand Hotel Dolder to enjoy the panorama with coffee and cake. He will muse, and I can adjust his scarf. You'll report about Sumatra. Very well, Klaus," she said, rising from her chair. "I have always thought you to be reasonable. No assault here. No emotional high tides. You surely understand the concerns of a daughter and organizer. You, of all people, should care about his work."

"A play about Luther?"

"We'll see. I am advocating for the continuation of *Krull*. The book hit its mark like a bomb. Finally, something exhilarating and witty for this country. There are lot of con men, but love is victorious with Felix Krull, possibly. . . . Duty calls. I thank you both very much. I'll send up two more bottles for you." She extended her hand to both of them and kissed them on the cheek. "Live it up this evening. No waving. No embraces. No contact. Just absence." She went to the exit. "I am counting on you, Klaus Heuser. Leave us in peace."

The door clicked shut.

Anwar fell back onto the sheets.

The air stood still. Flies circled around the lamp.

The Asian laid an arm over his eyes and breathed shallowly and rapidly.

Klaus Heuser stared from the dressing table to the balcony. Minutes passed like hours. His head was rattling like it did on his first day at home. The sparrows kept an eye on him from the railing. As if performing a little circus act, one hopped over his twittering neighbor. Excited and angry, Klaus Heuser tore up a sandwich and threw chunks of it outside. The feathered swarm seemed to be lying in wait for an evening snack.

Clouds persisted over the river. Wood creaked, floor panels or slats of the window blinds.

"Uninvited," Klaus heard from the bed.

"No. Never invited to begin with."

Libations on the Rhine

They were met by a roar of voices from the packed tables. The air could be cut with a knife. Cigars and cigarettes smoldered from mouths and ash-trays. As if pulled by magic, they followed a waitress carrying a tray filled with finely frothing *Altbier*[13] past customers' heads and through the Golden Ring brewery. The glasses of well-tapped beer were foggy. It would be quite a shame if they did not immediately find a seat so they too could be fogged by the cool libation. What was on the plates did not exactly look like light fare: sauerbraten, goulash, dumplings, little terrines with sausages, buttered boiled potatoes, sauerkraut with juniper berries. And yet: a lady over there was poking at a mixed salad with green beans. Across from a gentleman slicing a cutlet in aspic, a young man (maybe his son?) did the same to a conspicuous piece of white-bread toast topped with pineapple, ham, and scorched melted cheese. Hawaiian style. They followed the carried drinks into the Neusser Stube, where a half-open window provided fresh air. A few seats were free, perhaps to avoid a draft. The attentive waitress returned their glances and nodded in their direction. In sandals and a snow-white apron with strings that extended over her black skirt and plump, perky behind, she balanced her freight past guests who presumably were returning from the restrooms. A lady stowed her comb in her purse.

"Two beers. Two *alt*," Klaus called after the server. They sensed that she had understood even without turning around.

"Beer makes you fat."

"Not just one. The Ring brews its own."

The fresh-air corner was a bit dimly lit. Two amber-colored, if not smoke-covered, lightbulbs were screwed into dark wooden rings, which had all sorts of clever statements nicked into them: *Nothing slopped, nothing spilled.*[14] You could read the whole saying or guess the end of it only after walking half-way around the table: *Guten Appetit! Humans drink and horses guzzle—not in Bavaria, what a puzzle!*[15]

"Cozy."

"That's what they say."

"Opium den?"

"Oh never."[16]

They decided on a table in the back, hung up their coats, and sank down onto their chairs. "Was that her?" "I think so, yes." They were safe here, Klaus wanted to say, but one could not assume that any more in Düsseldorf. He handed Anwar a menu. "Do we have enough marks?" The financial overseer nodded. "We'll go whole hog. I need that. Shall we start with a schnapps?" Anwar shook his head halfheartedly. His finger slid down the list of entrees.

"Bratwurst," he deciphered. The waitress brought the beer. "To your health."

"Chicken fricassee?" Anwar ventured. Although the question was quite clear and came out fairly accent-free, she looked at Klaus as if she needed him to translate something. "If they don't have that, then order the Königinpastete." He looked up the small entrees, affirmed "good," and ordered: "For me . . . sauerbraten. For the gentlemen, two orders of the Königinpastete. You'll get an appetite when you start eating, I know from experience." The server made a note.

"Do you have Worchestershire sauce to go with that?"

"I'm sorry. But we have Worcester sauce. It's quite similar."

"Of course."

"And two caraway schnapps beforehand."

Remaining seated, they stretched out all fours. "Funny, one always says 'zwo'[17] in a tavern. Probably because it sounds more substantial." They didn't need to exchange any more words about the turbulent day. At least it had been prominent people who had badgered them, the author's daughter and a folkish poet.

"After Cologne we can keep going to Rüdesheim, wine country. I never went, because you just never go there. The crowds. But I'd like to see the Drosselgasse just once." Klaus pounded on the tablecloth with the end of his knife. Anwar hated such unchecked gestures. He had, somewhat successfully, been able to break him of another such habit: the occasional shaking of his left leg. When you yourself are no stranger to nerves, you react sensitively to others' nervousness. That could lead to undesirable exacerbations in their coexistence: "Quit that . . . !" "Then you break the habit of shuffling around in your slippers."

At least Klaus had stopped sniffling, and his ears appeared to be working too.

"Drosselgasse?"

"One medieval wine bar after the other."

"Everyone drinks like fish here."

"On the other hand, there's no opium. And intoxication is what made Europe great."

"Lots of ships run aground."

"But at least they were underway."

Anwar briefly touched Klaus's hand, who closed his eyes agreeably. "Happy couples are considered boring," he pondered.

"I not bored."

What did he mean by that?

Guests who were looking for the restroom eyed the dark gentleman with the light blue silk necktie in a relatively discreet manner. Anwar smiled back. Sometimes with an almost mechanical grin. His beautiful gold ring pleased him more and more, and the little Shiva on it could do no harm to a passive Muslim who had kissed holy trees and whispered along to the blessing in Dutch. The proximity of the bathrooms most likely explained the free seats and was moderately charming, possessing, on the other hand, a straightforward creaturely aspect.

"Hey, man, Karl, you old Swede, it's really you!" A hand rested on Klaus's shoulder. The ruddy face beneath thinning bread-blond hair leaned forward. His wedding ring seemed to have taken root in his flesh. Klaus started beaming joyfully, whereas Anwar was highly irritated by the reference to Swedish nationality. Had he been duped for unknown reasons all these years? Klaus turned toward the stranger, more cheerful, even spirited, than he had been for hours.

"I am truly pleased to meet someone, whom I unfortunately do not know and who does not know me. You see, I'm not Karl."

"Karl. No, Klaus."

Whose face froze.

"First the Scharnhorst School, then you were in the knife trade in Solingen. Wow, to see you here. In the evenings you commuted from Solingen to the trade school, you know, Bachstraße, right next to that pet shop with the gigantic tortoise in the window. You recognize me, don't you? It's Gert. Everything is still intact. And unfortunately, a lot bigger. We went to the movies a few times with Irmtrud. Yep, she now tends our cozy home. And our youngest is already twenty and works at the wharf in Papenburg. Wants to be a nautical engineer or something like that—Klaus! Man, let me give you a hug! You were a charmer. Irmtrud raved about you for quite a long time still: Klaus doesn't squish me like that when we dance and never steps on my foot . . ."

The light went on: "Gert . . . Klüser?" He twisted up out of his chair and stood in a rather contorted position turned halfway to the side. Gert Klüser appeared to want to hug him but then settled for a vigorous double punch on the arm.

"And you? Also in the shipbuilding industry?"

"No, no," he swept aside the absurd question. "Thyssen, what else? We are building really big now, high up, over twenty stories at the Hofgarten. Like New York."

"Great."

"You were in the Dutch class then too."

"I had to."

"And I'll never forget how you took me along when Irmtrud would invite you to coffee, although she had only set two places at first. In her mother's kitchen, remember? Her father, my father-in-law, never came back from Verdun."

"I was happy to do it. You two were right for each other."

"After our engagement we managed to become the youngest couple to get a place on a cruise of the *Wilhelm Gustloff.*[18] Bornholm, Helsinki. After trade school, Irmtrud specialized in hospital administration, hygiene, and, well"—Gert Klüser cast a glance sideways—"she made *Gaureferentin*[19] in the National Socialist Women's League. With her connections we were able to take breathers in South Tirol for a long time after that. And you, Klaus, were suddenly off the radar. Did they put the screws on you?"

As if he had remembered something, Klaus's classmate from before the war took his hands from Klaus's arms. "Irmtrud once saw you with Zwitschi Holzer, you know what they found out about him: *Volksschädling,*[20] warm brother. He disappeared."

"Yeah?" The blood shot into Klaus's head. "I was on the *Insulinen.*"[21]

Gert Klüser hesitated. This information probably had nothing to do with diabetes.

"Went to the Dutch East Indies in 1936."

"I'll be damned!"

Klaus's hip was already hurting from his twisted stoop.

"And then when it started?"

"Started?"

"Poland, France."[22]

"I stayed in Asia, of course. Bashing each other's heads in here? I improved my polo game somewhat."

"Polo? And you call what we did 'bashing heads in'? The *Volk* has bled to death. It gave its all. Fanatically. We overran the Frenchies and leveled the East to make *Lebensraum* and the fine gentleman here basks in a cheesemonger's hammock.[23] And who on earth is that you are sitting with?"

"I beg your pardon!"

"Don't look at me like that. I've knocked sense into plenty of other squirts. I should have suspected it: a draft dodger. What nourished you and made you great you simply leave in the lurch. For the life of me, I can't stand that: you grow up German and when it gets serious, you don't lift a finger. Our oldest daughter suffocated in a bunker when she was just a baby."

"What should I say to that?—Did you make the wrong choice?"

Gert Klüser seemed ready to grab Klaus Heuser by the collar; his hand spun around dangerously. "It's better not to give such garbage the time of day. Absconding in the middle of an awakening[24] and sitting back down at the table after we have been humiliated."

"You're the garbage," ventured Klaus, shaking. Anwar, hopefully, was ready to jump up.

"I was still there for the defense of Breslau."[25]

"Gentlemen, we are at peace here," came the voice of the waitress as she pushed her way between the two of them and put the caraway schnapps on the table.

"Went swimming with Zwitschi Holzer and ducked out," said Gert Klüser, tersely putting her in the picture. "I like to take a swim now and again and would love to duck out of the evening shift," countered the wonderful lady.

"We have lists for people like you.[26] You won't get anywhere here."

Anwar brandished a fountain pen.

"Mob!" Klüser appeared to be ready to take his leave.

"Say hello to Irmtrud."

His school acquaintance snorted.

"I mean it seriously," Klaus lobbed after him rather disarmingly. "New times, new greetings."

Gert Klüser needed only to take his hat from the hook and leave the restaurant. Apparently, he had already paid.

"The nose, the ear." Klaus Heuser had sunk back onto his chair. His hands lay shaking on the little table.

"Go now?" asked Anwar Batak. They downed the caraway schnapps.

"We should not have come back here."

"Dat weet ik vel."[27]

Notes

Translated by Gary Schmidt.

1. The German actor and theater director Gustaf Gründgens, who unlike the Mann family remained in Nazi Germany and continued to have a successful career. Erika Mann and Gründgens, neither of whom made a secret of their homosexuality, were married in 1926 and divorced in 1929. Erika's brother, Klaus Mann, wrote the novel *Mephisto* (1936) in exile, in which the protagonist Hendrik Höfgen is based on Gründgens. *Mephisto* was first published in the Netherlands, and twenty years later in Germany, in 1956, with the East German Aufbau-Verlag.

2. Notably, the composer Adrian Leverkühn, the protagonist of Thomas Mann's *Doktor Faustus*, was forbidden through his pact with the devil from partaking of "a love that warms." The German word "warm" also connotes homosexuality, as in the use of the term "warmer Bruder" (warm brother) for a homosexual male.

3. "Mielein" was a pet name used by Thomas Mann's children for their mother, Katia Pringsheim Mann.

4. "Joseph in Egypt" refers to the protagonist of Thomas Mann's tetralogy *Joseph and His Brothers*. Thomas Mann expressed his feelings for Klaus Heuser in a scene in which Potiphar's wife attempts to seduce the young Joseph.

5. "Krull" refers to the protagonist of Mann's comical novel *Confessions of Felix Krull*, which Mann himself referred to in his diaries as the gayest of all his novels.

6. "Du" is the informal second-person singular pronoun in German, as opposed to the formal "Sie." "Du" often connotes intimacy.

7. Thomas Mann was out of the country when the Nazis came to power in 1933 but had left behind diaries in the family house in Munich. He did not wish the diaries to fall into the hands of the Nazis.

8. Thomas and Katia Mann lived in Switzerland after fleeing Nazi Germany and later went to the United States and obtained US citizenship. During the McCarthy Era, they returned to Europe for a "second exile" in Switzerland.

9. Belawan is an Indonesian port on the island of Sumatra, at that time part of the Dutch East Indies.

10. Jupiter is the Roman equivalent of the Greek good Zeus, who is said to have abducted the beautiful young Ganymede to be his cupbearer on Mount Olympus.

11. "Lola Montez" was the stage name of Marie Dolores Eliza Rosanna Gilbert, an Irish countess who made a career as a dancer and actress and was also the mistress of King Ludwig I of Bavaria.

12. "Malkasten" refers to an artists' society founded during the Revolution of 1848, which sought German unification under a parliamentary democracy.

13. Altbier is a top-fermented dark beer, an older method of brewing than bottom-fermentation of other German beers.

14. In German, "Nix verschlabbert, nix verschütt."

15. In German, "Trinkt der Mensch, säuft das Pferd, in Bayern . . . ist es umgekehrt." The lines rhyme and play on the double meaning of the German verb "saufen" (to drink), which is used for animals, whereas the verb "trinken" is used for human beings, with the exception that "saufen" is used to describe generous consumption of alcohol by humans.

16. "Never" is in English in the original.

17. "Zwo" is an alternative form of "zwei," German for "two."

18. The *Wilhelm Gustloff* was a ship named after the founder of the Swiss National Socialist Party who was assassinated in 1936. The ship was utilized for the Nazis' *Kraft durch Freude* (Strength through Joy) program, which organized vacations for party members. Günter Grass's novel *Crabwalk* deals with both the murder of Gustloff and the sinking of the ship by a Soviet submarine (which caused the death of more than ten thousand passengers) from an early twenty-first century fictional perspective.

19. *Gaureferentin* is a district teacher and advocate for "feminine upbringing."

20. *Volksschädling* is a Nazi term based on the metaphor of invasive species that damage the integrity of the *Volk*. The term was codified into law in 1939 to allow for prosecution of individuals deemed to be subversive of the goals of Nazi ideology.

21. In English, "islands." Klaus uses a Germanized form of the Latin *insula*.

22. "Poland, France" is a reference to the German invasions of these countries at the beginning of World War II.

23. A "cheesemonger's hammock" is likely a pejorative reference to the Dutch.

24. In German, "Aufbruch," a term used by the Nazis to describe the ostensible revitalization of the German *Volk* starting in 1933.

25. Breslau was a city in Silesia that is now the Polish city of Wroclaw.

26. A reference to the so-called Rosa-Listen, or "pink lists" kept by police of known homosexuals.

27. Dutch for "I know that."

Anja Kümmel

Anja Kümmel was born in Karlsruhe, in southwestern Germany. She studied gender studies and Spanish in Madrid, Los Angeles, and Hamburg; since 2011 she has been living and working as a writer and journalist in Berlin. She is the author of five novels: *La Danza Mortale* (2004), *Das weiße Korsett* (*The White Corset*, 2007), *Hope's Obsession* (2008), *Träume digitaler Schläfer* (*Dreams of Digital Sleepers*, 2012), and *V oder die Vierte Wand* (*V or the Fourth Wall*, 2016), from which the following excerpt is taken. Set in London in a not-too-distant future in which all but a few of the city's inhabitants are chipped, the novel's protagonists are a young Mexican named Mesca, who has arrived from Los Angeles in the year 1980 only to find a dark futuristic metropolis, and Fenna, who has left an economically devastated Iceland to take a job as a contract killer only to find herself in a slightly warped London of the 1980s. In this excerpt, Fenna visits the legendary "V" Club in search of her victim, only to be drawn into experiences of a different kind.

from *V or the Fourth Wall* (2016)

When was the last time I was in a place without knowing who else was wandering around? What it looks like inside? Without at least clicking on my way there through playlists, guest reviews, acceptances and declines, galleries and livestreams?

Let me think . . .

Kindergarten?

The streets around V are dark and empty, doors and windows boarded up. Sulfurous slime collects between the cobblestones, a little like horse piss. *Spanish flu*, I think abruptly, and about a pimply boy whose name, like so many other things, doesn't want to come to me.

At the end of the alley, a flicker of neon. Some sort of emergency light. An exit sign inside of an airplane over a nocturnal sea. I feel my way toward it, along damp walls, torn faces. Robots, peacocks, silhouettes, clustered in thick layers over each other, share eyes, noses, mouths like brothers and sisters. The proportions aren't always correct. Different from MorphMe, the follow-up to MakeMe, which transformed friends, relatives, and lovers into monsters within seconds. White Vs slice through the names that stand over, under, next to the faces. *Ul . . . Si . . . xie and . . . Gar . . . shees . . . human . . . vox.*

One gap closed, another opened.

All of my memories lie in the future. None of them are stored anywhere; no one knows about them but me.

Fenna.

Ever since my name came back to me, I remember every little banal detail. The pimply boy, for example. But also the purple-striped jellyfish and the frustrated face of the Frenchman in the Sailor's Grave.[1] And the following thought: *Not being on LifeLine is like only being half alive.*

Funny that I thought that once. As though where I was offered an escape.

And yet only here is freedom complete.

I mean: When did I last have that? This blissful ignorance. This excitement. Top or flop? And yes, also this loneliness.

I am Fenna (again or still), but at the same time I'm someone else entirely.

Currently: an overripe Phoenix berry.

What should I wear? I asked Salem. And Salem said that I should keep the foil, make myself something nice out of it and then just put on some of those *blatantly futuristic* shoes. Whatever *futuristic* is supposed to mean in reference to something that was in style the summer before last—I have no other choice than to wear my GoldCaps; they are the only shoes that I have with me.

Upon getting closer, the neon flicker turns out to be a laser-blue V. Hard to tell if once there was more than just the one letter, and if so, what the word was.

A very similar V, but enormous and turned upside-down, has stood at the entrance to London's Chinatown since the second solar boom. *Should* stand there, I mean. The pictures were everywhere on the Net. Soon everyone knew it: the Chinese symbol for *person.*[2] In summer, the inverted V was made of water, in winter of light. Bamboo stalks swayed within; you could watch them grow.

I first ran around in that part of town a couple days ago. The guy who sold me the Little Fox[3] was Asian. Two run-down Chinese diners on Lisle Street. No sign of the watery V, of lanterns, or of dragon-décor.

A small stripe of neon white underlines the V. Looking at it nauseates me, a stabbing headache. The echo of quick steps, drunken giggles in the empty alleys—then, suddenly they're everywhere. As though someone had commanded "find freaks." Phenomenal output. Feathers brush against me. The first three hits: velvet, leopard fur, and silver paint. Like in front of the Rainbow: a bit Halloween, a bit retro-futuristic, a bit frilly porn. Plenty of rouge. And I always thought only the dead were so crassly made up . . .

I dutifully get at the end of the line, like in front of the Sailor's Grave. A pale being in front of me whose hair stands up like a black broom, behind me an overweight nun with violet lips.

No scanner at the entrance, naturally, not even here, futurism or not. Instead: a zombie-pirate with a golden cane. The corners of his mouth slide apart as though he had to vomit with the entrance of every single guest.

Oooooh! Vam-pir-a! And who is that? Miss Crêpe Suzette?

Boredom, if not disgust, makes his lids heavy. Nevertheless, he contemptuously knights his addressees. They gaze at each other, tear their eyes away, and scuttle inside.

The pirate twists his wound-mouth at me as well. C-3PO! he calls. And over my shoulder, little more than a hiss: look, the golden robot!

The four-hundred-pound nun chuckles into her lace cloth. I don my poker face, the only thing that always works for me.

And *that* there?

The pirate taps my left shoe with his golden stick. The GoldCaps spring elegantly back. For a moment, he loses his composure.

Xu Fan Rong, I say, as flat as the fins of a seal and without looking at him.

The pirate steps aside. Doesn't wave me through, doesn't tap me on the shoulder.

He does absolutely nothing, other than tightening his grip on his cane.

I push past him, into the V.

A staircase leads steeply downward. From below emerge noises that I recognize, a spherical synth line, covered thousands of times—if only I knew by whom. The finger-twitching ceases, *Catch-a-tune* has no meaning here.

Before my face hangs an old-fashioned train station clock with illegible numbers, lines, and Vs. Stylized Chinese?

The synth line brings with it an empty odor of ash, a little reminiscent of the smell a few days ago on the street, just more concentrated, along with a heat like the machine room of the Titanic—*i!Merse* makes you feel it, and also the cramped space, relentlessly. Otherwise there's no way to put up with old films. Everything undulates. For a moment the mass of people makes me seasick, the towering hairstyles, the impossible hats that collide with the lamps and cause the red light to sway.

There is a box, on the wall to the left, hands around cool metal, the forehead against smoky plaster. Lashes on the temples, sine curves on the retina.

Fenna! A voice that seems completely unknown to me calls out through layers of thinly hacked beats.

Sólrún. No—Salem. Salem is the only one who knows my name in this 1980.

Someone squeezes my jaw, and I—too weak, too startled to lunge out–open my eyes and mouth.

My double stands before me, headless. The head is that of another. Salem's. He looks completely different without the lampshade on his head, without the rabbit around his—something cold on the lower lip, a burning sensation on the tongue, some sort of caustic liquid.

I swallow, cough, and push his arm away, a few drops spray into my eyes, burn there even more.

Do you want to kill me, *Xiǎozi*![4]

Salem laughs, his glass raised out of reach, the torch of Lady Liberty. Now I see he's wearing a V-shaped arrangement of mirrored glass. The protruding shoulders are over-emphasized corners like one of the space figures that Yngvi liked so much as a kid. Apparently they've become ultra-cult in the meantime (about every third boy under twenty is using a *SpaceME* as a profile start). The coughing just doesn't stop.

There, take another drink.

Salem holds his glass out to me. I comply.

Whiskey?

He crooks a finger. Here, that means: follow me.

He, in front, I, stumbling behind him. *Ra-di-o-ac-ti-vi-ty*, drones a tinny voice on a loop. With it a stubborn synth and a penetrating clicking sound. A little like the pieces that Kjartan sometimes pastes together with X2_Retro-Sounds—not very professional, but catchy.

Salem stops, greets a—what's that called?—Geisha or something. Three little kisses. I polish off Salem's whiskey. Burning in my eyes and at the back of my throat. Not two seconds later, I hold a new glass in my hand. A smurf with a tuft of silver hair toasts me.

Plan 9 from Outer Space![5]

Plan 9 from . . . uh . . . *Outer Space*, I repeat. Maybe that's this place's version of *Samtakanu*,[6] an old-fashioned *Cheers!*

The smurf strokes his companion's laser sword, the movement somehow suggestive; turquoise dust falls from his eyelashes. Child's birthday party or orgy—the times here flow over and through each other like they do in my brain. Salem pulls me around the dancing people, by the green-white columns, red-white covered tables, chairs sloppily pushed in. Everything above the eccentric hairdos, the sweeping hats, lies in total darkness, severed by heavy, lacquered lamps on long cords. The lampshades, dark green on the outside, white on the inside, look like my grandma's ancient dishes that I was always disgusted to eat from. Lightless aquariums. I don't know where this underwater feeling comes from. Maybe because the last club I remember was in the tunnel to the new airport.

The dark wood chairs, the checkered tablecloth, the hip-high wood paneling—nothing about it bespeaks a trendy hipster club. More of a cellar pub, the belly of a ship, an air-raid bunker. Between half-empty bottles of red wine, cans of Red Stripe, and Marlboro cigarette packets—*tobacco* smoke, of course, it's *tobacco* that's burning my eyes like that!—someone sets two very white elbows. The part a shaky line, the fingernails bright red. Keeps stroking their own neck, the hairline, the shoulders, like someone on Qanuk[7] who doesn't have anyone else to grope.

That's Dead Marilyn, Salem calls over his shoulder.

Dead Marilyn lifts her head. Her dress looks like she's fallen in a slimy puddle a couple of times, her face bruised; twigs and leaves are stuck in her messy blond hair. She looks at me, or more accurately: right through me.

Qanuk means *Snowflake* in Inuit. But this here is 1980, or somewhere close.

And as far as I know, *Qanuk* was first made after the second crash—

Where is the living one? I ask.

Salem signals "Stop" with his thumbs; here that evidently means: look in this direction.

The living one leans on a box as tall as a person. Imitation wood. Next to it, a half curtain. Am I seeing this right? A . . . photobooth?

Dumb slut, Salem hisses. Stole my hairspray . . .

We push by her into a dark hallway that leads to the toilets.

In reality, the Living Marilyn is a man. I can tell from her shoulders, from the width of her wrists. I'm not sure about the dead one.

4 poses, 3 minutes. The red curtain moves slightly.

It's so . . . *retro,* I want to say, but thankfully Salem chooses this moment to drag me to the women's room.

It's suddenly bright here, in a piercingly blue way that summons my headache back up. Bright and full, it's hard to guess how full with all of the endless reflections of enormous hairstyles, each covered in a fog of toxic hairspray, certainly fuller than the dance floor. Salem wears a cube-shaped Grace Jones afro, slightly askew. I have no idea if that existed yet in 1980, whether Grace Jones was a thing yet. Someone shakes their mane; a sharp mist lands directly on my face. Idiot! hisses Salem's voice as he snags the spray bottle, a pink colored dildo-like thing, but his aim isn't any better. I turn away, sticky coolness on my neck and lips, a bitter film. Men's voices, women's voices, flat as tile and impossible to differentiate.

—Leichner, my dear, Leichner.[8] Rimmel's White Rose. Deep Midnight. I swear by Max Factor. Four pounds from John Lewis![9] Elnett. Wella. Raspberry red—all of these words bounce off of the tiles, find their way through plumes of aerosol, back onto the faces where they cling and become masks, second skins.

Reverberating beats, the floor vibrates; there is a disquiet like you get among rats on a sinking ship. I take a drink . . . *dreaming of her new love, and she hopes he'll be there soon*[10] . . . Another. Whatever-it-is. Around me: an exodus toward the dance floor. Harem girls armed with hairspray press by me; one of them has a V made of sequins glued to her forehead.

High tones cut through the walls, and the mirror rattles without all of the human bodies acting as insulation. Except for Salem, me, and two others who remain. Hardly more than schoolboys, girls in trouser roles.[11] Picture-perfect and very young. I only see their backs, tight butts, sharp elbows, fluttering hands making use of combs. Now and then their faces, inverted in the mirror, when they lean forward. I'm assuming they're boys. Brothers, or a gay pair. They look so similar to each other that each reflects and strengthens the beauty of the other. It is quiet now, without the hissing of the spray cans, the chatter of the harem girls. Quiet except for the voice from outside, singing: *There's no love inside the icehouse.*[12] So silent that I can hear the gold foil around my hips crinkling. Salem pencils in his lips with concentration. The two—boys, I'm almost certain now—turn to face each other in profile. One has black hair, the other blond. Probably not brothers. More likely gay. The blond is an inverted version of the dark-haired one. And vice versa. Both wear black, the blond in a black kepi and bright red suspenders, the other has a bright red tie over his black shirt. Their noses almost touch. They smile wordlessly, not at each other but at their mirrored beauty. A couple? I go with best friends, fuck-buddies at best. I would have thought *potentials* earlier, but not anymore, when something like HeartSync naturally . . .

By the way, are you into men or women?

I wince. Would most like to give Salem a smack. Even though he hadn't spoken inordinately loudly. He grins at me with a naïve happiness bordering on impudence with his purple lips that lie on top of each other like fat maggots. The two boys grin and lick over their combs, only a breath of air between tongue and teeth, and then put them away in one synchronized movement. Ah . . . I'm so frightfully distracted. Until now, I hiss, my gaze still submissively fixed on the dark-haired one, I was actually quite happy with . . . I can hardly say *my computer*, so instead I say: . . . with myself.

In this moment, I see the two boys coming closer in the reflection on Salem's V-armor. Here a piece of arm, there half a leg, in the middle me, my throat suddenly rigid. They already fill almost all of Salem's chest. I see my glance try and fail miserably to make a U-turn back through the skull. My back is brushed by a familiar scent, warmth believed forgotten. As though someone had given me a slap, our glances meet over Salem's heart. I know him. The dark-haired one. I'm not sure from where. The undercut, the tight curls that make his face slender and shadowed. The moist, over-ripe lips, the flesh of his cheeks. His cheeks, my teeth . . . in them . . . the final vestiges . . . baby fat . . . from inside, from—

The two are already past us. Salem's chest now a white, tiled emptiness. And I, strangely weightless.

Like angels, I want to say, but I say nothing.

The purple maggots part with a smack.

Half dead, murmurs Salem dismissively and moves me without a nudge back out into the heat, into the reddish light. My glass is already empty again, another song is finished. The smurf is nowhere to be seen. Ah, right, the bar! The bar!

What does one order here? Definitely not a Beijing Sling. Let me think.

Sunrise over Weihai, Shandong-Chardonnay[13] . . .

London Dry, orders a soft, rather high voice next to me.

The dark-haired one. He bends over the counter, standing close beside me, and the tip of his red tie sops up moisture. Our elbows . . .

Thank whomever for the reddish light.

London Dry. London Dry, of course.

Martini, I say and lay three blood-spattered bills on the bar. Thank you! Thank you very much indeed! For the reddish light.

In my thoughts, I run. Back to Clipstone Street, to the damn courtyard, the trashcan that I threw the photos into. If I didn't know it were impossible, I would think: Eden is standing next to me. Eden in his old form. Naturally that can't be true. It is 1980. And Eden wasn't even born yet in 1980.

There's a squiggly V on his inner wrist—now he turns his hand. His nail polish is pretty chipped. What remains looks like the starry sky over Vík[14]—by which I mean there are more stars in the sky than black, because there are no lights burning below them. Oval-shaped black flecks with silver glitter in different sizes that become more numerous and brighter the longer you look at them. I feel myself gravitating toward him, his fingers, these windows into a familiar—

Excuse me, "are 'friends' electric?"[15] he asks me suddenly, his voice almost drowned out by the music.

I want to reply, but then he answers his own question: "Mine's broke down, and now I've no one to love."

He holds a drink in his hand, his pinkie raised. I can't look him in the face, instead taking a gulp from my own.

Ok then, a brief glance. Up to his mouth. Teeth gleaming white. Lips so red they look like he's wearing lipstick. There's a small cut on his top lip. Already, we had it in biology class, a gateway to . . . *gay cancer* it was called in the beginning, and all the way until the 2010s and 2020s—

I should say something, but I can think of nothing but the tiny fissure that shines and gapes when he smiles, and how much I'd like to take my tongue . . .

Then about raw hands, the tender anus and . . . 1980. When did the shit begin? I don't remember, instead thousands of SIMs roll around in my brain, in which time travelers muck up history. If the Nazis had Pads, they would have won the war and so on. What all these miniscule details—

He abruptly turns his head.

Wanna make out with me?

He has the voice of a machine and eyes of flowing magma. Black, pupilless, like the eyes of a taxidermied animal.

Where have you been all this time? I hear someone ask in a heavily accented voice from far away.

He raises his well-groomed eyebrows. For a few seconds he stares at me as though I had Tourette's. Then he bends over and kisses me.

At first, I don't feel anything at all. But I also don't push him away.

I don't. Push him. Away.

He has no idea. He has no idea and just presses his lips on me.

His right canine. Pointed like that of a predator.

Fire and ice, deep in the chest. I think that's called *subglacial eruption.* I don't resist, I . . . feel his pointed tooth, the tip of his tongue, I press myself on him, or him on me, he himself on me, or—Fire. Ice. Completely impossible in this overly warm room full of—Not only do I not push him away, I run my tongue over his teeth, which are smooth and only sharp at the points, electrically charged memory. Gold foil crackles on my back, gold foil crackles everywhere.

Then he stops suddenly and turns away.

I'm sorry, I taste like gin and speed.

I'm light-headed, now only ice remains, in spite of the humidity, I cling to the bar, then to his arm. Gin and speed? *Sweetness and fire, sweetness and fire, sweetness and . . .*

His mouth is so red. Presumably I'll be marked, at least for the rest of the night.

I hold his wrist. It is almost like: *holding someone's hand—*

What does the V stand for? I ask him before I am overwhelmed by this revelation.

He grins. Teasingly? He leaves his wrist in my grasp without reluctance, as he simultaneously looks around the room and gestures with a vaguely circular motion at posters on the walls. Most are covered by tall hair, wide-brimmed hats, turbans, antennae, swans—yes, one guy has a swan on his head. I can only read one poster hanging behind us: "Keep Calm and Carry On."[16]

V1 and V2, he says. Retaliatory weapons of the Nazis. The V-night. The V-Spirit concept developed from that.

He leans heavily on his elbows across from me and presses his chin coquettishly against his shoulder. I still hold his wrist.

"Keep calm . . ."

And what . . . uh . . . does that mean?

Now he leaves all of these theatrical pauses between his words. Grins, sucks in air and repeats the words in my head: "Keep calm and carry on."

I feel his breath. It races into the tips of my fingers and toes. I recognize him unequivocally from his grin.

But in reality . . . he sways gently back and forth, a dizzy circling right before my eyes. . . . Well, here you see the reality. His pupils drift to the right as though he's calling up a post.

Anyone who doesn't know if he's going to survive the next few nights, he whispers almost conspiratorially, lives today even more intensely.

I nod, completely serious. "Keep calm and carry on."

I nod and pull him toward me. Until now I didn't know how such a thing was possible.

Two or three songs later he pushes me away to arm's length.

Just so that we understand each other. He clears his throat, takes a sip from his glass. No lipstick mark. All natural.

That was some kinda . . . his fingers imitate waves. *Status: absent.* I don't understand him.

Wager, he says then. Takes another drink and looks at me from the side. Some kinda wager, yeah.

Where the hell is Salem?

I want to say I know this guy. I slalom around the columns and the masked people, run into every lamp as though I had shot up from zero to sixty. I know him, his grin, without question. He floods through my veins like Q, only differently, evoking euphoria rather than calm, an unknown feeling, even when—

Of course, I can't explain the whole thing to Salem now. What it means: not even the spark of a desire to strike out. Not a thought given to lashing out, to kicking, pushing away, scratching, biting—well, ok, maybe biting. Licking, *eating up*, that for sure. For the first, *very* first . . . and then: Some kind of wager. A *wager*, damn it!

Notes

Translated by Simone Boissonneaul.

1. The Sailor's Grave is a club in Iceland.
2. In Chinese, 人.
3. "Little Fox" refers to a brand of switchblade knife.

4. "Xiǎozi" is a Chinese word used to refer to little boys or young men; usually derogatory but sometimes affectionate depending on context.

5. *Plan 9 from Outer Space* is a 1959 sci-fi horror film by Ed Wood, popularly referred to as "the worst movie ever made."

6. "Samtakanu" is an Icelandic toast.

7. Qanuk is a large island off the coast of Alaska.

8. Leichner is a cosmetics brand developed in Berlin in 1873, specializing in stage makeup, particularly grease paint.

9. John Lewis is a chain of department stores in the UK.

10. Lyrics from "Icehouse" by the Australian band Flowers.

11. Traditional theater part, a woman dressing in men's clothing.

12. Lyrics from "Icehouse."

13. Weihai is a city in China's eastern Shandong province.

14. Vík is a village in southern Iceland known for black-sand beaches and glaciers.

15. "Are 'Friends' Electric?" is a song by Tubeway Army.

16. The slogan "Keep Calm and Carry On" was used for a propaganda poster produced by the British government at the start of World War II.

IV

INTERCULTURAL ENCOUNTERS

Antje Rávik Strubel

ANTJE STRUBEL grew up in what is now Brandenburg, formerly part of East Germany. She studied literature, psychology, and American studies in Potsdam and New York. Her literary breakthrough came when she was awarded the Ernst Willner Prize in 2001 at the Klagenfurter Literaturtage, a three-day literary event held annually since 1977 in the Austrian city of Klagenfurt. At that time, Strubel added the invented middle name "Rávic," later changed to "Rávik," because she wished to give a name to the "absent presence" that appears when she writes.[1] She has published seven novels, all of which have received considerable critical acclaim, including *Kältere Schichten der Luft* (2007), for which she won the Hermann Hesse Prize, as well as three "user manuals" (*Gebrauchsanweisungen*) on Potsdam, Sweden, and skiing. Her episodic novel *Unter Schnee* appeared in English as *Snowed Under* (Red Hen Press, 2008). Strubel has translated four works by Joan Didion into German, including Didion's acclaimed novel *The Year of Magical Thinking* and, most recently, the national bestseller *Blue Nights*, which appeared in German in 2018 as *Blaue Stunden* with Ullstein in Berlin. Strubel is an avid reader of American literature; she has been inspired by authors ranging from Gertrude Stein and Djuna Barnes to Paul Auster, James Baldwin, and Vladimir Nabokov.[2]

Faye Stewart writes that "Strubel's novels offer an array of queerly gendered and sexualized figures, but they also invite readers to explore a literary style that reveals itself as queer in myriad other ways: through narrative voices and structures, in their thematic content, and by subverting traditions and negotiating geopolitical change." Furthermore, continues Stewart, "Strubel's fiction is socially critical in that it addresses divisive contemporary and historical issues, poses uncomfortable questions about violence, oppression, and human rights, and interrogates narratives of nation, citizenship, unity, and belonging."[3] These aspects of Strubel's writing are certainly factors why her novels have attracted attention from scholars of German literature to a degree equaled only by Michael Roes among the authors represented in this volume.

The following text is a chapter from Strubel's episodic novel *In den Wäldern des menschlichen Herzens* (*In the Forests of the Human Heart*, 2016), which follows a group of characters across North America and Europe in thirteen stories that, although interconnected, can also be read independently. In this particular episode, the enigmatic character Leigh is introduced. Like figures in other novels by Strubel, Leigh challenges readers' perception of the body and their compulsion to assign binary gender traits.

"The White Rock," from *In the Forests of the Human Heart* (2016)

Sequoia National Park, California, USA

They had booked a room in the Ponderosa Lodge. It was a spacious room with two large beds and a balcony. Sequoias stood in front of the window. The trees were so high it was impossible to see all the way to the tops, ancient giants with massive trunks and reddish-brown bark that looked like deerskin.

The trees were so famous that the area where they grew so abundantly was named after them and declared a national park. The entrances to the park were marked with red posts and had a boom gate that stayed open during the season. Signs warned about the dangers of the wilderness.

Visitors were reminded that they wanted to leave the park alive and advised to keep alert. Emily made fun of it. Wasn't that usually the point? To get out unharmed? Out of a car, a bed, an illness, a dream? As long as you lived, wasn't that the point? To get out of life unscathed?

Leigh had said signs like that were posted at the entrance to all national parks. They marked the boundary between what people thought was natural and actual nature, but they were basically just a barometer. The dramatic signs showed the degree humans feared the wilderness and varied according to the season, but they had nothing to do with life's real dangers. Emily nodded, since Leigh had more experience in these things than she.

They had parked the rental car in front of the Lodge and checked into their room. It was two in the afternoon, Tom wasn't there yet.

[. . .]

Leigh left the room and walked to the restaurant one more time. It was a down-to-earth mountain restaurant, a dining room with massive wooden tables, coarsely planed benches, and a long bar that also served as the reception area. Lots of whiskey and tequila bottles lined the shelves behind it, evidence that neither Mexico nor Texas was far away. Next to the bottle rack, somebody had stuck a piece of handwritten cardboard on the wall to cheer up the guests: "*If all else fails, there's always delusion.*"[4]

Emily grabbed the towels from the beds. They were of the same brown tone as the bedspreads tucked tightly into the mattresses. Despite the glaring sun, the room was dim. Emily brought the towels into the bathroom and then Leigh came back and said: "He's already here," and then he quickly gathered his things, the pad of paper with the list of questions, both books if he needed to look up quotes, the small recording device, and the scarf he had brought with him for all the other interviews.

"It's too hot," Emily said. "It's almost 90 degrees out there."

"I know. I'm not wearing it to protect myself from the cold. Clothes ought to be less about conforming to meteorology. The functions of things like clothing, and not only clothing, should be questioned more often. I think people should use them differently."

"Ninety degrees and a scarf?" Emily said. "Tom will think you're either sick or crazy. That's what I think."

Leigh looked at her. "I'll get us a table in the shade."

Emily liked being on the road with Leigh. She liked hitting the bars in Culver City with him on Friday nights, and staying there until it got light out and then they'd eat nachos for breakfast on the steps in front of his house, and she'd love nothing more than to be alone with him now.

[. . .]

At the beginning of the semester he was sitting in a poorly attended seminar. He wore baggy jeans, a jacket that protruded over the shoulders, a pair of round sunglasses on top of his short hair. Emily had felt she needed to be close to him. She didn't know him. She had never seen that student before. As she headed toward his table, he looked up calmly without smiling, gazed at her, "*a stop the mind makes between uncertainties . . .*"[5]

He made no attempt to talk to her, just pushed the scattered books with his arm over to his side of the table. But from the moment Emily sat next to him, she wasn't restless anymore.

[. . .]

As Emily crossed the parking lot to the trail leading to the oldest Sequoias, the bikers came up the mountain road. First one motorcyclist turned the corner into the parking lot. He was all in black. The handlebars and the exhaust pipe glistened in the sun. Then came the second, then more arrived, until the entire parking lot hummed from the powerful engines and Emily was surrounded by the machines.

"A burger 'n' coffee," the leader of the motorcycle gang shouted and took the helmet off his head. "You won't get me back in the saddle until I get some chow. My ass is killing me."

Over the glistening asphalt, which was intensified by the heat of the engines, the air melted and burned Emily's bare feet. Her toe started aching again even more. [. . .]

"Hey Roland," a bearded guy shouted. Did you order the babe for lunch?"

"So, how 'bout it?" he said to Emily. "Feel like takin' a spin with Papa Bear? He just looks nasty, but he's got a sissy bar for the ladies." He caressed the backrest on his Harley. "It's been a while since a gal's squeezed her sweet thighs on the old leather."

"Hey man, take it easy."

"Just sayin' it's been a while." [. . .]

Emily turned around and as she turned, she made sure not to brush against the hot pipes. She walked to the entrance of the restaurant without stopping, sat next to Leigh as though it were the most natural thing to do.

"What's going on?" Leigh asked.

"Nothing." [. . .] "Did the bikers ruin your recording?"

"They are messengers of the gods, Emily," Tom said. "You can always rely on the old gods. Otherwise, nobody can save you from yourself."

Tom was older than he dressed. Although he spoke slowly, almost sleepily, he gave the impression of being restless, a man strung through by a tendon.

"I was just talking shit, right, Leigh?" he said. "We were just bullshitting, but at least it wasn't digitalized for eternity."

"I thought you were doing just fine."

Tom snorted loudly. He leaned over the tabletop. "So, what's your opinion about the gods, Emily?"

"Don't have one, as long as their messengers are men on motorcycles."

"They're only in disguise," Tom said sleepily again. "We wouldn't recognize them without their disguise."

"Does that mean you've turned into a believer?" Leigh asked and checked the tape recorder and Emily looked at him. The way he sat there, looking so beautiful and the scarf didn't make him seem at all crazy or ill. Emily wanted to run her fingers through his messy hair. "I sincerely believe in everything I believe," Tom said. "I just can't always recall what."

"Well, I recall reading that you said that somewhere before," Emily said, even though she knew that it would get Leigh angry. [. . .] "Worded exactly the same way. . . . You've learned a couple of provocative sentences by heart and now you don't even bother listening to the questions."

"Emily," Leigh said.

"When I read your stories, I feel like everything is set from the start. All of your characters just repeat what we've heard a thousand times before. In a thousand other stories. They reproduce the same gestures, the same sex. Does that turn you on? Are you speculating on the 'been there done that' effect? Good for sales? Or are you fascinated by the idea that nobody escapes the predictable?"

The bikers noisily dragged a long beer bench into the sun, steaming boots lay in the grass.

"The one and only hope is that we're going to die someday," Tom said after a long pause.

"Believing! Dying!" Emily shouted.

Leigh didn't react. He didn't seem to hear her at all. He looked over at the men who had planted onto the tabletops their bulky, naked arms that were twined in tattoos like dark lichen. His face was tense. Only when the waiter came out and served the bikers coffee and nachos did the tension release, as though the appearance of the waiter meant he was out of danger.

"Are you a moral person?" he asked Tom suddenly, and Tom laughed and said one of the sentences he said in every interview. "I make fun of everything, of what I hate, and of what I love."

"Love?" Emily shouted. "In your books, you only describe sex, and you describe sex between a man and woman as though it were only about relieving yourself!"

Tom sat up as if somebody were pulling the tendon that ran through him.

"The poets, Emily, had two thousand years to tell us about love. To tell us about romantic love. And I'll tell you something," his right hand was raised, his index finger pointed at Emily, a bony finger that he looked at in astonishment, as though it were an alien body part, before dropping his hand heavily on the table. "Anyway," he said, and his fist made a dry thud on the wood, "we're done."

Leigh nodded.

"What's there to nod about?"

"The poets of the last two thousand years understood more about love than you do!" Emily said.

Tom looked at Emily, and Emily looked angrily back.

"Do you know what it means to yearn?" Tom said slowly, "To expose yourself? Surrender?" His fist lifted from the table. "Can you imagine what that means?" he said. "When the body burns?"

Emily was silent.

"When every nerve in the body is a burning thread? And what you long for is like snow?" he said. "Like snow that would melt if it came into contact with this burning thread?"

"That's good," Leigh said quietly. [. . .]

They looked at each other, Leigh and Tom, until Tom laughed. "Even the frogs are better at courtship than we are! All we know is: Zap and in with the drug. [. . .] Instead of making an effort, we indulge in absolute reification. Yearning! What does it amount to? Pornographically depraved, emotionless sex. . . . No demand for the unconditional, of one's own feelings, just cheap body imitation. Even though we only have one body, we confuse the simplest things. Wasn't there a time when sex was good for transgressing morals? And yet, of all things, we call feelings and sensitivity obscene. Kitsch and violence, nobody can tell the difference anymore. . . . Did I just say there are gods? At most all that's left of them is their messengers of death."

He threw down a few dollars next to the coffee cups, flimsy, crumpled bills. "Leigh, don't forget the White Rock!"

The bikers cheered.

The White Rock was two miles away from the Ponderosa Lodge. For the Chumash it had been a holy site. They had worshipped it before they were driven out and the authorities placed the area under their protection.

Emily and Leigh took the car.

They parked it in front of a boom gate in the woods, only rangers were allowed to drive farther on. Although it was late in the afternoon, the light fell starkly between the trunks and made them look slimmer. The leaves lying on the ground had jagged, shady edges.

They walked, one behind the other, Emily behind Leigh, and before they reached the rock she said: "Luckily, you got Tom to talk before I came."

"He was talking," Leigh said, "but he didn't say anything."

They followed a stream until the path branched off. It was exactly as Tom had described it to Leigh. After a short hike, they reached the edge of the forest.

Before them lay a large, flat, seemingly polished stone.

It stood out solitarily from the woodlands. It was completely white. The surface was slanted like a loge in an amphitheater hewn by nature, the proscenium opening out to the wide sprawling valley.

"I was furious," Emily said. "He didn't take you seriously!"

[. . .]

The valley lay before them dense with leaves, the crowns of the sequoias stuck out from the swaying green treetops.

"When the moon rises, it's supposed to be insanely beautiful," Leigh said, and Emily nodded, and then Leigh got undressed. He folded the scarf, pulled the T-shirt over his head, unbuttoned his jeans and took them off. He lost his balance and laughed, he dropped his jeans carelessly, stripped off his shorts, and shed the tight, sporty tank top.

The sun was glowing orange on the horizon.

Emily looked straight into the blinding center. When she turned back around, Leigh was lying next to her on his back on the rock. He had closed his eyes, and it was up to Emily whether to look at this body or not. It was a tanned muscular body, naked on a white stone.

Emily was still wearing her knee-length summer dress.

"It's insanely beautiful right now," she said softly.

It was warm and the scent of night-blooming jasmine hovered in the windless air.

"You never told me when you knew."

"What?" Leigh murmured.

"When you knew you're a boy."

Leigh didn't move. His arms were stretched out, the palms facing downward as though tracing the firmness of the stone. Only a small muscle that ran from the elbow to the wrist tensed briefly and, as if following an almost unconscious impulse, Emily leaned forward and kissed the spot where the muscle had just appeared.

"Not so long," Leigh said.

Emily's lips burned. It made her think of the burning threads Tom had talked about, and of the snow.

"And you?" Leigh said. "How long have you wanted to ask me that?"

"From the very first day. When you took off your sunglasses."

"I thought so. That's how you always looked at me."

Emily said nothing.

"I've known it since I first felt it," Leigh said. "First-hand. I've felt like I've outgrown everything ever since."

"Like a Sequoia?"

"Yes." Leigh smiled with his eyes closed. "Like a sequoia."

Emily poured cola into the two metal cups they'd brought and filled each of the cups with a generous splash of bourbon, even though the bartender had warned that Maker's Mark was too mild to mix with other drinks. Emily took a sip and didn't think the bourbon was too mild or the cola too sweet, the mix was exactly right.

"And now you view everything from above?"

"I wish!" Leigh stretched out an arm and Emily handed him the metal cup, Leigh lifted his head as he took a sip. He looked at Emily over the rim of the cup. "I don't view anything," he said. "I've outgrown everything, like clothes that are too tight."

"Can't you find new ones?"

"No."

"You don't have anything that's not too tight?" Emily asked.

"No," Leigh said.

"Then there's no exception whatsoever."

"No," Leigh said again and hit the rock with the flat of his hand. Emily stared into her cup.

"And what was it like when you noticed it?"

"I was twenty-one."

Emily swirled the whiskey-cola around a few times before taking a big gulp.

"She was two years older than me," Leigh said. Paused. "I needed to look at her all the time. I wanted to hear her voice, I wanted to inhale her, I wanted to watch her sleep." Leigh lay on his back with his eyes closed and Emily looked at him. "I wanted to sleep with her. On the floor, on a blanket in the woods, on the beach, on the couch, in the car. I wanted to be slow, I wanted to consume us, I wanted her to burn me up. Thighs, loins, my abdomen, my palms, it was so intense it hurt. As if my body was being expanded painfully. Tom put it nicely earlier." Leigh's chest and curved chin and forehead shimmered in the light that now was red, a reflection of the sun that vanished behind the trees.

"I couldn't think about anything else," Leigh said. "I kept imagining it all the time. On her, above her, over her, in her. Then we did it. She showed me. And it was right. Even though I didn't have a cock yet."

Emily focused on the arms. She studied Leigh's upper arms and elbows and then her gaze slid down his body to his feet, which were turned slightly outwards, the heels resting on the rock. They were sturdy feet with long slender toes.

"But you were already a boy," she said.

"Yes. The rest came later. Weeks, months later. When I bought my first pair of blue boxer shorts, and I found a gorgeous specimen at a dildo factory that suited me perfectly. That wasn't the main thing. It was just an addition."

"Show me," Emily whispered.

"The main thing was the longing," Leigh said. "This totally unprecedented longing had obsessed me completely."

"Show me," Emily said again.

Leigh laid there and said nothing, and the sky grew darker, and with the darkness came a chill. Leigh's nipples hardened, his shoulders had goose bumps.

"Just a little," Emily said quietly and without looking at Leigh. "Just while we're here on this rock."

"It doesn't work."

"Why not?" Emily asked after a while, but Leigh did not answer. She reached into the bag behind her and pulled out a towel. She carefully spread the towel over his legs and belly.

"You don't have it with you," she said.

Leigh grabbed a stone. "Somebody has to ignite it."

"And I can't?"

Leigh tossed the stone into the sky and they followed it with their eyes.

"You don't need to fall in love right away," Emily said.

Leigh pulled the towel a little higher up to his chest. Now his ankle peeked out from under the brown towel, which outlined the shape of his legs, the curvature of the knees, thighs, the hollow of his lap where the cloth gave way. The towel was not long enough to cover the breasts, and Emily thought about what Leigh had said earlier about the burning thread, and she thought about the stone Leigh had tossed in the air and that it hadn't landed.

"What's keeping the moon?"

They looked across the darkening valley. The green of the trees had transformed into a black wall, a single shadowy sequoia stood out in front of it. It stood out against the dark line of the horizon, which resembled a low fence by comparison. They stayed there for a while, their arms propped behind them, and watched for the moon to rise.

"Do you think Tom saw something?" Leigh said.

"Tom?"

"He was suddenly so different."

"What's a guy like him going to see?"

"He looked at me totally differently. As if I'd thrown him a fast one."

"But that wasn't you," Emily said.

Leigh sat up. He pushed the towel aside and Emily saw the beautiful dark body against the brightness of the stone one more time, before Leigh stood up to gather his things that were scattered over the rock. Leigh got dressed. First he put on his shorts and the jeans, then the tank top and T-shirt, and everything went in reverse motion. Leigh put his socks on last.

"Because of the scarf," he said. "Maybe it made me look crazy after all. Usually they turn it into a big deal when they realize something's not quite right. As if they suddenly can't recognize themselves anymore in the person sitting across from them."

"Who recognizes himself in anything," Emily said fiercely. She poured whiskey into the cups. The metallic gray blurred with the white shadow of the rock and she had to be careful not to miss the cup.

"No matter how you look. And Tom isn't exactly the smartest cookie in the jar about those things."

"Maybe," Leigh said quietly. "But what if you don't want to keep your illusions as the only reality anymore? Sure, you can pack your bags and take off. The question is where you'll end up. When in doubt nowhere," he said, *who are you to be telling us our home today is going to be someone else's home tomorrow*, shot through Emily's mind. "In the internalized outside of this great society in which you live. Tom definitely saw something."

"You sure are smug about it," Emily said.

"So, what do you think I look like?"

Behind them the rock sloped upward until it reached the edge of the woods, and before them was the valley, and if you wandered northward to the farthest end, it would lead into the desert. Emily shivered. Her summer dress was thin, and it got cold after dark.

"Anyway, there's no moon today," she said. "It should have appeared a long time ago."

"Just wait."

"Had we thought of it earlier, we could have gathered some wood so we could at least make a fire."

Leigh took off his scarf and put it around Emily's shoulders. "Better?"

"A little."

"You're right about looks. They don't matter. As long as you don't get hassled for using public lady's rooms."

"Urinal Seg-re-ga-tion," Emily said. "Cut the crap with your French theorists. When you read them, all you end up with is carbonated blood. But guess what I read? Scandinavians put hermaphrodite icons on their bathroom doors; stick figures with one leg in pants, the other in a skirt."

"The question remains," Leigh said. "Why we have this endless need to mark with a cultural gender code a basic necessity shared by every species in the animal world, given our pissing habits barely differ from those of a bear."

Emily drank the rest of the whiskey-cola.

"If the moon doesn't rise," she said, "we won't find our way back."

Leigh laughed.

"Seriously." It had suddenly grown dark. The blackness around them wasn't broken by anything, except for a very faint glow from the stone.

"Are you scared?"

"We don't even have a flashlight."

Emily thought of the warning signs in front of the park entrances. A while back in the Topanga Mountains, a family was mauled by a mountain lion. The Topanga Mountains were not Sequoia Park. But there were mountain lions everywhere. And in Sequoia Park there were also rattlesnakes and brown bears that sometimes were visible from the hiking trails.

"Tom knew we'd be in trouble without the moon."

"Bullshit," Leigh said. "If you want, I'll go and look."

Leigh stood up to look for the path they had taken. As long as he stayed on the white rock, his silhouette was visible, but after a few steps into the darkness it became one with it. The problem was finding the point where the dirt trail led to the rock. The path didn't have a sign, the transition from being out in the open to being enclosed in the trees at the edge of the forest had not been marked. In the afternoon, parts of the path were hidden by foliage from the previous autumn.

Emily wrapped the scarf tightly around her.

Her toe started hurting again. She was cold. The toe throbbed. She started to imagine what it would feel like to sleep next to Leigh, lie with him on the bare rocks, on his body, wrapped in the towels and in his scarf, protected from mountain lions and brown bears, and the disguised messengers of foreign gods. In a night like that she would get to know everything. The restlessness of spring would be resolved. She couldn't imagine what she *don't* would *learn anything*. But that was part of it *because it's always learned*, flashed through her mind, as long as you don't know something *of another person's body*, it is impossible to imagine anything.[6] Leigh knew that. He had more experience than she.

Emily listened into the night, it was still. There was no noise. The air didn't move, the darkness was a big balloon that expanded and she got smaller in its center. The points of contact with the rock she was sitting upon also got smaller, and in order to hold onto something, she turned around.

Notes

Translated by Zaia Alexander.

1. Beret Norman and Katie Sutton, "'Memory Is Always a Story': An Interview with Antje Ravic Strubel," *Women in German Yearbook* 28 (2012): 98–109, here 100.
2. Norman and Sutton, "Memory," 102.
3. Faye Stewart, "Queer Elements: The Poetics and Politics of Antje Ravic Strubel's Literary Style," *Women in German Yearbook* 30 (2014): 44–73, here 44 and 48.
4. A possible reference to Conan O'Brien's statement, "When all else fails, there's always delusion."
5. From the novel *Nightwood* by Djuna Barnes: "An image is a stop the mind makes between uncertainties."
6. All italicized words in this paragraph are in English in the original German text.

Marko Martin

Marko Martin grew up in East Germany. Six months before the opening of the Berlin Wall in November 1989 he was able to move to West Berlin, after having been prohibited from university study in the East as the result of his political viewpoints and his refusal to serve in the military. Martin studied German literature, political science, and history at the Freie Universität and Technische Universität Berlin, after which he began working as a journalist and critic, making contributions to a number of newspapers (including *Die Welt* and *Die Neue Zürcher Zeitung*) with essays and reports on his travels to Latin America, Israel, and Southeast Asia. He is actively engaged in human rights initiatives and the defense of writers living under totalitarian regimes. His first novel, *Der Prinz von Berlin* (*The Prince of Berlin*, 2000), depicts the German capital through the eyes of a young Lebanese man who, sent from his war-torn country to study in Berlin, discovers the freedom to live out his homosexuality. Martin's writing consistently addresses intercultural encounters by using a sophisticated and ironic narrative style, which draws readers' attention to the narrator's participation in the construction of the text. He has published seventeen volumes of fiction and nonfiction, including the collection of stories *Die Nacht von San Salvador: Ein Fahrtenbuch* (*The Night of San Salvador: A Logbook*, 2013), his "autobiographically based city portrait" *Tel Aviv: Schatzkästchen und Nussschale, darin die ganze Welt* (*Tel Aviv: Treasure Chest and Nutshell, in it the Whole World*, 2016), and the literary diary *Das Haus in Habana: Ein Rapport* (*The House in Havana: A Report*, 2019). The following story, "Was bleibt" ("What Remains"), is taken from the collection *Umsteigen in Babylon* (*Babylon Transfer*), published with Männerschwarm in 2016. The narrator, Daniel, who appears throughout the volume as an author figure attempting to construct a narrative, often in conversation with friends, reflects on a night spent in Tunis with his friend Florent and two local men.

"What Remains," from *Babylon Transfer* (2016)

What remains of this story—of the lonely ruin-keeper on the tiny cape behind the marina and the two men on the boardwalk—is nothing. What remains of the young man on the battlefield, on which Caesar held his ground against Pompey's men a half-century before the birth of Jesus, is also nothing.

What remains of the man, who, when he caught sight of you both from a distance, left the threshold of his clay hut and began to wander in feigned aimlessness across the terrain swept by January wind and afternoon sun, helped you over the little border wall with the rusted iron spikes looming toward the cloudless sky like skeletons, and pointed at the grave mounds, skull fragments, and pieces of bone, the other remains stored in plastic buckets behind his little house—what remains of that is nothing.

What remains of the young ruin-keeper with the unruly black hair under his baseball cap and the dust-covered Adidas pants, probably fake, bought on the cheap in the suqs of the medina,[1] who suddenly waived you inside the dim interior of his abode, where he grabbed your crotch and asked in guttural French if you wanted to smoke shisha, while outside Florent pretended to pursue his interest in the neglected graves from Roman times, is nothing.

What remains of that moment, after the wind slammed the door shut and the guard the barred window that afforded a panorama of the remains of what was once Ruspina,[2] forgotten outpost of the vanished empire; what remains of the clammy, tattered bed under the picture of the eternal president Ben Ali[3] that had been carelessly nailed to the wall, is nothing.

What remains of the sudden request for money, answered by you with a dismissive yet friendly smile, whereupon he shrugged his shoulders and quickly slipped his Adidas pants down to his ankles, which were already stretched like an arrow at the crotch, is nothing.

What remains of your amazement and his serious face, contorted as if by pain and vigilance, with darkly shimmering stubble, before the two of you stained the threadbare rug over the clay floor in the rhombus pattern of the last rays of sun and then at once said goodbye to one another with a forced, calloused slap of the hand, is nothing.

What remains of this occurrence on the hill protruding into the sea, is thus nothing.

And what remains of Mehdi and Mejid, the two curly-haired men wearing convincing knock-off Nikes and Armani jeans, they too strolling back and forth as if by chance, in genuine short black leather jackets, wherever and however they had bought them, is nothing.

What remains of them, when on your way back they approached you both in front of the restaurants on the boardwalk in their similarly gravelly-grumbly French, plunging their dark pupils into yours, is nothing.

What remains of their proposal to go at once to your hotel, where already in the lobby they were driven back out by that hate-filled, possibly just frustrated security man as both of you watched, a tiny bit touched by embarrassment, is nothing.

What, however, remains of their offer to rent an apartment on the marina for a measly forty dinars per night, your muted murmurings to each other weighing the potential peril, is also nothing.

What remains of the taxi ride that followed through the now darkening city, past the fortress, mosque, and dilapidated houses, only distinguishable in the variations of the presidential pictures mounted on their grayish white exterior walls, Florent being the one who pointed out with a whisper that one of the photos showed a bespectacled Ben Ali, probably aiming to project intellectual inquisitiveness but holding his ballpoint pen thrust so deeply into the gap between the index and middle fingers of a hand raised like Caesar that he could not possibly have written a single word; what remains of this discovery, which you both preferred not to share with the two men whose searching glances had lost no intensity, is still nothing.

What remains of the taxi's abrupt halt when you all climbed out in front of the parked night buses that were soon to drive down into the Sahara, and Mejid (the larger, stronger one) nonchalantly paid the driver a dinar coin, is nothing.

What remains of the cell-phone calls that began as Mehdi (the smaller and possibly gentler one) smiled knowingly, against an acoustic backdrop of muezzin calls and exhaust rattles, is nothing. And what remains of the techno version of an old Umm Kulthum[4] song coming from the inside of a CD store behind you and the clinking of the cups in the neon-bright, unwelcoming tiled coffee houses all around, full of men with hardened faces bent over card games and water pipes, if they were not dozing off or talking throatily at one another while never taking their eyes off the four of you out there on the street—is nothing.

What remains of Mehdi and Mejid, who once again climb into a taxi with you both and directed it to one of those offices still open at the marina, so that in strange proximity to the police station they could enter into negotiations in Arabic, shoving your IDs and theirs into a decrepit copy machine, after which you put the agreed-upon forty dinars in the hand held out by the apparent boss and in return received a key, before everyone in the smoke-filled room proclaimed "Yalla,"[5] is nothing.

What remains of your entrance into the block of buildings, open on three sides and a bit run down, with apartments and balconies, the little courtyards and concrete cross-bracing, what remains of the flaking white of the walls and the washed-out blue of the window slats, is nothing.

What remains of Mejids's disappearance from the apartment to which the key had fit, right after sitting down with you both on the corner seating of the otherwise almost empty, echoing foyer, what remains of the shirt and leather jacket Mehdi took off immediately, his hastily opened jeans and his dick popping out like an arrow from under his Calvin Klein knock-off briefs, his furrowed brow under his wavy, horizontally trimmed black hair, his lips only half open to your kisses and the rearing up of his body, is nothing.

What remains of big Mejid's unexpectedly quick return with a cigarette in the corner of his mouth and a transparent white plastic bag with six shrink-wrapped cans of local Celtic beer, along with dates and roasted *cacahuètes*,[6] wrapped in newspaper with the likeness of the eternal president, is also nothing.

What remains of how Mehdi quickly pulled up his pants after Mejid's return, of the slight shivering of his light brown hairless torso, his half-nakedness and arms draped casually over your shoulders, what remains of how we then emptied the beer cans, passed lighters around with thanks, lit cigarettes with closed eyes, then suddenly all stared awkwardly at Al-Jazeera and later MTV on the monstrous television in the middle of the bare room, what remains of the unspoken expectation and the conversations dragged out with such effort about Mejid's work as a truck driver and Mehdi's work as a painter, is nothing.

What remains of the ensuing *séparation*,[7] initiated by a snap of the finger, Mehdi accompanying Florent into the vestibule and you following Mejid onto the threadbare linens of the otherwise also completely empty bedroom, before you dry each other after showering with the only towel, is nothing.

What remains of the bedroom, where you, with the door carefully closed, afterward now also with Mehdi, the somewhat gentler one, the more appropriate one for you, discover the boundaries of transgressing the law, all the worried hands-away-from-my-ass gestures and the almost maidenly closed lips that nevertheless actually had the fragrance of canned beer and cigarettes, what remains of the naked, muscular and hairless body and the silky eyelashes, which in the moment of the highest, almost silent ecstasy fluttered open for a few seconds, is nothing.

What remains of his lips, which in that moment opened ever so slightly after all, or of his left arm, which held your shoulder in almost desperate tenderness, the inexplicable shimmering dampness in the corners of his eyes, is however nothing.

What remains of his quick jump up after the silent discharge, which conjured up the long forgotten guilt-ridden moments under the covers of your childhood bedroom, what remains of the somehow caught-in-the-act smiles on your faces, is nothing.

What remains of Mehdi's panic-driven flight as soon as Mejid flung open the bedroom door with broad shoulders and stiff dick whipping around as if in rage and blurted out a warning, while someone was already knocking urgently at the apartment door, is nothing.

What remains of your held breath on the tattered sheets while in the vestibule the rustling sounds of clothing pulled on hastily blended with the continuing booming knocks, the squeak of the door as it opened tentatively, and the entrance of one of the invisibles, again screaming in a raw throaty tone, is also, however, nothing.

What remains of the disappearance of the invisible voice, the slam of the apartment door and Mejid's return to the bedroom, pearls of sweat on his brow, what remains of how Mehdi fumbled around with T-shirts, socks, and pants as you too now quickly stood up, ran into the vestibule, and exchanged wordless glances with Florent, glances which yet again calm you in an absolutely inexplicable way, is nothing.

What remains of the haste of the four men, who climbed panting into their clothes, and what remains of Mehdi's injunction to wait for five more minutes after both of them had taken to their heels, since the voice belonged to the man from the real estate agency and had announced a police visit, is nothing.

What remains of the condoms, quickly hidden between rug and damaged terrazzo floor, is nothing.

What remains of Mehdi's and Mejid's disappearance, neither of whom found the time to give you at least a nod of goodbye, is also nothing.

What remains of their hobbled running, the laces of their gym shoes open like the zippers of the leather jackers over their T-shirts, put on inside out, is nevertheless nothing.

What remains of the discussion you had under your breath, your effort to remain composed with assertions of *there is no proof, they cannot do anything to us*, of how Florent, the epitome of composure, straightened the corner seating that had slid under his and the other man's weight and cleared the table of empty beer cans and the remains of *cacahuètes*, then emptied the overflowing ashtray in the garbage can, is nothing.

What remains of how you both left the scene and in a demonstratively casual manner returned the key to the office that mysteriously was still open and behind whose glass pane you now again also saw Mejid and Mehdi chitchatting, is nothing.

What remains of how Mejid and Mehdi slowly calmed down, then roughly put their hands on your arms and winked shyly under their silky eyebrows before they disappeared for good in the night, is nevertheless nothing.

What remains of your own now relieved walk, still somewhat weak in the knees—under the half moon over the silvery shining sea—back to the hotel, underneath the fortress walls, which had already deceptively served as the Jerusalem backdrop for Zeffirelli's Jesus and Monty Python's Brian, is nothing.

Isn't there perhaps the adventure of a foursome night?

Actually, no.

Isn't there a joyful, gasping, cheating of death, whose attempt to level everything I had sensed out there on that forgotten Roman cemetery between the anonymous grave mounds as the wind blew and sunbeams ran one last time over the steel-gray sea, while inside the clay hut you . . .

No.

Isn't there the tickle of being approached by the two twenty-year-olds instead of having to chase them, gasping like the older snooty European faggots with their label sweaters draped over their shoulders?

No.

Yet isn't there the vigilance we maintained when you hid cell phone, money, and passports under our unlabeled clothes in the hotel room, while I—unfortunately without success—tried to smuggle the two of them past the eagle eyes of the security guard with the imperious gestures and nauseatingly well-filed little fingernails from the lobby to the elevator.

Not that either.

Isn't there our spontaneous rage at this lackey and his decision to deny us a foursome night, perhaps more the product of his envy than his sense of duty?

Not really.

Isn't there our skepticism, in spite of our curiosity, that perhaps the two had quite a different hidden interest in us?

Yes. Actually, a little bit.

Isn't there the dawning foreboding that everything could end quite abruptly, in whatever fashion?

A little bit.

Isn't there our earlier annoyance about the many telephone calls, Mejid's resounding voice in the bare apartment and, before that, the lurking glances of the peculiar office employees around the copy machine before they—beneath the strict wall-photo-eyes of Ben Ali—finally gave us the key?

This too, a little bit.

Isn't there our skepticism when Mejid disappeared and our surprise when Mehdi then undressed so quickly that we hardly kept up, when he licked our nipples devotedly but did not want to touch our dicks, ran his fingers over our throats and in doing so did not lose his erection for one second and only softened a little, perhaps from fear of his own desire, when a tongue threatened to glide too far down his throat?

That too.

No. And not the splitting up after Mejid returned, the sex in succession, as if planned, since the two of them by no means wanted to see the other naked and under no circumstances in any sort of bodily constellation that could remotely be understood as passive.

All that was to be expected.

Does the sensation remain of being in bed with two young Tunisians?

Moderately, in light of their almost visible fear of losing control of themselves for even one moment, a surveillance mania, whether of a Ben Alian or simply traditionally religious nature, transferred to the sensual realm and still present even in the excess of drinking, smoking, and fucking, if you like.

And our mutual fear when suddenly there was a knock on the door?

Also to be expected, in spite of everything. Ultimately, our passports would protect us and the two of them their eloquence, their knowledge of the local tricks and customs. Mejid and Mehdi seemed anything but naïve.

Possibly the relief that the two of them did not demand some sort of payment in the hectic moment of departure but instead with some embarrassment mentioned the taxi that they had to take to their out-of-the-way suburb.

Relief because of a few dinars?

Come now. Relief because of their apparent honesty. Relief that this foursome night would at least not leave behind a stale aftertaste.

Had we ever experienced it differently?

No, but here we were in Arabia. And apparently, we were approached on the boardwalk not because of money.

So, relief that we did not have to pay some boys as once did Burroughs, Ginsberg, or Orton[8] in Tangier but were dragged off by young adults. And yet, at the same time, shame that afterwards we too dissect them in speech and writing in our compulsion to catalog, which we call an occidental ability to reflect and neither can nor want to give up?

Those now are your questions, Daniel. By the way: didn't you find it odd that the office was open so late, rather atypical of apartment rentals and on top of that in direct proximity to the marina police station?

Conspiracy, coincidence, pure incoherence? But that is by no means what remains . . .

Then what?

Our smiles the next morning! When at the breakfast buffet the all-inclusive vacationers once again scurried about loudly, fogging everyone with their banalities. Our smiles, perhaps even a little bit malicious, admittedly nothing more than a necessary defense before people who in word and habit live off of reducing everything to their level of raucous non-occurrence.

As if that isn't just as sweeping, Daniel! Following in Botho Strauß's[9] footsteps does not become you, you simply lack the gravitas. Better not even try.

You misunderstand me, our smile—so that's what remains—was less smug than melancholic.

Perhaps true, but why?

Because everything, the moments in the nocturnal apartment at the marina, our nakedness, the ensuing flight and even our weak knees . . .

Yes?

Did not just take place under the sign of a waning half-moon but also under the word "yet."

Says the mystic! Are you starting that up again?

Starting. . . . It's more like I'm girding myself for the foreseeable end of such stories, that's all. Something ends, something different begins.

Obviously and, in the end, the graves await each of us. Whether girded or ungirded, we go down the hole without memories.

You said it yourself. Carlos Fuentes said it! Life is short, even if the night is long. When we die, our past vanishes. It is what we lose, not the future.

And still . . .

Yes?

Under the starry canopy next to the bone houses and on the grave mounds there will still continue to be ruin keepers, there will still exist Mehdis and Mejids on the boardwalks, however happy or trapped in themselves they are.

You believe that, Florent?

I know that, Daniel.

Notes

Translated by Gary Schmidt.

1. Open markets of the old city; *suqs* is plural for *souk*.
2. Ruspina was an ancient town ruled by the Phoenicians, Carthaginians, and then Romans located in what is now Tunisia.
3. Zine El Abidine Ben Ali, president of Tunisia from 1987 until 2011, when he was forced to flee with his family to Saudi Arabia.
4. Umm Kulthum (1898–1975) was an Egyptian singer, songwriter, and actress who sold more than eighty million records and was dubbed "The Voice of Egypt."
5. "Yalla" is an Arabic expression meaning "come on," "hurry up," or "let's (go/do)."
6. Here and below, "cacahuètes" (peanuts) is in French in the original.
7. "Séparation" is in French in original.
8. Refers to William S. Burroughs (1914–1997), an American writer prominent in the Beat Generation; Alan Ginsberg (1926–1997), a famous American poet of the Beat Generation; and Joe Orton (1933–1967), an English playwright known for his black comedies and who was murdered by his lover, Kenneth Halliwell.
9. Botho Strauß (1944–), a German playwright and novelist who sparked a controversy with the conservative political views expressed in his 1993 essay "Anschwellender Bockgesang" (Rising Song of the He-Goat).

Gunther Geltinger

GUNTHER GELTINGER, who lives and works in Cologne, is the author of three novels: *Mensch Engel* (*Man Angel*, 2008), *Moor* (2013), and *Benzin* (*Gasoline*, 2019), all of which were published with Suhrkamp Verlag and received critical acclaim in leading German-language newspapers such as *Die Zeit*, *Süddeutsche Zeitung*, and *Die Neue Zürcher Zeitung*. Geltinger's novels include both intense self-reflection and an uncompromising eye on gay male subculture. Although addressing dark and difficult themes that may provoke discomfort in readers, Geltinger has avoided the fate of gay authors of earlier decades whose works triggered unease in the LGBTQ+ community and disinterest or rejection on the part of the heteronormative mainstream.

While writing *Gasoline*, Geltinger was inspired by the American author Paul Bowles's groundbreaking novel *The Sheltering Sky*.[1] While Bowles recounts the journey of a heterosexual couple southward into the Sahara, Geltinger's novel, dubbed a road movie by German critics, relates how a gay male couple seeks to overcome a relationship crisis on a vacation in South Africa and Zimbabwe. Alexander is a teacher and Vinz a writer: their plan to visit Victoria Falls provides Vinz with an idea for a new novel. And, unlike their gay friends in Germany, the two men wish to avoid the usual tourist routes, so they rent a car and drive northward from Johannesburg into the countryside. Already experiencing unease as a same-sex couple, the discomfort heightens when they apparently run over a man along the highway at night. Unami, a black Zimbabwean who has come to South Africa seeking work, joins them on their road trip. Motivated perhaps by both guilt and attraction, Vinz and Alexander take on Unami as tour guide, eventually crossing the border with him into Zimbabwe. Like *Man Angel*, *Gasoline* blends past and present, reality and fantasy, evoking haunting childhood images and allowing them to resurface in a concrete present, for example, the waterfall that represents both the channeling and destructive potential of sexual desire. Such images and the presence of violence and racism in Geltinger's novel suggest the significance of another potential intertext, namely Joseph Conrad's *Heart of Darkness*. In the following excerpt, Unami leads Vinz and Alexander into a canyon at one of South Africa's national parks.

from *Gasoline* (2019)

They walk through rapidly alternating light and shadow, Vinz in the lead, Alexander at a distance behind him, and Unami bringing up the rear, although he is the only one who knows the way. The narrow path prevents them from walking side by side. There is little chance they will lose one another here; the few existing offshoots end at the edge of the drop-off. Hikers have trampled them into the grass in order to catch a glimpse of the canyon. Behind the bushes, Vinz senses the vertiginous depths, the unpredictability of the landscape with its sudden precipices and the circle of the horizon in all directions. He walks precariously, conscious of each step he takes, the hangover from the sleeping pills like a sponge in his head through which the outside world is seeping more slowly than he is moving through it. The dry grass rustles under his feet, sometimes a rock breaks free and crashes downward, a branch snaps in the midday silence. Startled, he looks back to assure himself that the others are still there.

Down below he hears the river. Its distant murmur marks the border between path and chasm, an acoustic line that acts as his guide, as unreliable as the path itself. At the beginning it was a trampled-down hiking trail extending across makeshift steps through the rocky plateau. Now and then it disappeared between boulders, only to take up its course again elsewhere, narrower than before and increasingly overgrown. Soon there were only sporadic hints of faltering forays into the wilderness, as if all hikers who had undertaken a descent into the canyon had at some point turned around for fear that the path could lead into nothingness.

In the unshaded sections the sun is savage; he crosses these quickly, feeling as if his vision is still impaired. The day is like the inversion of darkness, a brightness that outshines all else. He stops under the next tree and looks around. The right word for the landscape would be: "breathtaking," a scenic binge. He had hoped for nothing less from this trip: nature that made his own being seem insignificant, calling upon him to see it in the right perspective. To write! For two whole novels he had mostly allowed the landscape to speak more often than his characters. Their actions remained dubious, but not nature's. If he was forced to choose one over the other, he could always let the landscape fall silent, for it was far beyond language or too old for words. When on occasion both coincided, there had been moments of truth. What remained were his days holding a finger over the delete button.

In spite of its beauty, the scenery is without luster, as if dulled by all attempts to narrate it. Eroded mountaintops line the high valley on each side, summits without peaks. Villages dot the slopes, between them expanses of green that are neither forest nor shrubland—not high enough to be the one, too tree-filled to be the other. Here they took a break and drank from the water bottle that they shared; Unami declined the offer every time. Alexander inquired about the name of a flower and sniffed herbs found along the path. Unami knew the names of some in English; most he didn't. In his language the names sounded more exotic than the plants themselves appeared.

For Alexander it was gentian-like or had the scent of lavender.[2] He put on his scientist face, dissected the umbel, and played the role of biologist. Vinz doubted that Unami knew what gentian blossoms looked like or how lavender smelled. Alexander was impressed by Unami's knowledge of botany and pronounced the names of the plants the way *he* heard him say them. Unami corrected his pronunciation; Alexander repeated after him, and their guide appeared to be satisfied. They walked longer and farther than Vinz was accustomed from his hikes with Alexander through landscapes they had crossed in lockstep. Hiking had always been a way to find their way back to each other when they were out of sync. After just a few minutes Vinz was in the lead again. When he turned around under the next tree, he was alone.

He waits for the others to catch up. The shade is cramped; he can smell his body, which he had last washed on another continent. Even Alexander's clothes are sticking to his skin, and Unami's face glistens as if it were varnished. Vinz follows the path of a drop of sweat that crawls over his temple, like the very viscosity of his movements. The blood that Vinz had dabbed off his forehead last night remained similarly indecisive on the wound, as if it still had plans for him.

[. . .]

Alexander plucks one of the waxy leaves that grew, like butterfly wings, in pairs on the branches. He tears it slightly and sniffs at it. Mopane, he says, and holds Africa provocatively under Vinz's nose. A piercing odor reminiscent of turpentine emanates from his hand. "Elephants go for it,"[3] Unami confirms. Since setting out they have not seen any animals, only a few birds and a nameless cricket-like insect shimmering garishly in venomous colors on a blade of grass. "As long as they don't go for us,"[4] Alexander says, and Unami laughs. Even the dumbest tourist in this country knows that there are no elephants at these altitudes. If it is really Alexander's plan to get rid of Unami by getting on his nerves, the further course of their trip depends decisively on their ability to behave like idiots: bumbling racist tourists like those you can meet anywhere in the world. Yet, he doesn't make it easy for them. When playing the hitchhiking game, they were both in agreement. The word for him was: beautiful. That kind of beauty that one could only keep at bay by constantly staring at it. Since setting out, Vinz has been sizing him up, as if he had to assure himself that Unami was still the same man they had almost run over the previous evening. A razor-thin nocturnal layer still lies like a filter between the man standing here and the one he had seen only in the dark.

[. . .]

"Are you sure, you'll make it?" Vinz points at the path that disappears among the boulders. Already the march has become an act of violence for someone who just yesterday lay bleeding on the road. If they wish to make him docile, they will have to penetrate him with their guilty conscience: their sympathy must amount to a rape. The deeper they go in, the greater his qualms. He would not be able to bring himself to cheat them if he felt that they too were acting out of need.

"Sure," answers Unami. The drop of sweat has reached the ridge of his cheek. Alexander offers him a handkerchief. He's flirting, Vinz thinks, he's slipping him things, a cigarette here, a flower there, and who knows how many compliments. It has been a long time since he has seen Alexander in such a good mood, the daredevil hunter to whom he had also succumbed *back then*, and he is appalled by the words "back then," which in the stories of the elderly warn the young that happiness exists only in the past tense. For example, when they first met at Alf's graduation party, in whose bed it seems they had both spent their nights for a while, independently of one another but in the same year and presumably in rapid rotation—as they recapped smirking on the balcony over cigarettes and small talk—such that the scent of the other, the trace of his desire, must still have clung to Alf's body, an image, as described in the corresponding passage of his first novel, that jolted Vinz like an electric shock and settled into his head for the rest of the evening, his gin-soaked synapses firing and sparking, causing him to hover close to Alexander, literally inhaling him when he pushed his way past him in the narrow hallway or squeezed in behind him in the buffet line, believing he could already taste and devour him, the tall, broad-shouldered blond, who also now took up the chase, until by chance they left the party at the same time, and in this scene he stumbles behind Alexander into the frosty February night, follows him jittering through the nocturnal city, walking in circles and making long detours, because both, as they would admit to each other later, are speculating on being taken home by the other, but in the entryway where they finally end up neither one of them has the right key, so they burst into laughter and press up against one another in front of the dumpsters, at the end of a chapter in which their story had little past and a lot of present moment.

Alexander reapplies 50 spf sunscreen, generously rubbing the lotion on arms and neck, then on spots not reached by sunlight. He passes along the tube to Unami, who laughs and says, "I like your jokes."[5] He also turns down the cookies that Vinz offers him, joking that they shouldn't waste their provisions on him. Their gear betrays their distrust in their own enterprise: hiking clothes and backpacks filled with supplies, whereas Unami is either relying on them or on a constitution that effortlessly endures long phases of privation. He has brought nothing with him, just his body. He has changed clothes, yet Vinz cannot say what he was wearing yesterday: cut-off jeans, a red athletic shirt and worn-out sneakers, the casual style of almost all young men here with their preference for Western athletic fashion brands, and yet Vinz caught himself instinctively looking at Unami's clothes for hints about his standard of living. He wears the arm sling as if it were a matter of course, a kerchief folded into a triangle in which his injured elbow rests. If this moment were a photo in their vacation album it would freeze his and Alexander's gaze on Unami and expose them in a similar manner as the picture of Bernd and Alf alongside their township guide,[6] their muscles—chiseled in the fitness studio—the main ingredient of the equipment that a gay man can acquire none too soon to gird himself against sexual irrelevance. Vinz knows that among all the other daddies, bears, and BBBs[7] that he quickly scrolls past on the dating sites, he too is becoming more and more invisible from year to year, whereas as soon as Alexander puts his profile picture online, with his naked torso and head cut off under the chin, the requests from slender students start to ring.

The path stretches out between glowing rock needles and then dives into shrubbery that closes over their heads like a tunnel. They find themselves again in a dense mountain forest, in fact a kind of jungle that falls off steeply before their feet. Solitary ruts between ferns and vines vaguely mark the path. Alexander steps ahead of the others and peers into the tangled green depths. Vinz can tell from his eyes that he is thinking the same thing: alone, the two of them would have turned around at this spot, and they had never shied away from choosing difficult trails. He tests the ground. Until now the hike had been spectacular without exception, Unami has kept his promise. Alexander climbs a bit ahead of the others and reaches his arm out to Unami to offer him support. He readily accepts the help, an ironic twitch in the corners of his mouth betraying that the gesture is a concession to the role he is playing. Vinz holds on tightly with both hands to the vines, which snap away under his grip. The murmur of the river has fallen silent, a muffled silence envelops them. Vinz doubts that they are going in the right direction. For a while they slide down in this manner, with twisted feet and flailing arms, their peculiar ballet dance with the centrifugal force of the abyss, which would no longer just be a metaphor the minute one of them were to take a false step. Vinz sees what is also seen by Alexander, what will be drilled into their brains when Unami straddles the boulders: his pointed, aggressive behind, the power of his body that has thrown them off track: look at me, his poses seem to say to them, you will pay dearly for this ass; and Vinz stumbles and grabs Alexander.

One after the other, they squeeze through a crevice, after which the path breaks off. Unami stops, turns around, and extends his hand to Vinz. He accepts, although he easily could have managed the step on his own. With the sudden closeness Vinz feels him tremble, senses the tension of his muscles. They lose their bearing on the mossy rock. Unami prevents them both from falling by stepping aside at the last moment. "Can you make it?" he asks and frees himself from Vinz's involuntary embrace. Even more than his dexterity at climbing, this self-confident avoidance of a contact that is too intimate seems to Vinz to be proof that Unami knows very well what he is doing. Even the fresh bandage peeking out from under the visor of his baseball cap seems like a jeering commentary on their real motives for taking on this murderous trail. "Sure,"[8] he says, sliding past Unami on the seat of his pants and taking the next rocky steps on all fours. It appears to him to be a basic stipulation of this hike that each of them knows about the vulnerability of the other, the hike leading them deeper and deeper into a landscape that will remain silent if they plunge into one of its crevices never to return. Alexander is standing down below and opens his arms wide to catch them. In the depths Vinz suddenly hears once again the familiar murmur of the water.

Notes

Translated by Gary Schmidt.

1. Gunther Geltinger interview with Gary Schmidt in June 2019.
2. "Gentian-like" and "lavender" are in English in the original.
3. "Elephants go for it" is in English in the original.
4. "As long as they don't go for us" is in English in the original.
5. "I like your jokes" is in English in the original.
6. Bernd and Alf are gay German friends of Vinz and Alexander who also traveled to South Africa recently.
7. "BBB" refers to *Bart, Brille, Bauch* (beard, glasses, belly).
8. "Sure" is in English in the original.

Yusuf Yeşilöz

YUSUF YEŞILÖZ was born in a Kurdish village in Turkey. He emigrated to Switzerland in 1987 and received Swiss citizenship eight years later. Arriving in Switzerland in his early twenties with no knowledge of German, he nevertheless devoted himself to mastering the language and decided to begin writing fiction in German in order to express himself to his new compatriots in his adopted homeland. Yeşilöz describes himself as a writer for socially engaged readers. His numerous novels, stories, and autobiographical works follow characters back and forth from Turkey to Europe, from rural to urban settings, reflecting on the dynamic relationship between place, language, culture, and identity. In addition to publishing fiction, he has directed eight documentary films on migration in the arts, politics, and everyday life, including *Zwischen den Welten* (*Between the Worlds*, 2006), which was awarded the Christian Berger Prize at the Innsbruck International Film Festival.

Yeşilöz, who identifies as heterosexual, was inspired to write *Hochzeitsflug* (*The Wedding Flight*, 2011) after a young man identified himself to the author as gay at a social event.[1] The novel tells the story of a young gay man struggling with coming out to his Turkish parents, who own and operate a *Döner* (Turkish kabob) restaurant in an unidentified town in German-speaking Europe. The situation becomes critical when young Beyto flies to Turkey with his parents to visit relatives, where he is told that he is to be married to his cousin Sahar, whom he concedes to marry but later abandons.

The well-known Swiss filmmaker Gita Gsell directed *Beyto*, a film adaptation of *Hochzeitsflug*, which premiered at the Zurich Film Festival in 2020. In *Die Wunschplatane* (*The Wishing Tree*, 2018), Yeşilöz continues the story of the Beyto family from a different perspective: a writer visits a Swiss town in order to conduct a creative writing workshop there and walks into the Beytos' restaurant to eat lunch. The restaurant owner sees in the writer a compatriot to whom he can entrust his son's story. The following excerpt is taken from *Hochzeitsflug*, which is narrated by young Beyto.

from *The Wedding Flight* (2011)

During the three weeks that taught me about the whole village and its deeply rooted traditions, it was as if I were intoxicated. I didn't communicate with Manuel or with my colleague in Bischofstraße.[2] During the day I would visit my friends from earlier times, most preferably Mofid, the level-headed one, who had a very calming effect on me. I had to listen to crazy Farda's questions about how good the sex was with Sahar: Was I letting her fly over the clouds? After three days I got used to his manner. He had no inhibitions in interrogating me about intimate details that were a big taboo for the villagers who were sane. At night I had gone to Sahar's bed, who had hoped that I would also make love to her after the wedding night. Instead, I lay next to her as if we were brother and sister, the length of a pillow between us. Directly after the wedding, Sahar and I had been invited to a different family's house every evening. An important custom, apparently, for the purpose of seeing the newlyweds together and acclimating them as a couple to joint social appearances. I became aware of the fact that in this village, a person attains their worth only after they are married and have children.

My father, who gave full credit to the village customs, had no use for gay men; he condemned them. Whenever he saw two men who were noticeably homosexual in his kebab house or on the street, my father always told the story of a man from his village. The man's name meant "blessing," and it was bestowed on him because he came after the birth of several daughters. But after his parents learned of his disgrace, they called him "Schmerz" (sorrow).[3] That man must have been about the same age as my grandfather Beyto; he was married and had several children, but he was caught in the act a few times in the village with a traveling salesman or a beggar standing behind him in bright daylight or at night in a stable. He must have left the village after a huge quarrel. It is said that sometimes villagers who were entering the military—and only for that reason—then undertaking long journeys, met him by chance in city bus stations, where he was selling rose water. But he pretended not to know the people from his village, who were his relatives. The rose-water vendor never returned to the village. My father never changed his attitude, even though he daily served gay men in his kebab house and thanked each of them when they ordered and when they paid.

My father also told another story about gay men from his time in the military. Although my father held hard-and-fast to his opposition to homosexuality and called it a disgrace, as he stressed repeatedly, he found the ridiculous way the military had handled the case of a man named Tarek to be abhorrent. He condemned how the military treated this young man who unknowingly let himself be seduced by Satan, as my father believed. In his words, one wouldn't do something so extreme . . . even to an enemy.

Father recounted Tarek's feminine behavior in the military, how he had been as coquettish as a female dove, flirting with every young man. With his demeanor and high voice he seemed liked a girl in makeup and long braids. He was indeed suspected of being gay. But no one had thought that he would turn himself in to the commanding officer.

Tarek did this only because he had found out that gays were exempt from military service due to psychosexual disorders. At first, they laughed at Tarek; some pushed him, others tried to use him as a love substitute, since they had not been able to touch a woman for two years while in the army. Young Tarek had to undergo many interrogations, stand in front of doctors, healers, and theologians, all of whom wanted to explain to him a better world without gays, and also in front of commanding officers who thought they were God himself. In the end, the proud military authorities would believe him and release him from the army. At first, he was against submitting to this monstrous procedure. Co-workers tried to convince him to change his mind. He was told to simply act normal during the months in the military. But Tarek was delusional and wanted at all costs to prove his homosexuality to his superiors, who beat him as if he were a donkey. He received a day's leave and went to a nearby city, where, after great effort, he picked up a guy whom he paid to take him from behind. In addition, he had searched long for a photographer who was willing to photograph him during the sex act. Eventually Tarek found one who, after having been plied with threats, was willing to photograph men loving each other. And Tarek was indeed released from service, because they finally believed in his homosexuality due to the photo. The said photo was passed around in the barracks like a playing card and was the source of much amusement until a higher, more devout commanding officer burned it.

After my first night of love with Manuel, I solemnly resolved to make it clear to my parents that I was homosexual. Manuel had given me an advice book on how to come out; coming out was a concept that was as renowned in our circle of friends as the moon landing. Later, however, I discovered with bitter disappointment that the Beyto family culture that I had grown into had left a more lasting mark on me than all the clever how-to books in the world.

I forged my plan while my parents were working at the kebab house. I went over all possible dialogues, performing them in front of the mirror in the small bathroom. I spoke my sentences as gently and amiably to the mirror as if I were uttering a plea. And the severe answers of my father in an angry raised voice that was both booming and commanding. Yet, in front of the mirror I could not presume how my father would take the news of my being gay, this great shame, this stain on the brow of the family. I noticed that I became embarrassed, although I was standing alone before the mirror. Yet, I found myself to be brave and believed I could face the wrath of my parents, an unprecedented storm.

On the day of my confession, I wore a brown suit. I was very elegant, the way my parents, above all my mother, always wanted to see their only son: dressed like men on television or at the bank. It was my intention to please them with my suit, for they were always complaining about my un-ironed pants that had stars embossed on the back pockets. I knew that my father wanted to close the kebab house somewhat earlier than ten o'clock that evening because he did not want to miss the gay television host's show, whom he called the "delicate flirtatious man with the tie." My father loved the man's gestures: nobody could flirt as well as he could, he said. My father's enthusiasm took on extreme dimensions when, from time to time, this man brought unusual characters on his show, and my father felt himself compensated for a hard day at work. Once the TV guy had welcomed a man to his show who rented himself out to women by the hour and even had a secretary in his service, an internet presence, and a glossy paper catalog with photos of himself half-naked. Father recounted this—from his perspective—strange story in his village with great zeal, much to the amusement of the men. He was still waiting for the flirtatious TV guy to come to his store, and father would invite him to have a spicy kebab and strong coffee and tell him about weird Ramo with the loose lips from his village. Yet, my father never found this TV guy to be respectable, because he was gay.

Before the show I went to father's shop. A few beer drinkers who had spent half their wages there were sitting at the bar in front of large brown beer bottles and smoking fat cigars. It was like the place was infested with smoke. My father looked back and forth from the customers to the clock.

He expressed his joy that I had come to help him straighten up and clean. When the beer drinkers wanted to order kebabs, my father responded that we were having a party and he had to close the shop. Cursing, the men went out into the cold, probably looking for another beer hall. In a rush, I swept the floor with a broom and mopped it with a rag. Father cleaned the tables and the meat knife.

When we arrived at our apartment, the flirtatious guy's show had already begun, and my mother had set out the tea in a double teapot[4] and her favorite narrow tea glasses with the gold rims, accompanied by roasted chickpeas, my father's favorite snack, and a pile of hard candy. Mother laughed at the show's first guest, a snake breeder who had tattooed a photo of one of his green snakes on his light skin.

She had cut up the pomegranate, her favorite food from back home, on a white plate and offered it to my father, who sang a paean to this noble fruit after each little piece that he put in his mouth. Then he gave us a lecture: the fact that this fruit did not grow in the West signified how cold the culture was here. Mother told him to quit spreading the dubious theories that a beard had recently been telling him. I too ate hard candy and drank black tea from the double tea pot. I sat on the sofa in front of the television between my parents, an image that they liked to see. I wanted to please my parents as much as possible before I shocked them. I had read in the newspaper that the moderator would be welcoming a gay couple that had adopted two children. The children were orphans. I imagined that my parents might find sympathy for the couple they would otherwise reject, because the two men had taken in two orphans. I saw a chance for myself. My parents, of course, did not know ahead of time whom the flirtatious guy was bringing on his show since they never read one of this country's newspapers. In fact, they avoided reading newspapers completely throughout their lives, as if reading the paper was an unpardonable sin.

The male couple—each man holding in his arms a child with a pacifier in its mouth—came on the glittering stage to great applause from the studio audience. At this very moment one of the children began to cry, and both men handled the little one so sweetly, soothing him with a milk bottle that they, with all four hands, thrust in his mouth. One held the child pressed tightly against him, and the other kissed it on the cheek while he stroked the child's neck. My father burst out laughing, but only because he was not used to men behaving like that. In his eyes, they were exposing themselves. My mother looked at the television skeptically and asked why we were even watching such a program: wasn't it enough that we daily served such men seduced by Satan? Father ignored mother; he took pleasure in the behavior of the two men, which in his eyes was demeaning and even ridiculous. For him, the couple was further proof, he said while slurping tea, that these people had no sense of shame. He had always said that shame had to be an unwritten law in society.

The couple on television was interviewed. One of the men had a soft voice and actually spoke in a woman's pitch: he played the role of the woman. Even I was confused by the strangeness of his voice, the unnaturalness of his mannerism. The second man was the taller one; he had a deeper voice and was somewhat overweight. The roles of man and woman were clearly assigned. They recounted the beautiful feeling of being parents, the satisfaction of raising orphans who otherwise would have fallen into the wrong hands in the East, their responsibilities toward each other as partners and, finally, the gratification of at last being recognized in society. The flirtatious man was visibly delighted: as he twice explicitly emphasized, he was providing the nation proof on his show of the progress of society. As the two men, each holding a child now fast asleep, took their leave and received a standing ovation from the audience, father changed the channel to a network from his homeland. At that moment a familiar old song was being sung and now mom got her just due. She waved her handkerchief back and forth rhythmically and sang along softly: "Give the bride a handful of roses! The bride with the golden belt and the narrow waist . . ."

My father said he liked this flirtatious man because he had of late gotten riled up about the xenophobic segments of society, but he would never be able to give this man high marks because it just wasn't okay, and it was shameless and completely unethical for a man to do it with a man.

Father gave us another lecture that evening. He spoke like a trained expert, saying, among other things, that being gay was a rich person's thing. Such a thing did not exist with us, because we were busy being breadwinners. "I know, father," I said melancholically to myself. "No grandson of Grandfather Beyto will turn out gay!"

I didn't contradict father and his theories, because I did not want to irritate him. On the television he watched dancers from our country and explained to me the meaning of the dance motifs. Three steps forward and two back meant you were always getting a step closer to man, the future, and to God.

I went to my room; standing in front of the bed, I briefly considered scrapping my plan. But I had promised Manuel that we would put our parents in the picture, so I remained determined to inform my parents about my love and thus make our relationship public. My coming out was more important to me than bread and water. I returned to the living room, sat down on the rug next to the sofa and told my father about a fellow countryman whom I had recently run into—by chance, I emphasized twice—in a café.

In point of fact, I had seen him repeatedly in corners of cafés frequented by Manuel and me, sitting with other men who were showing each other affection while speaking our language. It was from that man that I first heard friendly words about gays in our language, in which, for example, I knew at least ten terms for respect or sincerity. For the first time I heard a man say the words "we gays" in our language. At first, we, the fellow countryman and I, had hidden our eyes from one another, but later he approached me. Neither he nor I mentioned our names, the village we were from, or where we lived now.

I was naïve, hoping to use the story of this fellow countryman to tell my father my own story, thinking that father was intelligent enough to understand that I was actually talking about myself. The young man—I called him Alwan—had told me his story, I said. My mother's ears pricked up on the sofa. She used the remote to turn down the volume on the TV, just watching the men and women in the traditional costumes of their country and dancing hand in hand. Without turning her head away from the television, she asked me where I met such shady men. I pretended not to hear her and continued my story. Alwan, whose mother had pressured him to get married, had told her that he, Alwan, loved a man. His mother didn't believe him and claimed he was joking: only infidels could be like that, not the son of a devout mother who never failed in her duty to pray. But, when she saw his intimate photos with a man, she believed him and grabbed him by the collar, shaking him a hundred times and spitting a thousand times in his face. She cried and blamed herself for following her husband abroad and who had not wanted to return to the village; that's why her son had become so gravely ill. At first, she screamed at her son, then she threw him out, but a week later she invited him to come home. There, her son found her at midnight as she was attempting to take her own life. She was just in the process of slitting her wrists. He brought her to the hospital. Of course, nothing was said to the father or the other relatives. After a long period of suffering, the woman had now finally accepted the inevitable and had even started inviting her son's boyfriend over for dinner. And now, when first meeting him, she had even laughed at his jokes.

I wanted to put them in the right mood with this story before telling them my own. But I never got that far, for my father sat up straight and said to me with a voice so loud that it almost pierced the wall, "Son of the proud Beyto family: I work sixteen-hour days to send you to school, serving everybody from beer drinkers to gays, children and the elderly, drug addicts and xenophobes, so that you can waste your valuable time talking to sick people? Tell them, when you can, that there are enough good doctors and drugs in this country; they should seek help there. Alwan should remember his culture . . ."

At that point, my mother interrupted my father and hit the wall three times to drive away Satan so that he did not bring her such problems, uttering her famous words of astonishment: "Vah, vah, may God transform, God shall help him. As mother of this madman, instead of having to see and hear such a thing, I would rather gouge out both my eyes and rip off both my ears." It was a disgrace for the whole family, for all the offspring. "Your father also knows the story of the gay man from our village who became a rose-water vendor. His daughters were my schoolfriends, as beautiful as the moon they were, soft as silk, as precious as gold. Only, because of their bad father, they were only good enough to be second wives of old men who violated who knows how many women."

I returned to the topic of the show and said it was nice of these two men to offer a warm nest to orphans. It wasn't so bad they were a couple. Everybody had to live their own life, and nobody was allowed to interfere in other people's lives. Father contradicted me: there were enough men and women willing to take in the orphans. He, for example, would declare himself willing to support these two children, and my mother would gladly wash their clothes. He looked at mother, but she kept staring at the television. These two men were exploiting the children . . . to win back their reputation with people, he added, after popping a piece of hard candy in his mouth. I said these two men looked nothing but friendly; they had the best professions, ones we could only dream of. At this point, my mother interrupted me vehemently—her loud voice reverberated for a long time in my ears: being gay was something made for and by rich men, she screamed. I should stop defending the rights of these people.

If she had known of my intention! I stood up, poured more tea for myself and for father, who sat stock-still on the sofa. After I had returned to my seat, I told him I had read that gays were mentioned even in all the sacred books; it was a reality that existed in every time period and had to be recognized. Father did not believe that something like that could be written in the sacred books. Not in *our* book, for example; *that* had always been forbidden and belonged in hell. He stood up and left the living room, but he came right back with a book in his hand that I had never seen before in our household. I was so surprised that he had actually picked up a book: it was as if he had caught a star. He paged through the little book, pointing to a passage that was underlined in black. It appeared to be a quotation from a surah, a chapter in the Quran. He told me to read this section aloud. When I showed no inclination to do so, he recited it himself while setting the book on the table: the Prophet spoke here about the prophet of another people. Our Prophet, blessed be his name, had forbidden this sin of another people. One must, said the Prophet, fight this danger with all means, undertake everything to prevent the spread of this pestilence. God condemns all those who touch women and men from behind, and not even in the grave would he heed them. I was astonished, almost swallowed my tongue from astonishment, to hear these words out of the mouth of my father. Mother had listened to us without interfering. When her program, the one with the song she softly sang along with while she knitted—an occupation she had practiced since her childhood—was over, she said, laughing, that we should stop this senseless chatter now; such bizarre topics had nothing to do with us, why were we worrying our heads about this at such a late hour? She teased father: was he trying to make himself into an educated person by picking up a book? Father replied cheerfully that a fellow countryman who talked too much about God had recently presented this book to him.

Unfortunately, my advice book, in which well-read experts wrote about how to prepare one's coming out, there was nothing explicit about how to convince members of the Beyto family who were as rooted in their old customs as a linden tree. I felt beaten and had lost the courage to open up to my parents. The next morning, after my father had left for the shop, I wanted to grab my father's book, because I was astonished that he even had a book at home, but he had hidden it. The book had disappeared as if the earth had swallowed it up. Some days later I actually found religious writings in which it was stated that men had loved men even in the very beginnings of our religion, which for my irreligious father was only good as a means of discipline. I thought it was superfluous to pass this information along to my father. I had lost the strength to talk to him about it; I had to admit that to myself.

When my father felt like he was backed into a corner because he couldn't come up with any more arguments, he appealed to Grandfather Beyto. His sentence "It is not allowed to us as Beyto men" is famous. Grandfather Beyto is no longer alive, but his soul is sprinkled everywhere on the family members who never wanted to emancipate themselves from him. The question "What would Beyto have said about that?" was often asked, whether in the shop or in the marriage, whenever the question arose as to whether a girl or boy was worthy of being a Beyto. I even asked myself once what Beyto would have said about my love for a man. One day, when I was helping my mother in the shop, she was serving two men who were no longer quite so young. They stood hand in hand as they waited for their kebab. I joked with my mother about what Grandfather Beyto would have said about these men. My mother, who had met her sales quota for the day, walked, laughing, from the counter into the kitchen and said that the otherwise unrelenting Grandfather Beyto would have had to serve the two men dutifully because he, too, was dependent on sales.

Notes

Translated by Gary Schmidt.

1. Yusuf Yeşilöz interview with Gary Schmidt in June 2019.

2. Bischofstraße is the name of the street in the German-speaking city where the narrator's parents have their kebab house.

3. The singular form "Schmerz" in German can also mean "pain," although the plural "Schmerzen" is more commonly used to convey physical discomfort.

4. A "double teapot" is a traditional Turkish vessel for serving tea.

V

YOUTH

Alain Claude Sulzer

ALAIN CLAUDE SULZER was born in Basel, Switzerland, and currently lives and works as a writer, editor, and translator in Basel, Berlin, and Alsace. Since 1983 he has published numerous works of prose: the novels *Ein Perfekter Kellner* (2004), which appeared in English under the title *A Perfect Waiter* (2008); *Privatstunden* (*Private Lessons*, 2007), which was awarded the Hermann Hesse Prize; *Zur falschen Zeit* (*At the Wrong Time*, 2010); *Postskriptum* (*Postscript*, 2015); and the memoir *Die Jugend ist ein fremdes Land* (*Youth Is a Strange Land*, 2017), from which the excerpt "Soloist's Shower" is taken.

Sulzer's novels, which explore personal loss, discovery, and transformation in historical settings, have been praised by critics for their elegiac quality and masterful composition. In *A Perfect Waiter*, an aging Swiss waiter still mourns the love of his youth, until one day he receives a message from him—after thirty years of silence—asking for help. In *At the Wrong Time*, a young man notices a watch in a photograph of his deceased father. When he asks his mother where the watch is, she wishes to reveal as little information as possible, so he starts his own investigations and eventually travels to Paris to discover the truth of his father's homosexuality and institutionalization in a mental hospital in the 1950s. *Postscript* tells the story of Lionel Kupfer, a gay Austrian-Jewish film star of the early 1930s who is informed by his "Aryan" lover Eduard that he is no longer welcome in Germany.

Youth Is a Strange Land depicts Sulzer's childhood and youth growing up in Switzerland in a conservative, middle-class milieu by using short, crystalline vignettes, such as the following excerpt, which evokes a concise succession of images and also the inner world of the narrator in both past and present.

"Soloist's Shower," from *Youth Is a Strange Land* (2017)

Shortly before I was forced to leave the ballet school in the city theater—I was twelve, at most thirteen years old—I had an encounter that changed many things. It awaited me behind a door that I thought led to a toilet but instead turned out to be the door to the soloists' shower, which was not locked. Apparently, there were only two such showers, one for men and one for women. The showers were located in the entryway to the coat check on the second floor of the theater to the left of the toilets. The quarters were cramped in comparison to modern theaters, and there was a pervasive smell of cardboard, makeup, powder, glue, and rosin. The door was a normal door with a pane of frosted glass, nothing indicated the function of the space behind it.

I opened the door and found myself opposite a man without a stitch on his body. Hot steam hit me in the face. The man was wet and naked, wrapped in soapsuds, moist and resplendent. He had turned off the shower to lather up.

This encounter gave my life an unhoped-for turn. It created a reality that had previously not existed. It unearthed a fiercer desire, sometimes weaker and sometimes stronger but never ebbing, and in a way that I had never felt before. A desire that welled up into my throat and strangled me. It was still very new, but it was neither innocent nor childlike. I grasped almost instantly what I was seeing and feeling, and I had the impression that the man, who was almost twice my age, saw through me. He had recognized me. I was ensnared.

From that moment on I had an image before my eyes that differed from the secret thoughts I had occasionally toyed with because it was made of real flesh and blood, of bones and muscles. Not a photo, not a picture, not a face over a shrouded body, but a whole person. The man standing in the warm steam running his hands over his own moist skin was not my father, not my brothers, not my schoolmates, not my teacher. What I saw here was different. I had lost my innocence.

His chest, his stomach, his arms, his thighs were covered with lather. When I opened the door, he had one hand behind his head; the other hand, the one holding the soap, in his crotch. He looked at me somewhat surprised, then slightly amused, but he wasn't shocked by the intruder. He had not counted on anyone but nevertheless accepted my presence. I did not flinch back right away. He reached his hand out to the door to close it. He was used to having his body regarded by strangers, appraised, appreciated, and desired.

Right away it was clear to me that he was a dancer. Nothing was more natural for him than showering after a strenuous workout. The leaps and spins that he executed with apparent effortlessness owed themselves to the interplay of countless muscles and sinews that had to be trained daily. Here they were. His body—a perfect surface of skin and air—became, when dancing, a hunter that brought swans to life. He himself became a swan. Every day, this body had to be revved up. Every day, he desired to perform what was required. Every day, he stood under the shower like he did now. Every day, he touched himself. What could be more natural than wanting to touch this perfect surface? Yet what was more forbidden? I blushed, something for which I was known. I only had to reach out my hand to touch him.

In the few seconds that I had the privilege of seeing him alone, nothing escaped me, neither his neck nor his nipples, neither his hirsute arms nor his narrow hips, neither his shaved armpits nor his flawless calves, neither his testicles nor his large flaccid member. From head to toe everything was in admirable equilibrium, and since he was aware of this and of my undivided admiration, he could only smile at me and say: *Go ahead, look at me, touch me, my body belongs to you, kiss it, kiss me.* But, of course, he said nothing. He looked at me (amused?) and did not even ask what I was doing there or tell me I had opened the wrong door. He knew that I had made no mistake; on the contrary, I had opened the right door. I wanted to say, Sorry, I opened the wrong door, but of course I remained silent. He made no effort at all to cover his nakedness.

In that moment there was nothing but this moist, foam-covered, tanned, muscular body.

I see him before me, as if it were today. Never before had I come so close to a naked male body, not even at the swimming pool. The encounter lasted not even fifteen seconds, but in my reveries I drew it out to ecstatic lengths.

Afterwards I thought about him for days. I hoped to see him again, but the opportunity did not present itself.

Summary: His naked body was covered with foam. He was a dancer, around twenty-four. I thought it was the door to the toilet. I couldn't know that there was a shower behind it. I desired a stranger and I felt how much it hurt. The fact that it was only a body did not reduce the intensity of the desire . . . on the contrary.

I needed neither to know his name nor hear his voice to long for him. How long did I still have to wait?

Notes

Translated by Merrill Cole.

Antje Wagner

ANTJE WAGNER was born in Wittenberg and grew up in what is now Saxony-Anhalt, part of East Germany until reunification in 1990. She read literature and cultural studies in Potsdam and Manchester and served as an intern at Querverlag in Berlin. Querverlag published a volume of her short stories and two novels, including *Lüge mich* (*Lie Me*, 2001), which prompted a critic from the *Frankfurter Allgemeine Zeitung* to count her among the so-called literary Fräuleinwunder (miracle girls), a term patronizingly applied by the *Spiegel* critic Volker Hage to the generation of talented and successful young female authors who came of age in the 1990s.[1] Kiepenheuer and Witsch in Cologne published another volume of Wagner's stories, *Mottenlicht* (*Moth Light*, 2003), and then her novel *Hinter dem Schlaf* (*Behind Sleep*, 2005), described by Sebastian Domsch of *Die Tageszeitung* as "an artful fairy tale for adults in which dream worlds are not escapist flights from life but just a different way to be confronted by it."[2] In 2009 Wagner published her first youth novel, *Unland*, from which the following excerpt is taken. Other youth books followed, including *Der Schein* (*The Glow*, 2018) in collaboration with Tania Witte under the pseudonym Ella Blix, as well as the thrillers *Schattengesicht* (*Shadow Face*, 2010) and *Hyde* (2018). Wagner believes that writing good youth literature is more difficult than writing novels for adults.[3] Prominent authors of interest to her include Pat Califia, Joyce Carol Oates, Nicci French, and Jeanette Winterson. *Unland* is a young adult thriller centering on Franka, a teenage girl who does not conform to the expectations of femininity held by her peers. When she is sent from Berlin to a rural "alternative living project" for young people, she joins a family of misfits who are viewed with general suspicion by the rustic community members. From the farmhouse occupied by the family, one can see a kind of ghost town in the distance, which the locals call "Unland." In the excerpt, Franka accompanies twin sisters Ann and Lizzie to a spooky "lake"—the Mooschkolk—in the middle of the forest.

from *Unland* (2015)

The Mooschkolk wasn't a lake, it was a hole. It lay pitch black and grimy in the forest. Not at the wood's bright edges but deep in its dark heart, where the trees pressed closed up against each other and hardly a beam of sunlight made it through the canopy.

Here and there reeds licked the motionless water. The bodies that swam back and forth in the lake, throwing and snatching up balls, didn't make a single splash in the water. Instead, the water appeared to coalesce around each movement like oil.

I stared at the blackness.

"Do you like it?" Ann asked and grinned.

Dumb question. The hole there was as inviting as a gaping maw and radiated the joy of a cellar that had never been aired out.

"Let's call it what it is," said Ann. "The Mooschkolk would be a top candidate on a ranking of the hottest suicide locations."

This didn't appear to bother the residents of Waldburgen, who had divided into pairs and small groups around the edge of the lake. They lay on towels and blankets, read, dozed, chatted, laughed, played cards, or ran shrieking into the water, which silently swallowed them up.

"There's Christian . . . ," said Lizzie and looked at a handful of boys across the way who were sitting and chatting on a tarp with a pack of beer and bellowing something at a girl who emerged from the water.

"Christian?" I asked.

Ann gestured to a thin boy in the middle. On his upper arm was a prominent scar. "The one with the colorful Bermudas," she said. "He's Lizzie's boyfriend."

Protruding from the Bermudas were two thin, spiderlike legs, white like feta cheese. In contrast, his head and arms were bright red and peeling. "Wait a sec." Ann held me back by the hand for a moment. "Watch . . ." She nodded in Lizzie's direction.

"What?"

But then I saw for myself: as soon as Christian saw Lizzie, a baffling change came over her. Three of her fingertips fluttered back and forth against her lips, as if she had discovered something legendary: the Colossus of Rhodes or the Pyramid of Cheops, and she could barely contain a shout of glee. Then she removed her hand and called out with a voice that could only be compared with a dish full of melted butter: "Christian, Christian!

You're here too!" Even though she had known that he would be there! She had told us so more than once on the way through the fields. As well as the fact that she had only put on the very pretty but impractical handkerchief dress just for him. I saw how a smile appeared on her face and hooked itself onto the corners of her mouth, a smile that struck me as somehow peculiar, as though she had taken it from another face and placed it over her own. I saw how she hopped a little in the air and then ran over to Christian with the same bouncy step.

Oh no, I thought, aghast. Not Lizzie! Lizzie simply wasn't allowed to be the kind of girl who whenever a boy looked at her forgot that her head was filled with brains and not scrambled eggs!

"And—did I promise too much?" asked Ann. "She'd earn an Oscar for that, wouldn't she? *She*'s the perfect actor, not me . . ."

"Huh?" I looked at Ann in confusion. "Are you saying she didn't mean it seriously?"

"Wait a while . . . I'll explain it to you later. "

In the meantime, we had arrived where the gang was seated.

Lizzie was received boisterously by Christian, who groped at her butt. I immediately disliked him. Perhaps it was the irritating combination of bleach-blonde hair and naturally black eyebrows. Or the narrow-set eyes. Or the stupid butt grope.

Lizzie gingerly removed herself from Christian's grip, gestured to me, and smiled. "This is Franka," she said to the group. "She arrived at our place yesterday."

I hated it.

Lizzie couldn't have known, but I hated that. Whenever someone introduced me, something like this happened: the person opposite me was annoyed for some reason. The boys, at any rate, suddenly looked pissed off.

As we came closer, they had briefly scrutinized me with this typical glance that boys always use when viewing a newcomer: *What's he like, a loser, is he cool, and if so, could he eventually cause problems?*

All of them had looked at me like that and then assessed me as harmless but not a loser, paying me no further attention.

As casually as possible, I said "Hi."

Christian didn't answer for a while. "Ok, then, plant your butts." His smile came off as crooked. As if he was keeping half of it in his mouth.

As I let my backpack glide to the floor, making sure not to throw it or lay it down, since one could show uncertainty and the other annoyance, they all eyeballed me. Their stares zipped over my body like spotlights and every few centimeters seemed to set off some sort of inner alarm.

"Everything ok?" I asked the group sharply.

"Man, man, man," I heard. Then one of them laughed, and another belched.

I turned away abruptly and went toward the shore.

"Franka?" called Ann. She had followed me.

"It's fine," I said. They were still staring. Now I felt their glances on my ass. "I feel like a booger under a microscope, that's all."

With a quick motion I pulled my T-shirt over my head and removed my pants. For one brief moment I stood there in my swimsuit, dark green with long legs and white stripes, *Racer* in jagged lettering over my hips. I felt all of the glances on me, and even though I didn't want to, for a moment I saw what they saw: a mass of firm flesh, heavy bones, and muscles. A body, not like a slender pine but like a balled fist that exploded the concept of "girl." Then I ran into the lake.

In no time at all, the whistles and catcalls broke out.

The water was cold. It didn't matter. I didn't give a damn what they said about me now. I didn't want to hear it either, though. I dove under without taking the time to carefully get to know the cold.

I stayed under water until all of the air left me, and as I surfaced again I sputtered loudly and spat. Then I started to swim in a crawl stroke. I swam like a madwoman. I had always enjoyed swimming, but there had been few opportunities over the last year. My body felt comfortable in the water, fit and strong, more like a shark than a walrus. I was already almost to the other side, my breath flew, I hadn't swum so fast in an eternity.

At one point someone near me called out: "We'd better turn around. If we land in the reeds over there, we'll turn into blood banks. There are about a million leeches hiding in there.

I turned to the side. Ann swam next to me. Relaxed, athletic—she wasn't even out of breath. I hadn't even noticed that she'd gotten in the water.

"Okay," I said, turning around, and attempted not to pant.

"Don't let the guys get to you," Ann said. "They just aren't used to girls with baseball caps and bulging muscles. It makes them uneasy."

I said nothing.

In my old class, almost everyone wore a size XS. It didn't matter if it was their size or not. Skintight T-shirts I would have been afraid to breathe in.

Besides, it had looked as if the fabric might slip from their belly buttons up over their breasts if they moved their arms too quickly. I never got to see whether or not that was true. Most of them simply didn't move their arms quickly.

I wear XL. But not just because I want to raise my arms when I feel like it, but because I find it stupid when people look at my breasts rather than my face.

In contrast, almost all of the girls in my old class were convinced that their boobs were the most important part of them. There seemed to be a competition. They shoved their breasts up so high with push-up bras that they ended up peeking out of their collars like two bocce balls. Some dusted them with glitter.

"I don't get boys," I finally said. We let ourselves glide calmly through the water. We were all alone in that part of the lake. "I mean, do they lose their brains when it comes to girls? I mean, really: with cars it would be clear to them. They all know for sure that the most important thing about a car is the engine, not the paint! But with girls they all just stare at the paint. Seriously: if a nice chest or ass was really a guarantee of brain quality, someone'd have to offer Pamela Anderson a physics professorship!" When Ann laughed, she really laughed. She opened her mouth really wide and laughed loudly enough to silence barking dogs. And it was infectious. I couldn't help but laugh along with her, and I suddenly felt safe.

Notes

Translated by Simone Boissonneault.

1. *Frankfurter Allgemeine Zeitung* 31, no. 5 (2001): BS6.

2. Translation by Gary Schmidt. Quoted in *Perlentaucher*: https://www.perlentaucher.de/buch/antje-wagner/hinter-dem-schlaf.html.

3. Antje Wagner interview with Gary Schmidt in June 2019.

Ella Blix

Ella Blix is the open pseudonym under which Antje Wagner and Tania Witte have published two youth novels, *Der Schein* (*The Glow*, 2018) and *Wild: Sie hören dich denken* (*Wild: They Hear You Think*, 2020). In QueerBUCH, a German-language LGBTQ+ book blog, a reviewer writes that although *Der Schein* is not a classically queer book, it nonetheless "represents such a great number of diversities to a degree that is seldom the case."[1] Both Witte and Wagner believe strongly in the potential for promoting tolerance and diversity in youth literature.[2]

from *The Glow* (2018)

I ran quickly to the window. Kunze was standing on the gravel driveway in front of the house. He had changed his felt slippers for rubber clogs and was waving up to me frantically.

"I . . . I forgot something," he yelled up to me. "The lunchboxes for tonight are finished. You'll definitely still get cake too; after all, you missed the coffee. Go on over now to the cafeteria to my wi . . . wife, I mean Mrs. Tongelow. She's only here today until 4:30."

Lunchboxes? Sounded more like a youth hostel than a luxury boarding school. And "my wife" sounded more like a family business than an elite chateau school.

"I thought dinner was at seven," I called down.

"Not today. Today my wife has an . . ." he hesitated, "an important appointment. In any case, it's an exception. Hurry, maybe she'll still be there."

My stomach rumbled "Yes, sir." I nodded to Kunze, closed the window and opened the folder with the boarding school information. The last part consisted of maps of the grounds. House C, cafeteria. Let's go!

At least the cafeteria looked like the photos online. A dark hardwood floor, a large window façade on the right side, and round wooden tables arranged around the room, each with eight chairs. Across from the side with the window was a long counter with a glass shield in front of a half-open wall. Behind it you could make out the typical aluminum-colored funhouse of appliances of a commercial kitchen.

On the counter there were five solitary plastic boxes in a neat row. It was like at home: each one had a different color. Green, purple, pink, turquoise, yellow. There wasn't a black one. Pa would have peed his pants with glee. I was about to reach for the purple one when I saw the little card stuck on each box with a name and checkboxes. Lord help me! You couldn't even pick your own lunchbox!

Purple belonged to *Nian Wang*. Nian Wang ate gluten- and lactose-free, according to the card. *Mareike-Helene Hausmann*, right next to him, turquoise, was vegetarian and low carb. The yellow *Giovanni Esposito* didn't like pork and was allergic to pepper. It really was like at home. Berlin, I had once read, was the German capital of special dietary habits. Lukas was the best example: after all, he had been eating vegan for years! Lukas . . . damn it! I had to find internet access as soon as possible.

I scanned the signs on the boxes for my name. Mine was pink! *NO WAY!*[3]

A mistake could be ruled out: the name *Alina Renner* was written on it. A Post-it Note said: *Just in case: vegetarian. Extra cake.* Carefully I lifted the box lid. Salad, two rolls, cheese, fruit, a hard-boiled egg, and a wedge of chocolate cake. Some frilly things around it. Looked tasty.

The green box next to the pink one belonged to *Alexandra von Holstein*. Vegetarian was the only box checked. I looked around. The cafeteria was dead. I took the cake out of my box, put it in the green one, switched the cards, and was about to put the lunchbox back when a voice behind me asked, "Did they send you here for stealing?"

I froze. Immediately my face got hot. If I turned around now, for the next six months I would have to carry around the reputation of looking like a fire alarm. I had to buy time—and lose the red in my face.

"I don't steal," I said, facing the counter. "I actually wanted to . . . um . . . give away something."

"I see," said the voice behind me sarcastically. A girl's voice, pleasant and deep. Mareike-Helene Hausmann or Alexandra von Holstein, I thought.

"Ok, ok," I rumbled and shoveled the piece of cake back into my own box. I heard the soft jingling of bracelets behind me. Then I finally turned around. Long blue silk skirt. Tight silver top. Blue eyeliner. Curly, light blond hair, skillfully put up.

"Hi." A slender hand reached toward me. "Welcome!"

I didn't say anything. I didn't do anything. The hand was suspended in the air.

At that very moment an Asian boy came into the room, crossing it with long strides, saying to my counterpart in passing, "Hi, Gigi." He quickly looked me up and down and grabbed the purple box: *Nian Wang.*

"I think you are in my class," said my counterpart.

"Alina from Berlin, right?" The slender hand was still suspended in the air. I couldn't. I couldn't take it and shake it. After a while the hand reached past me and took the yellow box from the counter: *Giovanni Esposito.*

NOTES

Translated by Gary Schmidt.

1. QueerBUCH: Der LGBT+ Buchblog (February 9, 2018): https://queerbuch.wordpress.com/2018/02/09/rezension-der-schein-von-ella-blix/.

2. Tania Witte and Antje Wagner interview with Gary Schmidt in June 2019.

3. "NO WAY!" is in English in the original.

Claudia Breitsprecher

Claudia Breitsprecher grew up in West Berlin and studied sociology, psychology, and political science at the Freie Universität. As a social worker and teacher, she became interested in feminism and, since the late 1990s, has been writing both fiction and nonfiction. Her first novel, *Vor dem Morgen liegt die Nacht* (*Before Morning Comes Night*) was published in 2005, followed by *Auszeit* (*Timeout*) in 2011, for which she was recognized as female author of the year by the Autorinnenvereinigung (association of women authors), a nonprofit network for female authors of all genres from Germany, Austria, and Switzerland. Her nonfiction publications include *Das habe ich von Dir: Warum Mütter für Töchter so wichtig bleiben* (*I Get That from You: Why Mothers Remain So Important for Daughters*, 2002) and *Bringen Sie doch Ihre Freundin mit: Gespräche mit lesbischen Lehrerinnen* (*Bring Your Girlfriend Along! Conversations with Lesbian Teachers*, 2007). Breitsprecher is an active participant in the group Die alphabettínen, a group of female writers who have met regularly since the early 2000s to exchange experiences and ideas.[1]

The two following excerpts are taken from Breitsprecher's most recent novel, *Hinter dem Schein die Wahrheit* (*Behind the Appearance, the Truth*, 2017), the story of Jacob, a teenager who lives in rural Germany and goes missing after he is beaten up by members of the local soccer team, one of whom he has fallen in love with. In the first excerpt, Jacob's godmother Annette, who had fled her hometown years earlier to live openly as a lesbian in Berlin, is driving home to help Jacob's mother, Karin, look for her son. In the second excerpt, Jacob wakes up in the neighbor's barn, where he has been hiding to avoid having to explain his injuries.

from *Behind the Appearance, the Truth* (2017)

Annette

She knew the route well, Berlin to Eschenreuth, four hundred kilometers to the south, not too far away, but every time it was a trip into a completely different world, to where the hills, the houses, and the streets whispered their old stories. Where even today the glances of her former neighbors darkened when she smoked on the street, like thirty-four years before, when she was sixteen. Where the men missed no Reservist Comradeship meeting,[2] and the women cooked lunch after Mass as soon as they came home. All women. Karin too. Annette would have really liked to turn on her heel when she thought about it. Since her mother died and her father moved in with Rosi's family in Nuremberg, she didn't drive often to Eschenreuth anymore. Her sister had arranged everything: the family house over the bakery, from which her father had descended every morning at three, as well as the shop with the café, had long since belonged to a young family; and those people were the only ones in the village that Annette didn't know. All the others knew the score exactly with the so-called bird girl, who had flown out of the nest at such a young age. Flown out to a walled-in city in the middle of the Eastern Zone.[3] No man had the bird girl, but there was mumbling about that other thing, about which you couldn't really mumble at all, because there was no word for it in Eschenreuth. Probably people looked down their noses, or cracked jokes, or both, depending on day and mood. But when she walked through the town, old men lifted their hats and women nodded gently. Her father had baked all the day's bread for them, providing the few small bed-and-breakfasts with fresh rolls and creating many a wedding cake for the people. Her mother had always been friendly when she served people in the store or wrote down orders in the café, always in a good mood, always perky, and never sick. Yes, people greeted the bird girl, when she flew back again, sometimes for Easter, sometimes in summer, sometimes at Christmastime. If she passed by the village square, people looked at her like a rare species of vegetation, a flesh-eating plant maybe; and she clutched the steering wheel firmly with her hands as she imagined it.

After two and a half hours on the Autobahn, the fuel gauge slipped into the red area. It didn't suit her to interrupt the trip, but she had no choice and put on her blinker as the exit to the rest area came into view. Not until the gas was flowing through the gas tank nozzle did she feel how tired she was; she imagined how Grit would shake her head and how she would be filled with bitter ridicule. She had put Grit off with a story about Georgia O'Keeffe. Once more, no time because of work. There was nothing to object to about that, and Grit hadn't objected to anything. How was she now supposed to explain the sudden departure? A case of emergency, certainly. But with Karin it was always some kind of case: an exceptional case, a case of spontaneity, and mostly a case of relapse. *What more do you want,* asked Grit in a jealous tone, and Annette could give her no answer to that. Once this town had appeared to her like the dead end of the galaxy, and so she had headed out into the center of the Milky Way, which was surrounded by walls. She had dashed from one sun to the next, an exciting time, wonderful, dreadful, and then beautiful again. The suns had been hot and bright, but then they blew up and burned out, one after the other. Supernova. Star dust. And the village with all of its people was still there. Here, she had learned to run. Learned to read. Learned to love. Yes, also that.

When she had paid for the gas, she felt a pressing desire for hot coffee. She drove a few more meters and was soon juggling her tray toward a table at the window of the restaurant. Through the rain-soaked panes, she observed the monotone gray of the autumn sky at dawn. She pulled the lid from a tiny container of cream and put its contents in the cup, let a second one follow, and stirred. She took a small sip, but the coffee was still much too bitter, so she went back to the self-service counter and reached again into the basket with the packets of cream. The cashier, a young woman with a long blond mane and a horse's face, interrupted her bored examination of her fingernails and looked up. There was something reproachful in her gaze. A cup of coffee and three creams. *Immoderation* was the word glaring from her eyes. Why did they use this plastic garbage anyhow, thought Annette. She took the basket with one hand and rummaged in it with the other, pulling out one cream after another and considering the pictures on the lids. The Lorelei she put back, just as she did St. Bartholomew, but she chose Neuschwanstein Castle and the Hamburg Harbor, numbers four and five, which she surely didn't need. She put the basket back and smiled at the cashier. The horse inflated her nostrils.

The restaurant was still asleep. From the radio, a hit from last summer floated down out of the room's invisible loudspeakers. The parking lot was almost empty. Only a Mercedes van sat near her own car, a sapphire-blue Renault Clio that the rain had washed. On the sides of the delivery vehicle it said *Floor Coverings—Installation and Sales, Herbert Müller.* That was probably the man who was preoccupied with a slot machine not far from her.

Hunched up, he crouched on the barstool, the upper end of his behind peeking over the seam of his work pants. In his left hand he held a cup of the same kind that was in front of Annette; with the right, he shoved coins into a slot machine at erratic intervals. His eyes, reflected in the polished glass of the machine, pursued spellbound the blinking lights, fast and slow sequences accompanied by an electronically distorted ding-dong; alternating in quick succession, they either promised excitement or expressed regret. Too bad, unfortunately he didn't win. The next coin, please.

She observed how the man opened his wallet, then she turned back to her breakfast. She had chosen the most promising sandwich, but that also proved a bust. The sticky dough lacked salt, the butter was spread on it far too thickly, and on closer examination she could not help but notice that the cheese curled upwards at the edges and was wiggly in the middle, softened by the tomato slice that was supposed to serve as a decoration on the sad morsel but only completed the disaster.

The roll didn't taste good. Nothing tasted good to her after a night that was far too short. Jacob gone. Should she worry now, like Karin did, or should she get angry because the boy's disappearance was messing everything up? It was quite strange that he hadn't even said anything to her or written. Had her visits become too few and far between? She remembered how it had been when he came down with a bad flu, a sad, pale kid in a huge featherbed, his eyes feverish and moist. *My Playmobil knights are gone,* he whined, and she got him new ones for his next birthday. Jacob told her about Sascha, his favorite uncle, that dropout, as the people in the village called him. *Sascha makes colorful leather shoes in Spain,* he had whispered. *But don't tell anyone else.* Trust was good, but it could also put you in a bind. Whenever she came out of the boy's room, Karin gave her an injured look. Why don't you tell me what he says to you? Why don't you tell me? Silent questions, but Annette remained steadfast. After all, she had given Jacob her word of honor, and you didn't break your word of honor.

But now Jacob was no longer a child, and she sensed that he was closing himself off from her, or was it only because of puberty? Maybe she hadn't paid enough attention to him lately. All the events she wrote about demanded her attention: concerts and cabarets, openings and closings, readings, film premiers and theater evenings, plus all the private appointments. And Grit. Her life happened in Berlin—a life that Jacob didn't witness much of. His messages were just a few of all of those glutting her computer inbox. There was not much room for a teenager. And yet, with a young person it was just like with everyone else. You had to devote yourself to him fully or not at all. Everything else was wishy-washy: everything else just hurt.

She regarded the last morsel in her hand and sighed. She should eat much more slowly, buy another sandwich and another, no matter how it tasted. She should pile up a giant salad, load up scrambled eggs from the hot plates, and consume the entire buffet as if she had all the time in the world, just so she didn't have to drive toward this uncertainty. What if Karin was right and something had really happened? She felt it in every cell of her body. Nothing good was in store for her.

After all, it was cozy here with the horse at the cash register and with Herbert Müller, or whoever he was, throwing away his money over there. The machine in front of him was blinking now even more furiously. A siren howled. Herbert Müller placed the cup on a second stool next to him and concealed the events under the glass with his newly free hand, while with the other he pressed a red button in rhythm with the sounds. He pushed and pressed, slid back and forth. The stool wobbled, but he paid no attention to it. He nodded at the tooting and blinking and pressing, his black-gray curls vibrating on his head. A pillar of light rose on the machine, climbing over his hand, higher, ever higher, and finally the man sprang up. His fingers no longer pressed, but rather hacked at the machine. But suddenly they lost their rhythm. They were only a tiny bit too early, a tenth of a second. The machine wailed and the pillars plummeted. Numbers, aces, and the provocative wink of a bosomy blonde in a skimpy red dress all vanished. Herbert Müller stared at the empty compartment into which his winnings should have rained down and let his shoulders drop. Then he trotted to the checkout to get change for a bill.

He wants the jackpot so bad, she thought. He probably didn't need the money, but he would give everything for the one moment when the clink of countless coins could make him believe that fate means him well. The man forgot the bitter coffee, forgot the floor coverings and also the customers, who doubtlessly were waiting for him somewhere. He knew that he could only lose, but he didn't care about that when the lights danced before him. Maybe once, at some time, he had won, and the moment in which desire and reality became one meant more to him than any other. Joy. Happiness. Yes, she understood.

The song was over. Instead, only the day's headlines droned from the radio, announced by a young female voice. She spoke about the tax dodging of a top German executive, the growing influence of terrorists in Iraq, and an automobile accident with one dead and two seriously injured, but the speaker didn't forget for a second to send the painstakingly trained smile in her voice through the ether. She flirted with the microphone as if she had a screw loose somewhere. Annette got up, took the tray, and placed it on the shelf for dirty dishes, only letting Neuschwanstein Castle and the Hamburg Harbor slide into her bag, as the horse once more looked over to her.

On the short walk to the car she lit a cigarette. The rain had slackened. Stray drops fell on her auburn hair, which she had never made an effort to control. *Others spend a lot of money at the hairdresser's to look like that,* Grit had said, when she had awoken next to her that first morning. Annette pulled her cell phone from her jacket pocket, looked at the picture of her beloved on the display, and wrote her a brief message.

Unexpectedly had to go to Karin's. Emergency. Will call later. Kisses.

Just send. How practical. Her guilty conscience ate at her like a swarm of piranhas. She sucked in deeply the last drag of her cigarette. The nicotine spread into her bloodstream and relaxed her. A two-hour drive was ahead of her. Karin was expecting her, and maybe by morning Holger would also be with her. Then they would be together again, like so often, like always. She climbed in and drove slowly across the parking lot before merging into the sparse traffic.

Jacob

When Jacob opened his eyes, he saw the corner of the old blanket that his head was lying on, and lots of hay and straw. He squeezed his eyelids tight and opened them again. Oh yes, Götzl's farm, he remembered, and a film ran backwards: the climbing of every single rung of the ladder, the short stay at home, where he fetched his laptop, the long painful way from the pond. And the fight. Bullshit, it wasn't exactly a fight. In a fight, one person struck and the other fought back, and at the end both were somehow bruised. But how could he have fought back against three of them? Number Six and Number Eight[4] had held him for Philipp's first punches—he remembered that—until he hit the ground; afterwards the kicks came from all three of them. He focused on his left side. When he lay motionless on the floor, nothing hurt there. He looked at his wristwatch. It was a quarter after eleven, and it must already be morning, since the artificial light in the barn below was joined by a different light, penetrating through the roof hatch. The sky was bright outside, as bright as a November sky could manage. In any case, it was not night. Had he slept for seventeen hours? Had he not heard the farmer, who must have milked and fed the cows, or the mooing of the animals and water faucet, nothing at all? If so, he could say he was lucky that Götzl hadn't come up to him. That could have turned out badly!

Seventeen hours, he marveled once more and just now realized how thirsty he was. He sat up and opened his backpack with shaky fingers, retrieving the flask. Greedily he set it to his lips and drank, and the cold water first let him sense how dry his mouth had become. He took another big drink, screwed the flask closed, and set it next to him in the straw. The backpack lay open before him, appearing to want to invite him to reach into it again. The laptop. He got really hot with the thought that he needed to boot it up. That was why he took it with him, after all: to check online and be able to make sure. He pulled the computer tentatively onto his lap, opened it, and turned it on. If the guys had sent the video, he would certainly find it. Somebody would ask him what it meant, by e-mail, Facebook, Twitter, or Instagram. There were so many roads to ruin. Social networks, what a joke! What was so social about computer programs that could destroy him with a few clicks, just as he sometimes destroyed his opponent in his online game? And the Web never forgot. Had the blows not sufficed to torment him? His heart hammered in his chest as he opened the browser. The Wi-Fi signal was weak, but it was adequate enough to get on the internet, and suddenly the pain in his side was there again. He clamped his teeth together, barely daring to breathe.

E-mail, Facebook, Twitter, and Instagram—nowhere a message, a clue, a Tweet or commentary indicating that his video had been posted. He dug his fingers into his jacket and sighed with relief. Obviously, there was still a boundary that Philipp and his friends didn't want to cross. Beating, stealing, being cowardly—they seemed to be satisfied with that. Maybe they also feared that the incident would make waves when they posted it, and waves were unpredictable, sloshing here and there, possibly not just washing away Jacob but themselves too. In any case, last night's video had not surfaced, not during the night and not this morning. He was so thankful now for his long sleep, for the hours when he did not have to be afraid, until this moment. He closed the laptop and placed it next to the water flask. He crawled on all fours to the edge of the hayloft and looked below. The animals had fodder, the stable corridors had been swept, the feeding troughs filled. Suddenly Jacob got scared: the farmer must have noticed the vomit! And yet he hadn't climbed up the ladder to see if someone was sleeping in the hayloft? So really, the people in the village were probably right. Mr. Götzl was indeed a wacko.

Jacob got up very slowly. The muscles in his legs felt like cotton balls, but he had to look and see what was going on over there. Laboriously, he pulled a bale of hay up to the roof hatch and pushed a second next to it, then rested. As he got his breath back, he heaved a third bale of hay on the other two. The pain got worse with every movement. In spite of that, he climbed the steps he'd made, held fast to the handle of the roof hatch, and looked outside.

Well, well, wasn't that Annette's car parked in front of the carport? Of course, the Berlin license plate, the rainbow heart on the back. How horrible was that! The one time when he was not at home, his godmother, of all people, came to visit? Somehow everything was going wrong on this fucked-up weekend. If he had known that she was coming, then he would not have hidden himself away here. She could have stood by him when he revealed everything. And maybe stood by his mother too, who always behaved differently when Annette was with her, as if she were taking a vacation from her ego, or enjoying a break from her own strict rules and commandments. Sometimes Holger joined them, and then all three laughed together when they recalled the old times, or looked grim for the same reason. He couldn't understand it, but when he saw them together like that, he also wanted a friend, somebody with whom he could look back and ask, Do you still remember? He didn't understand himself why he couldn't find someone to spend his time with when school was out, someone he could talk to when everything in his heart and in his head was messed up? But no one would understand anyway. And maybe that's why he didn't search hard enough. How was he supposed to find a friend when he had to hide who he was? Gay. Already this word sounded like shit, or was it because no one opened their eyes with joy whenever the word was said? For "gay" one got no "I like it." What's said at most is "that doesn't matter." Pinched faces, concerned parents, wailing snot and water because they could not expect grandchildren from their gay sons or lesbian daughters, and if their oh-so-wayward offspring wanted to raise children, they really freaked out. He thought about things like that, but no one cared. Maybe Annette. He had missed her in recent years, even though she had written him e-mails or sometimes called. But that was not the same as her visiting. He needed a face he could look into, if he were to confide in someone. A face like Annette showed him, friendly and caring. Why today, of all days, did she have to . . .

Or is that exactly why she came? Because he was not at home? Or had his mother informed her about it? No coincidence, but a consequence of his flight? Yes, of course! Seventeen hours—more than enough time for panic and speculation, for a drive from Berlin to Eschenreuth. What did that mean? Had his mother gone out of her mind?

Oh shit. Slow down, ladies, don't make a big fuss, that is not what I meant! He turned around toward the ladder that led down, wishing he were home. Just down the rungs and out of the stable, once across the street, he could surely manage that. Yes, he had to go and explain everything. Come clean, eat something, and let himself be examined. And he had to go to bed. Why did he feel so sick? He hadn't known that a couple of bruises could rob him of so much of his strength. Or was it because of stress?

Once more he peered through the roof hatch. Oh no, not that now! He really didn't need that. But the A-Class Mercedes was headed for the house; slowing down, it turned into the driveway and came to a stop behind Annette's Clio. His A-Class grandma got out. She swung her purse over her shoulder and got a cloth bag from the trunk that appeared to be heavy. She rang the doorbell.

Oh no, that was not possible. As long as Grandma was hanging out over there, he couldn't take the field. Not in his condition, with his face covered in scratches and his wild story. He saw his mother open the door; his grandma went inside, and the door closed.

Fuck! Hopefully the old lady was not in the know. Then the shit would really hit the fan! He wouldn't tell Grandma anything anyhow; she was enough for him on ordinary Saturdays, when she was just checking to see if everything was in order, as she called it. Always the same game at the beginning of the weekend. Grandma came, stayed, and scrutinized, and when she was finally gone, Mother grabbed the pill bottle on the top left of the kitchen shelf. [. . .]

He could use the time to relax a little. He was still terribly tired, more tired than ever before in his life. Dog tired. Dead tired. This thing was more than a face covered in scratches and a rib perhaps broken, it hurt in a completely different place too, and it was this other deep pain that pulled the strength from his limbs. Man, Philipp, what did you think you were doing. I . . .

I . . .

He smoothed out the blanket, lay down on his back in slow motion, then stared up at nothing, thinking it over. He had to learn to think these sentences through and how to pronounce them, if he wanted to get out of the corner they had driven him into. A hideout over the cowshed, oh man, how embarrassing was that! He put his arm over his eyes and took as deep of a breath as his aching chest allowed. "Dude, Philipp," he muttered to himself, "I loved you."

Notes

Translated by Merrill Cole.

1. Claudia Breitsprecher interview with Gary Schmidt in June 2019.

2. In German, "Reservistenkameradschaft," local chapters of the volunteer Reservist Association of the German Armed Forces.

3. The "walled-in city" is a reference to West Berlin, which for thirty-some years was surrounded by East Germany, sometimes referred to pejoratively by West Germans as "Die Ostzone" (the Eastern Zone) or simply "Die Zone."

4. Soccer team numbers.

VI

RELATIONSHIPS

Peter Rehberg

PETER REHBERG was born and raised in Hamburg. He lived for ten years in the United States, where he studied Germanic languages and literatures at New York University and served as Max Kade Visiting Professor at the University of Illinois at Chicago and DAAD (German Academic Exchange Service) Professor at the University of Texas at Austin. He has taught gender studies, queer theory, literature, and cultural studies in Germany and the United States. His published fiction includes *Play: Geschichten aus New York* (*Play: Stories from New York*, 2002), *Fag Love* (2005), and *Boymen* (2011), from which the following excerpt is taken. In addition to his fiction, Rehberg has written numerous articles and commentaries for mainstream and queer media and served as editor of the magazine *Männer* (*Men*) until 2010. He lives in Berlin, where he is Head of Collections and Archives at the Schwules Museum (Gay Museum).

The narrator-protagonist of *Boymen* is Felix, a gay German man employed as a professor in the United States. Rehberg gives Felix the witty, ironic voice of a protagonist who is no longer a boy but not yet a man, not yet settled in a career but already in midlife crisis, and whose desire for a long-term relationship clashes with his disdain for bourgeois heterosexual norms.

from *Boymen* (2011)

In the airport terminal. Hollywood film set 1930, palm trees inside the terminal, not in front of it. The fans as decoration. Everyone in cream-colored, caramel-colored pants and shirts, as if they had been dressed for the very purpose of walking through the terminal in that moment, just for me. It is bright: the room glows. This is the way L.A. is supposed to look, exactly like that. L.A. itself, however, did not look like that when I got there. The city's sole attraction had disappeared for weeks, simply nowhere to be seen.

Gloom June: when in summertime the clouds darken the city. Without sunlight L.A. is like a third-world city: sad, broken down, a place you don't want to go to, better to leave at once. Stressful, without the reward you get for it in New York. Instead, San Diego looks like L.A. this morning.

I am at the airport taxi stand in San Diego, not in L.A. In San Diego I am not on vacation, I meet Marco, Anna's husband Marco, although she never says *my husband*. Whether married or not, I think *my husband* is conceivably the most embarrassing notion for someone you are supposedly close to and, ideally, someone you hopefully like. If a woman can utter such a thing without any irony, *my husband*, even if it is factually not incorrect, then something has gone wrong. The older you get, I think, the more unbearable heterosexuality becomes.

Marco is standing next to me; neither of us know what to say. I yawn demonstratively, although I am not tired. Not to make him think he's boring but because the pause in the conversation is so embarrassing.

You're just envious, Anna said and laughed when I came at her with the *my husband* argument. I had already been drinking a little. Because that's not so easy for you all, she said, because it's not so easy with you *buddies*, she actually said. Display of a sexual lifestyle. Got it. Straight people envy, she said, laughing again. And I don't know why she laughs all the time when we talk about the topic of "discrimination." I don't think it's all that funny. Not really. Some people would still much rather punch us in the face. Keeping your lips shut is better than getting a fat lip when you want to show yourself in public with your husband.

Marco gives me a cigarette. Since my first cigarette with Anna I have been smoking again. Marco smokes and gawks at the girls driving by in a convertible.

The straights could hold back a little with their display of a sexual lifestyle, out of solidarity, I think, but I don't say it. Like Brangelina, who didn't want to get married until the homos in the US were allowed to. I expect the same from my friends too, actually: a marriage and birth strike, until we are allowed to participate. If it doesn't work the other way around and we cannot do what they can do, they shouldn't do what we don't do. It's like that. But Marco isn't my friend at all. I don't even know who he is, actually. I don't want to know. We smoke.

What I'd most like to do now is put on my headphones and listen to Moby, Pet Shop Boys, or Fleetwood Mac, but I am not as impolite as all that.

I stand there silently with Marco next to me, as if we somehow belonged together.

My baby, Jack said to me. *Sweetheart.* Americans can pull that off. You believe it immediately. *My husband, he was my husband.* My guy, my man. The only heterosexual who can say "my husband" to her husband is Brigitte Mira as Emmi in Fassbinder's *Ali: Fear Eats the Soul*: What are you gawking at, you pigs, she said, that's my husband, she said, and then looked at El Hedi ben Salem alias Ali with eyes puffy from crying.

What is it always between you and Marco?

Since she finally figured out that the three of us weren't going to pan out the way she wanted us to, Anna became more and more unfriendly, more and more often. Couples paranoia, because your man took off, she says. Loosen up, why don't you.

Your husband, my husband. I would just never say "my husband." Ugh!

Get over it. Look for a new one.

It's that simple.

It's not that simple.

We can also argue, if you like.

Anna was sometimes terribly pragmatic. Or perhaps it was entirely the opposite: everything was just completely hypothetical. So inexperienced that she could never in her life give anyone good advice. What she could do was listen. And sometimes she told me stories. For instance, about her multiply handicapped acquaintance.

Marco starts talking now in front of me. Why California is not only the utopia but also the dystopia of the modern world. *Blade Runner,* film noir, all that. Why California is therefore the end of the world. I don't listen, not even with half an ear. I don't put on my headphones but my sunglasses and grin as nicely as I can. I can't summon up the courage for any more than that at the moment.

What Anna told me:

You might as well just have married a Turk, Anna's mother said, the first time she paid a visit in the Hamburg blue-collar suburb Pinneberg, and her mother saw that Marco was not a GI with blond hair and white teeth like 1945. Not even a colored. *Not even an American!* Anna's husband was just an *Ossi,*[1] which Anna's mother had not figured out right away. And it wasn't all that easy to understand, since Anna's husband, who at that time was still her acquaintance—*your acquaintance,* I still say, when I talk to Anna, if I don't say *the toad*—looked like the Turkish vegetable peddler in the shopping center in Hamburg-Niendorf, Anna's mother thought. A handsome man, she said, and such beautiful eyes. Nobody else says that. Anna doesn't even say that. Moreover, Anna's acquaintance made every effort at that time to speak with an American accent and not an East German one. Except for on television, Anna's mother had never seen another man with dark eyes and a dark beard whose name was also Marco (Marco—that was exotic in East German; everyone else was called Maik or Micha) and whose German didn't sound quite German. He's not an *Ami*,[2] said Anna, not a Turk, an *Ossi*. On the other hand, *Ossis* are the new Turks. So, Anna's mother was right, actually.

In the meantime, Marco is talking not so much to me as to the twenty-two-year-olds standing behind us at the taxi stand in San Diego whom he's about to take along to his hotel. Where do heterosexual men get their self-confidence, even the *Ossis*?—Or especially the *Ossis*? Even the handicapped ones. I would really like to have a drink right now, but unfortunately there's no minibar in the taxi.

Life is too short to waste on heterosexuality.

The four of us in the taxi. The twenty-two year-olds try keeping their traps shut for a while. Marco talks. He's acting now like he barely knows me. Maybe I should meet him sometime when I'm sober. Or drink with him.

We should have drinks together, he says to me in English, then climbs out of the cab with the two women, as if he could read my mind, totally pretentious, so the minors get it too. In the meantime, I'm thinking they aren't even eighteen. Marco turns around one more time. For a moment I think he wants to give me a kiss. I am staying at the Sheraton. Give me a call, he says then and looks directly into my eyes, which I suddenly find sexy, although I otherwise don't really think he's sexy. I shut the door quickly so Marco can't see me blush.

I shut my eyes.

I open my eyes again.

I take off my sunglasses.

What was that?

Onward alone, on the way from hotel to hotel, as if that's all there is here. Sometimes there are just more hotels around than otherwise; that was the difference between city and not-city in America. A few hotels on the Pacific, right on the coast, the highway immediately behind them, and behind that nothing more. A mock-up, not a city. What really used to be city and in San Diego is called *Gas Light District* and in New Orleans *French Quarter*, looks now like the imitation of a city. Not like the imitation of a European city, which it really used to be, but like the imitations of a European city in Las Vegas. Not for living in, just for looking at.

Nonsense, says Anna, when I actually am talking to her on the telephone from my hotel room and tell her I think San Diego is inane. Just as inane as New Orleans. What I don't tell her is that I just met her husband, who disappeared into his hotel with two eighteen-year-olds—now I think they were seventeen at the most—and that I blushed when he looked at me that way at the end and must have *flirted* with him.

Every winter at the MLA, the North American conference of the Modern Language Association. Literature destruction conference, says Anna, who comes only when she can't avoid it. This year she is staying home. I also would have preferred to stay home, yet:

I need a new job.

I need a new boyfriend.

But first a job.

So, I've come to San Diego for a job interview at the conference. Here you meet representatives of all the American universities that have positions to offer. Like at a huge sales fair. When they are interested in you, at some point you all hunker around in a stuffy hotel room and chat about Freud and Goethe. If it goes well, they invite you to a campus interview. There it is decided if you get the job or not. Either I get a new job or I'll have to go back to Germany after my one-year job in Ithaca. But I don't want to go back, not yet. America is my home, or at least I don't have any other one.

So, with a job I could stay in America. Even though work seems to me the most unreal of things, work that is always the same work, every day. Avoid the existence of a salaried employee at all costs, that whole broken life. You had to approach it ironically, of course, you had to first be able to do that. The day after tomorrow I have a job interview with Columbia University. Wasn't sure if I was depressed at the prospect or afraid that it wouldn't work out.

You have to get out of the hotel. Go outside. San Diego is beautiful. As beautiful as San Francisco, says Anna.

But San Francisco is a city for retirees, I think. I'm not at that point yet. In reality, for me there is only New York. Besides, I don't like cities where the sun is always shining. I stay in my room. I like hotels. More comfortable than my homeless shelter, and you can leave again right away. I have three days still.

I met your acquaintance, I say, to change the subject, *the toad.* Anna laughs, stressed.

You are running after him.

He is running after me.

We need to talk about Marco, she says.

I think so too.

But who wants to talk about problems? Not me, not Anna. Talking on the telephone doesn't work. In reality, telephone talk just doesn't work. What are you supposed to do if you don't want to talk but you have to because you are on the telephone? Breathe loudly on the other end of the line? That doesn't even work during telephone sex. So, then I talk a bit since I don't want her to hang up. Then I say what's happening with me, I mean what's *not* happening. Since I don't want to be alone right now.

Working at the university, living at the university. After a few years you can't even imagine anything else. Not because you're so happy but because in no time you become unsuited for anything else.

That's called a midlife crisis, says Anna, as if she'd already gone through that.

My career hasn't even properly started yet, I say.

Midlife crisis must mean: time is running out and so are the possibilities; now we'll see what you've made of your life. Why do you have a real problem when after an academic training period of approximately twenty years you get your first paid job around the age of forty? Because your professional debut coincides with your midlife crisis.

Anna says: I really have to go now. Give me your number. We'll talk later.

Alone in the hotel. Not an independent movie motel, like in a David Lynch film, but thirties glamour, Mae West and Jean Harlow. My room looks like in Hollywood, yet again everything is like in Hollywood. With a vodka Red Bull in my hand, I plop into one of the two cream-colored armchairs—not cream-colored, bourbon vanilla—directly in front of the window, with an ocean view, which today looks neither green nor blue. The ocean looks as if it were white. The light is blinding. Another vodka Red Bull. In half an hour the cash bar of the Queer Studies Association begins. A cocktail party for lesbians and gays, finally a few gays again, but you have to pay for your own drinks. It won't attract attention if I've already had a few. Most of them have already had a few.

That's called "social anxiety," Jack said, when we were still speaking to one another. I knew right away it was a mistake. I should never have told him that I like to drink. He would have figured it out himself at some point anyway. Booze after work, sometimes more, sometimes less. Am I an alcoholic? Is that why he broke up with me? I didn't really want to know exactly. In any case, I had the break up with Jack behind me. Anna and Marco still had theirs ahead of them.

San Diego, CA, December 26

We have a responsibility as intellectuals, I believe, believes the lesbian, who delivers the welcoming address at the queer cash bar, for we are the avant-garde, she says. I can't concentrate on what she's saying. I look at her plaid polyester scarf, base color beige, which, in spite of it being almost eighty degrees with high humidity in the windowless interior room, is wrapped cumbersomely around her throat. The scarf fits exactly once around her neck, but just barely, so that it falls down every two minutes, and during her twenty-minute-long greeting—even Americans sometimes have no sense of timing—she has to push it back up, as if that were fashionable. It's not fashionable, it's stupid, totally stupid.

Falsely understood vanities of fashion-challenged lesbians, at least twenty years behind the times. Vanities that first become recognizable as vanities because they have not worked as fashion for such a long time. The false belief in lesbian scarf selection, that unfashionable vanity, is less recognizable as vanity than the fashionable kind. Untrue, it's exactly the reverse. I go to the bar.

Vodka Red Bull.

We don't have that.

Okay, vodka.

We only have wine.

Give me a glass of white wine.

The fat man looks at me through his greasy glasses. At first, I think he wants to flirt with me. Then I understand that he's worried. Because I look so drunk.

Queer Studies is mainly a cover name for Lesbian Studies, not Gay and Lesbian Studies, for there are no men here. The thing with lesbian and gay solidarity didn't work out at the university. The men took their leave. Gay men indulge in the luxury of staying stupid. The three that remain are butt ugly. Bellies already at thirty-five, no haircut (like Anna), everything lost, the end. I stay with my half-empty glass at the bar and think that under different circumstances I could have found that poignant, the scarf with the lesbian on it, or at least funny. In this milieu not at all, sorry. That's depressing. That was terror!

Can I have another glass of wine, please.

The greasy glasses look at me and say:

I think you had enough, Sir.

Only Jack talks to me that way.

I would have liked to pour my wine over his glasses, but my glass was already empty.

When I ask her about her aggressive misbehavior, the academic lesbian justifies the relevance of her performance by saying she is not subject to the dictates of fashion, not as a lesbian, not as an intellectual—a clear twofold *no* to fashion—and distances herself clearly from the average heterosexual woman who is seduced by brand-name fetishism. As an intellectual Turkish lesbian, she says, she parodistically imitates fashion. Totally wrong speech sound. Lesbian offender, not Turkish lesbian, I think, but I don't say it, looking sheepishly at the lesbian scarf. That's the moment when I really feel excluded as a homosexual man.

I belch.

Apparently, I no longer have my bodily functions completely under control, like an old fart, and am not certain if the lesbian realizes it. A corner of her mouth has now sagged. She must have noticed it.

What kind of music do you listen to, I ask quickly, so that my belch is forgotten. I ask the lesbian offender, who is called Ingrid and who actually looks a bit like Ingrid Bergman ("my father is from Istanbul and my mother from Flensburg"), which doesn't improve the situation either, and she has no idea what I want and no answer to my teeny question. To distract from the dilemma, she fixes her slipped scarf. This time it helps a little. The scarf helps add more expression to the rather thin ideas of the lecture through a dramatic submissive gesture, and it serves to fill embarrassing breaks in communication.

When you hear the right music, then the styling works too. I bet the lesbian listens only to country music and only knows Kylie and Madonna from gender seminars. It doesn't work if you cut corners with the legwork. Real music is a good antidote to styling accidents, I say out loud to Ingrid and consider whether I should help her this time to readjust the scarf, which has slipped again. Perhaps that would change something in her situation. I come a step closer. Ingrid says nothing but laughs. Laughs in a way that you really don't know if she is laughing or not laughing, how the lesbian laugh is to be interpreted, because she herself has not yet decided if she should take my comment as ironic or insulting. She looks at me once again, maybe she looks at me for the first time even, but at the same time for the last time, and then she decides—different from Anna—on being insulted and knots her too-short polyester scarf—which after the lesbian fake laugh has slipped again—tightly around her throat and leaves the windowless conference hall without saying a word. So much for gay-lesbian solidarity, I call after her.

The people around me laugh. They think it was a joke.

I should go now.

It occurs to me as I enter the elevator, still hung up on the lesbian plus scarf, that you don't just have to know how you *don't* want to live. The lesbian cannot help me out. True, insulting her is great fun, but it's also adolescent. I can't forget how adolescent it is and that you can't get stuck in a stifling eternal adolescence. That's not a solution either. You have to be able to imagine how you want to live, even when adolescence, which lasts a bit longer on average for faggots than for the control group, at some point actually does end.

The elevator door opens and in comes Jack.

In the elevator in front of me: in a bright blue tank top, shiny white shorts, and five-o-clock shadow. *Forty-year-old gays who waste their free time in the gym,* I think. Jack grins. How I hate that grin. Every time he grins like that, every time I fall for him again at once, whether I want to or not. I don't want to.

Hi.

Hi.

I didn't know we were in the same hotel.

I didn't know you were here.

How is it going?

Good. You?

Very good.

You look great.

You too.

Thanks.

I have a three-hour flight behind me and have been drinking for the last four hours. My eyes are red, my skin is shiny. I was too lazy to shower. Jack has just showered. I can smell it. He showers before working out. Before and after working out. He always smells good. How I hate that. He is standing close in front of me. The elevator is cramped; I get dizzy. *I could use a kiss from him. I would feel much better.* Although Jack's German is better than my English, we usually speak English with each other. I close my eyes briefly. *Never say goodbye.* Stupid, but true. Looking for love. Being in love. Grieving for love. My love stories always become heartache stories. (Who said love makes you happy?) What I'd most like to do is press my forehead against Jack's head, behind his ear, at the hairline, where he smells the very best. The elevator stops and the door opens.

See you.

I rub my eyes as if I had just dreamed. I would most prefer it to have been a dream. I decide it was just a dream. Everything else would be too complicated right now. Thinking about Jack. Anything is better than thinking about Jack. I will cry for him until I find someone else. But at the moment I have more important things to do. I should prepare for my job interview.

You know, I really don't need a boyfriend right now. I don't.

I go to my room.

Not completely fresh in my head, I try by myself to start the discussion that I had just not had with the lesbian. That I never had at the MLA. Criticism and art. Art and criticism, what is the difference between them? It's actually an important question. It is actually about something. It's actually about something for me. Criticism itself is not enough, I think then, as I think about the lesbian and her styling. Then criticism of criticism, and so forth. Who cares about that? But it's not enough either to just criticize the lesbian like an adolescent, or the *Ossis*, or the straights. You have to imagine how you can become happy. How becoming happy works.

1. Truth

Criticism can tell us how not to live. Art must tell us how we can live. How to make aesthetic decisions, not moral ones. I want to be an artist and not a thinker. Academic depression: true, but comfortable. You have to risk being happy. Happiness is the post-religious person's justification of existence. Glamour is the religion of narcissists.

In the minibar there is no wine, but there's tequila.

Tequila doesn't taste good out of the bottle.

I drink it anyway.

You have to risk being happy.

The lesbian can't help you out with this. Jack was able to help me out. Felix and Jack.

Shortly before he broke up with me, I thought it could all be different again. As if when we talked we still believed that everything was okay, that everything was still okay. As if we weren't careful to avoid sentences we already knew, sentences that got us into trouble.

Can I have another drink?

I think you had enough.

When it wasn't okay anymore.

The last time we sat across from each other in the café. How good he looked all of a sudden, I thought. In this light. Like my husband. My handsome husband, I thought, when I looked at him, handsome and sexy, as if that was a contradiction.

What's wrong? he said and laughed, as if I shouldn't do that: look at him when he laughs, as if that were too intimate.

As if we were seeing each other for the first time, as if we had just fallen in love, as if it were love at first sight, like the first time again, at first sight, every time, now.

As if he didn't remember yesterday evening, all the other evenings.

Or it didn't bother him. It didn't bother him when we had nothing to say to each other. As if he didn't think it was not okay. That you had to do something about it, contradict, work on it, whatever, I didn't know. You couldn't accept it.

He must have thought: that's life.

He wanted to tell me something, but he stopped in midsentence.

As if he'd changed his mind and preferred not to speak after all.

What's the word? But then it didn't come to him.

It won't come to me, he said.

Why was saying nothing so beautiful then, although it was otherwise a problem, at least for me? I was almost happy and he looked happy too.

The next morning, he broke up with me.

I'm drunk.

I call Anna.

I thought we were a perfect couple, I say.

Anna doesn't say anything.

Everything was like in a fairy tale!

I almost bawled, but then I paused briefly to calm myself down again.

What did we do wrong?

Perfect couples do not exist, says Anna.

When I'm drunk, she gets monosyllabic. Her AA buddies no doubt told her she's not allowed to have contact with alkies. And she thinks I'm one. When I was drunk I always argued with Jack.

People will go on dangling for years in front of one major choice. Often having to do with employment or love object. Being too smart could easily mean you have no direction in life, Jack said—like a know-it-all during one of our last arguments—because you don't really believe it. One of his sentences that were both a compliment and the opposite at the same time.

Jack was not especially talented. He didn't have new ideas in his head every morning when he got up. He was just sure of himself. He didn't have to ask himself over and over who he was. Already before drinking his first cup of coffee his head was as clear as mine would only be for two or three hours a day at most. I needed breaks, distractions. I lost and found myself again—when I was lucky. I say to Anna:

We had been in the new house for only a few days when the job offer came from Yale. He decided immediately. Yale was better than Cornell. So off to Yale. Not because he was a careerist but because he noticed that something wasn't right about our suburban idyll. He noticed it just as much as I did. I think he knew that I was not really available for the suburban idyll. He knew it before I did. For me, that life was an experiment; for him the experiments were over. For him it was the life he wanted. I didn't fit into his life anymore. I didn't fit into my life anymore.

Then he was gone.

Maybe he was right, says Anna.

I don't know what she means.

You have to have a goal, then life is better, she says.

Oh, I see. Yes, of course.

I was envious of people who knew what they wanted. From the outside, that always looked great. Although this strategy can easily make you into a liar. Besides, sentences with which you want to prove the strength of your will never sound truly intelligent. Not wanting anything, like me, isn't unmessed-up either. I took another gulp from the tequila bottle.

For me, life means waiting and sometimes being lucky, I say to Anna.

Both are privileges of youth, she says.

And then she asks: and what do you want to be when you grow up?

I had no answer.

I hope something better will occur to me, I say.

Anna says: better to be an alcoholic with money than without it.

And at that moment I had no more arguments against a job at the university.

San Diego, CA, December 26

Sometimes I have to remember that I am free and can do what I want, like an adult man. I go by myself to the hotel bar. Marco is sitting there without the sixteen-year-olds. Norah Jones comes out of the speakers with "One Flight Down." I consider for a moment if I should turn around, then I join him at his table.

Marco grins. Is he plastered too? The peculiar thing about Marco's grin: that when he grins the corners of his mouth don't go up, which is what you would expect from a grin. The corners of Marco's mouth go down when he grins.

Hi.

Hi there.

Looks like he wants to grin and suppress a grin at the same time. As if he were ashamed of grinning. Why is he so nervous all of a sudden? Normally he likes to let himself go. It's always somehow strange when we see each other.

Marco grins/doesn't grin.

Before they were married, Anna had a theory that Marco had a harelip, like Jürgen Habermas, she said. When Habermas speaks, you can't understand a single word. Two hundred and fifty students sit in the room and take notes when he talks, although you can't understand anything, truly not a word, nothing at all. I don't know what they write.

But recently no more jokes about Marco were allowed. After all, they were married. Only Anna could make jokes about Marco.

What are you drinking, Marco asks.

Vodka Red Bull.

You can understand what Marco says, that's not the problem.

Only why the corners of his mouth go down and not up—that you can't understand. If it really means that he's ashamed of his friendly grin, then that was an insult. Instead of being greeted by him amiably you first get insulted.

Marco does strange things sometimes, as if he was unfamiliar with the most basic rules of social interaction. For instance, when he speaks, he always puts his face so close to you that you think he is about to kiss you. Anna thinks that's "cute."

I don't, I said loudly and clearly. It's not cute, not at all. Besides, I don't want the harelip around my own mouth. Marco looks, at best, sexy from a distance, I decided, when he's so bored and cool, almost angry. Then you can imagine he's an *Ami* or a Turk (which was Anna's mother's opinion). I think he only makes the angry face when women are in the room.

Where are your two girlfriends from this morning? I ask.

Marco grins, corners of his mouth lowered. With that face I can't even imagine he wins points with women.

Preparing for job interviews.

Apparently boozing was only allowed at the MLA for those who already had a job. Everyone else sat around in their rooms anxiously and had to resort to the minibar.

Students of yours?

Marco grins/doesn't grin.

I really don't have anything to say to straight guys. Women, fucking, and soccer is out, and the straights that I know are intellectual duds. Straight guys have the unique talent of immediately making any topic dead boring.

How does that work with you all, in the darkroom, I mean.

He is apparently plastered.

I actually feel completely lucid.

I look at him.

How do you do that: sex, without saying anything beforehand?

You all. I particularly love being addressed as a representative member of a minority. What's this turning into? Minority solidarity between homos and *Ossis*? And are *Ossis* even a minority? It seems to me that the opposite is true. Marco isn't grinning anymore. *Obtrusive curiosity from plastered straights at the hotel bar,* I want to write down, but I don't have my notebook with me. Without the grin Marco doesn't look angry but, instead, a bit boorish.

Grab the crotch, pull out the dick, and run from one to the next, I say and look at Marco, although his face is still too close to mine.

Do you get hard fast?

What?

Why gay sex is fascinating for women is clear. Gays and women want the same thing and used to be allowed to talk about it only in secret. A sex stud's existence, although in and of itself always unpleasant, is a liberation for women and homos. But for straight guys sex talk is taboo. Nobody wants to know the way men talk about women when they are among themselves. And gay sex usually causes hysteria among straight men. Stupid jokes were as far as it went. But Marco continues.

Do you have a big one?

Drunk babbling, obtrusive East German curiosity, or is he somehow affected by the homo question in a way I had not suspected? Marco's face is still close, much too close.

The sixteen-year-olds must have put liquid ecstasy in his glass or something.

Come on, let's go to the john.

It was supposed to be a joke.

He grins/doesn't grin.

Mine is not so big, he says.

Thanks for sharing.

Talking about dick sizes with my best friend's husband, I'm not sure about that.

I stand up, and Marco grabs my arm.

What do you want?

Another round.

Marco looks at me. His face too close to my face.

At the moment, I don't find him so multiply handicapped.

Anna goes to bed at ten and turns the light out. Like women who already have two pregnancies behind them.

And now I have to listen to that! Gays as gay mom for straights.

And they don't even have children.

Has he now grasped that he has to look boorish/angry and cannot grin under any circumstances?

Another vodka Red Bull.

For Christmas I gave her a latex suit. She tried it on. Then she looked at herself in the mirror and died laughing.

Why is he telling me that?

Women are different than men, I think, or women aren't different than men. Everybody is afraid of getting old. That was the important moral test:

that for fear of death you don't do anything too stupid. That you don't panic and do something wrong, life insurance, condo, all that garbage.

In reality every relationship has failed because of sex. No more sex, sex only with others.

Nobody, in reality, has the pornographic self-confidence to put up with that.

Two more schnapps, I say and turn around.

Marco's face too close to my face.

Too close to my face.

Your place or mine?

San Diego, CA, December 27

Every morning should start like a morning in the hotel. Wasting no thoughts about how the room should look the way it did yesterday and ready for the next night and the next day. Every day like a new day and no consequences from the old one. What happened yesterday didn't have to make sense, along with what happens today and tomorrow. I get up and go into the bathroom. Three of the four walls are covered with mirrors. Clear light falls from the low voltage halogen spotlights onto the light brown tiles. I am standing on the heated floor. I look in the mirror. I turn from left to right and back. I get views of my body that I've never seen before. Other people can see me relentlessly in a way I can't see myself. You had to forget that so you could go outside without fear.

There are days when my face avoids my own glance. My face is a human face; slowly it's changing. Actually, I think getting older is awful. Nobody admitted how completely awful getting older was.

The telephone rings.

Not Anna.

Not Marco.

It's Jack.

Jack?

What's up?

Just checking in.

You looked confused the other day.

Confused?

He probably meant drunk but didn't want to so say. Americans always have to be so polite.

So, I was just wondering if you're okay.

Yeah, I am good, I am good.

Did he have a guilty conscience? Or was he really worried about me? It was, I should think, still too early for the "let's be friends" thing.

Just feeling, I don't know—a bit old today, I guess, I say.

I had a headache. I hadn't showered yet. I almost told him about last night. Just because I always told him everything. But that seems like years ago now.

You are pretty enough to mourn your youth, says Jack.

Again: one of those compliments that was the opposite at the same time. Problem: when you actually don't have anything more to do with people who know you well but still confront you with such truths.

I guess the end of our relationship was the end of my youth, I say.

Jack laughs.

Drama queen. Now it's my fault that you are getting older, *boy*? When we talk it's like nothing has changed. As if everything would always stay that way. Can't it just stay that way? The two of us always talking on the telephone? We'll have a telephone relationship. That would be lovely!

Yes, of course, it's your fault.

He laughs again but doesn't say anything else.

I needed a drink in order to continue. But it was too early for that.

We really need some time.

Distance.

What do I know.

How do you do it, I mean, getting older?

I didn't want him to hang up yet.

Since I turned forty I do the man-thing, Jack says, completely seriously.

Forty-year-old boys aren't that successful.

He talks as if you could control these things, as if you could be the director of your own life, fill in a role, know the right gestures, and then make it your own. That exists, that's called *identity*. And if nothing else works, then you let yourself go and become a *bear*. Old and fat, hair growing all over. Gays have the talent of making a fetish out of truly everything. But for Jack getting old was not a free-time fetish. It wasn't about superficialities for him. He meant it seriously.

You have to break off with things in order to get free, he says.

Theoretically correct but, practically, the exact wrong thing to say to me.

Besides: I don't want to give up the idea of living in different worlds. I want to have the feeling that everything can start over again from the beginning.

As if there was no cost to life. That's childish, no question. And somehow the game doesn't work anymore.

You should stop falling in love with pretty pictures. You should look for a real partner.

I think it's a bit mean to hear that from your ex-partner. After all, I used to think Jack was that: a real partner.

This is a serious conversation.

Sorry.

So polite again.

Then we'll be polite.

It's nice talking to you.

Just wanted to say hello.

Let's talk again, soon.

Yes.

Bye-bye.

Bye.

Bye, baby, I almost said.

Jack led a life without great passions. They made him insecure, I think. He wanted security. For that he needed someone he could count on. That's what he wanted from another man. I had come to understand that. He wanted a *man* and not a *boy*. Although not necessarily a fat bear with hair on his belly and in his ears.

He was a man, and he wanted a man, whatever that was, however you do that.

If you don't define it in reference to women.

In reference to power and money.

How else then?

He didn't want one who didn't know what he wanted. Didn't I know what I wanted? I was looking for a prince although even the word I thought was *shitty* (and *shitty* was my new favorite word). *My prince*—totally shitty. I wanted one who would save me. I would do what the prince wanted, my guy, my husband. Totally shitty. I led the life that Jack wanted. It wasn't my life but his, my husband's life. Without him that life became meaningless, because it wasn't mine.

Job and money and life in the suburbs, the heterosexual rites of becoming a man. Jack had no problem with it. That was his life. He wanted to participate, but it didn't work. At least I still had that much independence, apparently. It had to work differently if it was going to work. A gay man.

How do you become *a gay man*? I scribbled the words on the hotel notepad next to the phone, as if they were vocabulary words I still had to learn.

A gay man.

As if that was an assignment that could not be completed. Gay and young was easy, but gay and old was a real challenge.

Assignment: Remain gay under the current living conditions. Do not become old and stupid as a gay man. Survive.

You should look for a real partner.

Jack makes me sad. I could also get good advice from Anna.

I think it's better if we don't talk anymore.

I want to break up with you.

Now I can say it too.

I look in the mirror. I make faces. I want to laugh but can't. I examine my face with a stern glance. I have to look away. I close my eyes and brush my teeth. Sometimes it helps to keep going. Just do what you always do and believe there is a duty. Get up, wash, work out, sleep.

After the first cup of coffee I remember a few words again.

2. Truth

If I had to choose between good food and good sex I would always choose good sex. But if I had to choose between sex and thinking I would choose thinking. Since you automatically get uglier with time that means you can concentrate on thinking again in old age. I don't need much money, I just need to straighten my head out.

This thought makes me happy, as if it were already a plan for the future. I almost smile. I open the sliding shower door. I turn on the shower. The warm water runs over my neck and farther down my back. I close my eyes and turn around.

Notes

Translated by Gary Schmidt.

1. "Ossi" is a slang and at times pejorative German term for someone from the former East Germany, whereas "Wessi" denotes a West German.

2. "Ami" is a slang German term for Americans, sometimes affectionate and sometimes pejorative.

J. Walther

JANA WALTHER, who writes under the name of J. Walther, grew up in rural Saxony, formerly East Germany, where she continues to live in her ancestral home with her partner. She studied social pedagogy and has worked with perpetrators of domestic violence. Since 2008 she has written numerous short stories and novels. Her first published novel was *Benjamins Gärten* (*Benjamin's Gardens*, 2010), whose protagonist, nineteen-year-old Benjamin, lives alone in the house of his deceased parents wondering how his life will unfold until another young man arrives in the village to give him a new perspective. The two novels *Phillips Bilder* (*Phillip's Pictures*, 2013) and *Nur eine Frage der Liebe* (*Just a Question of Love*, 2014) form a trilogy with *Benjamins Gärten*. Walther's stories have appeared in the series Mein Schwules Auge (My Gay Eye) with Konkursbuch Verlag and the collection *Liebe und andere Schmerzen* (*Love and Other Pains*, 2013) with Größenwahn Verlag. Important for Walther as a writer and reader is, above all, the authenticity of the characters portrayed.[1]

The following excerpt is taken from *Im Zimmer wird es still* (*A Hush Falls over the Room*), first published with Bruno Gmünder Verlag in Berlin in 2011. Peter and Andreas had settled down as a couple, buying a house in the country that they envisioned as the setting for their future life together. When Peter is diagnosed with terminal cancer, Andreas suddenly finds himself in the role of caregiver for his older partner. The excerpt begins from Andreas's perspective, switching later to Peter's. With sparse but evocative language, Walther depicts the reality of illness and its effect on the inner life of the two men.

from *A Hush Falls over the Room* (2011)

For Christian

Sunlight pushes through the curtains. He stays in bed for another moment, prolonging the beginning of the day, pausing between dream and memory.

It's cool in the room. He turns on his other side, snuggles up under the blanket. He closes his eyes, feeling the nearness of sleep once again creeping up on him. But he must not fall asleep again, because then it will be too late.

He stands up abruptly and feels dizzy for a moment. He runs his fingers through his hair and goes straight into the living room, suddenly restless. He opens the door; evenly filtered light lies over the room. Peter is lying there with his eyes closed, his head bent backwards, his mouth slightly open. Strangely lifeless. He becomes frightened, standing still at the door. The sight meets him fully unprepared. Anxiety clinches his neck, paralyzing him. He knows that it can happen any day, any night, and yet it is a shock. He ought to go now, find out what's wrong. But he still can't move. He can't step closer. He is afraid of death, afraid of a dead body. It terrifies him. He feels chilly. The cold spreads through his body.

Then he gives himself a jerk. It can't be. It's imagination. He walks to the bed and without hesitation, quickly touches Peter's hand. It's warm. Peter opens his eyes, recognizes him, and smiles. He smiles back, feels how clenched his jaws are.

He turns around and pulls the curtains open. The sun is still hiding, but the sky is beginning to brighten. The light is gentle. He stands for a moment at the window, then goes into the kitchen to prepare breakfast. He puts the water on for the coffee, places plates and cups on the tray. Then he cuts oranges.

He finds himself staring expressionlessly into space. He remembers moments like the one he just experienced. Shorter, less intense moments, but they had been there. Perhaps only nightmares that scared him in the night, or fleeting, repressed fears. But it has always been the same paralyzing horror, sometimes only brief, a wave that rushed through his body. Always quickly repressed. Now he admits to himself that he's afraid to come into the living room and find Peter dead.

When he imagines being with him, the moment isn't so sudden, a leave-taking. But Peter as a dead body, without transition, is incomprehensible and frightening. He looks at Peter, who lies quite peacefully, his eyes half-closed. Slowly his horror and paralysis give way. Peter is still breathing. He brings jam and honey and gives Peter a quick kiss. Then he juices the oranges, toasts bread, and gets milk out of the refrigerator. He sits down to breakfast with his legs crossed on the couch.

"Are you all right?" Peter asks him.

He makes an effort to seem less absentminded. "Yes."

After breakfast he finally goes to the bathroom and gets dressed. Just in time to let Nurse Annegret in. As she enters, the sun breaks through and lights up the dewy courtyard behind her.

He leads her into the living room and offers her a coffee. She refuses immediately, looking hounded for a moment, something that he has never seen in her before. Then she gives Peter her hand, looks peaceful and friendly again, as he has known her.

He brings her a bowl of water. Nurse Annegret pulls the blanket off. He overcomes his impulse to leave. He will soon have to help her change the diaper. She is deft and nimble with it. He looks away, trying to switch himself off inside. He is ashamed, but he can't bear it: the smell, the loose, unhealthy skin. The body that is no longer the body he knows.

The nurse puts a fresh shirt on Peter. It has a hideous, hospital-green color and is open in the back. "Now the sheet."

He has already gotten it ready last night and gives it to her. He turns Peter gently on his side, getting closer to him, as close as possible. He holds him, while she pushes back the old sheet and places the new sheet underneath with skillful movements. The sore spot on his butt is there. He can't help but look as the nurse treats it. It's the sight he's most afraid of. The spot is already painful for him to look at: shiny, red like raw meat. A hole in Peter's skin, big as a thumbnail. Since Peter is no longer being taken care of in the hospital it has become smaller. Peter's hand clutches his shoulder, and he knows that his own pain is not the worst.

Carefully, he lets Peter roll back down again, knowing that he is causing him new pain. He walks around the bed. It's not yet over. He turns Peter carefully toward himself, now needing all his strength to do so. With a tug, the nurse removes the old sheet and pulls the new sheet flat. She smooths out the wrinkles, and then Peter is able to roll back. Peter has closed his eyes. A wave of pain is reflected on his strained face. The nurse injects morphine. No one speaks. He presses Peter's hand. His face slowly relaxes again. His clenched brows and tightly pressed lips go slack. Peter open his eyes, thanks Nurse Annegret, who pats his underarm. Then she looks up at the clock and says goodbye with a cheerful, intimate nod.

He clears away the wash water and the old sheet. Peter asks for a bowl of warm water, because he wants to shave. He brings him everything needed for it and places a small mirror in front of him on the tray. Peter begins to shave. He observes him furtively. Only with difficulty does Peter manage to hold the razor and guide his hand over the skin with the right pressure. At the sideburns, he slips and cuts himself, then washes the blood off, a few drops mixing with the wash water. He gives Peter a paper towel and steps behind him, taking the razor out of his hand and quickly shaving the spot neatly. Peter smiles at him through the mirror. Then he washes the foam off and applies cream.

He clears the tray away. Peter is visibly exhausted. He tightens his shoulders and goes back to him.

"Rest a minute," says Peter.

"No, no, I have to . . ."

"Come on, for my sake."

He wants to list what he has to do, but then he gives in, only too gladly gives in. He lies down on the couch. The exhaustion sits on his neck, creeps up behind his eyelids. He struggles against it but then closes his eyes for a moment. Peter whispers, "Come here," but he hears it only from afar. He sinks down. His dreams become heavier and darker, collecting from the bottom of his soul.

He stands at the hospital bed, kisses Peter. He hesitates a moment, closes his eyes, kisses him one more time, his mouth slightly open. Peter's lips become soft. The kiss is wet, sensual. His tongue feels its way forward, meets Peter's tongue. The kiss becomes deep, passionate. He breaks loose, breathes heavily. Peter whispers, "Lie next to me." He stretches out next to him. He searches for Peter's mouth again. Peter's hand squeezes into his pants, freeing him from the tightness. He breathes hard into Peter's mouth, moans. Peter's hand feels hot. In his hands he is safe.

He wakes up with a dry mouth, his eyes open and having lost his bearings. This dream felt safe and intimate, and he had permitted it, but now he feels ashamed. It is an embarrassing, inappropriate idea.

He opens his eyes. Peter appears to be sleeping. He ought to get back up, but he cannot brace himself for it. Peter's face seems quite peaceful, but his hands are somewhat clenched.

The bell rings, he stands up reluctantly and opens the door. It's Mark. Happy to see him, he gives him a hug. They stay standing for a moment in the sun, leaning on the wall next to the door. He looks at Mark from the side. The lines around his eyes today stand out more clearly. A few gray hairs have mixed into his temples. He lets his gaze wander around the yard. They don't speak: they know each other too well to feel silence as unpleasantness.

Almost at the same time, they break away from the wall. He leads Mark quietly inside, in order not to awaken Peter. Then he makes coffee. Mark hugs him from behind.

"Hey sweetie, are things going well for you," Mark whispers. His warm breath tickles the hair on his neck. He puts his head over his shoulder. "Yes, they are now."

Mark laughs and kisses his ear. "It feels good."

"What? My ear?" he grins.

"Oh, well."

The coffee machine hisses. Peter wakes up and Mark goes over to greet him. They kiss each other and Mark sits next to him on the bed and holds his hand, while he exchanges a few words with him.

He brings two coffee cups over and they sit down on the couch. He leans his back against Mark and drinks his coffee. Mark begins to massage his neck, kneading his tense muscles. He closes his eyes. Mark's strong fingers find the hard knots and loosens them. He lets himself fall, relaxes. Mark's hands become softer, stroke his shoulders, his neck, scrub his hairline, let chills shiver through him. He opens his eyes, feels embarrassed. Peter smiles encouragingly. Mark's fingers push up to his collarbone. Suddenly he longs for Mark's embrace. He closes his eyes and swallows. He is agitated. Repressed emotions bewilder him. Then Mark strokes his back reassuringly, and he manages to control himself. He scoots away a little from Mark.

He tries to shake off the feeling. There was nothing there at all. After all, he can hug Mark, be held by him. Yet the intensity of his desire has scared him. He tries to give it a name, to legitimize it, but remains confused. Mark drinks his coffee. He looks out the window, holding his coffee cup tight.

Mark says goodbye, since he has to go to work. He kisses him goodbye and feels a tingling as Mark's lips press against his. He brings the coffee cups to the sink and turns the faucet on. He stares at the water running into the cup, reaching the rim, until it's spilling over.

He thinks about how he was once in a club with Mark. They had danced and sweated, and he held onto Mark's arm to scream a few words into his ear. They laughed and flirted with the men around them and touched each other while dancing. At some point they kissed on the mouth. It had the veneer of a friendly kiss, but he was almost at the point of giving Mark a real kiss. Their mood was crazy and exuberant, and it occurred harmlessly and naturally.

Peter calls something to him and he notices that the water is still running over. He turns the faucet off and banishes thoughts of Mark from his head. Then it comes to him that he has promised Katharina to help pick apples. He tells Peter and goes outside.

The ceiling has a crack. It extends from the window side to the edge of his field of vision over his head. The crack is fine as a hair; probably only the paint is cracked. The white ceiling seems to have grayed, especially toward the walls and around the lamp. The paint is already seven years old.

The mailman comes. Peter sees only his upper body in the blue-and-yellow jacket and hears the clicking noise as the mail falls into the box. Then he sees his back, because he turns toward the Mertens' front door. Hopefully, he doesn't have a package, since they are all in the backyard picking apples. They would hardly hear the bell. But the mailman goes back to the van and slams its doors shut.

It is quiet. He hears the clock tick. It chops up the minutes. He tries to reach the remote. It lies farther back on top of the cabinet. He cannot grab hold of it, and a box of medicine falls to the floor. Then he has the remote and is able to lay it on the blanket. He pushes the red button, but the TV doesn't react. He picks up the remote, holding it in the right direction, then tries again to push the button, but his finger slides off. His fingertips feel numb. He tries with another finger, but he can't manage to push the right button. His stubborn hands resist.

He lets the remote drop. He observes his hands, which have cramped. He remembers a necklace that his hands had created. A necklace made of entwined silver wire and tiny pearls, bound in an irregular, luxurious cascade. A businesswoman bought it for her girlfriend. He remembers designs, drawings of rings on big sheets of paper, filigree lines, shadings with a soft pencil.

He remembers how the warm structure of gold felt under his fingers, how it bent to his will, assuming the form that he had imagined. Bent to the precision of his hand. He remembers the showcase lighting that made his most beautiful pieces glitter.

His glance drifts over the furnishings of the living room, the chairs at the dining table, of which he sees only the backrests, the sideboard, and the couch. The pillows are pushed flat. On the cabinet stands a vase, in which the dahlias have shriveled up at the edges and will soon be dead. The linden in front of the window filters the sunlight that falls into the room and makes it softer.

The light in the hospital was always severe. At noon, blazing sunlight came in, heating up the room. Then the sun disappeared behind the side wing. In the evenings, his roommate's TV cast a blue gleam on the wall, preventing him from sleeping. In the night he woke with a start whenever the nurse turned on the lurid neon light. The nights were long. Never dark. The orange light of the lanterns on the grounds easily penetrated the thin venetian blinds. The man in the bed next to him snored.

When Andreas was there, they spoke about the weather, Andreas's work, then searched for other topics. They were often silent.

The doctor wanted to speak to Andreas. Only after arriving at the hospital had he filled out a living will for Andreas. He recognized from the nervousness of the young doctor what was wrong. He saw it in Andreas's face when he came back.

The treatments stopped. He convinced himself that the doctors first wanted to wait to see their effect. He believed that medicine could still improve something. They would find a new treatment, a completely new medicine.

Then he was no longer able to lie to himself. He asked the doctor for honesty but shied away from talking about it with Andreas. What was he supposed to say? He knew that he himself was guilty, because he hadn't gone to the doctor earlier. He was angry with himself. There was nothing left for him but to accept his illness, to be strong now.

He tries to think of something else, a beautiful memory, wandering through pictures of the past. Sunlight that fell through the branches of an olive tree, the glittering snow on the roofs of the city. He searches for the intense memories that he sometimes has, triggered by a detail, a sunbeam in the window frame, a half word, the little hairs on the curve of Andreas's neck.

He cannot manage to grab hold of any memories. Only a mood, a blurry image, and a longing that hurts. The tighter he closes his eyes, the more he tries to hold and penetrate them, all the more mercilessly do they slip away. Only in his thoughts can he cautiously pause at that point where he feels the memory that was perhaps just a dream, a fantasy, or a hazy sentiment. He cannot force it.

An unpleasant memory pushes forward, overlays everything. As he lay there watching himself half-naked, there was a feeling, just a strange parallel that remained abstract. Now he knows it. And the memory is present, detailed. Not eroded by the years.

"Do you like my body?" he asked, not for the first time, but this time more demandingly. It had gone on too long already for him to ask in an understanding or indulgent manner. He had put on only his pajama bottoms, turned out the light, and climbed in next to Andreas under the blanket.

"You already asked that—yes." Andreas's cool hand began to stroke his chest with even, firm pressure.

This time, he was the one who lay there quite peaceful and passive, tracing the pressure of the hand. The fingers stroked his nipples, his abdomen, went lower. The touches triggered little warmth in him, but he felt his body react. He shoved the blanket down and observed in the weak glimmer of light from the window his own beautiful, aroused body. Then he pulled down his pants and Andreas's hand enfolded his dick. He closed his eyes and began to breathe hard.

Then he opened his eyes again and saw his boyfriend's face in the weak light. Everything within him suddenly became cold. Andreas was observing his body like a piece of flesh, on which he conducted a mechanical performance, fully disinterested.

"I can't stand how you look at me! So indifferently."

"Then don't look," Andreas answered impassively.

He heard the smack of the slap, without a clear thought, saw Andreas's head fly sideways. He had hit with all his strength. A further remark and he would do it again.

He covered himself. "Then don't look!" He spit each word out. He shouted at Andreas. He felt wounded. By the cynical words. By this impassive face to which he had been exposed in his nakedness and his lust. They quarreled. They threw insults at each other. They flung out their frustration, disappointment, and fear.

But, finally, they both calmed down, said nothing more. Still in the dark, each by himself. After a while Andreas stood up and dressed hastily. "I'm going then. I'm really sorry. It was a mistake from the beginning."

His voice sounded painstakingly composed. He heard the bedroom door shut, only just now realizing it. He put on underwear and crashed into the hallway. He found Andreas collapsed against the wall next to the apartment door, sobbing. He walked toward him. "What did you say?" he asked loudly. Andreas lifted his arm over his head protectively, his body tensed.

He became frightened and tried to speak softly. "Come, sleep on the couch, it's already late." He gently pulled him up by the arm and led him into the living room.

The next morning, they gratefully accepted the normality of drinking coffee together in the kitchen. They treated each other delicately and spoke no more about what had occurred between them the night before.

He shuts his eyes, glides away for a moment, nods off. Then he jerks awake again, doesn't feel refreshed. Outside it gets noisy: a child laughs, probably the Mertens' little one.

Andreas comes in beaming. His face is reddened by the fresh air. His hair is a little disheveled. He smiles at him. This is the only option remaining for him to express tenderness: his smile, the warmth of his eyes. Sometimes the sound of his voice, his words. Only rarely now his enfeebled hands.

Andreas steps closer, straightens the blanket. He strokes his hands. The fingers are a little dirty, probably from the garden, the skin on the knuckles raw. He runs his fingers over the back of his hands, strokes across the bump on his wrist. The little hairs of his lower arm tickle his fingertips. He strokes his arm. The skin is warm from the sun, and the other side of the arm is quite soft and sensitive. Andreas takes his hand, holds it, and strokes the fingers with his thumb.

He enjoys every second. When Mark hugs him, he senses how much he longs for a touch. When Andreas strokes him, he often stifles the desire, because he can hardly bear it. Because he longs for more, for greater intensity, for closeness and tenderness. Andreas's touches are too seldom and too short. He often has a lot to do, has to do it all alone, has no composure to sit with him. Sometimes he feels his dread. A certain restraint, perhaps from uncertainty. Perhaps, though, he simply feared the intensity of the desire, like him.

Andreas says something about lunch. Their hands disengage, lose contact. Andreas turns and goes away. He follows him with his eyes, while he goes into the kitchen. Then he only sees his upper body, his face and legs cropped by the kitchen furniture.

Onion skin rustles dryly, a knife cuts through tough vegetables, striking hard on the wooden board. The oil begins to hiss as the onion is added. A spicy scent wafts across the room. The wooden spoon hits the edge of the pot with a clink. The roasting noises are muted. As more vegetables are added, the scent becomes milder. Water patters, and the sounds ebb away.

He closes his eyes.

Notes

Translated by Merrill Cole.

1. J. Walther interview with Gary Schmidt in June 2019.

Jürgen Bauer

JÜRGEN BAUER lives and works in Vienna, Austria. He studied media studies, theater, and film in Vienna, Amsterdam, and Utrecht, specializing in Jewish theater. His study *No Escape. Aspekte des Jüdischen im Theater von Barrie Kosky* (*No Escape: Jewish Aspects in Barrie Kosky's Theater*) was published in 2008 in Vienna with Sachbuch, Edition Steinbauer. After working in the theater, Bauer decided to write novels. The excerpt is taken from his first novel, *Das Fenster zur Welt* (*The Window to the World*, 2013), in which Michael, an unemployed actor who has just broken up with his boyfriend, takes a road trip to Germany with eighty-year-old Hanna to find her first love from the time just after the end of World War II. In the following excerpt, Michael decides to visit a sex club in Vienna after his breakup. Bauer has published two additional novels, *Was wir fürchten* (*What We Fear*, 2015) and *Ein guter Mensch* (*A Good Person*, 2017).

from *The Window to the World* (2013)

After such a long time, it felt forbidden to be here again.

Michael opened the door and stepped through the heavy black curtain. Beside him, a few men were standing in the entrance area. He looked around and went directly to the counter, paid for the admission, and received a plastic bag. The dressing room, a small space with a few benches, was not very busy. He hadn't come here for the past few years and, even before that, had only infrequently boarded the express train that brought him here. Usually the train ride lasted longer than the stay. Whatever he might find here was easier to get in other ways. He wondered how a bar that, based on its function, promised so much excitement, would have an entrance area so unspectacular, almost making it look respectable. It felt like being at the box office. Michael took his clothes off: shoes, jacket, sweater, jeans, T-shirt, underwear.

He kept on only his socks. Then he stuffed everything in the plastic bag and put his high boots back on, which were so popular here. He paused for a moment, looked down at himself and considered, was he cold? No, here they were vigilant about the temperature; at the very least there had to be that much accommodation.

He went naked to the coat check and handed in the plastic bag. The young man there laughed anxiously, took Michael's clothes, carried them into a separate room, and came back with a number, which he pressed into Michael's hand. Did it portend anything that the young man didn't check him out? Wasn't he still quite good looking? Unsettled, he forbade himself further thoughts, thanked the man, and went through the door into the bar area.

Here sat a few men narrowly pressed together in somewhat separated cabins. Others, less unattractive, Michael discerned, leaned against the bar or sat on barstools and drank beer. Michael had almost forgotten how ridiculous it looked when grown men stood lined up and naked and acted as if it were the most natural thing in the world that others were having sex with each other right in front of them. He liked this conventionality, this stuffiness. Of course, everyone was naked, of course, most of them wanted sex. But that made the whole thing no more exciting than the corner bar shortly before closing time. The two men having their fun right at the bar were not worth a glance from the others. Out of jealousy? Probably, because in reality it was not an especially exciting sight. The one still had his half-full beer in front of him and took a gulp now and again. It had always disgusted Michael that completely self-confident, ugly men got the most sex because they didn't mull over it or it didn't matter to them, and they simply took what they wanted.

Michael passed by the bar; he had not come for a beer. At the end of the room, stairs led to the basement, and he wanted to go down there. A young man leaned on the railing, examining each one who passed by him on the way downstairs. Probably he was considering who to follow. True, that was actually cheating, but what should Michael have said? He pushed past him, went swiftly down the steps, and pushed the curtains aside. He gave his eyes a short moment to adjust fully to the darkness, then groped his way through the room and waited in the dark to be touched. Michael tried to imagine how the whole scene looked from outside. Like an act of desperation to get over the separation from Ernst and forget. It was just a few days ago when Michael came back home to find that Ernst had cleared out the apartment. Or was it more like a sexual high that choked off the feelings of deep loss with superficial stimuli, at least for a short time. Would he then not wail and call Ernst's name, which would echo from the naked black walls into nothing? It would be more dramatic to rush naked out of the club and into the rain—it wasn't raining—stopping at some point, completely wet, to squint at the sky and burst into tears. Too bad for Michael that tears had always been difficult. He simply couldn't cry on cue.

Michael was happy that it was so dark here and that he saw and recognized no one. He was here because he liked the feeling. The feeling of many hands on his body, the unexpected contingencies, which he could not anticipate in the darkness, the surprising reactions of his body, which were more intense here. That changed nothing about his feelings for Ernst. It also covered nothing up. It wasn't a high at all. It was most likely a massage, a massage by other means. He also didn't have a bad conscience. He didn't feel dirty. At most, he felt a little bit crazy. It changed nothing about missing Ernst. It was just an attempt. And he was not fully into it. The place became boring once the hands touched him a little longer. After a while, he decided to peek in the bar and felt his way slowly to the door.

As his eyes adjusted again to the dim light, he saw a naked back at the bar that he could not mistake. Ernst had truly not waited long to search for quick sex here, but it would have been ridiculous on his part to allow himself to think this way. After all, he was standing here just as naked. Ernst was alone, leaning on the bar and drinking a beer. Michael was not sure how one should behave in such a situation. He quickly considered going to the exit and hoped that Ernst wouldn't notice him, but he remained standing there, waiting to see what he should do. He was too curious now to simply disappear.

After some time, Ernst finally turned around and immediately caught Michael's eye. They both remained standing where they were, making no move toward one another but not pretending they hadn't seen each other. Michael did not want to show any weakness. The thought appeared absurd to him. After all, they were standing naked in front of each other . . . two men shortly after breaking up. Still, he wanted to preserve some dignity, however ridiculous the attempt would come across here. He examined the man who a short time ago had been his partner, looking him over from head to toe. The sight of his naked body caught him completely off guard, and the feeling frightened him. On the one hand, he knew Ernst's body, having gotten fully accustomed to it in the last few years, and even now the sight immediately awakened smells and tastes that joined him with Ernst. Michael could do nothing about it. He sensed how Ernst's body had always felt next to his and immediately had the familiar smell in his nose, from across the room. On the other hand, the sight also seemed completely new to him and almost uncanny. The body that he had been so intimate with in the last year appeared to have been cut out and pasted on this background, giving it an utterly new aura. Should they be ashamed of themselves, have a bad conscience, or was this the definitive conclusion of their relationship, the tragedy having become a farce? Ernst was still looking into Michael's eyes and then slowly began to laugh. It was a warm, almost benevolent laugh, an intimate expression that drew Michael into his spell and at last brought him to move toward Ernst. Only after a few steps did he believe to recognize something else in the laugh, a knowing concession, an understanding condescension, like you often see in the way parents look at their children. But now it was too late.

"Did you come here to prove something to me?"

"Hello, Ernst."

"Because of the note? Are you here for that reason?"

Michael wanted immediately to turn around and disappear. He wanted to run away from the reproachful tone in Ernst's voice that revealed both aggression and arrogance but yet wasn't completely loveless.

"Or are you here to prove something to *yourself*?"

He was talking about the note that he had left behind. The note that Michael had found on the refrigerator after returning to the emptied apartment where he had lived with Ernst.

You never do anything.

I think that you're not gay at all.

The strangest two farewell sentences he could imagine.

"I am not here to prove anything."

Strangely, he had never missed anything during his relationship with Astrid. The unruly desire for men that he had felt early on had become a deeply concealed memory from his teenage years and only fully emerged after he broke up with her. Only after their separation had he admitted to himself that he was indeed gay. But was that true? Were there not enough men who lived with women and, in spite of that, had sex with men? The two farewell sentences had affected him in quite an odd way. Not because of their brutality, and also not because of their coldness. No, they touched him because a disturbing question had been posed: Who was he, if he was not even conscious of his body and its needs?

"I'm here to have fun."

"Can you ever have that?"

"I've had it until now."

He was lying.

"I have the feeling that you want to be unhappy at all costs."

"You know, I know few people who knock out sentences like that as naturally as you do," said Michael.

A song was playing in the background that sounded like plastic. Michael didn't know it. He hadn't listened to new music for years, but it made the conversation even stranger.

"Did you go there? Did you speak with her?"

He didn't know who Ernst was talking about.

"To the doctor. Did you go there?"

Ernst had arranged an appointment for him with a psychologist he had found on the internet. He had had to coax Michael for weeks until he finally agreed.

"Did you?"

"What?"

"Speak with her."

"Of course, I spoke with her. After all, you paid enough for it. I assume. But are we really standing here and talking about my shrink?"

"And?"

"And what?"

"What did the doctor say?"

"Doesn't that fall under confidentiality?"

Michael struggled into a friendly gesture and pulled up the corners of his mouth.

"I only want you to be okay."

Now Michael had to laugh out loud. A pair of men nearby turned around, even though the music still droned from the speakers. Loud laughter wasn't customary here; glances were enough for communication.

"You want me to be okay? Life is wonderful for me. You're through with me, but everything is wonderful. In the evening I come home and half the apartment is empty, but life is wonderful, life couldn't be better. Jobless and alone in an apartment that I don't know how to pay for. Don't you think that's wonderful too? A note on the refrigerator, nothing else. No word, no conversation, no call. You want me to be okay? Why should you care, as little as you feel for me?"

"I love you."

Unbelieving, Michael glanced from one corner to another, letting his gaze range over the naked male bodies, from the bar to the exit, from the steps to the darkroom to the toilet door. But no one heard him, gawked in disbelief, or was disturbed by these words, which surely no one had ever pronounced here. Everything continued as usual.

"You were the single decision in my life that I have never regretted," said Michael.

An old Madonna song played in the background. Ernst's face twisted.

"That was simply too much for me. No one can bear that alone."

Michael didn't know how to answer.

"Do you know what I wished for more than anything else in the last year? A normal boring evening."

"I wanted nothing else."

Michael wasn't lying now. It was what he had wanted. Still wanted. But it was obviously not what he could do. Ernst puffed. It sounded like coughing. Michael looked him in the eyes.

"I should have played it better," he said.

"Played?"

"Played. Played being happy. At some point that works. Like in theater. Pretend until a genuine emotion arises."

"You would have had to change so much. Done so much differently."

"I could have just pretended that everything had changed. I was simply too honest with you."

"I am not your audience."

Michael tried to cry, but it didn't work. He couldn't find any emotion in himself, nothing that could squeeze out these tears. There was only this dull feeling, a heaviness under the eyes. Ernst turned away.

"I just wanted to have a normal evening again. Like before. Nothing spectacular, no proof of love. Just a normal evening with you. But every evening, no matter how it had begun, at some point simply went off the rails, without any drama. Out of control. And I could do nothing to stop it. Nothing at all. I was simply helpless."

"And I was guilty. As always."

Michael knew he was guilty. But he always became aware of his guilt only afterward. Too late. Only then did his share in it become clear to him. He had let Ernst run aground. Again and again. Not out of malice, not out of desire for argument, also not out of anger or rage, but plainly out of the inability to do anything else. How often had he sat at the table with Ernst and noticed his smile, which seemed like new to him. Every time he found himself fully unprepared for the sight: this bright, engaging smile, utterly without irony, with an openness that could have no ulterior motives or malice. This beaming face that he had immediately fallen in love with, back then. When everything had been simple, uncomplicated, and effortless. How often had he wanted to say something nice—just a trifle, more wouldn't be necessary. But how often had he said something else. Something that once uttered could not be taken back, however much he wanted to. Seeing yourself so precisely, and knowing what you wanted and what signs and actions you had to set in place for it, how could you act against everything that you felt?

Michael looked down at the floor like a small child caught in a lie. He always knew his share in a quarrel, in an injured silence. And he could never act otherwise. How would he describe that? As a driverless train? As a car without functioning brakes? Michael looked at Ernst. It was almost uncanny how similar they had become after all these years: the short hair, already thinning on the forehead, the three-day beard. They had even adopted the same posture. Like dog and master, he thought.

"You would have needed something. A perspective," said Ernst.

Michael knew that.

"A vista. Something new. But you simply did nothing. Nothing at all. You canceled everything and backed out. We didn't sleep together anymore. Why do you believe I wrote you those sentences?"

He felt trapped.

"We would have just needed a new beginning."

That was also clear to him. And nonetheless, how should he have responded, except:

"I already know what I need. You don't have to tell me that. You are no longer in my life."

"I've missed you," said Ernst.

"I was always there," answered Michael.

"You pulled me down. Me and you. Because of nothing. I tried to understand it. To understand you. I made every effort."

That he had, and Michael nodded.

"But it didn't work. I didn't get to the bottom of it. What makes you tick." It was getting harder and harder to listen to Ernst.

"I gave you time. It didn't help. I was with you. I was sympathetic. I was tough. I booked a vacation. It didn't help. I looked for a new apartment. Always the same."

Michael knew that Ernst was right, but still he was defiant, angry.

"But you didn't want to live the life with me that would have made me happy. You just want to finish me off. That is your only goal. Even now."

"Can you imagine that there are people who only want to be happy? Why couldn't you allow yourself that?"

Michael wanted to say something, but he couldn't bring himself to do it.

"Did she help you?"

"Who?"

"The doctor."

"I never went in. I ran away when my name was called."

Michael only wanted his clothes back. He felt naked.

NOTES

Translated by Merrill Cole.

Lovis Cassaris

Lovis Cassaris was born in southern Italy and grew up in Switzerland. They studied German literature, philosophy, and English literature in Zurich, Berlin, and Potsdam, and are currently completing a doctorate in gender and queer linguistics in Zurich. They work as a communications manager and freelance journalist.

Cassaris identifies as a queer-feminist activist. Their literary texts challenge social conventions and explore gender identities outside the constraints of heteronormativity and gender binarisms. Their short stories have appeared with Konkursbuch Verlag Claudia Gehrke, an alternative publisher based in Tübingen, Germany, which addresses sexuality, culture, and politics, including in its annual collections *Mein lesbisches Auge* (*My Lesbian Eye*) and *Mein schwules Auge* (*My Gay Eye*). Cassaris's debut novel, *Ein letztes Mal wir* (*Us for the Last Time*), appeared with Querverlag in Berlin in 2016. In this novel the protagonist Alexandra Roth finds a companion to tell the story of her partner, who chose to end her own life after suffering a terminal illness. The following unpublished story, "Bonnie in Clyde," explores the efforts of an aging lesbian couple to reinvigorate their sex life.

"Bonnie in Clyde" (2016)

17 . . . 18 . . . 19 . . . over her bed floated twenty red jellyfish. That's what the little decorative lights hanging from the ceiling over the bed looked like to Hilde and which were supposed to radiate something like a warm, romantic evening light. For quite a while now, Hilde had been aware that during sex with Louise she had been constantly counting the jellyfish while she lay on her back and her sweetheart rubbed against her upper thighs. 18 . . . 19 . . . 20 . . . And then again from the beginning. 1 . . . 2 . . . 3 . . . She used to count the jellyfish only when, already wet with arousal, she was lying

naked in bed waiting impatiently for Louise to finishing cleaning so she could join her.

Hilde the wild one. That's what Louise affectionately called her, and she had come by that title honestly, for it was a fact that Hilde had a name that did not exactly radiate the sex appeal of a Dita Von Teese[1] and the body of a woman who, by now, had a few years behind her. Hilde had not abstained from any kind of indulgence during those years, and she had continued to maintain the sexual curiosity and lust that she knew from her youth.

It was this very Hilde who was now lying in a bed that had seen and heard pretty much all possible kinds of kinkiness in the repertoire of a professing lesbian—and was bored to death.

"Everything ok with you?" asked Louise uncertainly.

"Everything's great. Just keep going."

"You were just counting out loud."

"No, I wasn't."

"Yes, you were; I heard it quite clearly, my love."

"It's . . ." Hilde didn't think about it for long. "It's something new."

"Something . . . sexual?" Louise continued her questioning salaciously.

"Yes," answered Hilde and immediately regretted her statement.

"What exactly are you counting? I am quite curious," said Louise, laying her head on Hilde's chest and starting to use her thumb and index finger to play with her nipples.

"I'm counting . . ."

"The seconds to orgasm?" Louise completed the sentence.

"Exactly." Slowly Hilde was getting nervous. Because she didn't know how she should answer the next question. Because Louise continued nibbling on her nipples. Because . . .

"And how do you know, when you . . ."

"OK, enough!"

Louise abruptly stopped her nibbling.

"Sweetheart," started Hilde as lovingly as possible. "I think something's not ticking right with me anymore."

"Where isn't it ticking right anymore? You mean down there?" asked Louise amused and pinched Hilde's labia with her thumb and index finger.

"That thing down there has a name. And yes: I think I'm gradually entering the change.

"That doesn't mean you can't be aroused any more. Am I doing something wrong?" asked Louise, now alarmed.

"No, no," Hilde assured her and pressed a tender kiss on her partner's forehead. "But . . ."

She paused.

"Say it!"

"But I have the feeling that we . . . have become an old married couple. That's exactly what we didn't want."

"But that's not true!"

"Dearest. It always starts like this: we get undressed, lie in bed, then you kiss me, work first on my left then my right nipple, slide down, use your tongue, until . . ."

"Dammit, your right! We fuck like we're following a script."

"I'm so glad you recognize the problem."

"Yeah, now that you mention it." Louise continued mulling it over.

"And now?"

"And now . . ." Hilde repeated helplessly, "I have no idea."

When Louise returned home on a Tuesday evening from her monthly coffee date with friends, with the same guilty conscience she had every month since Hilde's retirement, since money was actually always tight, always much too tight for things like *café mélange* and Black Forest Tort, she discovered a nondescript black box on the small coffee table in the living room. "What is that?" she asked in astonishment. Hilde was seated on the sofa, her legs crossed and her arms stretched out over the back of the sofa, a mischievous smile on her face.

"Open it!" she eagerly prompted her partner.

Carefully, Louise took the box in her hand, almost not daring to shake it. Very slowly, she removed the lid, laid it gingerly on the table, and couldn't believe her eyes.

"What's that?"

"That's a double dildo," Hilde responded with pride. "With it we can, when we . . ."

"I know what a double dildo is," Louise responded in annoyance. "But we don't have the money." No way did coffee and cake cost as much as a sex toy, Louise said to herself.

"Don't be a spoilsport. Come sit over here." She patted the seat next to her several times with the palm of her hand. "Feel how silky it is. And so ergonomic."

"Ok, it does feel really great," admitted Louise.

"Wait until it's inside of you, sweetheart. We will definitely have a lot of fun with it," Hilde said as if she were in an infomercial.

Louise couldn't suppress a smile. "But it must have been expensive."

"It wasn't."

"Then it's a cheap cancer-causing Chinese product."

"Definitely not."

"Was it a special offer?"

"You could say that."

"Quit being so mysterious. What did you pay for it?" Louise was slowly getting impatient.

"Nothing. I paid nothing for it." Hilde locked her eyes on her partner, who stared back expectantly.

"I . . ." She hesitated, then took a deep breath. "I stole it," she finally blurted out, suddenly feeling relieved.

"You did what?"

Hilde could smell the trouble.

"You said yourself that we don't have any dough. But our relationship is important to me. I don't want us to die of boredom one day. Sometimes you have to make small sacrifices for love." After uttering this sentence, Hilde felt like a hero. Like a Robin Hood, who took from the rich and gave to the poor. What was objectionable about that?

Louise looked at her questioningly.

"How could you?"

"It's just a bit of silicon. They definitely won't miss the thing in the shop."

Louise shook her head. "How could you do it without me?"

The beige trench coat that Louise had wanted to donate to charity because it was out of fashion and actually much too big for her small hips now found a meaningful use. It had large outside pockets and spacious, inconspicuous inside pockets. She put on a hat that, together with the coat, was strongly reminiscent of Paddington Bear. Hilde was wearing the same black duds that she had already worn during her first theft. They brought her luck. Why should it be different this time?

"Maybe we should forget the whole thing." Louise's voice shook slightly with excitement. She hopped back and forth nervously, causing the glass doors of the shop to keep opening and closing.

"Nonsense. Nothing is going to happen to us. Who will think the two of us old ladies are capable of ripping off sex toys?" Hilde whispered with a wink of the eye.

"OK, then," Louise sighed.

"And remember the list. If we can manage it, I'd like to have a few Ben Wa balls." She took her girlfriend by the hand and pulled her away from the glass door and directly into the shop.

"Act normal, like you're just looking around. And take what appeals to you. But keep your eyes open!"

"Eyes open," repeated Louise and disappeared behind a set of shelves. She observed the sales clerk behind the register. She was checking some product lists and placing orders on the telephone. Perfect, thought Louise and slid a pack of Ben Wa balls into the gigantic pockets of her coat. She felt her pulse beating everywhere in her body. This was easy, she thought, and positioned herself in front of a clothing rack, directly in the sales clerk's line of vision. Louise noticed how she was starting to enjoy the game. Would she get caught? How far could she go? She waited until the clerk lifted her head and when she looked down again immediately pocketed several undergarments. After all, she didn't know what size Hilde wore by now. She almost dropped a hanger when she felt Hilde's warm lips on her neck.

"A fantastic yield!" rejoiced Hilde in contentment. "We are getting better and better." Vibrators, several dildos, stimulation chains, Ben Wa balls, anal plugs, leather handcuffs, and even a schoolgirl costume were all lying on the bed. After their third theft, the bedroom was now full of sex articles.

"Not bad at all," Louise asserted and felt how proud she was of herself. "We are a little like Bonnie and Clyde."

"Oh, Clyde!" called out Hilde in an ironic tone of voice.

"Oh, Bonnie!" answered Louise and pulled Hilde toward her onto the mattress.

"Do we want to try something out again?" she suggested and reached for a toy.

Hilde shook her head. "Today I want to feel you like this." They had found one another again. And they had both noticed that it wasn't the new toys anymore that brought them to dizzying heights. It was stealing together. And up until now everything had gone off without a hitch. No one in the shops had noticed anything.

"Do you have time tomorrow?" Hilde asked.

"I have a date with the neighbor to have coffee downtown, but I'd be happy to postpone it."

"Which shop shall it be this time?" She felt desire overcoming her, felt that it was the same for Hilde. Then she heard the ripping sound of the zipper and felt Hilde's warm hand between her legs. She had been wet already the whole time, even in the streetcar on the way home. She remembered the glances of the people that she happened to look at and her fear of standing out with their loot. And immediately she came.

"We actually don't need anything more," Hilde ascertained somewhat irritated.

"Maybe they have a new assortment of items."

"We were just here the day before yesterday."

"The orders in Shop Number 3 are always placed on Tuesday and Thursday. New goods usually come on Monday. And today is Monday," Louise insisted.

"Alright, then." Hilde gave in. After all, Louise had completely blossomed in the last three or four weeks, and it couldn't be foreseen how long this second spring would last. Besides, she couldn't deny the fact that Louise's enthusiasm aroused her in a strange way, and the sex since the first joint coup had become much more creative and intense. Hilde had not counted the jellyfish for a long time.

"You know how it works," said Louise. Hilde nodded.

She felt her labia swell with arousal and tried when she walked not to look like she had an invisible horse between her legs.

Their gazes met. Hilde imagined how hard Louise's nipples must be by now under the wide-cut trench coat but set her mind to concentrating fully on their new theft. Her hands had become agile, her ears more attentive, her eyes sharper; they both felt like two unbeatable ninja warriors, and a smile appeared on Hilde's face when she imagined herself with her old round belly in a tight black body suit. It was the beginning of the week; nobody bought sex implements after the weekend and certainly not in the middle of the day. They were practically all by themselves. Completely laid back!

Louise knew right away where she had to go. She had learned how to play with the sales clerks, test boundaries, fool security cameras, and she looked for the ultimate kick that would later set them aloft in bed and enable her to fuck Hilde's brains out again.

They observed each other pocketing new sex toys and with every flip of the wrist their arousal seemed to get stronger, their desire barely containable. They felt a little like their pocket seams, which threatened to pop.

"Hey, what are you doing there?" Louise asked. "You are getting cocky."

Hilde embraced her girlfriend from behind and suddenly pressed her not very gently against one of the shelves of DVDs, which immediately began to wobble. "Hilde!" Louise moaned.

"Let's go try this on," Hilde whispered in her ear and wagged a lace bra in front of her face. Laughter from both of them. Then she shoved her girlfriend toward the changing rooms. What a feeling! It was as if they had been born again. Louise almost ripped down the curtain. "It's ticking right again with us, isn't it?" Hilde said, amused, and grabbed Louise's waist even tighter. "I want you now!"

"Not so loud," Louise pleaded with Hilde, who had gone crazy, but Louise couldn't control herself either. They barely made it to the changing room. After some acrobatics, Hilde pulled her lover down and they found each other again on the dusty floor of the narrow corridor. In the meantime, Louise's heavy trench coat had opened up. With every wild gesture of love some of the stolen goods fell on the floor. They didn't care. Hilde charted a path between Louise's thighs, suddenly lay on top of her, lavished her with kisses and, for her part, was pampered with caresses. Hilde opened Louise's patterned yellow-green blouse one button at a time and took one of her already hard nipples into her mouth.

"Stop laughing," Louise complained. "Otherwise . . ."

"I'm not laughing at all!" And then they both understood that the laugher was neither Hilde's nor Louise's.

Notes

Translated by Gary Schmidt.

1. Dita Von Teese is an American model and burlesque star.

Sources

Jürgen Bauer, excerpt from *Das Fenster zur Welt* © 2013 Septime Verlag, Vienna.

Ella Blix, excerpt from *Der Schein* © 2018 Arena Verlag GmbH, Würzburg.

Claudia Breitsprecher, excerpt from *Hinter dem Schein die Wahrheit* © 2017 Krug & Schadenberg, Berlin.

Lovis Cassaris, "Bonnie in Clyde" from *Mein Lesbisches Auge 16* © 2016 Konkursbuch Verlag, Tübingen.

Gunther Geltinger, excerpt from *Benzin* © 2019 Suhrkamp Verlag, Berlin.

Joachim Helfer, two excerpts from the unpublished novel *Das Dritte* © 2021 Joachim Helfer.

Odile Kennel, excerpt from *Mit Blick auf See* © 2017 dtv Verlagsgesellschaft, Munich.

Friedrich Kröhnke, unpublished text from 2015 © 2021 Friedrich Kröhnke; excerpt from *Ciao Vaschek* © 2003 Ammann Verlag, Zürich; excerpt from *Nach Asmara* © 2011 Jung und Jung Verlag, Salzburg and Vienna.

Anja Kümmel, excerpt from *V oder die Vierte Wand* © 2016 Hablizel Verlag, Lohmar; English translation by Simone Boissonneault.

Marko Martin, "Was bleibt" from *Umsteigen in Babylon* © 2016 Männerschwarm GmbH, Hamburg.

Hans Pleschinski, excerpt from *Königsallee* © 2013 Verlag C.H. Beck, Munich.

Christoph Poschenrieder, excerpt from *Das Sandkorn* © 2014, 2015 Diogenes Verlag AG, Zürich.

Peter Rehberg, excerpt from *Boymen* © 2011 Männerschwarm GmbH, Hamburg.

Michael Roes, excerpt from *Zeithain* © 2017 Schöflling & Co. Verlagsbuchhandlung GmbH, Frankfurt am Main.

Sasha Marianna Salzmann, "Berlin, September 18" © 2018 Sasha Marianna Salzmann.

Angela Steidele, excerpt from *Rosenstengel* © 2015 NSB Matthes & Seitz Berlin Verlagsgesellschaft mbH.

Antje Rávik Strubel, "Der Weiße Felsen" from *In den Wäldern des menschlichen Herzens* © 2016 S. Fischer Verlag GmbH, Frankfurt am Main; English translation by Zaia Alexander.

Alain Claude Sulzer, "Solistendusche" from *Die Jugend ist ein fremdes Land* © 2017 Alain Claude Sulzer, Galiani.
Antje Wagner, excerpt from *Unland* © 2015 bloomoon, an imprint of arsEdition GmbH; English translation by Simone Boissoneault.
J. Walther, excerpt from *Im Zimmer wird es still* © 2016 J. Walther.
Tania Witte, excerpt from *beziehungsweise liebe* © 2011 Querverlag GmbH, Berlin.
Yusuf Yeşilöz, excerpt from *Hochzeitsflug* © 2011 Limmat Verlag, Zürich.

GARY SCHMIDT is a professor of German at Coastal Carolina University, where he teaches German language, literature, and culture, as well as intercultural studies and LGBTQ+ studies. He is the translator of Joachim Helfer's *What Makes a Man* and the author of *The Nazi Abduction of Ganymede: Representations of Male Homosexuality in Postwar German Literature*, as well as many essays on contemporary German literature and cinema.

MERRILL COLE is a published poet, literary theorist, and queer theorist. He is the author of *The Other Orpheus: A Poetics of Modern Homosexuality* and the translator, from the German, of the 1923 naked dancing magnum opus *Dances of Vice, Horror, and Ecstasy*. He teaches literature, creative writing, and queer studies at Western Illinois University.

www.ingramcontent.com/pod-product-compliance
Lightning Source LLC
Chambersburg PA
CBHW060627310726
48982CB00003B/697

* 9 7 8 0 2 9 9 3 3 3 8 0 5 *